SOJOURNER

A NOVEL

Formerly Titled
The Witch of November

By Daniel L. Copeland

Enthralling! Copeland has the exceedingly rare ability to write a fast-paced novel with character depth and believability, while making the reader see and feel everything as the story unfolds! Another masterpiece by this incredibly talented author!

Rod Leonard.

LOVED, LOVED, LOVED IT! I started this book in hard copy but made the mistake of reading a few passages to my husband, who then wanted to check it out himself. Enormous mistake. He was so enthralled, he said we should share it.

It had me on pins and needles, so to keep marital peace, I bought the Kindle version! *Sojourner* is excellent. The best book I've read in a while. It has just the right blend of action, lots of intrigue, and a tantalizing element of science fiction—other worldliness. Be careful though, it might mess up any plans you have until you finish it.

Victoria Southwick

"*Sojourner* is a great mystery and much more. Copeland did a masterful job developing several characters, each of which seemed somehow connected to others. There were many surprises throughout the book! I found it difficult to put the book away. I highly recommend *Sojourner* if you enjoy mysteries!"

Steve E

Sojourner, a novel
ISBN: 978-1-970773-01-9
IngramSpark Edition

Published by *Daniel Loran Copeland and Chipping Away Publishing*

PUBLISHING HISTORY

Dedication:
The work is dedicated to the kind hearts and gentle souls trying to make the world a better place.

Leading causes of premature death:
Borders drawn in sand
Idols chiseled in stone
Gods created on paper
Flags
Greed bred in the heart
Hate fabricated in the mind

Danl L C

PART ONE

CHAPTER 1

Tommy felt alone. Not just lonely. Empty.

Outside his kitchen door stood a scene vastly different from that of their farm on the Kansas Plains. A waist-high chain-link fence surrounded a small patch of dead grass. On one side was an oil-stained, one-car concrete pad that stretched to the gravel alley. His twelve-hundred-acre paradise reduced to brown grass, hard dirt, and a rectangular pad of greasy concrete. The brownstone house Mom had rented on the East Side of Cleveland shared little with their Kansas home, except a few pieces of furniture that made the journey in a U-Haul truck.

Suddenly, across the street, something moved in the shadows. Tommy stepped closer, peering through a windowpane covered with glistening droplets of water, which shattered the porch light into a thousand miniature rainbows, but whatever he'd seen was gone.

Maybe it was Paul's adventure plans that troubled him. Mom had told them not to leave the house, but after three days of Paul's pestering, Tommy caved in. Tommy was almost 14. Paul was 18 months younger, but Tommy was the cautious one. A fact Paul pointed out half a dozen times during the last three days.

Paul promised they wouldn't go too far. And besides, Halloween didn't begin until midnight. Yet despite Paul's reassurance, something vague and distant nagged Tommy, and it wasn't just disobedience to their mother's warning.

"I don't know about this," Tommy said. He stood by the back door, made of thin wooden panels and a window of single-pane glass. The door seemed old and fragile, and Tommy wondered how it had survived so long. He grabbed the doorknob. It wobbled as if something were missing inside.

"Wuss!" Paul grinned, zipping his denim jacket.

Tormenting Tommy was Paul's favorite pastime, especially for anything resembling a dare.

"I ain't a wuss," Tommy hissed, trying not to awaken their mother.

"Are you scared about the stories Dad told us?"

"What stories?" Tommy asked.

"Halloween stories about the witch in Cleveland."

"What witch?"

"The one Dad told stories about. The witch that comes on Halloween and kills people on the lake."

Tommy shook his head. "Not that kind of witch. You don't understand."

Paul sang, "Tommy's scared of the witch, Tommy's scared of the witch. It's not Halloween yet. So, no witch. We going, or are you chicken?" He flipped his collar against the back of his neck, then turned and trotted down the stairs.

"I ain't chicken," Tommy called out softly. "But maybe we should— I mean, we've only been here a week. You know, wait till we know the place better."

"But it's a full moon. Come on, we never miss a full moon."

The practice of venturing out under the full-moon's light evolved, as many children's games do, from a single spontaneous episode in the not-so-distant past before their dad died. Thinking about the past was something Tommy tried to avoid, but no matter how hard he tried, some things caused him to remember. For some reason, he never understood, the full moon was one of those things.

He remembered standing on a grassy knoll. A cold eastern wind rocked him back on his heels. Before him, square, freshly dug pieces of sod tilted up from the earth at odd angles. Clutching a bunch of wildflowers, which were mostly weeds, Tommy stared at his father's name engraved on gray granite. He laid the flowers on the dry grass in front of the tombstone and then whispered, "Goodbye, dad."

A chill from the night air crept up Tommy's back. With a shiver, he returned to the present, bit his lip, and studied Paul's face. Tommy said, "Mom knows about us playing outside during the full moon."

Paul shrugged his shoulders, turned, and walked away.

Tommy glanced back into the house and then stepped into the damp night air. But no full moon greeted him, only the dingy yellow hue of sparsely placed streetlamps. Blue-gray clouds pressed down on the city like thick ropes. Even the air smelled bad, but Tommy couldn't find words to describe the stench. Tommy tightened his muscles against the cold and damp. He took one last look over his shoulder at the door to his new home, which vanished from view as he rounded the corner and turned onto the street.

"You said not far."

Paul pointed to the horizon. "Hey, look! The Rock & Roll Hall of Fame is over there somewhere."

"You said not far."

Paul said nothing.

Now Tommy knew how Dorothy felt. This wasn't Kansas. This wasn't their farm. Acres of corn and wheat didn't surround them. No distant lights shone from the homes of friendly neighbors. Instead, only two-story brownstones stacked like cordwood on either side of the street. Each had ten concrete steps leading to small platforms and two identical brown doors that led to separate homes. If not for the house numbers, people wouldn't know which one was theirs.

They continued in silence, down one block, across a deserted street, then down another block. Tommy said, "I'm cold." He shoved his hands deep into his coat pockets. "Let's go home."

"Sure," Paul agreed. However, Paul's route home would be set using his adventurous navigational skills, which meant they'd be taking the alleys and side streets, the closest comparison to the rows of farm machinery, sheds, and haystacks of their farmyard in this strange land.

Tommy heard distant thunder. But not thunder, something else. Something odd. Paul didn't seem to notice or ignored it. "Something's not right." Tommy slowed, but Paul walked on with short, quick steps.

"You're a wuss." Paul spun around to face him, walking backward.

"This ain't like home." Tommy stopped.

"No shit. Wasn't my idea to come here." Paul turned on his heel and walked faster.

"Mom didn't have a choice." Tommy jogged a few steps to catch up.

"We could have stayed. She wanted to move back to the city. She never liked the farm."

"Mom said we were broke."

Paul didn't answer.

Both boys stopped dead in their tracks. A low, thumping sound vibrated their bones, pulsed in their ears, impossible to ignore any longer. Each beat brought their eardrums to the threshold of pain. They looked at each other but said nothing. Was this something from the inner city? Or from the far reaches of outer space? One thing for sure. It was close.

Shaking off the invisible chains that anchored him to the sidewalk, Tommy grabbed a handful of Paul's jacket and jerked him into an alley. Reflections from the wet street danced on business windows that flexed with each dull thud. It came from everywhere, careening down the streets and reverberating off the buildings, but other sounds mixed with it. It—it sounded like—music.

Rap music.

Headlights lit the intersection half a block away. The rap struck like crashing ocean waves. An old pale-blue Chevy, not over three inches off the ground, turned the corner. Its chrome wheels threw wild splashes of light down the street and up the walls. The Chevy crawled toward them. Inside the car, Tommy saw the heads of four men, all sitting low, veiled in thick blue smoke. The car stopped, the rap ended, and the motor fell dead quiet. Tommy pulled Paul into a narrow doorway. Neither moved. Neither breathed.

Both rear doors flew open, and smoke boiled from the car. Within seconds, the smoke reached Tommy, carrying a sweet, sickly scent that hinted of something familiar yet strange. Then a more familiar scent mingled with the first. It smelled like dad's old truck that used a half quart of oil from the field to the grain elevator. Two men rolled from the backseat, one on either side. The closest man landed on all fours, his butt sticking up in the air like a baboon Tommy once saw at the Kansas City Zoo. The pair wore similar clothing: baggy blue jeans, white shirts buttoned at the collar, and no tie. Their skin was dark, but not black. Baboon wore a red bandanna around his head, and the other man wore a black baseball cap turned backward.

Tommy had little experience with people of color. Mostly white folks lived in Sweet Water, Kansas. In the coffee shop one morning, some men in a nearby booth said bad things about dark-skinned people. Dad said they feared anyone who was different. Tommy had agreed with his father—until now. *These must be the people they were talking about*, Tommy thought.

With great effort, Baboon stood. Taking two exaggerated steps into the street, he stopped, wobbled from side to side, and then made a slow, unsteady turn. With his body leaning forward, his feet followed in shuffling steps until he smacked into the Chevy's rear bumper. His buddy laughed. The laughing man held his sides, pointed, and roared. Baboon stood with his back toward the alley, where Paul and Tommy shivered in the shadows. Struggling with his zipper, Baboon threw his head back as piss streamed off the bumper and splashed onto his shoes.

Paul struggled against Tommy's embrace, and Tommy's arm felt like a piece of waterlogged driftwood. Paul's breathing became a high-pitched wheeze that grew louder with each breath. Throwing his free hand over Paul's mouth, Tommy wrapped his dead arm tighter around Paul's waist and pulled him deeper into the shallow doorway. Tommy felt a cold steel door against his spine. Then the laughing stopped.

The laughing man stepped from behind the Chevy and stared into the alley.

Straight into Tommy's eyes.

CHAPTER 2

For several months, Karen Parker had not slept well. After three hours of fitful tossing, she accepted that sleep had eluded her again. Staring at her transparent reflection in the kitchen window, she tried to still her thoughts. She sipped a mug of hot chocolate as she thought about her fourteenth anniversary, which occurred a year ago. Life seemed perfect then. Roger owned the farm of his dreams. She wrote for a weekly newspaper. Her days teemed with worthwhile things for a mother to do: church volunteer, soccer coach, PTA leader, and chief cookie baker. Roger and Tommy and Paul and Kansas fulfilled her every aspiration.

Almost.

Karen still reeled at the speed with which cancer overtook her mate. Forgetting might have been easier had it not been for a poorly timed argument. Roger stomped off to the field. A few hours later, Karen cooled down, planned her apology, and fixed him breakfast. However, Roger didn't come home.

She found him slumped over the steering wheel of his tractor, stalled in a drainage ditch at the far end of the field. His skin felt cold and clammy to her touch. His face had turned bluish black from settling blood. A condition called postmortem lividity, which she'd seen hundreds of times at the scenes of accidents and homicides and suicides. Scenes she'd pursued without hesitation, fear, or remorse, for those were the scenes of the stories that Karen reported. Yet, despite the hardened emotional shell she cultivated when she was a Cleveland television reporter, she couldn't shake this last image of her husband.

The cascade of misfortune didn't stop with Roger's death. After selling the farm, the home, and the equipment, enough money remained to pay the debts, move what was left of her family to Cleveland, and rent a brownstone on a not-so-good side of town. She returned to pursue the only profession she knew—journalism. She wasn't the rising star of fifteen years earlier but was a journalist again, starting at the newspaper as she did before. Karen Parker vowed that, like the phoenix, she would rise from the ashes.

Of one thing, she was certain. She'd spent far too many nights like this. If only she could shut off her brain. Fatigue stiffened her muscles.

She sipped the last of her chocolate, which had grown lukewarm. Easing down the hall, she went to check on her boys before pursuing the sleep that evaded her. She hated bringing them here, hated taking them from the only life they knew, and hated that they didn't have a father to help them become men.

For a moment, she stood silently outside their bedroom, straining to hear the soft sounds of their breathing. Earlier, she'd grown cross, snapping at Paul when he failed to heed her final warning for civility at the dinner table. At bedtime, she told Tommy and Paul that she loved them, but somehow, it didn't seem enough.

The old hinges creaked as she opened the door. A dim glow, cast by the 40-watt hall lamp, spilled into the room and fell across the bunk bed, shoehorned into the corner.

Karen gasped. "Oh, shit!"

CHAPTER 3

Tommy tried to become invisible, but it wasn't working. The men peered into the alley. Their eyes searched the darkness, trying to locate the source of the sounds. *Which way to the brownstone?* Tommy wondered. Two blocks behind them, best he could remember. The men inched closer until they stood in a semicircle outside the alley entrance. Only one option.

Tommy screamed, "Run!"

Dragging Paul out of the doorway, Tommy sprinted down the alley, pulling Paul behind him. Paul cried. Sounds of heavy feet slapped against wet pavement behind them.

"Get the little bastards."

Tommy bolted from the darkness into the glow of a streetlamp. The footsteps closed in right behind them. Paul screamed, and then a rough hand caught Tommy by the collar, jerking him to a stop.

"Let me go," Tommy cried out, twisting desperately to free himself, but the man held him fast.

"What you boys doin' out so late? You could get hurt. Right, guys?" Laughing Man taunted.

Driver held Paul's arm like a chicken's wing, forcing Paul up on tiptoes. Baboon fell on all fours and vomited on the sidewalk. A fourth man pulled something from his pocket, flicked his wrist to the side, and produced the shining blade of a knife. Knife said, "You boys lost?"

"Leave us alone!" Tommy screamed, kicking and flailing his arms in the air as Laughing Man held him.

"Yeah. What you gonna do if I don't?" Laughing Man hooted as if it were the funniest thing he'd ever heard. Tommy swung his fist, finding only the cold night air.

Knife moved closer, lowered the edge of the blade along Paul's chest, stopping at his heart. With a quick jerk, Knife popped a button off Paul's jacket. Paul wet himself.

Driver tried to back away and continue his grasp on Paul at the same time. "Hey! The little bastard pissed on me."

Knife backhanded Paul on the side of his head. Paul hollered as blood streamed down his neck.

The sight of blood on his little brother turned Tommy's fear into rage. Raising his leg, he stomped down hard on Laughing Man's foot, and then twisted violently, freeing himself. He ran at Knife, but Knife spun around, catching Tommy across the face with the back of his hand. Tommy fell to the pavement. The taste of blood filled his mouth.

A flash of white-hot light filled the street. When Tommy's eyes adjusted, he saw a man silhouetted against a streetlamp's reflective glow.

The new guy seemed to have come from thin air, as if he'd materialized from vapor. The New Guy moved silently toward them. Knife stepped away from Paul and snarled, "What in the hell do you want?"

"You gentlemen should leave now." New Guy's voice cut through the night, sounding as if he were right inside Tommy's head.

"Fuck you!"

"You should go," New Guy said with a voice firm as stone.

Maybe he was a cop and would pull a gun. Tommy saw that happen all the time on television.

The men turned their backs to Tommy and Paul, focusing their attention on this man in the street. A glint of light reflected off Knife's blade. Laughing Man held a tire iron next to his leg. He and Driver fell in silently behind Knife.

Laughing man circled New Guy, swinging the tire iron in tight circles above his head. "Get your ass out of here."

New Guy turned, cutting Laughing Man off. They stood face to face, and then New Guy said, "This doesn't need to happen. You can drive away and lose nothing."

Laughing Man raised the tire iron high in the air, slamming it down, missing New Guy's head but striking his shoulder. Tommy heard a bone snap. *Please! Fight!* Tommy screamed in his mind. *"It's not my place,"* said a voice in return. *"Go. Now!"*

Swinging his arm like a windmill in a stiff wind, Laughing Man struck New Guy again and again and again until New Guy sank to his knees, blood streaming down his face and dripping from his chin onto the road. New Guy lifted his head and looked straight into Tommy's eyes, and Tommy felt as if he had known the man forever.

Laughing Man's breath came in quick gasps, and the tire iron hung to his side. Knife pushed Laughing Man out of the way, grabbed New Guy by the collar, jerked him to his feet, and then, with rapid jabs, thrust the blade deep into New Guy's stomach. The slick sound of splitting flesh filled the air.

Paul whimpered softly as Tommy pulled him halfway down the alley to a large garbage bin on wheels. They squeezed between the bin and the wall. Tommy gagged at the stench.

New Guy fell into the street. Laughing Man kicked him in the head. Then the Chevy Guys stood there admiring their work.

"Hey! Where'd those damn kids go?" Laughing Man asked.

"Shit. They ran off." Knife cuffed Driver on the head. "Why weren't you watching, dipshit?"

Knife walked backward across the street. "Let's get out of here before the cops show up." Then he yelled, "This ain't over, you little bastards. I'm going to find you, and when I do, I'm going to cut your guts out. Do you hear me?"

CHAPTER 4

For the third time, swearing like a drunken sailor, Karen Parker ran from her bedroom to the kitchen, then back. *Where are those goddamn keys? Think! Purse!* Turning her purse upside down, she dumped years of accumulated odds and ends onto the kitchen table.

Damn. Think! Coat!

Karen flew back to the bedroom. Searching her coat pockets yielded the same thing that emptying her purse had.

Nothing.

★★★

The Chevy was gone. The street grew quiet. Paul cried softly. Tommy held him. In the dimly lit street, New Guy's body lay surrounded by a sea of red. Tommy eased his grip on Paul, slowly drifting toward the fallen man.

"What do we do?" Paul whispered.

"Is he dead?" Tommy asked cautiously, stepping closer.

"Let's get out of here." Paul's voice quivered.

"Wait…." He signaled Paul to stay put, but Paul glued himself to Tommy's side.

Nearing the body, Paul said, "Nobody needs to know about this. It wasn't our fault."

"We can't just leave him! We gotta do something." Puffs of vapor formed as Tommy spoke. Their shoes squished and squeaked on the wet pavement as they moved closer. Tommy listened for the rumble of rap music. In the distance, he heard a siren, but it faded into the night.

The man wasn't dressed remarkably well. He wore a faded shirt with green and blue stripes, jeans, and tennis shoes—not Nike, but some generic department store variety.

Tommy glanced over at Paul, and it was as if he saw him for the first time. Paul's shoes were untied, with the laces in large loops and the unraveled ends trailing on the ground. His shirttail hung from under his wrinkled Levi jacket, and a tuft of blond hair stood straight up on the right side of his head. Paul wasn't a fearless adventurer, like Indiana

Jones; he was a little boy. Not just any little boy, his little brother. *How could I have let this happen?*

Unexpectedly, there came a deep, gurgling noise. Paul jumped back. "What was that?"

"He's alive!" Tommy kneeled next to the man, touching his shoulder softly. "We need to get help."

"I told Mom we needed our own cell phones, but she wouldn't listen. Let's go home. It's through that alley." Paul pointed across the street.

Tommy traced an invisible line from Paul's finger to a drugstore, and next to the drugstore, something rarely seen—a payphone.

CHAPTER 5

Karen raked her fingers through her hair, pulling it up into a wild, shaggy mass. She saw the damn things as the scream she stifled erupted. In plain view, on the kitchen counter, lay the wad of keys for which she'd been searching. But she found them too late. Hearing a noise, she spun around as her two pale-faced boys walked through the back door.

"Where in the hell have you been?" Karen raged. Before either boy could respond, she saw the terror in their eyes. She dropped to one knee and gathered them in her arms. "Are you okay? You scared me to death." Tears streamed down her cheeks.

She pulled back, studying her sons with intensity. Wiping the tears from her cheeks, she said, "What were you two thinking? I told you it was dangerous here!"

"We're sorry, Mom," Tommy offered, trembling.

"What happened?" She heard sirens. The red lights of an ambulance flashed through the window.

Tommy glanced over his shoulder, then sucked in a deep breath.

Paul said nothing. Keeping secrets was easier for Paul than for Tommy, so Karen's eyes focused on Tommy.

"Just exploring." Tommy shrugged his shoulders.

"Exploring!" Karen said, almost shouting. She closed her eyes, took a deep breath, and then continued in a tone so calm it sounded unnatural. "Tell me what happened. We'll talk about your *exploration* later."

"It was a full moon. We walked. Then this sound. Boom, boom, boom." Tommy spoke in staccato, hands chopping the air. Fighting back tears, he occasionally bit his lip, recounting the night's events.

A thought crossed Karen's mind. She dismissed it, but it returned.

"We're in a lot of trouble, huh?"

"You said it. We'll talk about your punishment later." She rose from her knees and sat on the couch, staring out the window, chewing on a fingernail. There was a story here. *Two boys, fresh from the farm saved by a stranger in the middle of the inner city.*

"What is it? Mom?"

"Did those men follow you home?" She pulled her cell phone from her purse.

Calming down a bit, Tommy explained in more detail. The men drove away. He called the police, and then they ran home. The streets were deserted—no one followed them.

How could she think of work at a time like this? But regaining her former status as Cleveland's top reporter meant more money than the fashion-show-social-event-garden-club writing job she'd taken. And more money was important for her children, so she was thinking about them. Right?

Tommy said, "Dad told me what you used to do. He said you were a reporter here before you moved to Kansas. That's what you're thinking about, isn't it?"

Karen glanced at her phone. "No Tommy. I'm not thinking about that. I'm thinking about how I almost lost you two." She walked to the sink, filled a glass of water, sat it on the kitchen counter, and stared out the window.

"It would be a good story." Tommy put his arm around her waist. "We'll be okay. You'll be leaving for work in a few hours, anyway."

Karen's eyes moistened. Many challenges lay ahead, not the least of which was finding a balance between career and motherhood as a single parent. "I can't leave you guys."

Tommy glanced at Paul. "If you got your old job back, would it be more money?"

"Yes, but that has nothing…."

Tommy cut her off. "If you made more money, could we move away from this side of town?"

"I suppose."

"Then you must go. I want out of here as soon as possible. We're safe now. You go."

Paul started to say something. Tommy gave him a stern look.

"Go!" Tommy waved his hand at the door, then folded his arms across his chest.

Karen ran a brush through her hair, dressed, and gathered her things. "Get some sleep. Okay?" She hesitated a moment, then walked out the door.

The rain had stopped. A southern breeze warmed the air. She drove to the area Tommy described, which proved easy to find because police and paramedics swarmed the street. Bolting from her car, she met a thick hand at the end of a large cop's outstretched arm.

"Crime scene. You can't go in there."

Karen shoved her shiny new press ID in his face. "Press!" She insisted and walked on.

"Sure. Have it your way." He flipped his wrist as if he lacked the strength to argue.

She took photos in rapid succession. After taking a dozen shots, a familiar face caught her attention. The detective's hair had grayed, and his stomach strained against his belt more than she'd remembered, but he hadn't changed so much that she didn't recognize him.

"Who called it in?" The detective called to another officer, who scribbled on a notepad. "Somebody saw this, and I want to know who. Whoever it was, called from that payphone over there. Who in the hell uses a payphone nowadays? Get the lab people on that."

"Alex Madden?" Karen asked tentatively.

"Do I know you?"

"It's Karen Parker, I mean, Delulio. Well, used to be Delulio."

He squinted. "Well, I'll be damned. So, it is. I thought you were long gone."

"Well, I'm back." She turned one hundred eighty degrees, waving her outstretched arm at the street. "What happened?"

"Man got beat and stabbed, which ain't nothing unusual for this neighborhood." Alex surveyed scurrying police officers and paramedics as he chewed on a weathered toothpick and stared at Karen. "What are you doing here?"

"Working." She turned to see his steadfast eyes. The toothpick in his mouth flicked like a nervous twitch.

"So, I figured. I mean, how did you get here so fast?"

Big mistake. Alex Madden was a serious cop who missed little. No, that wasn't right. He missed nothing. She should have kept her mouth shut. Now, what was she going to do? "I heard the sirens. I live a block over." She pointed toward the brownstone.

"I'd wager you hear sirens at all hours in this neighborhood. Why venture out in the middle of the night for this particular siren?" Glancing to where Karen pointed, he saw a lab tech dusting the payphone for fingerprints.

"I don't know. Instinct? It was so close." She shrugged her shoulders, then glanced away. "Was he robbed?"

"Somebody saw what happened. Called it in. Know anything about that?"

Karen shook her head.

Alex pulled the toothpick from his mouth and flicked it into the street. "I don't know if he was robbed. I do know he was beaten and stabbed."

After a long moment of silence, she turned to face him. "Alex, it's good to see you. Maybe we can have coffee sometime?" Karen shifted her weight as he studied her. Before Alex could respond, Karen nodded toward her phone and said, "I better get some shots." She eased away, clicking random pictures, unaware of what images she shot.

She hadn't thought about anyone questioning her. What would the police say if they knew her two young sons were almost killed and now, they were home alone? She hadn't thought about that. She damned sure hadn't thought about running into Alex Madden.

She shuffled toward the body. At first, she doubted that what Tommy said was true. Even his wild rambling about this stranger being some sort of hero seemed to make sense now.

A firefighter sprinted to the ambulance. His departure gave her an unobstructed view. Her hand flew to her mouth. Hero or not, the man was a pulp of bloody flesh in a puddle of blood. *How could he still be alive?* One paramedic, holding a bag of clear liquid, kneeled near the man's head. A front-page photograph, but her phone hung at her side.

Two ambulance attendants and two firefighters hoisted the victim onto a waiting stretcher. One paramedic held the IV bag while another shouted orders as they rushed to an ambulance that waited with gaping doors. The doors slammed shut, and the paramedic, who'd been shouting instructions, slapped the rear doors twice, signaling her last act in this rescue. Red lights danced off the buildings and glistened on the wet street as the ambulance sped off toward St. John's Hospital. Karen shivered.

A firm, warm hand kneaded her shoulder. It was Alex.

"You, okay?"

"Fine," she said, struggling to keep her voice calm. "It's been longer than I thought."

"What do you know about this guy?"

She glanced at her shoes, then down the street. "I don't know what you mean."

"Get your story ready for the afternoon edition. I'll be around later. We'll talk. And Karen, I'm glad you're back."

He looked into her eyes, and for a moment, she thought he wanted to say something else, but he stuck his hands into the pockets of his rumpled tan coat and walked towards his car.

★ ★ ★

Staring out the window, Tommy didn't hear his mother open the back door. She eased beside him, putting her arm around his shoulder.

"You all, right?" Karen asked.

He nodded.

"He's alive," she said. "I'll stop by the hospital on my way to work. I'll call if I learn anything."

Tommy nodded but said nothing.

Karen walked to the couch and kneeled beside it. Paul slept under a patchwork quilt that his grandmother made for his birthday a few years back. She kissed his forehead, then returned to Tommy.

"I'll be home right after work. Are you sure you're all, right?"

"We'll be okay." Tommy's voice was flat and emotionless. He had gotten Paul into dry jeans but didn't mention that. "Go to work. Don't worry about us. I can handle everything."

She touched his shoulder, then departed as silently as she had arrived, out the back door and into the night.

CHAPTER 6

Early morning was the quietest time at St. John's Hospital. Karen grabbed her notebook and donned her dark-blue blazer, which contrasted with her faded blue jeans. She liked the look. Every profession calls for a certain amount of seduction. The look was somewhere between Saturday night and Monday morning—her faithful Levi jeans and a fitted navy blazer.

Pausing at the door, she rubbed the third finger of her left hand and the gold band that she refused to remove. In addition, the band served another purpose beyond the emotional tie to her late husband. It kept men away. She wasn't interested in meeting anyone—not now, not for quite a while, maybe never. However, she had work to do, and in the real world, a bare ring finger might make a difference. Working the ring over her knuckle, she stuffed it down the front pocket of her jeans.

Taking a deep breath, she pushed the heavy glass doors open. They opened slowly, and she felt like she moved through molasses. Inside, the white tile floor glistened with a freshly buffed coat of wax. On the wall, a bright yellow sign with bold red letters read FAST TRACK. Red arrows on the floor marked the way. Karen followed them to a small waiting room where two large nurses sat watch at the admissions desk. A young Hispanic couple sat on tattered brown chairs, and each held a sleeping child. The parents looked pale and scared. Somewhere beyond the closed doors was a third child, either injured or ill. It could be her sitting there, worrying about Tommy or Paul.

Karen marched towards the emergency room door.

"May I help you?" The larger of the two nurses stood, causing her chair to skate several inches.

Karen walked on, pretending she didn't hear the woman.

"Hold on there!" the second nurse said, louder and more calloused.

Karen took a deep breath. Holding out her ID, she said, "Press. I'm following up on a man an ambulance brought in moments ago."

"Not in there, you aren't. No one is allowed in the ER, except emergency room personnel. That includes reporters, Missy." The woman paused, as if hoping Karen would give her an excuse to throw a cross-body block. After a long minute, the nurse said, "If you give me the patient's name, I will tell you his condition. That's how it works." The nurse moved within arm's reach and stood with her hands planted firmly on her hips.

"I don't know his name. Someone stabbed him and left him for dead. The ambulance brought him in a few minutes ago."

"Sounds like you got yourself a John Doe. No name, no info—that's the rule. Besides, they rushed him into surgery."

At one time, she would have screamed, demanded to see the administrator, threatened litigation, and done whatever necessary to reduce these two Neanderthal guards, posing as nurses, into apologetic and humble little people with a new understanding of the phrase power of the press. Had she lost her touch? Stupid question. She turned away, her feet sliding along the floor as she gazed down, seeing little other than the white vinyl tile passing beneath her. She passed a fast-track sign and moved deeper into the hospital.

When she looked up, she realized she was lost. Before she found her bearings, she heard voices, one male and one female, coming down the hall toward her. She slid into a room marked HOUSEKEEPING. She heard the man say that the patient had multiple stab wounds—a real mess. Karen's heart pounded in her chest, and she found it hard to swallow, as if someone had stuffed a thick cotton towel down her throat.

Karen eased from the closet and followed at a safe distance until the man and woman disappeared through a set of swinging doors marked SURGICAL SUITE 13. Next to the doors, a stairway labeled OBSERVATION AREA led up and to the right. Bounding up the steep steps, she smiled. A few minutes earlier, a brick wall dressed in white stopped her cold, but now she was about to watch the forbidden operation from the observation suite.

Karen Parker was back.

CHAPTER 7

At the top of the stairs, Karen found the doctors' observation area overlooking the surgical suite. Thick burgundy carpet covered the floor, oak wainscot paneling covered the walls, and overstuffed chairs with striped upholstery of deep green and burgundy sat empty. On the opposite side of the suite was the students' section, furnished with mismatched plastic chairs, thin blue carpet, and off-white walls. Two women, reading thick textbooks, occupied two of the plastic chairs. Alex Madden and a young detective Karen recognized from the crime scene sat in the front row. She had never entered the doctors' section. The students' section had changed little since the last time she was here when she watched Senator Andrea Ross die on the operating table, fifteen years ago, at the beginning of the end of Karen's career.

Alex raised his thick hand. Karen gave a little wave in return. The hard-plastic chairs looked more inviting than the overstuffed chairs in which she sat, but there was no way to get to them from here.

Below her, the surgical suite buzzed with activity, and at the center of the pandemonium, a man lay on a stainless-steel table with tubes and hoses and wires connecting him to monitors and medical gadgets, making him appear more like a science fiction bio-mechanism than a human being. One man watched monitors and twisted valves, and two nurses counted bright stainless-steel hardware and porous brown sponges. A third nurse arranged the instruments fastidiously on a cart covered with a blue cloth. The smell of antiseptic solution assaulted her nostrils. A nervous din echoed through the suite, creating a grave sense of urgency.

Two doctors burst through the double doors. A moment later, the light of halogen bulbs bathed the room. Everyone squinted but continued working as if it were nothing extraordinary. Karen's eyes adjusted. A nearby monitor flickered. The screen, initially bright blue, filled with the image of the victim's body. She thought back to the last time she was in this room, but she remembered no monitors. *They must be recording this,* she thought.

The story of the senator's assassination should have brought her national recognition. Instead, it sent her packing. For nine months, Karen had shadowed Senator Ross's presidential campaign, a woman destined for the White House, until an assassin's bullet pierced her skull. Ross was not yet buried when Karen started her own investigative story, and she soon realized something even more sinister than mere assassination lurked in the shadows of this event. She was getting close to the truth when a man from Washington, D.C. arrived to take over the case. His name was Sam Henry, and he had a nasty case of CIA-007 attitude. "Back off your investigation, or go to jail," he had said. She should have stood her ground. But she crumbled. Something inside her had continued crumbling ever since. However, that was fifteen years ago. It no longer mattered.

A nearby monitor displayed a close-up of the victim's abdomen, riddled with small slits where the knife struck. The surgeon announced the date and time, then introduced himself as James T. Wellington.

He said:

```
The patient is a Caucasian male
approximately forty-five years of age,
weighing one hundred and seventy pounds,
six-feet tall. The police found him on the
street after being alerted by an anonymous
911-call. He has two lacerations,
approximately forty-five millimeters running
laterally on the left side of his skull, each
begins near the left temple, and extend
parallel approximately twenty-five
millimeters above the left ear. These are
about a week old. Our patient, it seems, is
no stranger to violence.
```

Wellington introduced his assistant, Dr. Benjamin Cray. Dr. Cray nodded as if to affirm both the announcement of his presence and Wellington's description. At Dr. Wellington's command, a technician recited the patient's blood pressure, pulse, and body temperature, both historical and current. With that done, Wellington droned on. Karen tried to listen, but the doctor gravitated into medical babble beyond her comprehension. Occasionally, she could vaguely translate something he said. She understood the patient had been close to death since he arrived at St. John's, and at one-point Wellington noted that the man's condition seemed like that of a hibernating bear.

Raising her eyes, she studied her peers across the room. The students stared at a glowing monitor, and the detectives, slouching in their chairs, looked like dictionary definitions of boredom. Wellington finished his dissertation.

Time to begin.

Whether to watch the real people below her or the monitor posed a tough decision for Karen. The monitor provided more detail, but she found watching the people more intriguing. The experts across the room focused on the monitor, so with some effort, she did the same, but blocking the real people from her mind remained a challenge.

Wellington asked for a scalpel, which an assistant delivered to his outstretched hand. He handled the surgical instrument with great familiarity and then announced, for the record, what he was about to do. The medical terminology subdued the reality of the act, which was to slice the man open.

He drew the scalpel across a small patch of flesh below the man's sternum, then paused, and said, "Son of a bitch." Raising the scalpel, he studied it, and said, "What's wrong with this piece of shit?" After a moment, he tossed it on a nearby cart and asked for a new one.

On his next attempt, a small incision appeared under the glistening blade. He stopped, peered at the insignificant opening, and said, "This guy's skin is like an alligator's."

A gnat-like buzzer sounded. A technician said, "There it is again."

"There's what?" Wellington asked, craning his neck to see the woman and her machine.

"It's the heart monitor. Like there's something there, and then it's gone. I don't know what it is, but it's strange."

Wellington gave his head a little shake, as if something bothered him.

Someone cried out, "We're losing him!"

"Goddamn it," Wellington said, above a piercing alarm. "What have you got?"

"Flat-lined! He's in arrest!"

"Paddles! Stat," Wellington shouted.

"No! I've got a pulse, but it's weak."

"Adrenaline!" A nurse handed Wellington a large syringe with a long needle. Wellington pointed the needle toward the ceiling, squirted liquid from its tip, and then sank it deep into the man's chest. Removing the syringe, he said, "I'm going in."

"We need to stabilize him first," a technician fired back.

"He's bleeding out. You do your job, and I'll do mine," Wellington snapped, and then he quickly sliced the man from sternum to navel.

"He's coming back," someone said flatly.

Wellington looked at Dr. Cray. "Spread him."

Cray slid a stainless-steel paddle under each rib cage. Despite his education and training, Dr. Cray performed nothing short of manual labor, spreading the patient open until the veins in Cray's arms bulged like writhing snakes.

"Jesus," Wellington whispered.

Unable to watch the monitor any longer, Karen leaned forward, resting her elbows on the banister. She wished she could remember Biology 101. She counted organs, ticking them off on her fingers, but what do they really look like? Different, she was certain, then the glossy pictures of a textbook. She wasn't an expert, yet nothing she saw connected with the images stored within the corridors of her memory.

Nothing.

Wellington stood motionless, staring with wide, unblinking eyes. Cray paled behind his green mask, his eyes darting between the patient and Wellington. Other members of the team leaned in to see, each with a different reaction. The nurse, who handed surgical instruments to Wellington, stared, frozen like a statue. Another gasped, then retreated. A third glanced, then fainted. A technician, who didn't seem overly involved in any particular activity, caught her before she hit the gray concrete floor.

"Um, we—eh, have a—well, this subject," Wellington stammered.

"What now?" Cray was the first to string together a sentence.

Holding out his hand as if to calm his assistant, Wellington said, "I have exposed the abdominal cavity for exploration."

Karen bit her finger. Wellington sounded like a prerecorded message one might hear in an airport, and she decided he was reciting by rote as he continued.

"There is evidence of trauma to the internal organs consistent with the lacerations seen on the exterior of the abdomen. The lacerations here, however, are in the mid to late stages of the healing process."

"Son of a bitch! There it is!" A female technician blurted out.

"What?" Wellington turned. His voice was subdued.

"A second heartbeat. Syncopated with the first, but just as strong."

There must be a logical explanation. Karen couldn't anticipate any other possibility.

Dr. Cray stated the simple truth. Sliding the paddles out of the man's abdomen, Cray sent them clanking to the concrete like cymbals in the silent room.

Stepping back, Cray stared into Wellington's eyes and said, "He's not human."

CHAPTER 8

The bed felt wet. The nightmare familiar. Wiping the perspiration from his face, Sam Henry stumbled to the bathroom, filled a cup with water, and gulped it down. His reoccurring nightmares involved a mission in El Salvador, on which everyone died except him. The most haunting aspect was an image of a man carrying him to safety. Sam kept seeing the man's face and the name badge sewn on his shirt. After Sam healed from his wounds, he tried to find the man. However, it was as if the man didn't exist.

✱✱✱

Dr. Wellington raised his eyes, staring across the operating table at Benjamin Cray. An uncomfortable moment of silence passed. Cray asked what he was supposed to do.

"Close," Wellington whispered.

Cray asked a nurse for an instrument. She fumbled with the shining tools. Maybe because closing was out of sequence, perhaps because of something else. Karen couldn't be sure. Cray touched the patient, then glanced at Wellington, who was backing away.

"The incision is healing from the inside out," Cray said.

Wellington continued his retreat, bumping into the wall two feet left of the exit door. Feeling along the wall, his eyes remained fixed on his patient. Before disappearing into the adjacent room, he looked at Dr. Cray and said, "Stay with him, Ben."

✱✱✱

This was huge, and Karen had to get it in print fast. What was the real story? Was this a rare human anomaly? A mutant-humanoid weapon from the CIA or KGB? Or a sojourner from a distant world? First

Contact? God. She didn't know where to begin. No, that wasn't true. Before she could begin, she had to get the hell out of there.

Across the room, Madden's arms fanned the air in reckless animation as he talked to the younger detective. Madden pointed at Karen, and then his young assistant, Jerry Faulkner, bolted for the door. She understood what was happening.

The medical students didn't think about escaping. Instead, their curiosity got the better of them as they peered over the edge of the banister, hoping to see something with the naked eye that they couldn't see on the monitors. As if by osmosis, they sensed they had lingered too long and turned toward the door, but Madden quickly blocked their escape.

"Hold on." Madden stuck out his large hand like a traffic cop. With his other hand, he peeled back one side of his blazer, exposing a gold detective's shield. "We need to talk."

"You have a warrant? I'd like to see it. If not, get out of our way!" The younger of the two women decided it was time she used the expensive university education her dad was paying for. This was straight out of Arrogance 101. A technique she'd watched doctors use daily since they accepted her into medical school. But she learned that this skill required practice. To say it had less than the desired effect on Madden was an understatement.

Madden explained the facts of life to them, and although delivered in a few terse sentences, his monologue contained enough insight that it should have earned both students three class credits.

Five minutes later, Madden was standing in the hospital security manager's office, explaining the situation. Madden told the security chief most of the story but failed to mention that he'd already commandeered one security guard to imprison the two students and another to round up the surgical team. And, of course, he left out the one minor detail that the hospital's most recent surgical patient might be an alien from another world, instead opting for an innocuous explanation about there being evidence of a rare infectious disease. For the moment, things were well contained, save for one renegade reporter. With the security manager's help, hospital security staff would seal the exits.

Then Madden had one more detail.

Call it insurance.

***

Karen prayed Madden's partner wasn't coming as she sprinted down the hall. She stopped at an intersection with another hallway, its size suggesting that she had reached the main corridor. "Careful," Karen whispered, inching forward, and peeking around the corner. About ten yards down the hall was an elevator next to a nurses' station. That's where Madden's partner stood talking to a woman wearing a pink-striped dress. The woman pointed down the hall and motioned with her hand to the left, at the spot where Karen stood.

"Shit," Karen swore under her breath. Turning to run, she saw a white metal door with the words EXIT PARKING stenciled in red paint.

★ ★ ★

When Jerry Faulkner rounded the corner, he heard a door latch click shut. Easing the steel door open, he smelled the scent of damp concrete and automobile exhaust. Drawing shallow breaths, he heard only silence and traffic in the distance. He closed the door and moved on.

CHAPTER 9

Sitting in an old blue Chevy on a deserted street in old town Cleveland, Carlos Garcia crumpled a beer can, then tossed it at a stop sign. The streets were still quiet. Morning commuters had not yet begun their ritualistic travel. The homeless slept in doorways, and the slightly more fortunate slept in rundown project apartments. Carlos studied these patterns. His business success depended on knowing his city and its habits. The few souls who might venture onto the streets wouldn't recognize his car, not at this time of day, not in this neighborhood. If he hung around too long, the gangs that ruled these Cleveland streets would investigate. Carlos knew that as well. He wouldn't be staying that long.

"Hey little cousin, you look freaked, man. Don't you wimps party in Colorado?" Carlos ruffled Julio's hair.

"We party. I'm tired from the trip and all."

"You're a farm boy. We'll whip you into shape. Now, let's make some money, and then we find those two brats." Carlos pulled a revolver from his belt, a Brazilian-made 38-special, with nickel plating and a two-inch barrel. With his thumb, he pushed the release button, then flicked his wrist to snap the cylinder open. Six rounds gleamed in the light of a streetlamp. Slamming the cylinder shut, Carlos returned the pistol to his belt.

Carlos handed Julio a compact 380 cal. semi-automatic pistol he'd pulled from his boot. "Here, mi amigo. This one's for you. I'll get you a real gun, but for now, you can use my backup."

Julio turned the small gun over in his hand, staring at it.

Carlos showed Julio the safety. Eyeing his driver, Eddy, and his lieutenant, Miguel, Carlos said to Julio, "You know how to shoot, right?"

"Yeah," Julio said.

Carlos laughed. "What do you farm boys shoot? Turkeys?"

"Pheasants," Julio corrected.

"Well, you won't be shooting any pheasants here," Carlos said.

***

Abraham White flipped the sign in the door from closed to open, then turned on the lights and started the first day of his 30th year in his small grocery store in old-town Cleveland. Abraham had no more than toggled the light switch to on when a pair of headlights appeared in front of his store.

"Right on time," Abraham said to himself.

William Harkness's arrival never varied over two minutes unless something was wrong in the neighborhood. William—no one called him Bill—was a Cleveland police officer on the graveyard shift.

"Coffee?" Abraham asked as William walked through the front door. A steaming cup was already waiting by the cash register.

"You know it." William picked up the cup, cradling it with both hands, holding it near his face, savoring the aroma.

"How's Cleveland this morning?"

"Normal. A robbery, a few assaults, one murder, but our neighborhood, thank God, was quiet." William and Abraham held their normal conversation, the weather, and the Browns. William invited Abraham to go fishing with him on the lake. Abraham had to tend the store.

"You're going to die in this damn place," William said, draining his second cup of coffee, then adding, "You should sell this place and retire, but you wouldn't know what to do with yourself. You gotta learn how to relax. Think about it. Go with me to the lake. I know where the big ones are." William stretched out his arms as far as he could reach, showing Abraham the size of the fish he contemplated catching.

"Think about it." Then with a wave, William walked out the door. William's patrol car disappeared around a corner.

William is right, Abraham thought. *I need a hobby*. Once a week, Gloria nagged him to sell the store so they could travel while their health was still good. She'd be up in an hour or so. Maybe he'd talk to her about watching the store so he could go fishing.

✱ ✱ ✱

"There he goes," Carlos said. "Yeah, just like every cop. They must have cloned these stupid bastards. Every morning, they stop at their favorite spot for coffee and donuts, and then they go screw around until it's time to go home. Idiots." Carlos adjusted his sunglasses. "Time to go, Julio."

Julio protested, but Carlos said, "Initiation time, little cousin. Blood in, blood out. Understand?" Julio turned his head enough to stare down the barrel of the pistol in Carlos' hand.

"I understand," Julio said.

***

Abraham unpacked canned peaches and placed them in neat rows on the top shelf. The bell at the front door rang. Stepping from the aisle, he saw two young men enter his store. They weren't from this neighborhood. Abraham knew everyone who lived in this little corner of Cleveland. One wore a black hoody, the other a faded plaid shirt. They had an hour before the local men started making their way to paying jobs. If these two were still hanging around, there would be trouble for them.

"Can I help you?" Abraham made his way to the sanctuary of his counter. Neither boy answered.

The boy wearing plaid worked his way to the back of the store. Abraham watched. Something wasn't right. The black hoody boy was reading the ingredients on canned chili. The plaid-shirted boy disappeared into the back-storage area, and then Abraham heard the back door open and shut. It was locked from the inside. Did the kid leave or let someone in?

"Hey, Pop."

Startled, Abraham spun around to find the boy wearing a black hoody standing at the counter. "Yes?"

Suddenly, Abraham was looking down the barrel of a gun. "Julio," the gunman called. "Get your ass out here." The gunman craned his neck, trying to look around the store, but the gun remained pointed at Abraham's chest. "Julio! You chicken-shit bastard! Get out here, or I'm going to shoot your ass."

The gunman mumbled something and said, "You got a plastic bag, old man?"

"Yeah, sure," Abraham said with an uncontrolled quiver. He reached to the plastic bag holder and pulled one free. He held it out to the gunman.

"Fill it." The gunman motioned toward the cash register.

Opening the register, Abraham emptied the cash drawer. When he finished, Abraham held up the bag. "I don't want any trouble."

The gunman smiled. "That's good, because neither do I. You have a nice day." With that, Carlos pointed the gun at Abraham's chest and fired six rounds. He tucked the pistol back into his belt. On the way out, he picked up the only thing he'd touched and put it in his sack. Chili for lunch.

CHAPTER 10

Tommy's stomach growled. He was hungry, so he begrudgingly left the warmth of his cocoon on the chair in search of food. Pulling a bag of cereal from the cupboard, he searched another cabinet, then the dishwasher, for a clean bowl. As the generic puffed rice spilled into the bowl, Tommy realized this was another adjustment he'd have to accept. Before his dad died, Mom bought name-brand cereal. Tommy figured generic cereal wasn't the most challenging change he would face.

It had been a tough night. Although he was safe at home, he'd suffered two nightmares, both involving the knife-wielding maniac from the street. As he poured the milk, he sensed someone on the back steps. Outside the door, the light from the kitchen lit a man's face. Tommy recognized him. The man from the street. The one Knife tried to kill. "I need your help, Tommy." The man spoke, but his lips didn't move. Then he was standing in the kitchen, like magic.

"I must be dreaming." Tommy rubbed his eyes.

"More like an apparition." The stranger studied Tommy's face for a moment and then added. "A hologram, a vision. Do you understand?"

Tommy nodded his head and said, "Who are you?" Tommy leaned away until his weight forced a step backward.

"A friend."

Tommy took a deep breath.

"In a few minutes, a policeman will come. He'll take you to the hospital."

"Is Mom there?"

"Yes. However, that's not important. We'll talk again when the time is right. For now, just do as they tell you." The stranger faded, then reappeared on the back porch.

"Wait! What's your name?"

The man paused before stepping into the darkness.

Without turning around, he said, "Nigel."

Then he was gone.

CHAPTER 11

Carlos wiped his plate with a butter-soaked piece of wheat toast. Robbery made him hungry. Murder made him ravenous. By now, he should have been home, but he had unfinished business that needed tending. The two little punks who witnessed his first Halloween kill got away. It wasn't Halloween just yet, but close enough. Last Halloween, Carlos killed a rival gang member in a drive-by shooting. It pleased him so much that he made killing a Halloween tradition, and he hoped to increase the number of victims each year. Killing those two boys and the store clerk would triple last year's count. He didn't enjoy killing kids, but they were gringos, and two fewer gringos wasn't a bad thing. Besides, it was Halloween, so kids were fair game. Carlos made the rules up as he went. Then there was that chicken-shit cousin. There wasn't much worse than a brother who ran out in the middle of a heist. But a blood relative? That was damn embarrassing. He'd have to make an example of Julio. Merely killing him wouldn't be enough.

Carlos stood. "Pay the bill, Miguel. I gotta piss."

"I'm beat. Let's go home," Eddy stretched his back.

"We can't go home, dumb shit. We got business." Carlos threw a fifty on the table, then turned to walk away.

"What? Those kids? How we gonna find them?" Eddy rubbed the small of his back with the knuckles of his fists.

Carlos turned back. His face twisted in an evil sneer. "We cruise."

"What? Drive around? What they gonna do, flag us down? Shit," Eddy said.

Carlos placed both hands on the table and leaned into Eddy's face. "They got to live close by. Two little pricks like that ain't gonna be far from home at that time of night. They'll come out sometime. Walk to school. Play some hoops. We'll find them. Then we're gonna find that worthless cousin of mine. He's gonna pay."

* * *

Tommy didn't expect to fall asleep but awoke to find that predawn gray had replaced the blackness of the night. His stomach remained knotted from the persistent nightmares that plagued him since his father's death.

Standing at the kitchen sink, he filled a glass with water and took a long drink. It tasted like a swimming pool. Maybe the entire night was a nightmare—a hallucination caused by the homemade pizza mom made last night. The kitchen clock said it was 6:05.

He heard a knock at the front door. That would be the police. *How did I know that? That was just a dream, wasn't it?* He peeked out a slit in the curtain and saw a police officer standing at the front door. A black and white police car waited at the curb. *We must be going to the hospital.*

"Hello," Tommy said through the opening of the chained door.

"Hi, I'm looking for Mrs. Parker's kids. Is Karen your mom? I'm Officer Ricks, David Ricks. You can call me Dave."

Tommy closed the door, undid the chain, and let the police officer enter. He'd been told, in no uncertain terms, to never open the door for anyone and to never go anywhere with a stranger. But this was a police officer, and Tommy was expecting him, wasn't he? Saying nothing more, Tommy walked down the hall and disappeared into a room.

"Wake up," Tommy said, firmly shaking Paul's shoulder.

"What?" Paul asked, peering through thin slits in puffy eyelids.

"We gotta go see Mom," Tommy explained. "There's a policeman here to take us."

"Is she okay?" Paul asked, dragging himself from under the covers, rubbing his eyes. Paul had not bothered undressing before climbing into bed, but that wasn't unusual.

"She's okay." Tommy tried to comb Paul's tangled hair with his fingers, but it was hopeless.

Tommy led Paul into the living room. "This is Paul. I'm Tommy."

"Hi, boys. Don't worry, your mom's fine. It's just that—well, something's happened." David Ricks didn't know why Detective Madden sent him to fetch the Parker boys—something about an insurance policy.

Tommy didn't ask questions. Instead, he held the door open, waiting for Officer Ricks to realize he and Paul were ready to leave.

"It's against policy, but you boys can ride up front with me," Ricks said as he opened the passenger door.

"Cool," Paul said as he slid in.

Tommy wondered how Paul's night was. So far, he was taking the night's horrors well, like he took Dad's death, or so it seemed. The car's gadgets engrossed Paul. Ricks pointed to things and explained their purpose. Tommy couldn't remember a word the man said.

* * *

"There're the little pricks. That cop's taking them. Probably headed downtown to give a report." Carlos pointed at Tommy and Paul crawling in the front seat of the police cruiser.

"Shit. What we gonna do?" Eddie asked.

"Follow the bastards. We'll get our chance."

CHAPTER 12

Karen grabbed the exit door handle and pulled, but it didn't budge. She gave it a yank, and the door popped open with a loud scraping of metal against metal. A second later, the sound echoed off the far wall, then continued through the garage like a ripple on a pond. Swearing under her breath, she peeked through a thin slit in the doorway, scanning the parking area for men in uniform. Seeing none, she eased into the garage, which was half-full, mostly Mercedes and BMWs parked in front of PHYSICIANS ONLY signs.

Click! Whoosh!

On the opposite side of the garage, an elevator door slid open. Karen slammed her back against a nearby concrete pillar. Muffled voices of two men mingled with the sounds of distant traffic. The voices grew louder, and the sound of footsteps joined the mix. One man's footsteps sounded as if he wore metal taps on his shoes. She took a deep breath, picking out the words from the encroaching conversation. Positioning the men from the sounds they made, she eased around the pillar to conceal herself from them. That is when she noticed that the door to the stairwell had not closed but was still partially open. Her heart raced, watching as the door slowly closed against the resistance of a pneumatic control arm.

"Why do the police want her?" she heard one of them say. He sounded like a teenager.

"I don't know, and I don't care. Don't let her get away."

"Should I search the area?" The younger man asked.

"I don't think that's necessary. We're way ahead of her."

About twenty feet away from her sat a black BMW sedan with tinted windows that reflected images of the two men. The younger man wore the uniform of a hospital security guard; the other wore a black suit. As she watched, something crept into her consciousness—that something was her own reflection. If either of the two men looked at the BMW, they could see her just as clearly as she could see them.

"Promise you won't shoot anyone."

"Sid," the uniformed man said as he slapped a holster that hung to his side, "you ain't gotta worry about me, or old Pete, here."

"I ain't worried about old Pete if you keep it snapped in." With that, the second man walked away. At the elevator, he paused and said, "Don't shoot her." The elevator door closed.

The pneumatic arm overcame the resistance of the warped doorjamb, pulling the exit door shut with a distinctive sound that echoed through the garage, startling the young guard. In the BMW's reflection, Karen watched him stalking toward the door. He drew his pistol and swept it from side to side. With a sudden lunge, he kicked, planting his foot in the middle of the door. The door held tight. His gun fired. Karen jerked, covering her ears, and quickly tightening her muscles to keep from peeing her pants. Her ears rang as if a town square bell were implanted inside her head, and the rancid scent of gunpowder filled her nostrils. The guard pulled the door open. Crouching, he waved the gun with exaggerated arches. Satisfied that no one lurked in the stairwell, he blew the end of the pistol's barrel, then stuck it into its holster. He did two more quick draws, each followed by a slow pivot on bent knees.

The man holstered his pistol and touched the bullet hole with his finger. He then studied his finger as he walked toward where Karen hid. When he stopped, she could see him in her peripheral vision. She could hear him breathing. The scent of his Old Spice aftershave mingled with spent gunpowder. After a few moments, he turned and walked toward the street entrance. She estimated the garage would soon swarm with police, but as the seconds ticked past, none came.

She knew Alex would be pissed that she ran, but what could he do? Nothing. However, she never thought some pimply-faced, gun-toting psycho security guard would ruin her escape. How many more like him are out there? A chill shot up her spine. She had not factored lunatics into her estimate of danger. Certainly, this fool was the worst she'd see— an underpaid want-to-be cop. She'd write a story about him someday. She looked at her watch: 6:15.

The guard walked toward the entrance, where he paced, looking at his watch every few seconds like a nervous tick. A few minutes passed, and then he sprinted up the ramp and disappeared. Karen eased along the wall toward the entrance. Halfway up the ramp, she peeked over the concrete wall and saw an espresso vendor in a faded yellow Kombi bus. The hospital guard stood waiting in line. *What an idiot.*

Nothing could prevent her escape now. She'd get away clean.

Walking from the shadows into the first rays of morning sun, Karen resisted the urge to watch the security guard order coffee and flirt with the pretty barista. Karen felt young and alive. Blood surged through her veins. At the crosswalk, she punched the button and waited for the light to change. Nothing could stop her this time. This time, she'd write her story and make her mark.

A police cruiser rolled into the intersection and stopped in the right-hand turn lane. Karen turned away, but not fast enough to avoid meeting the eyes of a young boy sitting in the front seat. The light changed, and the cruiser continued toward the hospital entrance.

Paul did not see her.

But Tommy did.

CHAPTER 13

Alex Madden had found her Achilles heel. Manacles were unnecessary. Madden had her boys. Fighting back tears, Karen thought about the many contradictions in her life. She longed to be a tough reporter and a fearless truth crusader. But she was a mother, and fearless, she was not.

A young man wearing a light-blue security shirt stood sentry at St. John's front entrance. Thin, with a slight case of acne, he couldn't have been over twenty years old. He looked like a clone of the idiot in the parking garage.

"Excuse me. I'm Karen Parker." The young man showed no interest in her. "I must find Detective Madden."

"Sorry, Lady. I don't know Detective Madden. If you'll excuse me, I'm busy." His eyes darted back and forth, sifting through people exiting the hospital. Wet rings formed under his arms, and a nervous twitch overpowered his left hand. He was looking for her but didn't see her standing right in front of him.

Perfect.

She roamed undetected on the first floor for ten minutes and had just arrived on the second floor when Madden's sidekick spotted her in the hall. Approaching her calmly, he introduced himself as Jerry Faulkner with a pleasant smile and a deep, resonant voice that didn't match his youthful age. He led her to a conference room, where she saw the surgical team and two young boys holding white Styrofoam cups filled with steaming hot chocolate. Alex sat between her boys. Large and burly, Alex looked more like a grandfather than a hardened Cleveland cop.

Tommy's eyes opened wide, and with open arms, he flew to her. "Mommy!"

★★★

Sam awoke from yet another nightmare. Over the years, he'd learned to live with them. What choice did he have? They were dreams, and dreams can't hurt you. Still, it took hours to shake them. Sometimes it took all day. A quick glance at the alarm clock confirmed he was late again.

Sam staggered to the shower, wondering if a counselor might help, knowing that he would not talk to one. Instead, he'd drink strong coffee and pretend everything was okay. Hot water poured over his head and streamed down his neck, and he remembered a time when he couldn't tolerate being late. Now, it didn't bother him. The obscure job they'd stuck him with was a joke. No one noticed what he did or didn't do.

He'd already proven that.

* * *

"These young gentlemen must belong to you," Alex said as Tommy released Karen from a fierce hug.

"Yes." Karen sat. Her boys moved to either side of her. "This is Paul and Tommy."

"Sorry, I had to bring them here. I hope you can understand my dilemma. I must talk with them," Alex said.

Karen said, "You had to make sure I didn't get away."

Alex shrugged. "That too."

"I would have made it this time. You couldn't have stopped me. Had it not been for my boys."

"I'm sure you would have. But we're still friends, right?"

"The best," Karen confirmed.

"You're still hurting, I see. It was ten years ago."

"Fifteen," she corrected.

"See, fifteen years ago. Karen, you did the best you could. No one can fault you for that. It's over. Let it go." Alex shifted his weight and moved closer. "Hey, you were young. Scared. Hell, you still don't understand what you were up against, do you?"

"What do you mean?" Karen shifted Paul to her other knee, so she faced Madden squarely.

"I mean, Sam Henry. He wasn't just a cop. He was a powerful man in a powerful position. What else could you have done? You couldn't fight the United States government."

Tommy listened. What did that mean? Mom never talked about what happened to her in Cleveland, except once when she got mad and launched into a fit about some guy named Henry. Tommy didn't understand what she was talking about. Still didn't. The United States government? What was she—a spy?

* * *

With everyone secured, Alex set out to find the hospital administrator. The administrator's assistant ushered Alex into the office. On a massive cherry-wood desk sat a thick brass nameplate engraved with the name David Johnson. Alex assumed that Mr. Johnson had heard about the surgical crew and security by now. Sticking out his hand, he said, "I'm Detective Alex Madden."

Johnson stood, glaring, and said, "What in the hell do you think you're doing? Imprisoning my staff? Locking down my hospital? Commandeering my security force? I'll have your badge."

Alex didn't react to Johnson's barrage of anger, he expected it. He'd expected worse. He's right. But what was I supposed to do? Let people go their way, telling everyone about the alien in Cleveland? And what could the department do? Force me into early retirement? Alex smiled at the thought.

Johnson's nostrils flared, his face flushed red, and his hands shook. "You think this is funny?"

"Not at all. I'm sorry, Mr. Johnson, that was inappropriate. I was thinking of something else." Since he couldn't think of a plausible explanation for his sudden Cheshire-cat grin, he forged ahead. "Once I explain our situation, you'll understand. Serious decisions must be made. That's why I'm here." Alex spoke with a calm baritone voice, soothing and reassuring. "I'm really not prepared for a situation like this. I don't know the protocol. You know—what steps must be taken and who must be called?"

Alex told of the events of that morning, beginning with the 911 call and ending with staff being confined in a second-floor conference room. It took him five minutes. "Mr. Johnson, you have a serious situation on your hands. It's your call." The color had drained from David Johnson's face, and if Alex judged correctly, his color wouldn't soon return.

"Mr. Madden, now that I know the entire story, well—you did the right thing." Johnson sank into his leather chair. Rubbing his forehead, he continued. "What's next? I'm not sure. We prepare for all kinds of emergencies, but not for this. Yet, in training, we're told that no matter what kind of emergency one faces, the initial response is always the same: verify and contain. It appears you did it right."

Johnson paused and then continued. "I think we should call the National Center for Infectious Diseases. The CDC may not be the right place to call, but they will know who is. That's how the government works."

"You're the boss, Mr. Johnson." Alex took a deep breath and sat in a chair facing Johnson's desk. Something didn't feel right, but it was Johnson's hospital, and he was probably right, the feds would take care of things. Then he could go home, get some sleep, and forget this ever happened.

CHAPTER 14

A doctor emerged from the kitchenette, gliding his feet along the floor. Karen thought he looked funny wearing surgical scrubs, playing waiter, carrying a paper plate that bent in the middle and threatened to collapse under the weight of several pastries. In his other hand, he balanced two cups of steaming coffee.

"James Wellington. Friends call me Jim."

Karen introduced herself and her boys.

Wellington took a seat next to Karen. "Hungry?" He handed Karen a cup of coffee, offering Paul the first choice from the plate. "Why are you here?"

"That man saved my boys. Now, I guess we know too much."

Wellington grunted. "I guess we all know too much." He turned to the boys. "I'm a doctor, a surgeon."

"You operated on him?" Tommy fixed his eyes on Wellington's face.

"I tried. I didn't do such a good job."

Tommy bit his donut. "He's not human. Is he?"

Wellington looked at Karen, then back at Tommy. "I don't think so."

* * *

It was 7:02 a.m. when the phone rang at the CDC's administrative office in Atlanta, Georgia. Linda Moore, an Administrative Communications Officer, the current acceptable title for a switchboard operator, answered the phone.

"This is Dr. David Johnson," Johnson said as if she'd recognize him. "I'm the Administrator of St. John's Hospital in Cleveland, Ohio. I have a problem here." Or was it an emergency? He wasn't sure which was more accurate. "I must speak to someone who can help me with…." His voice trailed off. *What exactly do I need help with?* "We have something here that we don't understand. Eh—it's something extraordinary." He couldn't say much to a switchboard operator, and he realized the difficulty of explaining the patient in his hospital. No, that wasn't true. Telling the story was easy. Believing it was difficult.

"I'll connect you with Diagnostic Support," she said without the slightest hint of trepidation. "Maybe they can help." With that, the line converted to elevator Muzak. Punching the speakerphone button, Johnson laid the receiver in its cradle, drumming his fingers to generic Calypso music.

A man's accented voice erupted from the speaker on Johnson's desk: "Diagnostic Support, Dr. Jahan speaking. How may I be of assistance?"

Johnson frowned. "This is Dr. David Johnson, Administrator of St. John's Hospital in Cleveland. That's in Ohio."

"I have been to Ohio, Doctor Johnson. How may I be of assistance?"

"Yes, well, we have a rather unique situation. Is there a supervisor I could speak with?" Johnson looked at Alex and flashed a knowing smile.

"I am a senior research specialist assigned to the Epidemic Intelligence Service. I am the team leader, and I'll be most happy to help you if you would only tell me what is troubling you this morning in the fine city of Cleveland."

Before Johnson could respond, Alex leaned toward the phone and said, "Doctor, I'm Detective Alex Madden. Maybe I can give you an overview of what has happened here. I can't tell you the medical details, but perhaps starting at the beginning would be helpful." He paused. "This is difficult to explain." Alex cut his eyes to Johnson. Johnson nodded his approval.

"That would be most helpful, Detective Madden. I prefer starting at the beginning. You'll find me a most patient listener."

Alex cleared his throat and tried to picture the man on the other end of the line. The name sounded Indian, or maybe Pakistani. Alex pictured a small guy. Although he spoke with a heavy accent, his words were clearly enunciated, his voice pleasant and melodic. Alex felt comfortable, although he had no reason to. He hoped Jahan wouldn't dismiss him as a lunatic.

Alex had spent years explaining events, both large and small. Beginning with the 911 call and proceeding through the operation, he told the story like the master storyteller he was, a consequence of being a police officer for twenty-five years. His dissertation gained polish with each recital, and, as with his disclosure to David Johnson, this one also took five minutes.

"That would be a most interesting development," Jahan said. "I would very much like to be speaking with the surgeon in this matter. Is he available?"

Alex gave Johnson a nod.

Eager to convince the CDC official of his call's authenticity, Johnson blurted, "Yes! I can have him here in a few minutes. Would you like to hold?"

"No, I'll call back. In about ten minutes?"

"Ten minutes then." Johnson disconnected the call.

"You want me to get Dr. Wellington?" Alex asked.

"That would be great. Thanks." Johnson breathed easier, sensing that he'd passed some magical milestone that would return his hospital to normalcy.

That hadn't gone too badly, Alex mused as he walked toward the second-floor conference room. Things felt controlled for the first time since Wellington opened the stranger's abdomen. All the witnesses had been secured, and to the best of Alex's knowledge, there were no leaks. If this continued, they might not fire him after all.

Johnson shook Wellington's hand like a long-lost friend. Wellington's arm moved like an old-fashioned water pump. "James! Good to see you. How are you holding up under all this? I've talked to the CDC. A specialist named Jahan. He'll be calling back soon." Johnson pulled out a chair and waved for Wellington to sit. Wellington remained standing.

Johnson said, "Detective Madden told Jahan what happened, but Jahan wants the medical details from you."

On the way to Johnson's office, Wellington began a slow burn that started at the base of his neck. Johnson's unjustified confidence in the correctness of his actions caused him to erupt. "Damn it! You don't realize what you've done."

"Now, calm down, Jim. Everything's under control. The people at the CDC are on this now. We'll turn matters over to them and get back to normal."

"You don't understand," Wellington whispered as he sank into the chair.

The three men sat around Johnson's conference table, a star-shaped speakerphone being the table's lone embellishment. Johnson jumped when the phone rang. His hand darted for the receiver, then froze, allowing it to ring a second time before he punched the button and said, "Hello, this is David Johnson."

Using a secured line, Jahan was also recording to facilitate a quick transfer of information to interested parties, whoever they were. "Hello, Dr. Jahan here. It is good to be speaking with you again."

The soothing bounce of Jahan's accented voice was unchanged. "When we last talked, you were to retrieve the doctor who performed surgery on the subject who concerns you greatly. Dr. Wellington, if my memory is serving me."

"Yes, that is correct. Dr. Wellington is here. Also, Detective Madden has rejoined us."

"Hello, Dr. Wellington and Detective Madden, it is 7:21 a.m. Eastern Standard Time. I am happy to be speaking with you this morning about what appears to be a most interesting case. Dr. Wellington, Detective Madden, was able, during our first conversation, to explain in good detail the events that have occurred there. However, it would be most valuable to learn your observations." Not telling colleagues they were being recorded bothered Jahan, but there were policies to follow.

"Where should I begin?" Wellington asked.

"Begin as if you were talking to students. I understand you are a teaching surgeon." Jahan didn't elaborate on how he knew that, and at the time, no one in Cleveland thought to ask.

Wellington sucked in a deep breath. "The ER doctor's triage found extensive trauma, including head lacerations, a compound fracture of the clavicle, and thirty-two puncture wounds to the lower abdomen. Shallow breathing, heart rate forty-five and weak. He couldn't even get a blood pressure reading. I don't have the file, so I'm recalling this as best I can."

The file! Shit! Alex jumped from his seat, signaling to Johnson that he'd return. Johnson acknowledged him with a nod.

"You are doing fine. Please continue."

"They rushed him to surgery. I was on call. My team had him as ready as possible within 20 minutes."

"What do you mean, ready as possible?"

"The lab couldn't match his blood type."

"Most interesting. Continue."

"My assistant, Dr. Cray, examined the X-rays. Considering the extent of the head trauma, the skull was free of fractures, but his left clavicle had a clean break. Compound fracture. The bone broke the skin, and the other half pointed downward, threatening to puncture a lung. Cray wanted to stabilize the clavicle before surgery, but he found it wasn't fractured. There was a red spot on the skin, but no broken clavicle. Cray figured the ER mixed patients and X-rays. It happens. The ER gets a little crazy sometimes."

"Are you now believing that the first X-rays were correctly attributed to this patient?"

"I talked to the ER doc before surgery. This was his first patient, and he saw the broken clavicle himself. I didn't have time to investigate."

"I understand," Jahan said in a reassuring voice. "Continue."

"As I said, the man was savagely beaten. His head and face injuries appeared consistent with being on the losing end of a fistfight. The X-rays supported that hypothesis. However, I've learned that he was beaten with a tire iron. From the description of the assault, he should have been dead long before the assailant used a knife on him."

"Excuse me. For a moment, I am confused. How is it you now suspect the victim was beaten with a tire iron?"

"Two boys witnessed the attack. I was talking to—Tommy, I believe that's his name."

Alex appeared in the door carrying a file and returned to his seat.

"Dr. Wellington, you have told me about a rugged man with a rare blood type and an odd diagnosis by an emergency room doctor, but nothing that indicates the man is anything other than human. How do you support the notion that he is something extraordinary?"

"When I opened his abdominal cavity, his anatomy was not human. The organs were different, and the wounds were already healing. Then his second heart started bea …"

"Did you say—second heart?"

"That's correct."

"My anesthesiologist noticed it first. She kept muttering that something was odd. In fact, she said something about it before the patient crashed. The anesthesiologist thinks the patient was alternating between hearts. Then both hearts started beating in a syncopated rhythm." Wellington talked uninterrupted for another five minutes.

When he finished, Jahan said, "Dr. Wellington, accept my apology. I do not know what you're dealing with, but you have convinced me it is abnormal."

Johnson leaned forward with both elbows resting on the table. "What do we do now?"

"I must contact the appropriate authorities, and I want to investigate this myself. Yet, how do I convince my administrator that I must travel to the City of Cleveland without revealing too much, if you understand what I am saying? You have taken the correct measures. Continue as you have begun. I will be in touch."

With Jahan's last words, the line went dead, as did the sound in David Johnson's office.

After a few minutes, Johnson looked at Alex and asked, "Did we do the right thing?"

"I don't know," Alex replied. "But I think we're going to lose control soon."

"You think?" Wellington rolled his eyes.

"I want to call a friend at the FBI," Alex continued. "I'd be more comfortable with someone I trust. Maybe the FBI can keep things from getting out of control."

"Do that. I have a bad feeling about this," Johnson said.

CHAPTER 15

To Jahan, it was just one of many emergency numbers in a dusty manual on a bookcase that he'd never had reason to call. He wondered if anyone had ever dialed this number. After two rings, an automated voice answered.

A Pentagon computer recorded the call at 07:45, Eastern Standard Time. The procedure, developed years earlier, began its automated process, triggering a cellphone clipped to the belt of the man designated to be the commander of field operations if the nation ever had alien contact. When his cellphone's vibrator erupted, Sam Henry almost spilled coffee in his lap. If not for routine tests and an occasional quirky sighting, Sam wouldn't have known if the damn phone even worked. He didn't recognize this number. This was no test.

Sam almost caused a multi-car accident as he pulled to the side of the road. Angry drivers shook their fists and shouted obscenities as he selected the applicable contact number on his iPhone. His other hand disappeared into the pocket of his suit coat, retrieving a stick of gum. He listened to a message recorded by Dr. Jahan from the Centers for Disease Control.

With trembling fingers, Sam punched a seven-digit number on the keypad of his phone. When a computer answered, he entered seven more digits, followed by four followed by three. He touched the pound key, and the sequence was complete. Milliseconds after his fingertip left the keypad, the First Contact Protocol became official. By virtue of an obscure Federal Act, Sam Henry became the second most powerful man in the United States.

CHAPTER 16

In the conference room, police officers and medical staff stood in separate huddles like opposing teams, filling the room with nervous chatter. Paul cuddled at his mother's side, and Karen rested her chin on top of his head and closed her eyes.

Tommy watched his mother and little brother for a few minutes, then walked to the room's large windows, where he crawled into the farthest window from his mother and wedged himself in the opening. On the drive from Kansas, Mom talked so much about Cleveland that he felt as if he'd once lived here himself. When his mother was eight years old, riots erupted on the East Side, and four people died. Tommy couldn't remember anything remarkable happening when he was eight years old. From the window, he could see Washington Park and the Cuyahoga River, which divides the West Side from the East Side, where he now lived.

Outside, red and gold leaves rustled in a light morning breeze, some on the trees and some skittering along the ground. Flowers blazed red, purple, and yellow. To the north, he saw downtown's high-rise buildings of mirror-like gold and black. In the distance, Lake Erie shimmered in the morning sun. At regular intervals, jets carved their path over the lake, setting their approach to the airport. He wondered who rode in these planes and why they came. Closing his eyes, sadness crept in, its weight pressing on his chest until breathing became difficult. He missed his dad. He didn't know if he could live without him. Didn't know if he wanted to.

***

Sam Henry pulled onto Pennsylvania Avenue, turning towards Andrews Air Force Base. He looked like an ordinary D.C. worker commuting to a mundane job, but he was not average, and the work before him was far from mundane. Since they relegated him to this stupid post, he'd mostly investigated swamp gas and things that went bump in the night. However, this was straight from the CDC, real doctors, and a real hospital.

This is what he prepared for.

He called Terri Wilson, the only person he trusted with such information outside the chain of command. Terri didn't answer. He left a brief, prearranged message that would seem ordinary to anyone. Anyone but Terri.

He rubbed his sweaty palms on his pant legs, realizing it had been many years since his last mission. No previous call had ever warranted the Level One Alert he activated via the Strategic Emergency Communications Array, which was called SECA, a high-tech satellite orbiting five hundred miles above the earth's surface.

★★★

Alex hung up Johnson's phone after talking to Eric Key. Alex met Eric when they were young, eager, and inexperienced. One hot summer day, unbeknownst to each other, they entered a warehouse at precisely the same time as a drug dealer had instructed. At the time, communication between the feds and local agencies was almost nonexistent. The dealer had discovered Alex and Eric were narcotics officers. He then hatched his plan, hoping they would kill each other in a shootout.

The dealer's plan failed. Eric and Alex survived, and a lifelong friendship was born. From that day forward, Alex trusted few men more than he trusted Eric Key.

★★★

Madden and Wellington left Johnson's office in silence. Unaware of their lockstep, each man was lost in his own thoughts. The fate of the patient troubled Wellington. Something entirely different bothered Madden.

In the grand scheme of things, Madden's thoughts seemed insignificant, and that bothered him too. Still, something was eating at him, and Alex Madden wasn't a man given to letting things go unsaid. "You seem to hit it off with Karen."

Wellington glanced sideways at Madden. "Sorry, what was that?"

"Karen. You were hitting on Karen Parker."

Wellington looked puzzled.

Alex glared at Wellington. "Karen? The boys? Tommy? You said Tommy told you about the attack?"

"Oh, right. Tommy's mother, Karen, is it? I'm terrible with names. Scary, eh? Doctors are supposed to be smart, but I have a hell of a time remembering names."

"You could at least learn a woman's name before putting the make on her."

"Excuse me?"

"Don't bullshit me. I saw you."

"Saw me what?"

"Don't give me that shit! I know a move when I see one."

Wellington rolled his eyes. "I don't know what you think you saw, but I was not putting the move on her."

"I saw what I saw."

Wellington grabbed Madden's arm, jerking him to a stop. "I was making small talk. I figured they were scared and could use some food. It's the doctor in me, I guess, always trying to fix things. Sorry if I was invading your territory, but I was trying to be friendly. That's all it was. Okay?"

Madden studied Wellington for a moment. "Karen's a lot tougher than you might think. She used to be a damn fine crime reporter. Tough as nails, when necessary, or a real charmer when the occasion called for it. We were friends back then." He paused for a moment. "Father/daughter relationship, just so you don't get the wrong idea. Sorry, Doc, maybe I jumped to the wrong conclusion. It's just that…."

Wellington put his hand on Madden's shoulder. "No further explanation is necessary. My guess is you're a good man to have as a friend." After a moment, he felt awkward and removed his hand from Madden's shoulder.

They resumed their walk toward the conference room. "What's going to happen to my patient? What's going to happen to all of us?"

"Worries me too."

"We need to start trusting each other and quickly."

CHAPTER 17

Dr. AJ Jahan called the CDC director's office, but she wasn't in, and that meant Deputy Director Dr. Art Burns would act in her stead. In addition, that made Jahan's task even more difficult than he had initially thought. Burns was a tight-ass. Born of wealthy stock, Burns had never faced the adversities of the working class. Known for his cold analytical approach to even the most human of acts, Burns was not well liked by the CDC researchers.

AJ called ahead, telling Burns' secretary that he must see the deputy director, and yes, it was important, and no, it couldn't wait. However, AJ knew Burns would never authorize travel to Cleveland without an explanation—a detailed explanation. If Burns knew what was happening, he'd go himself. AJ struggled to concoct the perfect story. He was sure it would not work.

* * *

Some nineteen hundred miles and three time zones away, Katherine Davis, director of the CDC, made final preparations for her address to the Western States Medical Association. This year the association's congress was held in Park City, Utah, a ski resort outside Salt Lake City. She was about to step to the podium when she was called to the telephone. The Secretary of Health, Education, and Welfare was on the line. Their conversation was brief. She had a thousand questions but was told to ask none. Her orders were explicit: place one phone call, relay one simple message.

Stunned, Katherine hung up the receiver. Her concentration was shot, and delivering her speech would be difficult.

* * *

Burns' secretary simply said, "The Director is on the phone." Not unusual, Katherine liked to stay in touch.

Burns tapped a pencil against the edge of his cherry wood desk, staring at the blinking red light on his phone. After a full minute, he picked it up. "Good morning, Director." Checking his watch, he ran a quick calculation in his head, then said, "Why aren't you giving your speech? Is something wrong?"

"Arthur, listen carefully," Katherine began, her tone uncharacteristically severe. "Get Dr. Jahan on a plane to Cleveland immediately. Order him, I repeat, order him to keep this strictly confidential. AJ is to contact a man named Sam Henry at St. John's Hospital. He is to talk to no one about this, and that includes you."

"What's up?" Burns asked. He couldn't remember hearing Katherine sound so somber.

"Arthur, this is a direct order. Do you understand?" Her tone telegraphed the message more clearly than her words and the words—Direct Order—conveyed a clear message to any government employee, helping Burns understand, with great clarity, the consequences should he fail to obey. Washing dishes in a federal prison held no interest for him.

"Consider it done," Burns said, setting the receiver in its cradle. "What the hell?" He said under his breath.

★ ★ ★

"Good morning, Sarah. And how are you this fine morning?" Dr. Jahan asked, trying hard to remain optimistic.

"Good morning, Dr. Jahan," Sarah said. "Dr. Burns will see you, but you have little time."

"I will make it as quick as I most possibly can." He didn't like the sound of this already.

"I don't think you understand. There's a flight to Cleveland in less than an hour, and you're on it. Alicia is getting a car. She'll be at the front door in five minutes. You'll need to hustle to make the flight. And Dr. Jahan," Sarah added, "discuss this with no one. A direct order, from the director, I think."

AJ merely stood with his mouth hanging open. Looking at his watch, revealed that less than thirty minutes had passed since he called the 800 number he had found in that dusty manual. He managed to say thanks before stepping into the deputy director's office, where he heard a quick repeat of what Sarah had just said, including the direct order, which was delivered officially from Burns. Burns explained the obvious—that AJ had no time to pack—but Burns assured him that he'd be taken care of and not to worry.

"AJ," Burns never called people by their first name, "whatever it is, good luck."

AJ turned silently and walked out just moments after he'd arrived. He stopped briefly at his office and threw some things—he did not know what those things should be—into a briefcase before rushing to the car that awaited him at the front door.

Jesus Christ, whoever is driving this has some serious juice, he thought as he flopped himself into the front seat of the agency's Ford, driven by Alicia Cortez.

"Flight leaves in less than an hour. What's up with that, AJ?" Alicia asked.

"I can't say," he whispered, staring straight ahead.

Alicia pulled the gear selector into drive and said, "God, it must be something big."

CHAPTER 18

Glen Harris, the special agent in charge, surveyed the FBI conference room. His administrative assistant had heaped the credenza with pastries, bagels, and fruit, plus, two stainless-steal coffee canisters and two pitchers of juice: one apple and one orange. Glen prepared his meetings with meticulous care. This session of the Greater Cleveland Task Force on Gang-Related Crime would prove no exception. There should have been two pitchers of orange juice, because the apple would be untouched. Glen knew the reality. Cops hated meetings, save the donuts and coffee. A few would drink juice, orange, not apple.

Glen didn't like making presentations, and local cops were the worst audience, having heard far too many empty promises from far too many federal bureaucrats. But Glen had information about a new gang that ran its operations from inside federal and state prisons. The public believed that locking everyone up would solve the crime in America. If they only understood that the street gangs selling drugs and terrorizing every city in the nation started in the California prison system, then maybe they'd be more open to discussing other solutions. However, that wasn't going to happen anytime soon, and it wasn't Glen's problem today. What he needed at the moment was a bit of solitude before his presentation. However, that wasn't going to happen either, because, as was her practice, his administrative assistant hunted him down.

The FBI director was calling on the secured line.

Glen's conversation with the director lasted less than five minutes. Glen slowly lowered the phone, rehearsing in his mind what the director had said. Glen needed his best agent. He needed Eric Key.

If Jedi Knights were real people, Eric Key would be a Jedi Master. Eric had won numerous martial-arts competitions, taught self-defense to FBI agents, and operated his own martial arts school. Often, new agents tested Eric's mettle only to be introduced to the mat. Even then, Eric never used his hard-martial arts skills, only self-defense techniques he taught agents. Putting agents in the hospital wasn't Eric's job.

Glen often turned out to watch recruits' first encounters with Eric, wondering when the man or woman would arrive in the Cleveland office who could put a chink in his armor. To date, none have. Maybe Saldana, the new guy, would be the man. Saldana was a big, burly kid who didn't seem intimidated by Eric.

What unnerved Glen most about Eric wasn't his size, speed, or ability, but the cold confidence in his eyes. But these were thoughts for another day. Glen had not seen Eric this morning. Eric hated meetings more than most, and Glen was pissed that Eric had picked this morning to dodge one.

Glen gulped one last swig of coffee. Half of it went down his chin, appearing as a brown stain on his white shirt and red tie. What else could go wrong? Dabbing at the front of his shirt with a napkin, Glen entered the conference room. Eric still wasn't there.

Glen's cell phone rang.

"Special Agent Harris," Glen said, turning his back on the room and walking back into the hall.

"Good morning, Glen," Eric said.

"Where in the hell are you?" Glen asked in a demanding whisper.

Eric wanted to say he'd forgotten the meeting, but he abandoned the idea upon hearing Glen's voice. "Huh, Glen—I got a call from an old friend over at CPD. He has something big happening and needs the bureau's help. Glen, I owe the man. He saved my life once."

"Where are you?" Harris asked with measured words.

"St. John's Hospital."

"I'll be damned. Who's the cop?" The pitch of Glen's voice raised an octave.

"Alex Madden."

Glen remained silent for a moment. "This is crazy. It just so happens that the director called me. He ordered me to have an agent contact Detective Alex Madden at St. John's Hospital." Another pause. "Since you are already there, it only makes sense that I assign it to you. Eric, don't screw it up. You're to assist Madden until a guy from DC shows up. Whatever's happening there, keep a lid on it. Top secret." Glen paused again. "The guy from DC is Sam Henry."

"I'll be damned," Keys whispered.

"Keeping it quiet includes me," Glen added after another pause. "If you need to contact the Bureau, call the director."

*　*　*

Maria Esperanza watched her son inspect a bug on the window as she stuffed a crème-filled cupcake into his lunch box. Maria held a teaching degree, but she cleaned houses for a living. Teaching was her passion, but she made more money cleaning houses. Maria never dreamed she'd be a single mother running a one-woman enterprise.

Eight years ago, she and her husband were driving to a Christmas party but they never arrived. She awoke in a hospital bed with a tube stuck down her throat and a cast up to her ribs. The bulging tummy that held her unborn son was now flat. Using a notepad, she asked about her husband more out of duty than need. She already knew the answer to her question. The nurse shook her head. Tears streamed down Maria's cheeks. She didn't dare ask about her baby. The nurse started to say something, then turned, and left the room. A few minutes later, the nurse returned with a small bundle in a blue blanket. Mike was her firstborn and her only child. When she held her son for the first time she thought: God has something wonderful planned for this one.

*** * ***

Military jets weren't meant to be comfortable. Sam Henry decided the designers at Northrop had succeeded on a grand scale because the T-38 Talon and comfort were irreconcilable. However, it was fast, and speed was more important than comfort. In less than twenty minutes, Sam made the prerequisite contacts and was strapped into the advanced trainer jet bound for Cleveland.

The flight crew gave him a tight-fitting flight suit. He sandwiched two compact black cases between his knees. The seat was hard, and he was one uncomfortable man. The flight wouldn't take long, but it would give him time to think.

The pilot turned the Talon onto the runway, straightened it out, lined it up, and pulled the trigger. Fuel poured into the General Electric turbojet engines. Sam felt like a pancake as the plane rocketed toward launch speed. The nose rotated, and the pilot pointed the Talon into a near vertical climb, then kicked in the afterburners.

Closing his eyes, Sam thought about how he'd come to this obscure job and what he'd learned along the way. He hated the term UFO. When they dumped him in the position, he thought the move was chicken shit. UFOs? What a bunch of crap! He studied his far-fetched enemy and learned it wasn't so far-fetched. Sam now believed that contact with aliens was inevitable.

Over one billion trillion stars burn in the known universe, and in our galaxy alone, it is estimated that one hundred billion planets exist. Given those numbers, Sam decided there must be other intelligent life. Yet, even if they had achieved space travel capabilities, and there was no reason to believe they had, why would they travel here to a small rock circulating an average star?

Aliens might scan the galaxies for signs of life, like radio waves, as we do from the New Mexico desert and other places around the globe. However, since radio waves take time to reach deep space and since we've only transmitted them for about ninety years, the math dictates that contact would not happen soon.

Sam decided his reasoning had a big hole in it. The hole was pure ignorance or arrogance, depending on one's interpretation. The error was thinking that alien life would be like us, think like us, move like us, and obey the laws of nature as we do. That thinking was plain stupid.

Sam believed that the Earth would receive visitors one day, but unlike the movies, it wouldn't be pretty or exciting. And it wouldn't be the first time.

Sixty-five million years ago, a space traveler came here. This traveler had no plan, no motivation, and certainly no remorse. It was not a probe from an alien world. No one piloted it here. It just came.

This spaceship was nothing more than an enormous, cold rock twelve miles across. It slammed into the Earth's surface at fourteen thousand miles per hour, sending a flash of deadly heat around the globe in a matter of minutes and propelling a cloud of dust into outer space. The impact created a crater one hundred twenty miles across. A dust cloud mushroomed from the detonation and cloaked the Earth in a blanket of death that wiped out over seventy percent of the Earth's population. Entire species gone forever.

Yet, contrary to popular opinion, life is a powerful force, an odd contradiction, fragile yet hardy, and over time, it has proven itself virtually indestructible. However, that point of view is unique to the survivors. Sam harbored no illusion that humanity would enjoy the survivors' point of view under similar circumstances.

First contact might be with a virus or bacteria, or something different from life as we know it, perhaps a crystal. It need not come from some distant galaxy. It might be floating in the upper reaches of our atmosphere, waiting for a ride to the planet, or deep in the ocean, evolving until its collision with life on the surface.

A vast lake under the Antarctic ice served as a perfect example. A survey plane beaming radio waves at the ice cap discovered it. Sophisticated satellites later validated the finding. Roughly the size of Lake Ontario, the Antarctic lake is trapped under two-and-a-half miles of ice. Within its sixteen-thousand-foot depth lurks a complete ecosystem teeming with life, sealed from the rest of the world for over two million years. Many things can change in two million years.

Sam looked out the window. The ground drifted by far below him. The pilot said they were halfway to Cleveland.

Another theory was that man might have already experienced his first and last contact with an alien life form that was so incompatible with humans that the two couldn't coexist on the same planet. People have traveled to places they were not welcome, discovering life previously unknown. Ebola and AIDS viruses had remained hidden in the jungles of Africa long before man encroached on their world. Ebola burns quickly through its human hosts. Victims bleed to death as their internal organs liquefy in two weeks or less. With modern air travel, Ebola, or some related virus, could circle the globe in thirty to forty-five days, killing eighty percent of humanity. After the collateral deaths, Sam figured a few humans would survive—maybe five percent.

AIDS has killed five million people. It kills much slower than Ebola. Many people believed it was a malady of drug addicts and homosexuals, so they ignored it. On the fundamentalist fringe, some even declared it a curse, or blessing, sent from God to rid the planet of sinners. What if the AIDS virus mutated, as viruses often do, and became an airborne pathogen?

Sam believed humanity would survive AIDS as well. In California, doctors found a boy immune to HIV. Drugs now slow the disease's progression for HIV victims. Nevertheless, if AIDS or Ebola mutated, either might claim ninety-nine percent of the world's population before human antibodies conquered it. Humans would adapt, and a few survivors would start over.

The jet's engines changed pitch and Sam's mind floated back to the mission at hand. Everything was well contained. The remaining loose ends were significant. Witnesses included medical staff and police. How many were involved? He thought it strange that he recognized a name Dr. Jahan had mentioned: Alex Madden. They were never friends. Enemy was a more fitting description. Their one brief encounter was fifteen years ago, during the aftermath of the Ross incident. Sam never felt right about that mission. Madden didn't understand, and national security dictated that he never would. Then there was that poor young reporter. She had spirit. Sam did not remember her name. Carrie, Carly, Karen? He wondered what had become of her. With her talent and determination, she probably went on to do grand things.

CHAPTER 19

Wellington wanted to see his patients. That was his job, and he thought it was more important than staring at the walls of the second-floor conference room. But when he asked to make rounds, Madden pitched a fit. After Wellington's considerable professional pestering, Madden agreed with the proviso that Jerry Faulkner, Madden's partner, tag along wearing scrubs, posing as an intern. Wellington's first stop was his last patient, the one he'd left on the operating table. A Cleveland police officer stationed outside the room did not surprise him, but the shotgun-toting cop inside the room pissed him off.

Damn paranoid cops. This man was a victim, hero, and patient, not a damn criminal. Wellington couldn't shake the feeling he'd failed his patient.

Benjamin Cray was in the room. "How's he doing, Ben?" Wellington asked.

"He should be dead."

Wellington reached up to inspect a bottle of clear liquid hanging above the man's head. He sniffed the air. It smelled sweet, like fresh-cut flowers, but there were no flowers in the room.

"It's him, Jim."

"What?"

"The smell. You noticed, didn't you?"

"I did." Wellington scanned the room again as if there must be some logical explanation. There was not.

"What is he?" Ben asked.

"I don't know. But I owed him my best, and I didn't give it to him." Wellington moved closer. As a surgeon, he had to be distant and clinical, but after surgery, his patients became real people with lives and names. Years ago, he started taking before and after pictures with each patient, keeping them in a photo album. Emergencies didn't have before photos. Only photographs of the operation and, of course, the shots afterward. He kept some afterward photos in a special section—the tombstones of those who had trusted him with their lives. He frequently visited his photo collection, especially the tombstone section, to remind himself of his responsibility. No one knew about his tombstone section. It occurred to him that such a habit was macabre, something his colleagues would frown upon as unhealthy. However, Wellington cared little about what others thought.

"You did the best you could," Ben offered.

"Not good enough," Wellington said, meaning more than his performance at the operating table, which could have been in a regular surgical suite, one without an audience and cameras.

Wellington touched the man's arm, the same as he'd touched hundreds of patients each year, trying to impart something he couldn't explain. That's when he felt it. He'd felt it at the operating table, or had he imagined it? He wasn't sure. It was something wonderful. In the operating room, he didn't say anything, fearing his team might think he'd dipped into the pharmacy's psychotropic drugs.

"You feel it?" Ben asked.

"Yes, I do."

★★★

"I think you're going to make it," Alicia said, zipping between two cars while traveling sixty miles an hour. Her maneuver earned her a waving fist and a blaring horn from a man in a red Ford truck. He wasn't the first driver she'd pissed off on her breakneck race to the airport.

"You're going to have a few citizen complaints waiting when you get back to the office," AJ observed. "I'm not sure whether to thank you or file a complaint myself." AJ's attempt at humor wasn't entirely successful. The situation didn't lend itself to that, but the effort earned him a halfhearted grin from his driver.

"The way they put it to me," Alicia responded, "missing this flight wasn't an option. I don't think a few complaints are going to mean much as long as you're on that plane when it takes off."

"Sorry, I can't tell you about it."

"Burns made that clear." Alicia knew AJ didn't enjoy power trips the way some men did. She liked that about him.

They entered the U-shaped highway that funneled travelers into and out of Hartsfield-Atlanta International Airport. The traffic wasn't heavy, and it flowed ten miles an hour above the posted speed limit. Still, AJ felt as if they were crawling along the blacktop.

"Here you go." Alicia eased to the curb near a Delta sign that hung from the terminal's veranda. "Whatever's going on, good luck and be careful. And remember, I love you." She planted a kiss on AJ's mouth.

"I love you, too," AJ said, but his mind was miles away. Later, he'd regret that he wasn't more attentive.

With that, he turned and raced toward the Delta entrance.

Alicia watched. She paused at the curb until the throng of travelers absorbed AJ. She prayed he wasn't facing a level four pathogen. Alicia Cortez-Jahan eased back into the airport traffic, wondering what could be so terrible that its secret couldn't be shared between them. Their marriage was still the best-kept secret at the CDC.

Please, come home, AJ. I have a surprise for you, she thought as she blinked tears from her eyes and patted her stomach.

In the northeastern sky, cumulonimbus clouds rose five miles above Lake Erie's surface. From up here, Erie looked more like an ocean than a lake and rightfully so, because the Great Lakes acted more like an ocean than a lake. They covered ninety-five thousand square miles, created their own weather, and had claimed their share of ships and lives.

The T-38 Talon banked, dipping its left wing toward the water's surface, then settled back into its descent. Cleveland arose on the horizon. Soon, Sam would arrive at St. John's Hospital. He'd gather information, secure the witnesses, and arrange the next leg of their journey.

Then he'd look upon an alien from another world.

What a fantastic job!

Alex found Eric waiting in the second-floor break room, standing separated from the other occupants. A solid handshake reunited the old friends. Alex poured himself a cup of coffee, which he never touched as he told Eric the high points and revealed the reason he'd called for help. Alex studied his friend's face, then dumped his coffee down the sink. "Follow me."

"The doc says he's still in a coma." Alex pushed the dimly lit button on the elevator panel. "I have officers posted outside and inside the room. It seems a little ridiculous considering the man's condition." The elevator doors slid open, and they stepped inside.

"It's okay, Alex," Eric offered, the strain clear on his old friend's face. Alex's story was hard to believe. There was a simpler explanation. However, if there was, why was the director involved? Something else was bothering Alex. Of that, Eric was certain.

"This man, or whatever he is, saved two little boys. I mean, he walked in the middle of a bunch of gangbangers and saved them," Alex said.

Eric thought he saw a slight quiver at the tip of Alex's chin. "Alex, there's nothing more you can do. Someone is coming from Washington who knows how to handle it. Then we can get back to what we do best: catching bad guys. We'll start with the assholes that did this."

"Yeah, I guess you're right. It's just that—well, it's hard to explain," Alex said, his voice trailing off.

Eric reached past Alex and touched the elevator stop button. "There's something you need to know. My supervisor didn't know any details, but he told me the director called and ordered him to send an agent to St. John's Hospital to assist a detective named Madden. Get what I'm saying? This is national-security-level shit. The director doesn't get involved in petty stuff."

Alex pursed his lips and stared for a moment. "The hospital administrator contacted the CDC. They must have activated an emergency response system." Alex shrugged his shoulders. "No big deal. Just how it works."

"Alex, my instructions were to keep this quiet until a guy showed up to take over."

"You said that's what we wanted. Right?"

"The man is Sam Henry."

Eric released the button, and the elevator started moving.

Alex gritted his teeth, unable to speak. Just when he thought things couldn't get worse, they did.

CHAPTER 20

The POTUS marched down the corridor, followed by his entourage, on his way to address the American people. However, General Edward Powers, his National Security Advisor, caught him in a hallway near the press room. Powers grabbed President Beckman's elbow, dragging him into a broom closet. Powers toggled the light switch, and a twenty-five-watt bulb on the ten-foot ceiling cast a dim light. The room smelled of damp mops and pine-scented cleaner.

Powers talked, his hands chopping the air. Powers' voice and mannerisms bothered Beckman, as did talking to a military man in a room meant for janitors. Beyond that, Beckman wasn't listening.

Powers explained that an alien or some high-tech humanoid was confined in a Cleveland hospital. A full-scale activation was underway at the National Security Council Crisis Center. Sam Henry was aboard an Air Force jet bound for Cleveland. Beckman nodded, suppressing a yawn. He had important business. Half the Senate faced replacement at the hands of American voters, and as their president, it was his responsibility to help voters pick the right candidates. Candidates who would back his agenda and turn a blind eye to things that didn't concern them.

What he didn't need was a media circus over some Halloween hoax stealing his thunder. Military people always thought of worse-case scenarios. Everything was a crisis to them. Maybe that's why he disliked them so much. Military types wanted him to overreact, and they worded everything to that end. That's why he'd learned never to give military people what they wanted. If they said don't bomb, he bombed. Military people didn't get it. They believed that their purpose was to protect America. Beckman understood their actual purpose was to make money for military contractors and manufacturers of military equipment, who in turn gave lots of money to men like himself.

"Is that all we know?" Beckman asked, reaching for the doorknob.

Powers placed his hand on the door, holding it closed. "Nothing is coming out of Cleveland yet. It's quiet there. We think local law enforcement has it contained. We are treating this as top secret."

"Okay. This—eh, whatever it is, is guarded? Right? Go to the crisis center and get on top of it. I want a full briefing when I arrive."

Powers stared at him.

Beckman took a deep breath. "You said this is top secret. If I walk out of this press conference, every damn reporter in town will camp on our doorstep, demanding answers. Then we'll have a mess on our hands." Beckman looked at Powers' hand, and Powers withdrew it from the door. Cracking the door open a few inches, Beckman checked his watch.

Powers said, "I agree, but cut it short. We'll need executive decisions during a situation like this."

Beckman frowned. "I'll be there."

"Sam Henry is a good man," Powers said. "I take comfort in that."

Beckman had paid little attention to detail during his tenure. He was a master-plan kind of guy. Yet he didn't share Powers' optimism. Beckman never liked the idea that someone had a reputation superior to his own. For that reason, he never liked Sam Henry.

"Sam hasn't been tested under pressure for a long time," Beckman said.

"I'm not sure I understand your point," Powers said.

Beckman pulled the door closed. "One man isn't enough. We need more firepower than that. After the Sears Tower incident, I ordered the establishment of an elite light-infantry unit specializing in counter-terrorism tactics. I want them nearby. Just in case."

"Yes, sir," Powers nodded. He knew about the counter-terrorism unit because they were his idea, but Beckman would never admit that. "I'll activate them and let Sam know they're coming."

Beckman shot him a stern look. "No. This needs to be a black operation. No one can know. Not even Sam Henry."

★★★

Madden and Key found Dr. Wellington in his office, sitting behind an old walnut desk. Madden's young protégé turned medical student sat nearby. They had finished rounds, which included three checks on John Doe. Alex introduced Eric Key and then plopped himself in a chair facing Wellington's desk.

A decanter of single-malt Scotch sat on a walnut credenza behind Wellington's desk. The doctor stood to refill his glass and offered Eric Key a sample. Eric declined.

"How often do you FBI boys come across an extraterrestrial being?" Wellington poured Scotch into three additional cut-crystal tumblers.

Alex swore and took one from Wellington.

Eric shrugged his shoulders, taking one, as did Jerry Faulkner. "Not often," Eric admitted. The four men lifted their glasses, clinked them together, and savored the single malt as it bit their tongues and warmed their throats.

"Did you see John?" Wellington had named his strange patient John.

"We just came from there. How's he doing?" The concern in Alex's voice was unmistakable.

"I don't know. He's in a coma, we think. However, we know nothing about him. He's opened his eyes a few times, but I don't know what that means. It may mean nothing." Wellington stared at his glass and swirled his Scotch for a moment before saying more. Looking straight into Alex's eyes, he said, "Tell me. In the room? Did you feel it?"

Alex looked at Eric and then back at Wellington.

"I did."

Eric nodded and sipped his Scotch.

* * *

The Air Force jet jolted when the pilot raised the flaps, creating an air dam that felt like applying the brakes of a car. A few seconds later, they were on the tarmac, and Sam Henry climbed down a ladder the ground crew had pushed to the plane. Sam worked his iPhone with both thumbs and bounced a signal off the SECA satellite, encoding his call and making it impossible for eavesdroppers to hear his side of the conversation.

A woman answered in a singsong voice. "St. John's Hospital. How may I direct your call?" It took her a few minutes to find Detective Alex Madden's last known location.

The phone sitting on the walnut desk rang. Wellington pushed the hands-free button and talked toward the phone. "Dr. Wellington."

St. John's receptionist's voice floated from the speaker. "Dr. Wellington, is there a Detective Madden with you?"

"Yes, he's sitting right here." Looking at Alex, Wellington sipped his drink.

"I have a call for him. Would you like me to put it through?"

"Who is it?" Madden asked.

"He said his name is Sam Henry."

A chill ran through the room that Wellington didn't understand.

A moment later, Madden said, "Put him through."

Wellington pushed the button, stared at the phone, and waited for it to ring again. It always took a few seconds to reroute a call. Not because of any lengthy delay in the internal circuitry, but Marie, the receptionist, would without fail, explain to the caller that, yes, she found whoever she was searching for, and, yes, they would take the call, and thank you for being patient, and in the unlikely event that the call did not ring through, please call back. Wellington realized that all of this took only seconds, but for some reason, it felt like hours before the phone rang again.

"Hello, this is Dr. James T. Wellington," he said, lowering his voice and winking at Alex.

"Good day, Dr. Wellington. My name is Sam Henry. I'm with the federal government." Sam didn't name the agency, which was a one-man dog and pony show. "I'm in Cleveland to investigate a report from the CDC." Sam paused. "Doctor, is Detective Madden in the room?"

"This is Detective Madden." Alex attempted to replicate Wellington's booming bass, but his voice sounded strained.

"Good morning, Detective. Who else is in the room?"

"Dr. Wellington, FBI Agent Eric Key, Cleveland Detective Jerry Faulkner, and myself."

"No one else?"

"That's correct." Alex's brow furrowed.

"My side of the conversation is encrypted. Your side is not," Sam began. "With that in mind, please limit your responses. How are things going?"

"That depends on your point of view," Alex said. "On an average day, I'd be on my way home. I'd probably stop along the way to enjoy a warm bagel and fresh coffee. Compared to that, it's not going worth a damn. However, considering the situation, I'd say things are going as well as can be expected."

"I understand, Detective. I'll see what I can do about that bagel later. How secure is the situation? How many people are involved?" There would be no bagels, but he needed to make it sound as if they would all be back to normal soon.

"There's the surgical team." Alex closed his eyes, counting silently on his fingers. "Seven, including Dr. Wellington."

Wellington gave an affirmative nod.

"A woman," Madden was careful not to say reporter, "and her two boys, two interns, one FBI agent, and eight police officers."

"That's everyone?"

"Most of them are in a conference room on the second floor. A few others know bits and pieces, but nothing substantial. That's everyone."

"Who's monitoring the media?"

Alex shifted in his seat when another voice chimed in.

"Mr. Henry, this is Eric Key, FBI. We have people at our office monitoring television, radio, social media, and print. They report any unusual activity. If agents are involved, they give us a heads-up. If the duty officer heard anything, he'd call me ASAP. He hasn't contacted me, so we assume no leaks."

Alex nodded and smiled.

"Detective Madden, how much does your department know?"

"They don't know anything," Madden said with a hint of satisfaction.

"How is that? That many officers assigned to the hospital must require authorization." For the first time, Henry's voice raised above the calm, almost nonchalant tone he'd used throughout the conversation.

"It was pretty easy. Everyone here is off the duty board. As far as anyone downtown knows, they are all home by now. The captain's an old friend."

"Excellent. You mentioned a woman and two children. What is their connection?"

Alex looked at the floor, shaking his head. *How damn strange is this reunion?* "The woman is a reporter. She showed up at the scene, then followed the ambulance to the hospital. She sneaked onto the observation deck while Dr. Wellington was performing surgery. Nothing was out of the ordinary at that time." Alex took a deep breath, then let it out.

"She learned about the attack because her boys witnessed it. The man saved the boys from gang members, almost getting himself killed. The woman's name is Karen Parker." Alex paused. "Her maiden name was Karen Delulio." Alex wondered if the name would mean anything to Sam. Probably not.

Wellington frowned. Apparently, this information was relevant, but he couldn't imagine why.

The line remained silent for a moment. "Interesting. And where is the—man?"

"He's in a private room guarded by two police officers. A member of the surgical team is there too. The man is in a coma."

"I'll be landing at the hospital heliport in ten minutes. Could someone meet me?"

"I'll be there," Alex said.

"Great." For several seconds, nothing was said. Then Sam cleared his throat and added, "Mr. Madden, this doesn't have to be like the last time."

Before Alex responded, the line went dead.

CHAPTER 21

The blue helicopter waiting on the tarmac was a Hughes 500, which Sam recognized as a Hughes OH-6 light-observation helicopter that was also marketed as a civilian craft. Sam had flown in both the military and the civilian variant and liked neither of them. On the chopper's side, bold yellow letters read GREAT LAKES HELICOPTER. The pilot introduced himself as Val Feldner, a man of slight build with black hair and thick black eyebrows hidden behind mirrored aviator sunglasses. Sam shook the pilot's hand and introduced himself. Feldner helped Sam aboard, showing him where to stow his bags.

In the reflection of the helicopter's glass bubble, a thin smile appeared on Feldner's face as he cranked the motor to life. The Allison 250 turboshaft engine spun the five-blade rotor to takeoff velocity. The distinctive sound triggered Sam's memories of El Salvador. Sam tried to clear his mind. Thoughts of El Salvador were always unwelcome, especially now. He didn't need the distraction. So, he focused on something that bothered him since his conversation with Alex Madden. A young reporter named Karen Delulio.

✱✱✱

Edward Powers entered the new National Security Council Crisis Center, a place where the President of the United States and his advisors could take on the world. It was the nerve center of the most powerful military force on the planet. Edward Powers influenced the center's design, and he beamed at the thought of being here for its first genuine test.

Across the street, the old crisis center had waited forty-some years for the inevitable war that never happened between the United States and the Soviet Union. Over the years, it became a cobbled mosaic of old and new technologies. It lacked the sophistication required for computerized warfare. That was not the case here.

Powers understood what most men did not—wars are won on the ground, not on a computer screen. Enemies could be forced back, armies pummeled, and national resources rendered inoperable, but such attacks don't defeat countries. They only weaken them. Such were the tactics of recent skirmishes, push the enemy back, blow up its power plants and oil fields, punish the people economically, but not defeat it. Politicians don't understand war. Most weren't alive the last time they fought a real one. Yet politicians and their rich donors run the country. It made Powers ill.

Powers wouldn't be in command for long. President Beckman would take control, and that bothered him. Beckman lacked military experience. Powers wondered how a man like that could lead a military operation.

At the far side of the crisis center, Powers stared into a retinal scanner that identified him as one of four people—the secretary of state, the vice president, the president, and himself—who were authorized access to the next room. A transparent door, twelve inches thick, and constructed of alternating layers of Lexan and oil, slid open, allowing him entry into the secure command center, or SCC, the most secure room in the Capital. From here, he could run a covert operation within a covert operation. No one could monitor the words or transmissions generated in this room.

Picking up a blue phone, he entered a series of numbers, then listened as the electronic code sped silently through relays and fiber optic cables toward its destination. Beyond the thick glass, young soldiers stared at their computer monitors, creating a scene that looked more like a high school classroom than a military command center. A click suggested someone had picked up on the other end. Powers cleared his throat. He spoke with clipped sentences. His eyes remained riveted on the young soldiers' faces in the other room. When he'd finished, he slowly lowered the handset into its cradle. Soon, the most elite counter-terrorism squad in the world would be en route to Cleveland, Ohio. A waste of resources, but waste wasn't new to military operations.

★ ★ ★

When Tommy awoke, he realized that something was wrong. An unearthly racket, like a cross between a jet engine and a record played backward, filled his ears. Everything he saw was blurred and warped. He stuck a finger in each ear and closed his eyes. The sound didn't go away, but he was able to acclimate just enough to think. When he opened his eyes, his brother and their mother appeared as blurred images on the couch. The others in the room talked in slow motion, twisted and out of focus, tracers trailing their movements. One small sphere of clarity appeared at the door leading into the hall.

"Tommy, I'm ready now."

"Who's there?" He looked around. His own movement felt stiff, almost mechanical, as if his neck were in a brace.

"Time to go."

"Where? Where are you?"

"Hurry. I don't have much time."

Tommy looked at the door. Again, the center of his vision cleared.

"Follow the pathway."

Tommy stood and walked on a clear path through a tunnel surrounded by a kaleidoscope of swirling images. The tunnel led to the door. He felt dizzy, scared, and disoriented.

He opened the door and saw the same clear tunnel. It led him down the hall to the elevator. Every number on the elevator keypad blurred beyond recognition, except the number four, which he pushed. The elevator started upward with a jerk.

* * *

Alex hadn't waited long when the distinctive whop of a helicopter's rotor caught his attention. He shielded his eyes from the sun and located the incoming chopper at two o'clock. His watch read 10:25.

Swirling dirt and pulses of pounding air disrupted his thoughts. The helicopter eased toward a yellow X painted on the asphalt. Before its rotors stopped, the side door opened, and a compact man jumped to the ground. He wore a brown tweed sports coat over a blue denim shirt, not the attire one would expect of a D.C. bureaucrat, not the black suit Alex remembered from fifteen years ago. The man retrieved two black cases from the chopper, then ducked his head and ran under the menacing rotor blades.

Alex felt uneasy. He had hoped he'd never again see Sam Henry. Their last encounter nearly ended in a fistfight. For fifteen years, Alex wished he'd thrown the first punch.

"Detective Madden?" The man shouted over the chopper's ascent. He dropped a case and extended a hand.

"Mr. Henry." Alex grasped the extended hand, gripping it firmly. The two men stood for a moment with shoulders hunched and eyes squinted shut as the fierce, man-made wind assaulted them. The torrent settled as the helicopter rose into the sky. Both men relaxed and opened their eyes.

"Anything new?" Henry scooped up his cases and hurried toward the hospital.

"Nothing's changed."

"Tell me again, who knows?"

"Beyond those in Wellington's office, there are six surgical team members, two students, Karen Parker, her two boys, the officers, and the video technician."

"Say that again?"

"What?"

"Video technician?"

"This is a teaching hospital. They video surgeries and use them in the classroom."

"Is that video secured?" Sam asked with a calm tone.

"There's an officer in the editing room with the video tech. Oh, add another officer to the list. The technician is enhancing the video. He should have it finished in about thirty minutes. Don't worry. It's secured," Alex said.

Sam held his questions as they passed three hospital workers loitering in the hall. When they were clear, he asked, "How about lab work, emergency room staff, files?"

"I have the file. A lab tech couldn't find a match for the man's blood. He's curious, but he's not thinking it's the blood of an alien. He thinks he will be written up in the New England Journal of Medicine for discovering a new blood type."

Alex stabbed at the elevator button. The doors slid open, and both men stepped inside. Everything was under control. Even Sam Henry seemed less aggravating than he'd expected.

★ ★ ★

Tommy stopped in front of a hospital room. A man stood by the door, distorted and unmoving. Inside, he saw the blurred images of two men. One dressed in dark blue, like a cop. The other wore green, like a doctor. Tommy could see the man clearly on the bed. He was hooked up to a machine. Tubes protruded from his nose, a larger one stuffed down his throat and needles stuck in his arms like porcupine quills connected to more tubes, which led to bottles that hung above the bed.

"Tommy." Tommy looked around, pivoting on his heel, searching the corners of the ceiling.

"Help me."

"Who said that?" Tommy spun a circle, almost falling to the floor.

"I'm sorry. I forget you don't understand. You're hearing me think."

"Hearing you think?"

"Come closer."

Tommy stood at the foot of the bed, unwilling to move.

"They say you're not, eh, human." Tommy shuttered, talking to a man with a tube down his throat.

"I'm a visitor, but to say I am not human is incorrect."

Tommy thought for a moment and said, "What do you want?"

"Your help."

"What makes you think I can help?"

"Will you try?"

Tommy studied the man. His eyes were closed, his skin ashen, and his chest rose in cadence with a machine at the side of the bed.

"What can I do?"

"Help me escape."

Coldness crept over Tommy's skin and under his clothes. It occurred to him that he was crazy or dead, so it didn't matter what he thought, or what he thought he thought. Nothing mattered, and he didn't care.

CHAPTER 22

The room held a strange fragrance, but Tommy saw no flowers. Yet, the odor wasn't flowers. It didn't smell like anything Tommy had experienced before. He must be dreaming.

"Tommy? It's time," the voice said. The breathing machine whooshed and wheezed with the rise and fall of the man's chest. Tommy said, "I can't help you."

"You won't help me." It wasn't a question.

"I said, I *can't* help you!" Tommy felt dizzy and, for a moment, thought he might fall. He grabbed the bed rail to steady himself.

"What the hell?" Tommy released the rail and stepped back, bumping into the blurred, swirling mass of color that surrounded him. He pawed at it, but it was like trying to swim through a spider web that wasn't there.

"Leave me alone. I can't help you." Tommy wept softly.

"Don't worry. You did your best."

Why did he say that? "You did your best."

Those four words rattled around in Tommy's head. He waited for them to fade, but they would not. They were the words his father often used, except his father said them as a question. As a challenge. *You did your best?* And every time Dad said those words, Tommy looked inside and asked if he had sincerely done his best. And in most cases, he had not. So, he would always try again, and when he did, his father would smile from a place that seemed much deeper than the mere expression on his face.

How dare this man, or alien or whatever, use his father's words? Why couldn't Tommy let those words go? His father was dead, but the seed father planted was not. No, he had not done his best. He had not even tried.

"How could I help?"

"Pull the tube from my throat. That machine is killing me."

Tommy looked at the machine and watched it breathe for the man.

"Pull it out. I'll die soon if you don't."

It was only a dream. Might as well see it through—get it over with. He'd awaken soon enough. Tommy moved to the edge of the bed, and with both hands, he gripped the corrugated plastic hose and pulled it from the stranger's throat. The machine sounded an alarm. Tommy punched at the machine's buttons until the buzzing stopped. Air escaped from the man's lungs with an involuntary gurgle and then silence. His chest didn't move.

Tommy shuffled backward on rigid legs—his eyes wide and his breath short. *I killed him. Please let this be a dream. Crazy! Extremely crazy.* He reached for the door handle but couldn't find it. He spun around but saw no door, only a swirling blur of color. Turning back, he saw that the man's chest remained still.

The swirling colors of the room slowed. Tommy watched as the men's faces become recognizable. They began moving.

Suddenly, the man on the bed sucked in a lung full of air. At first, his breaths were erratic, deep, and strained, but they grew stronger and quieter until he slept. The swirling color intensity increased. After ten minutes, the man opened his eyes, looked at Tommy, and smiled.

Tommy's heart still raced, but his fear subsided as he removed the thick leather straps that secured the man to the bed. The man sat upright and quickly began removing tubes and wires.

Removing the last needle from his arm, the man eased himself to the floor on unsteady legs. "Thank you," he said.

"Are you Nigel?" Tommy put the man's arm around his own shoulder for support.

"That's me."

"Nigel, what?"

"Just Nigel." Nigel steadied himself, using Tommy as support.

"Now what?" Tommy asked.

Nigel shuffled to the door, sliding his feet along the floor like an old man. "Bare."

"This is Cleveland, Ohio. There ain't no bears around here."

"Not bear, *bare!* My ass is bare. I'm cold. Need clothes."

Tommy walked at Nigel's side, out the door and down the hall. The same distorted blur continued around them. Only a small, round space like a tunnel in front of them was clear.

"How are you doing that?"

Nigel looked over at him. "Doing what?"

"That!" Tommy waved his arm at the distorted image that surrounded them.

"Oh, that. It's hard to explain."

"Try. I'm freaking out."

"Freaking out? That doesn't sound good." Nigel waved his hand. "It's like a wrinkle in time, but it's not that. We're out of phase with other people or with the universe. That's the best explanation I can give. I'm not actually doing it. It's more like it's being done through me. But don't worry, they can't see us. They don't know we're here."

"How long can you do that?"

"Not me, but not long. Bad things can happen if the portal is open too long."

They found a room marked: LINEN. Inside were stacks of folded sheets, blankets, pillowcases, green uniforms, and slippers. Nigel put on a uniform and slippers. He looked good. Not too young, not too tall, head held high, back straight—he'd pass for a doctor easy enough. Nigel was a handsome man. Anyway, Tommy estimated he was. Brown hair trimmed, chiseled features, and determined blue eyes. Tommy's excitement prevented him from wondering why no head wounds remained from the savage blows of the tire iron.

* * *

Karen opened her eyes, squinting at the sunshine flooding through the windows. Paul's head rested on her shoulder. She eased him to one side, as only a mother can do, without disturbing his slumber. Stretching her arms, she arched her back and wiped the sleep from her eyes. With a slight tilt, she walked to the coffeepot. Someone had made fresh. Inhaling the rich aroma, she realized something was wrong.

Empty windows.

A quick scan of the room.

Tommy was gone.

* * *

Nigel smoothed his new clothes, then ran his hand over his hair. "Tommy, you've done all that I asked. I can't ask for more. Go to your mother now."

"I'm going with you." Tommy paused and then whispered, "I'm afraid."

"Nothing wrong with that, Tommy. I'm afraid as well. That's why you must go to your mother." Nigel rubbed Tommy's shoulder.

Tommy looked up into Nigel's face. "You don't understand. I'm afraid of what will happen to me if I don't help you. If I don't do my best."

Nigel studied Tommy for a moment and said, "If you insist. Now, we must go."

★ ★ ★

Karen raced toward the door, but an officer caught her by the arm. He said he was sorry, but she could not leave. Her first attempt to explain was nothing more than sobs and babble. Finally, she strung enough words together, so the officer understood Tommy was gone. The officer surveyed the room and swore. After ordering another officer to guard the door, he and Karen hit the hall running.

★ ★ ★

Alex led Sam Henry to Wellington's office, where they found Eric Key, Jerry Faulkner, and Wellington waiting. The glasses of whisky were gone. Sam positioned himself across from Wellington, and then Alex said, "Dr. Wellington, this is Sam Henry from the National Security Council. He's here to take over."

"Mr. Henry," Wellington said, extending his hand as he stood.

The men shook hands. "What's the condition of your patient?" Sam Henry asked?

"He's in a coma. It doesn't look good."

"I want to see him. How sure are you that this man isn't human?"

"As sure as I'm standing here. His anatomy is all wrong."

"That's it? You decided the man is an alien because his insides are a little different? There must be other explanations."

Wellington shifted his weight slightly forward. "Listen. You are probably damn good at whatever it is you do for the government." Wellington noticed a subtle change in Henry's expression, but he couldn't read its meaning. "Well, I'm damn good at what I do as well. His anatomy wasn't a little different; it's a lot different. It's not human—stomach, spleen, liver—not human. He has two hearts, and he healed a broken clavicle on his way to the operating room." Wellington sat then continued, "I know this sounds crazy, but I'm telling you, whatever this man is, he's not human. Maybe he's some experiment from one of your buddies."

"Our government has nothing like that," Sam said.

"How about somebody else?" Wellington waved his hand in a circle above his head. "Hell, we aren't the only ones who experiment with everything in God's creation."

"I'd know about it if they did, and they don't."

"How can you know about every top-secret experiment in every country on this planet?"

Sam's eyes closed to thin slits, and for a second, he looked as if he had something to say. Finally, he said, "You'd stake your reputation that this thing is an alien from another world?"

"I already have."

"How many people know about him?" Henry reached into his jacket retrieving a package of gum and offering a stick to Wellington, who declined with a wave of his hand. Sam stuck a stick in his mouth, then tossed the wadded paper onto Wellington's desk. Wellington frowned, grabbed the wrapper, and pitched it in the trash.

"There's my surgical team. One of them is with the patient, and the others are in the second-floor conference room." Wellington explained the composition of the surgical team, all of them trusted employees who must maintain strict medical confidentiality. Further confinement would be unnecessary. He was confident of that.

"What about others, lab techs, ER personnel?"

"The ER crew knows nothing," Wellington said. "They did triage but saw nothing out of the ordinary. The lab people only know that he has a rare blood type." Wellington looked at the ceiling. "Let's see, there's the media specialist. He shoots video footage for training. Oh, and the administrator, David Johnson."

Alex closed his eyes. Sam was staring at him. The glint in Sam's eyes said more than most men could say with words.

"Cell phones?" Sam asked.

"Collected them," Alex said.

"Anyone else?" Sam was staring at Wellington.

"None that I can think of." Wellington felt relieved, for reasons he couldn't explain, that his first exchange with Sam Henry had ended.

"Detective Madden, you didn't mention David Johnson. Where is he now?" Henry's voice exuded a cutting quality that Hollywood would patent if such patents were possible.

"I forgot him," Alex mumbled. "He's the one who called the CDC, so I assumed you knew," Alex lied, hoping to make his oversight seem less obvious. Alex's head dropped. "I don't know where he is now."

Henry stroked his chin. "Is anyone with him?"

"He isn't under arrest," Alex snapped, wishing he had not.

Wellington leaned forward in his heavy wooden chair, and it creaked with an ancient sound of wisdom passed on from the many souls who had thought countless thoughts as they sat and pondered things that men ponder when they sit in heavy wooden chairs. "Mr. Henry, I understand your concerns. However, believe me, David Johnson wants to keep this quiet as badly as you do. Maybe more so." Wellington's voice grew stronger with each word. This was merely a D.C. bureaucrat, little more than a cop with connections. "Detective Madden made it clear that Mr. Johnson wasn't to speak to anyone about our patient."

Sam Henry breathed out. "I'm sure he did. Thank you, doctor."

"Agent Key," Sam said. "Find David Johnson and bring him here. Don't let him talk to a soul."

"He's a very busy man," Wellington interjected.

Henry raised his hand for silence, then stared at Eric until he left the room.

* * *

Walking out of the hospital proved easy, but Tommy knew it wouldn't remain easy for long. Their escape would soon be discovered. The cops wouldn't be happy. Soon he and his new friend would be fugitives.

Cool.

Think, damn it, think. Where can we go? How are we going to get to wherever we're going? He only had the ten bucks that he'd stuffed in his pocket last night before they left on Paul's little excursion into the dark. It was last night, wasn't it? It seemed like months ago. Where to? How was he supposed to know? He'd only been to three places since they moved to Cleveland, the brownstone, his aunt and uncle's house, and their cabin. *Well, four now, counting the hospital.*

That's it! Aunt Alice and Uncle George were gone for two weeks, and he had fare for the bus. They walked into the sunshine, and everything in his vision zipped back into focus. Walking down the sidewalk, a smile exploded on Tommy's face. *We are free.*

"We need to get on the bus," Tommy said. He saw that Nigel's face had turned ghostly, the energy oozing from him into the morning air. The sight reminded Tommy too much of his father during the last days of his life. "I know a place you can rest."

"Thank you, Tommy. That's all I need. Then we can go our separate ways." Nigel spoke with a soft, almost inaudible voice.

"There!" Tommy tugged Nigel's arm, pulling him toward a Cleveland Rapid Transit bus. They would need to run to make it in time. Nigel moved slowly, dragging his feet like a drunkard.

"Hey! Wait! Wait for us!" Tommy screamed, flailing his arms in the air. Each time he let go of Nigel, Tommy had to go back and get him. Nigel no longer moved forward under his own power. Their hopes of escape hinged on catching that bus.

* * *

Across the street, in the hospital's parking lot, three sets of eyes followed Tommy and his friend.

"Shit," Miguel whispered. "Isn't that the dude from last night? That's wacko. Let's get the hell out of here."

"Looks like the dude," the driver, Ed, said, lifting his shades and then setting them back on the bridge of his nose. "What's up with that? The dude's friggin' Superman or what?"

"That's loco. Let's get the hell out of here," Miguel repeated.

"They're both toast. This time, we do it right. Then we find that wimp-ass cousin of mine and shut him up too." With that, the third man, Carlos, drew the blade of his knife along his own arm. A thin line of blood appeared in its trace.

* * *

Karen and her officer escort found Dr. Wellington's office. The officer rapped on the door, and when it opened, Karen rushed in and threw her arms around Alex's neck.

Sobbing, she said, "Tommy's gone."

PART TWO

CHAPTER 1

Sam recognized her when she burst through the door. He'd hoped for and dreaded this moment. Why he remembered her, he could not explain. Conflicts and intimidation happened often back then, but she was a fiery woman with steel nerves, talents wasted on a journalist, talents etched in his memory. Too bad her path had not taken her into law enforcement or intelligence. He knew any encounter with Karen Delulio would result in a barrage of unbridled rage, which he planned to absorb and then say he was sorry, thus putting to rest another reconciliation from his past, as if it were that easy.

However, something about Karen didn't seem right. She had changed. He sensed that the fire that once burned inside her had diminished. What changes a person like that? Children. She was a mother now, and her son was missing. She had reasons for concern. The thugs who tried to kill John Doe wouldn't want witnesses, and Tommy was a witness. Could the perpetrators track Tommy and his brother here? Sam felt a chill in the air.

Alex wrapped his burly arms around Karen and rocked her gently. "We'll find him. He can't be far."

Alex looked at the officer who had brought her. The officer shifted his weight from one foot to the other, trying unsuccessfully to avoid Madden's gaze.

Finally, the officer said, "I don't understand how he slipped out."

"Explain it to me," Madden said.

"We were right there. One minute the kid was asleep in the window, and the next minute he was gone." He turned his palms up in frustration. Silence followed. He shifted from foot to foot, glanced at his watch, and tapped at its face.

***

In a hospital room on the fourth floor, Officer Sean Camp had a headache. He shook his head, trying to rid himself of the cloud that floated between his eyes. Slowly, things sank in. Empty bed. John Doe was gone.

"How in the hell?" Sean watched Dr. Cray rub his eyes. They exchanged a look and dashed from the room.

"Did you see him?" Sean asked the officer in the hall.

"See who?"

"John is gone." Sean pointed at the empty bed.

***

Dr. Cray burst into Wellington's office. Between gasps for air, Cray said, "He's gone."

Sam didn't know who this person was, but he already knew that Tommy was gone.

"What happened?" Wellington asked, leaping to his feet.

Cray blinked. "I'm—I'm not sure,"

"He's dead?" Wellington asked.

Karen's crying became hysterical, and she would have crumpled to the floor had Alex not been holding her.

Sam stood. "What in the hell are you talking about? I thought the boy was missing from the conference room."

Cray looked confused.

Wellington said, "He's not talking about Tommy. He's talking about the patient."

"The patient?" Now Sam looked confused. "You mean the alien?"

***

On the Cleveland Rapid Transit bus, Tommy and Nigel fell into empty seats. Inconspicuous, they were not. Nigel's skin had turned pasty white, as if life were leaking out of him. An elderly woman with blue hair gathered her purse and moved to the back of the bus. Nigel snored in unison with the diesel's groan. In a few minutes, Tommy would ask the driver if the bus was going to Brandy Island, but first, he needed to think. His mother would be worried sick and angry too. Why was he doing this? It made little sense, but he didn't have a choice.

CHAPTER 2

Edward Powers stood in the crisis center with his hands clasped behind his back. His crisp uniform and statuesque pose portrayed a man from a past era. Surveying the room, he marveled at the techno-wizard soldiers who operated the center's gadgetry. They all seemed busy, and he didn't know why. He had not yet given any orders. Computers seemed to generate work all by themselves. Powers accepted the necessity of computers, but he didn't like the damn things. In addition, fighting men no longer fit the image etched in his mind. In fact, half were women, and with each passing year, the men looked more like schoolboys. Damned if adapting to the new military didn't cause him some difficulty.

He took a deep breath, expanding his chest, and took comfort in the fact this wasn't a genuine crisis. He didn't believe in little green men. When Sam Henry arrived on the scene, he'd probably discover the doctor had indulged in too many syringes of something from the hospital pharmacy. Mostly, he prayed that the first test of the crisis center didn't end too soon. A thin smile formed on his lips. Despite the frivolousness of this so-called crisis, this is what he lived for, and he was damn sure going to enjoy every minute.

***

The CRT bus snaked through the streets of Cleveland. Bathed in a brilliant autumn sun, the city took on a new look. Golden leaves glistened in the morning light, celebrating their deaths with a vibrant dance in the wind. Purple flowers stood against an emerald sea of trimmed grass, and the air smelled fresh after the night's rain.

When his father died, the world grew dark, but now everything glowed as if scales had fallen from Tommy's eyes. For three bucks each, they had tickets to anywhere in Cleveland. Tommy felt free.

***

Half a block behind the CRT bus trailed a blue Chevy slung low to the ground. A traffic light turned yellow as the bus passed the intersection, then turned red for the Chevy. The Chevy sped up. A woman stepped from the curb, and the Chevy's front fender clipped her bag, sending groceries flying across the intersection. She spun around, landing on her butt halfway into the lane of traffic. A delivery truck slid to a stop two feet from where she sat.

★ ★ ★

Sam Henry's historic First Contact at St. John's Hospital had been contained: one restrained alien, no deaths, no injuries, nobody ill, no news media.

Perfect.

Now, it had all gone to shit, and Sam couldn't prevent it from spiraling out of control.

This was more like it.

Adrenalin coursed through his veins.

Eric Key returned with a flustered David Johnson.

"Can someone tell me what's going on? I'm a busy man," Johnson said.

"Mr. Johnson, I'm Sam Henry. I'll explain everything, but we've outgrown this space. Can you lead us to your office?"

David Johnson shook his head but obliged, leading the way to his office. Karen fell behind the procession, weeping so hard that she almost collapsed. When the convoy entered the administrative area, Mandy Olsen, Johnson's secretary, frowned, then followed them into her boss's office.

"This will work," Sam declared, dispatching a pile of papers from Johnson's desk.

"Those are important." Mandy gathered the papers Sam had displaced. Mandy had been Johnson's secretary for ten years. She was loyal, as good assistants tend to be. "I'll put them on my desk, Dr. Johnson." She stormed from the room.

"Why don't you give your secretary the day off?" Sam suggested. "We don't need more people involved in this."

"She already knows what's going on," Johnson said before he could contemplate the wisdom of revealing the fact.

"She what?!" Sam glared at Alex, who was already glaring at Johnson, causing Sam's look to be wasted.

"Mandy has been with me for ten years and is my most trusted employee. I've trusted her with many secrets over the years. She'll be a great asset," Johnson said, cutting his eyes to the floor.

Sam took a deep breath. He had to control his emotions. He knew that. *Damn it! Control yourself, Sam.*

Karen's constant crying grated on Sam's nerves like fingernails drawn across a blackboard. However, he felt disappointment. This wasn't the woman he remembered. Time may have distorted his memories. Perhaps something else bothered him that he couldn't discern. Whatever it was, she had to go. She'd be of no help. She was a distraction.

"Forgive me. I was harsh," Sam said with an even voice as Mandy returned to the room, unaware of the dissension her mere existence caused. Sam looked at Mandy and said, "I'm sorry, I didn't catch your name."

"Mandy Olsen."

"Mandy, Mrs. Parker is quite upset. Would you take her to your office and make her comfortable? But neither of you leaves. No calls. Understood?"

Mandy nodded her agreement and, with one arm around Karen's shoulder, escorted her from the room.

With the women gone, Sam glanced around the room and asked, "Is there anyone else I don't know about?" No one spoke. Satisfied, Sam moved to a large whiteboard mounted on the wall and erased what was written there.

Johnson started to protest, but Sam raised his hand, calling for silence. "Let's identify what we know."

Sam felt in control again, at least in this little corner of the world. "We must conduct a thorough search. Pair up and search every inch of this place." Sam wrote: Search Hospital.

David Johnsons said, "You were to explain. Why do we need to search the hospital? That will be traumatic for patients. What are you searching for?"

Sam said, "Sorry, I forgot you missed that part. Tommy Parker is missing."

"That explains the crying woman, but surely we don't need to search the entire hospital. He's just playing or perhaps went looking for a soda."

Wellington said, "John is also missing."

"The, er—patient?" Johnson asked. "How is that possible? His room was guarded."

"Tommy was also guarded," Wellington said.

Johnson looked puzzled. "It seems strange they both disappear at the same time."

Sam said, "Yes, it does. Thus, the reason we are going to search. Can we move forward?"

Anticipation mounted. The men were eager to begin the hunt.

"Remember that those thugs might be looking for the boys," Alex interjected. "So be careful."

Sam surveyed the room and noted affirmative nods from everyone. "Somebody ask Karen if she has a picture of the boy." On the board, Sam wrote: Photograph.

"Done." Eric dashed out of the room. He returned a minute later with a picture of Tommy taken the previous year. Sam grabbed the photo from Eric's hand and stared at it for several minutes.

"Can you make a copy of this?" Sam held the photograph in the air, directing his question to Eric Key.

Key took the photo, then left the room.

"Dr. Wellington, how long will it take to search the hospital?" Sam asked.

"I don't know. Forty-five minutes?"

"Be careful, be thorough, but be quick about it." Forty-five minutes was too long, but he didn't have a choice. He prayed the boy got bored staring at the walls and wandered off, as young boys often do. Somehow, Sam knew better. Tommy did not wander off. So how did he slip out unnoticed? Well, kids are clever. It could happen. However, Sam feared Tommy left the same way John Doe did, and that was difficult to explain. For now, Sam would keep his fears to himself.

Johnson didn't have a partner for the search, but Sam had a task for him. "Mr. Johnson, could you ensure that hospital security has the exits covered? And give them copies of that photograph while you're at it. I can't stress the importance of keeping the reason for the search secret." Sam followed Johnson to the door, where Johnson lingered for a moment as Mandy handed him copies of Tommy's photograph, their fingers touching as the photocopy passed between them. *Interesting,* Sam thought, becoming the first person to notice there was more between the man and his secretary than mere professional courtesy. It took Sam less than ten minutes to discover what had eluded an entire hospital staff for two years. Sam expected nothing less from himself.

With everyone gone, Sam withdrew into the office, locking the door behind him. He opened his black cases, and within five minutes, a small dish-like antenna was set up on the corner of Johnson's desk. He hung his jacket on a coat tree, staring out the window as his laptop raced through its startup applications.

★ ★ ★

"Sir, we have a message from Mr. Henry," Corporal Jane Peck announced. Eighteen years ago, such an announcement would have come from a man, not a 20-something-year-old woman. Nevertheless, today, Jane Peck, corporal, US Marines, monitored the communication link between Sam Henry and the crisis center.

Powers walked toward her station with a calm confidence that only time and testing can temper in a soldier. The words he was about to read on her computer's monitor would destroy his composure, although he'd do a fine job hiding it from his troops. If one could call the gaggle of pimple-faced computer jockeys—troops.

Powers leaned down, peering over Corporal Peck's shoulder, savoring the scent of expensive perfume mingled with a mild odor of tobacco smoke, pure heaven. Maybe the new army wasn't so bad after all.

"On screen," the corporal said in her most official voice.

Powers read the message.

OBJECTIVE NOT SECURE
OBJECTIVE NOT SECURE
CONTACT IS ON THE GROUND
CONTACT IS CONFIRMED

"Son of a bitch," Powers swore under his breath. Only Corporal Peck was privy to the crack in Powers' military demeanor.

"Okay, people. We have a new twist. The contact is on the ground." This meant that Sam Henry had no goddamn idea where the so-called alien was. Powers had a way of inflecting the width and breadth of a situation with the mere tone of his voice. The room became a flurry of activity, if for no other reason than that it seemed a necessity to do so. Powers marched across the room toward a young sergeant who stood at attention next to a rather ordinary-looking black phone. Powers' eyes locked on the sergeant from halfway across the room. "Get the White House."

In less than a minute, Powers had Beckman on the line. He tried to brief the President, but Beckman cut him off. "Too busy, reporters to talk to, elections to win, handle it, I'll be there soon," Beckman said.

Powers suppressed a smile. He'd be in command longer than anticipated.

CHAPTER 3

The CRT bus rumbled away from the curb, its diesel engine straining against the effects of weight and gravity, slowly launching the bulky, swaying carcass into the morning traffic. Nigel slept, his head resting against the window, swaying in unison with the massive machine as it oscillated along the uneven city street. Other than the blue-haired old woman who fled to the back seat, no one paid attention to Nigel. Back in Kansas, a man wandering the streets in surgical scrubs would have drawn considerable attention to himself, but not here. City folks keep to themselves. *Understandable,* Tommy mused, considering last night's lesson. Their indifference suited him fine. The only people in Cleveland that Tommy needed were his aunt and uncle, and he needed them to be out of town.

Tommy's aunt worked as a lawyer, and his uncle ran his own business. At least Tommy thought he did. They didn't talk about Uncle George's business. Aunt Alice called it the Company. Tommy didn't know what kind of lawyering Aunt Alice did, but it must have been for the military because she worked for some attorney who was a general.

Now that he'd thought about it, going to his aunt's home wasn't such a hot idea after all. Mom would figure it out. But it was the only other place in Cleveland that he knew. First, the police would check the brownstone and then his aunt and uncle's home. There must be a better place. The bus turned south, heading away from Brandy Island, which wasn't an island but a small peninsula stretching like a finger into Lake Erie. Uncle George said that Brandy Island sounded better than Brandy Peninsula. Tommy couldn't argue with that.

Turning onto Erie Avenue, Tommy saw a tall building with a pyramid-shaped top. Mom called it Tower City, and Tommy wondered what people did there. A few blocks later they turned onto I-90, traveling away from the grandeur of skyscrapers, away from Lake Erie, and away from Brandy Island.

* * *

Ed kept his distance, matching the speed of the bus. "Where in the hell are they going?"

"Like, I'm supposed to know?" Miguel laughed. Miguel laughed at pretty much everything.

"Doesn't matter how far they're going. It won't be far enough," Carlos said from the back seat.

***

"Incoming message, General. Sam Henry again," Corporal Peck announced.

Powers crossed the room with deliberate steps, his well-starched uniform rustling. "On screen."

"On screen now, sir."

Powers leaned over her shoulder, a little closer this time, his hand resting on the back of her chair.

INSTANT AREA SEARCH UNDERWAY
POTENTIAL JUVENILE HOSTAGE
ACTIVATE WITNESS PROTOCOL 3.56

Powers understood witness protocol 3.56. Everyone else in the center flipped through the green manuals, looking it up. Protocol 3.56 meant that all witnesses must be confined at a high-security government installation. A request Powers anticipated, if in fact, they had discovered an actual alien. For now, Powers had to assume there really was an alien. Why else would Sam Henry initiate 3.56? Three-point-five-six required the president's authorization, but Beckman wasn't here.

Powers understood the game. Policies were written to ensure that acts like Protocol 3.56 were not initiated without proper authorization. However, people don't consult policy manuals during actual emergencies. They assume the other person knows what he or she's doing. Therefore, Powers called the Secret Service duty officer, ordering him to gather a transport team comprised of agents and Marines. The duty officer assumed Powers knew what he was doing, and in a manner of speaking, he did.

Next, Powers called Andrews Air Force Base, where he found an old friend on duty. "Morning, Barry," Powers said.

"Morning, Ed. What's up?"

"Barry, I need to transport a team to Cleveland ASAP. They will pick up civilian passengers, then head toward the West Coast. The final coordinates will be given to the flight crew after they leave Cleveland. Better figure around forty people total." Powers explained the covert nature of the mission. "Barry, this is a need-to-know, top-secret mission of national security interest. I need your most trusted flight crew. And Barry, the crew might not return for a few days."

The reply came without question. "They'll be airborne within the hour."

***

Sam's screensaver flashed pictures of the Earth, and then an icon popped up indicating he had received an e-mail. Reading the message, he breathed easier. Most presidents would be slow to incarcerate American citizens without due process, even in an emergency. Richard Beckman, however, never seemed concerned with people's rights or following the constitution.

Sam took no pleasure in locking these people away, but they complicated his mission. He couldn't waste his limited resources keeping them quiet, and he knew that despite his best efforts, something would leak out. Then he'd have more trouble. The only way to ensure silence was to get them into a controlled environment. He knew just the place. He didn't like sending them there but weighing the importance of this discovery against violating a few people's rights made his decision easy.

Now to decide if any of them would stay with him or if they all must go.

CHAPTER 4

Dr. AJ Jahan arrived at St. John's Hospital in a green taxi. Jahan eased from the back seat, his black hair shining in the midmorning sun. A brown leather briefcase appeared toy-like, dangling next to his 6'5", 250-pound frame. Staring up at the hospital, he considered what he was about to see. A man unlike any other. Impossible. Could this be contact with an extraterrestrial? Probably not. His analytical brain eliminated that as a possibility on the flight from Atlanta. There must be a logical explanation.

AJ noticed two security guards at the entrance, probably there because of the hospital's unique patient. At the reception desk, a silver-haired woman greeted him, then placed a call to the administrator's office.

"Excuse me," Mandy said, easing into Dr. Johnson's office. "A Dr. Jahan from the CDC is on his way up."

Sam Henry seemed to be in a daze. He returned to the present. "I'll let you know when I'm ready to see him. Have you heard from any of the others?" The others meant the men searching for Tommy Parker and John Doe.

"Not yet." Mandy lowered her eyes to the floor and left the room to return to Karen's side. The two women sat on a small Victorian couch, covered with a blue floral print. Mandy's routine included greeting guests, sorting mail, writing memos, and helping her boss navigate the undercurrents of human emotions as he supervised the diverse hospital staff, everything from arrogant doctors to under-educated janitorial workers. Today was not one of those days. She'd often wondered how doctors coped with telling parents that their child had not survived. She thanked God it wasn't her job. She prayed that such a message wouldn't come here, not in her office, not to this woman.

* * *

Powers retreated into the SCC. He needed space and time to think. He was thinking about Sam Henry, wondering if Sam could handle the task. Requesting the 3.56 protocol was a bold move, classic Sam Henry.

Yet, Powers believed Sam had changed, and the problem was he didn't know how much. He hated to admit it, but Beckman might be right. Perhaps Sam wasn't up to the job.

A commotion in the crisis center interrupted his contemplations. "All rise!" A marine demanded as the President of the United States entered the center. Two angry-looking Secret Service agents followed in tight formation. Their right hands concealed in their navy-blue blazers, no doubt resting on the pistol grips of automatic weapons. Everyone stood as Richard Beckman marched into the crisis center.

"At ease," Beckman said with a paternal tone.

Beckman had never served in the armed forces and knew nothing of military protocol. He'd never been a judge either and had confused the customs of the two professions. No one bothered explaining it to him. Or if someone had, Beckman had not paid attention.

"What's the status?" Beckman asked Powers as he emerged from the SCC.

Powers squared his shoulders. "To the best of our knowledge, the contact remains at large."

"At large! You mean he's escaped?"

"Yes, Mr. President. When we last spoke, I said the contact was on the ground. That means at large," Powers said in a neutral voice.

Behind Beckman's back, soldiers rolled their eyes.

"I know that," Beckman lied. "I thought he was still in the hospital. Now you're telling me he has gotten away? Son-of-a-bitch! How did that happen?"

"We don't have the details. The hospital is being searched. We don't know if he has left the hospital."

"That sounds better. So, you're saying it hasn't escaped?"

"I'm saying we don't know." Powers paused, glancing across the room. "There's a possibility that the alien has taken a child hostage."

"Oh," Beckman said, as if the information were irrelevant.

"That's what we know so far. Sir, I need to brief you further in the SCC." This meant Powers had something confidential to say. Sam Henry designed the SCC security and assured Powers that the security was failsafe.

Once inside the SCC, Powers explained the complexity of the situation in simple terms. Sam Henry had requested the witnesses be sequestered, which sounded better than imprisoned at a facility in Nevada for debriefing, which sounded better than what would happen there. Powers explained the constitutional issues associated with

Witness Protocol 3.56. Beckman only needed to sign an executive order, which Powers had already prepared to make it legal.

Beckman signed the form without question. Powers filed it in a fireproof cabinet, which contained thousands of preexisting forms and orders, all part of the extensive planning that went into the crisis center. Powers wondered if anything had not been considered when they developed this room.

Probably not.

CHAPTER 5

In the Old Executive Building, another protocol was in motion. The analysis of the people involved in the incident. Lessons learned the hard way proved that even skilled agents could break under stress, so now everything was second-guessed in real time before, rather than after, something went wrong. Intelligence officers began sifting through files. Steve Howe, a rookie, shed his green wool suit coat, loosened his tie, and undid the top button of his starched white shirt. He'd read until his eyes refused further cooperation. His protégés, Graham Morton and Parris Turner, had kicked off their shoes.

Steve wasn't ready for that level of comfort. His shoes remained on. He had finished Sam Henry's CIA file. Some of it said little. Some of it read like a movie script. Most intriguing was information that wasn't there. The stuff that was missing.

The CIA had its share of rules and regulations. However, some secrets were so dark that even CIA officers weren't trusted with them. To satisfy the record keepers' penchant for record accountability, it wasn't a secret that the secret was secret, so when information was pulled from a file, a form signed by the director stood in testimony to the authorization of its removal. An understandable necessity that had a certain irony.

Of interest was a report removed by authorization of the late Clarence Harding. The removal authorization read: Senator Andrea Ross, assassination, Cleveland, Ohio. It was dated fifteen years earlier.

Parris stretched until she appeared as rigid as a two-by-four. Her toes curled inside her sheer nylons, and a dusty green cotton sweater and wool slacks clung to her willowy frame. Steve tried not to gawk but failed.

Graham stood, arched his back, and then walked to the coffeepot. "Find anything interesting?"

Parris said, "I'm reading about Sam Henry's latest project. His alien detection toolkit. He has airtime on the military's most recently deployed Strategic Emergency Communications Array satellite, the XV-E." Parris continued with a ten-minute history lesson on the SECA program. This was the customary briefing process that NSC intelligence used. Bring all present up to speed on the background, even if they already knew the information. Make no assumptions. Graham no doubt already knew about the SECA satellite, but he hung on every word. Such concentration was a learned skill. Focus wasn't a problem for Steve. This was the first time he heard such classified information.

"SECA was a black project." Parris paused, allowing that to sink in. "We learned that the French company, Demers, launched a United States military satellite last fall. Demers trained a highly screened unit of Americans to load the satellite into the cargo bay of their Liberty deployment rocket. Demers employees weren't even allowed on the complex until just before the launch. We weren't supposed to know about it." Parris smiled. So did Graham.

"Other than that, we know little about SECA," Parris allowed. "But then, neither does anyone else. Sam compartmentalized it. Even the development teams worked in isolation from each other. They tested it in Nevada, and we know how secretive those people are."

"How can they keep things that secret? Surely the people who built the damn thing knows what it can do." Graham had been in the intelligence business for twenty years, FBI, CIA, and NSC, and keeping something that clandestine was unheard of. He was having difficulty believing it was possible.

"You're the Deputy Director of Intelligence, NSC. Twenty years in the business. How much do you know about Operation Deep-Six?"

Steve Howe sat straight. He only knew one thing about operation Deep-Six—it was an operation he'd seen in Sam Henry's file, and someone had removed all the information regarding it. One secret too dark to tell—fifteen years ago. It was the code name assigned to Senator Ross's assassination.

Graham's jaw glistened with corrugated ripples of muscle.

Parris leaned forward. Her eyes grew dark, and she spoke in a deep whisper. "That's how secret they can keep things if they want to."

★ ★ ★

The military anti-terrorism squad, called Unit-11, germinated after an attack on the Sears Tower in Chicago. General Edward Powers was among the first to walk through the aftermath of the attack. The bodies of men, women, and children who were slaughtered slowly and painfully while the police waited, and the politicians negotiated. Afterward, it became clear that the terrorists never planned to negotiate or survive. Surprisingly, a few escaped despite a ferocious firefight with police that left twenty-five officers dead and thirty wounded.

Inside the building, Powers found a little girl clinging to life. Lying naked in a pool of her own blood, she had been raped, disemboweled, and left to die a slow death. A message to western capitalist pigs. Edward Powers heard their message, but they failed to anticipate his reply.

Avenging that little girl's death became Powers' personal crusade. He vowed that his country would be prepared to face this new threat. Therefore, he created a small, elite counter-terrorist force—Unit-11.

When Unit-11 was ready, Powers turned to the CIA and the FBI for help. With their combined intelligence efforts, Powers found the terrorists in Lebanon. What happened next was more like surgery than a massacre, skillfully removing the terrorists from this world and sending them to the next.

Their crimes at the Sears Tower were not adjudicated in a court of law, but photographs found in the terrorist camp and DNA tests proved Powers killed the right people. He'd hunted the bastards down and made them pay. He'd not lost one soldier in the process, and he'd done it on foreign soil. It was a victory that could not be shared with the American people, but the message reached those who needed it most. The rules have changed.

The Sears Tower incident taught him a second lesson. Politicians couldn't be trusted to make quick decisions. He vowed to face a court martial before he watched another event like that. Terrorists were not domestic enemies, and dealing with them was not a job for civilians. He'd not wait idly while politicians weighed the effect of their decisions on the next election. That's why he also designed the Secure Command Center. So, he could run a covert operation within a covert operation.

Unfortunately, Beckman also knew how the SCC worked. And now this marvel of technology served as an office for his private calls and political chicanery.

CHAPTER 6

The bus undulated gently. Tommy rested his head against the back of the seat, watching Cleveland slip by and thinking back to their first day here. When they arrived, the brownstone was a mess. Mom wouldn't stay there until she had scrubbed and painted. One weekend, while the paint dried, Uncle George took them for a ride on his boat. What a boat! The whole family could have slept on it; except they didn't have to because Uncle George took them to his cabin on the shores of Ontario.

Uncle George had shown Tommy a spare key and cash hidden on the boat in case of an emergency. It was a little weird, as if he expected something bad might happen. Uncle George did something else that Tommy thought was strange. After they got on the boat, he insisted everyone call him Dutch. Dutch was an odd guy, but sort of cool. Tommy grew to like him. Uncle George, Dutch, got cooler the farther the Santa Anna—Dutch's less than original name for his boat—got from Ohio. It was as if a weight lifted from his shoulders, free of some darkness that haunted him. A weight lifted from Tommy as well, because now he had a plan. They could hide on the boat and get a little rest, then head for Canada. Perfect, unless Mom found him before they got the boat on the water.

The only problem now was that the bus was going in the wrong direction. They needed a different bus. The air brakes hissed as the driver swung the bus to the curb. Tommy tugged Nigel to his feet and led him off. Nigel shuffled behind him, squinting in the intense sun. Outside, the sunshine felt warm on Tommy's face. A wooden bench sat under a three-sided shelter constructed for commuters using the Cleveland Rapid Transit system. Tommy eased Nigel onto the deserted bench. Now, all he had to do was get them safely to the Santa Anna. That should be easy enough.

★★★

At the intersection of Roosevelt and 27th Street, the bus pulled away from its stop.

"There! That's them!" Miguel hung out the window, raising himself to see above the cars parked along the curb.

"Where?" Carlos and Eddie said in unison, craning their necks to see through cars and pedestrians.

"Right there!" Miguel pointed.

"I don't see them," Carlos said from the back seat. "You're still stoned."

"Bullshit. You're friggin' blind. They're right there in the little bus stop, thingy."

"Ah. So, they are. Perfecto." Carlos smiled, then picked a kiss from his lips with his fingertips and blew it toward his prey.

The light turned green, and Eddie started forward. Carlos slapped him on the back of the head and said, "Where you going, dumb shit? They'll see us."

"But the light changed. What am I supposed to do? Sit here?"

"Exactly. Just sit here, man. So, I can think. These bastards can go around." Carlos slapped Eddie in the head again and said, "Shit, man, wave them around. Do I have to do all your thinking for you?"

Carlos ignored the motorists as they passed, honking their horns, flipping them off, and mouthing obscenities. Eddie peered over his shades as he calmly waved people around. Miguel sat on the edge of the door halfway through the window, turning so he could face the passing cars, and yelling obscenities of his own.

The light turned red.

"Where are they now?" Carlos asked.

Raised up through the car's window, Miguel looked at the bus stop and said, "Still sitting on the bench."

"Perfect. Sit down." Carlos pulled a revolver from his belt. "Get your piece, Amigo."

Miguel pulled a 9mm Browning Hi-Power from under the seat. Together, they had nineteen rounds.

Carlos pulled himself to the front seat, so he was almost even with Eddie and Miguel. Now Carlos could see his prey. The boy and man were sitting alone on the bench. Carlos didn't notice or care if there were others in the line of fire. He pointed. "When the light turns green, don't move until it's about to turn red. Then go and pull up right where the bus stops. When Eddie stops, we shoot. When I say: go, you haul ass." The car was silent. Carlos gripped Miguel by the shoulder. "Miguel, my friend, you have more bullets than me. If you have any of them left when we're done, I'm going to shoot your ass."

Carlos slid back into his position by the window.

Miguel gripped his 9mm with both hands. He wasn't much of a shot, but at this range, and with fourteen rounds, he had to hit them a few times. The light turned green. Horns blared behind them. Eddie cranked up the radio. When the light turned yellow, he hit the accelerator.

* * *

From the other side of the intersection came a ruckus of blaring horns, but Tommy couldn't see what was causing the commotion. Probably a stalled car—hardly anything to get so worked up about. He wondered if all city people were so uptight. The traffic light changed. He heard a motor rev from the direction of the stalled car. The sound of the motor reminded him of something, but he couldn't quite place what it was. Suddenly, he heard rap music and squealing tires. He knew those sounds without seeing the car.

Turning toward the sound, Tommy saw a low-slung blue Chevy lurch through the intersection. Laughing Man and Knife leaned from the windows. Both held pistols in their hands. Nigel sat with his head tilted back and his eyes closed. By the time Tommy turned back around, the Chevy had cleared the intersection. Knife was in the back seat. His eyes were wild, and his teeth glowed with a vicious smile.

Tommy's mouth fell open.

He couldn't move. It all happened so fast.

The Chevy swerved toward the curb, tires locked, sliding toward them. For a moment, Tommy thought the Chevy was going to run right over him, then the front tire hit the curb, and the car stopped dead. The first shot hit inches above Tommy's left shoulder, exploding the bench with a shower of splinters that stung the side of his face and neck. Tommy pushed Nigel to the sidewalk, gunshots popping like a string of firecrackers. Tommy heard people screaming and saw them diving into stores and doorways. The concrete tore at his knees as he pushed Nigel along ahead of him. Tommy's chest felt as if it would explode from the pounding of his heart. This was the real deal. He was going to die right here.

Tommy scrambled toward the cars that lined the street. Sharp stones stabbed at his hands. He pushed Nigel between two parked cars. Blood stained Nigel's side. Tommy propped him against a car bumper. "You're shot."

"Are you okay?" Nigel's eyes drooped halfway shut.

"Yeah. I think so. We gotta get out of here."

"Sounds like a good idea. Got a plan?"

Tommy could hear cursing down the sidewalk. No time. Whatever they were going to do, it had to be fast. He peeked around the side of the car nearest the sidewalk. Knife was already out of the car, yelling at the guy in the front to get out. Tommy glanced at the street. "Let's go!"

Without looking, Tommy dashed into the street with Nigel in tow. The closest car slammed on the brakes, turning sideways, and barely missing them. The next driver's reaction was too slow, and he smacked the first car, sending it lurching toward them. Tommy jumped, the front fender missing him by an inch. He heard a shot and kept running. The air was filled with the sounds of squealing tires and blaring horns and the smells of gunpowder and burned rubber.

They reached the other side, ducking into a department store. People stepped back when they saw Nigel's blood-soaked side. Tommy kept moving, pulling Nigel along to the far side of the store, out into a corridor that connected additional stores, and then exiting onto the next street over. A green and white taxi sat at the curb. Tommy pulled the rear door open and pushed Nigel inside.

The driver turned. "What's this? The man. He's hurt."

"Can you take us to Brandy Island?"

"But your friend needs a doctor."

"He is a doctor. Look, mister, I need to get to Brandy Island. Can you take us, or not?"

"Yes. I will take you, but what of your friend? What happened?" The driver pulled from the curb with a jerk, accelerating into traffic.

Tommy didn't answer. Nigel slumped against the door. Tommy lifted Nigel's shirt. A hole the size of a quarter was oozing blood. "Please hurry," Tommy said, glancing out the back window.

"Your friend, he's been shot. In my country, I saw many such wounds. Your friend needs a hospital. I'll take you there."

"No! We can't...."

A streak of pale blue flashed past the window. The driver snapped the steering wheel, jerking the taxi to the right, but not far enough. Sounds of grinding metal and breaking glass filled the car. "What the hell?" The driver shouted.

"They're trying to kill us," Tommy yelled. The Chevy swerved away, then headed back toward them.

The taxi driver turned into the Chevy, smacking them hard. "Hold on," he shouted. He slammed on the brakes and cranked the wheel. The taxi spun around in the middle of the road. Cars skidded around them.

With the accelerator slammed to the floor, the taxi headed in the opposite direction. Tommy looked back and saw the Chevy mired in the snarl of traffic the taxi driver's stunt created.

"They shot your friend?"

No use lying, Tommy reasoned. "Yes."

"What did you do to piss them off?"

"Long story. We witnessed a crime."

"My name's Franco. I'll take you to the police."

Three blocks later, Franco looked in the rearview mirror and swore. Tommy turned. The Chevy was right behind them. Tommy wasn't sure if he was going to piss his pants or throw up. Either might have been an improvement.

CHAPTER 7

The taxi rocketed forward when the Chevy smacked them from behind. Franco floored the gas pedal. The taxi drifted to one side, tires clawing the pavement. The force threw Nigel to the floor, and Tommy landed on top of him. Nigel groaned. Tommy felt sticky, warm blood soaking through his own shirt. Pulling himself back up in the seat, he glanced back at the Chevy. A man jutted out of the Chevy's window and fired two shots.

"They're shooting at us," Tommy screamed. A bullet struck the taxi's back window, punching a hole the size of a silver dollar and peppering Tommy's face with glass shards.

"Get down," hollered Franco, spinning the wheel and sliding the taxi sideways into an alley. Sparks flew amidst the sound of grinding metal as the taxi glanced off a building. At the cross street, Franco kept the throttle floored, bouncing through the gutter, missing a truck headed south by inches. Crashing through several trash cans in the next alley and then at the next street, he turned left, then right at the intersection. The Chevy was still close. Tommy saw a puff of smoke lift from the barrel of the man's gun, and Tommy ducked. The rear glass shattered. Franco screamed and hit the brakes, sliding to a stop. Seconds later, the Chevy slammed into them from behind.

* * *

A rap came at the door. Sam remained silent. The door eased opened. Mandy leaned halfway into the room and said, "Excuse me, Mr. Henry? Dr. Jahan has been waiting to see you."

"How's Mrs. Parker?" Sam asked. He never gave much thought to people's feelings. It was a handicap in his line of work. Why had that changed? He didn't know.

"She's doing okay, I guess." Her voice was flat and lacked emotion. "Show Dr. Jahan in."

The large man passed through the doorway into the office. He had the rumpled look of a man who just finished a long flight, but for some reason, Sam thought the disheveled appearance was a permanent condition. Jahan's sports coat looked like it had shrunk in the wash. So did his shirt and tie. Sam motioned him toward a chair.

Sam extended his hand. "I'm Sam Henry. I'm the one you called."

"Then the call, which I was making, was the correct one?" Jahan's hand dwarfed Sam's, but his grip lacked spirit, and it was loose and damp.

"You could not have handled it better." It was true, Sam realized. The system worked as designed. Everything was perfect. So why had this alien disappeared with Tommy Parker?

"I am so enthralled by the possibilities here. I must see this man right away. Are you sure it's an alien life form?"

Jahan sounded giddy—an innocent excitement that Sam found refreshing. Before the alien and boy disappeared, Sam felt much the same. Reality, however, prevented him from sharing the moment.

"I'm afraid we don't know where he is." Sam turned his back, walking toward the window. Looking out across the city, he said, "Dr. Wellington seems certain that he's not human. I didn't get to see him."

"He has escaped?"

Sam gazed across the lawn at an edging ablaze with red and yellow flowers dipping in the breeze. "It may have taken a young boy."

"It kidnapped a child?" A hint of anger seeped into Jahan's voice, causing Sam to turn from the window and study the CDC doctor for a moment. Sam thought the anemic handshake concealed Jahan's strength. Dr. Jahan, Sam decided, was not a man one should have as an enemy. "We are searching the hospital."

Sam explained how John Doe had been in a coma, guarded by police officers, and then vanished. The Parker boy disappeared too, also under the watchful eyes of several police officers. Articulating the events helped to cement things in Sam's mind. The alien and Tommy walked by dozens of people without being seen.

"They vanished?" Jahan's voice turned analytical. "The metaphysical possibility of transporting living tissue through space and then reorganizing it is unlikely. It looks good in movies, but I have difficulty conjuring a theory to support it. My guess is that they walked out."

"How do you explain that no one saw them?"

"I would hazard a WAG." Jahan smiled. "A wild-ass guess." His honesty prompted an involuntary curl on Sam's lip. Sam liked Jahan already, which was both unusual and unexpected. He tried to stuff the thought. It could make dealing with Jahan more difficult.

"Our John Doe could possess an ability to shift cognition or prefrontal cortex manipulation," Jahan said, an ominous timbre woven into the texture of his voice.

Sam held up his hand. "Simple version."

"Mind control."

"Mind control?" Sam thought he'd considered every possibility, but mind control? Sam shuddered. If the alien possessed such power, how could Sam trust anyone, including himself?

"But how?" Sam walked to Johnson's desk and sat on its edge.

Holding his hands in front of his chest, Jahan pressed his fingertips together. "Consider the human brain. It comprises eighty-six billion neurons, about ten times the population of Earth. Some studies show that the average person uses a small percentage of those cells. What if we could use the brain in its entirety? Consider that our most advanced computers lack the capacity to duplicate all the body functions and the fluid movements of a child running and kicking a ball. The average adult does things a thousand times more complex every day, never giving it a second thought."

"That's interesting, but so what?" Sam shifted his weight on the desk.

Jahan leaned forward. "Scientists believe that electronic impulses firing across the synaptic nerve endings control short-term memory. It might be possible to disrupt those impulses, which would affect a person's short-term memory.

"Somehow, short-term memory is converted to long-term memory. How this occurs is not clear, but scientists believe that long-term memory is generated by complex chemical sequences that can reproduce the same memories long term.

"That has some foreboding considerations. For example, a few years ago, in California, after ten years of research, a scientist injected the brain cells of a quail into the brain of a chicken. Afterward, the chicken moved its head like a quail and even made sounds like a quail!" Jahan paused. His lips curled upward as he continued. "This is a lot of effort to fool a chicken, but interesting just the same."

That raised a smile from Sam. All things considered, that was quite a feat.

"This discovery has amazing potential and unparalleled terror. For example, if I knew the exact chemical codes, I could give you an injection, and poof, you have the dictionary implanted in your long-term memory. Using an aerosol bomb, I could convince an entire city to kill themselves. Or turn an army on itself. Scary, eh?"

"You're saying our visitor might have controlled people's minds and walked right past them?"

"Yes, you are understanding me correctly," Jahan said. "A superior race might be able to disrupt the electronic impulses in the brains of those nearby. Especially if those nearby are of lower cognitive functioning, and we may well be of lower cognitive functioning to this being. The bottom line is this: if there's no short-term memory, there is no long-term memory."

"I'll be damned." Sam stood. He had not considered the possibility of mind control, at least not that he could remember. *If it were true, what else could it make people do? Could this alien be controlling me right now? How would I know if it were?* "Doctor, what do you suggest?"

"I am not having enough information to speculate on such a question. I am just offering you an explanation for how this alien might have walked away unnoticed. There could be many flaws in my assumptions. For example, if what I have said is true, why didn't he just change those individuals' minds last night? Thing is, I could be dead wrong. Oh, and the name is AJ."

"Good point. I suppose we'll be doing a lot of guessing," Sam said. *AJ had an astute mind. Might he be an asset?* Another question Sam couldn't answer, but he had to find answers quickly.

Sam picked up the phone. AJ needed to be occupied, and Sam needed to think. "Mandy? Could you check with the video man? Tell him we have a doctor from the CDC who needs to see the video of the operation."

Sam explained to AJ that a video and some blood samples were the only physical evidence they had now. Next to nothing compared to what he had moments earlier, a living alien.

Mandy appeared at the door. "The officer who's watching our video tech asked if he should escort Dr. Jahan to the lab."

"No, can you take him?"

Sam started a list of those who would stay and become part of his team. Everyone else must go. He expected a fight when people learned they were being sent away, but Marines were good at winning fights. It wasn't his problem anyway, was it? Give the Marines the list and let them handle it. Still, he couldn't divorce himself from the trauma he was about to inflict on people. Thinking like that wasn't a good sign.

CHAPTER 8

Tommy raised his head enough to peer out of what had once been the taxi's rear glass. A veil of rising steam concealed the Chevy. Horns blared around them. The sweet scent of antifreeze filled his nose. Franco was still screaming, holding his hands over his eyes. Blood trickled through his fingers. A bullet had hit the rearview mirror. The shattered glass must have sprayed Franco in the face.

Behind the rising steam, car doors slammed. Not much time. Tommy scrambled over the seat, pushing Franco to the side. He had driven tractors on the farm. A taxi couldn't be much different. Movement in the side mirror caught his attention. A man with a gun stood a few steps away. Tommy's breath came in quick gasps. Squeezing the steering wheel, he stretched his leg and peered up over the dash. He pulled the transmission into gear and pushed the gas pedal to the floor. The motor groaned, and the tires squealed. Gunshots rang in his ears, but each pop grew more distant as the taxi accelerated. He'd bought them a little time, and that was all. Tommy couldn't drive like Franco, and Franco had been unable to lose them.

* * *

Alex knew they would not find Tommy in the hospital, so he gave his partner a half-ass excuse for not finishing the search together and then headed for Johnson's office. When he arrived, he saw Karen sitting alone in the secretary's office. He sat next to her. She leaned her head against his shoulder. He held her and said everything would work out. After a few minutes, he stood and walked into Johnson's office. "Heard anything?"

Sam's head jerked up, his hand covering a sheet of paper on the desk. "No," he said.

"We won't find them in the hospital."

"I know. Mr. Madden, we need to talk." Sam relaxed and waved Madden into a nearby chair.

"I've got a tough decision to make." Sam glanced at the list. "President Beckman has signed an executive order placing the people who know about John Doe into a witness protection program. Just temporary. They'll be sequestered until we know more."

"What are you saying?"

"There's a jet in route from the Presidential Air Wing out of Andrews Air Force Base. Onboard is a group of Secret Service agents and marines. They will take the witnesses to an undisclosed location."

Alex stood; fists clenched. "You bastard!"

Sam didn't move.

"Same crap as the last time I dealt with you," Alex growled. "You come here telling me it's going to be different this time, and then you lock us all up. Goddamn it! I won't stand for it, not again. Who is your boss? I want to have a word with him."

Sam raised his hands in surrender. "Alex, calm down. This is a national security issue. I answer to the NSC. That's the president, vice president, secretary of defense, and secretary of foreign affairs. President Beckman is my boss. You think you can call him on the phone? Have a little chat? Damn it, Alex, pull your head out of your ass. Those Marines will be here within the hour, and they won't screw around. Disobeying an executive order is treason. Treason with a capital T. You know, prison time. These folks take their orders seriously. Damn seriously."

Sam knew Alex served in Desert Storm. And Sam knew Alex would follow orders from his commander, even if he didn't like the orders. Soldiers never forget how to do that.

"Alex," Sam breathed. "These people will be scared as hell." Sam motioned toward Karen in the next room. "We need to help them through this. They're going to be fine, but I need your help. We have our duty." Sam picked up the list. "I got to be sure I'm making the right decision. Here's my list of who stays to help and who goes."

The redness drained from Alex's face. Thirty years lifted from his features as the soldier within stirred to life. Alex stiffened his spine. Sam was seeing the true character of the man. The unseen force that made Alex Madden who he was. Sam liked what he saw.

The door swung open. Sam and Alex looked to see who had invaded their conversation.

It was Mandy, her face pale. "Where's Karen?"

"Son-of-a-bitch." Sam reacted with a flash of anger. Karen must have heard them. Now she's on the run.

"Call security and have them watch the exits," Sam demanded. Mandy bolted from the door.

Sam looked at Alex. "Go to the conference room. She won't leave without Paul." Then Sam darted out the door.

Not the elevator, too obvious.

She knows the exits are blocked.

The stairs! She'd take the stairs.

CHAPTER 9

Tommy drove two blocks, barely avoiding a dozen collisions. He craned his neck to see the side mirror. The Chevy was closing fast. Ahead, cars blocked both lanes. The far right-hand lane was a clear path, so Tommy took it. The road curved to the right and then started climbing back to the left. It appeared to be some sort of entrance to a highway, and then Tommy saw why it didn't have any traffic. It was closed.

A barricade blocking the road exploded as Tommy drove through it, sending a plank of wood crashing into the windshield. He squirmed around, trying to find a place to see out of the spider-webbed glass. A gunshot cracked right next to his ear. He looked in the rearview mirror but saw nothing. Another shot shattered the driver's side window. Pieces of glass peppered his neck. He glanced to the left. The Chevy edged within three feet of them.

Tommy pushed the gas pedal to the floor, swerving toward the Chevy. The taxi rocked as the two cars met. The Chevy careened against a guardrail. For a moment, he was free of them. Then, through a small section of the windshield, he saw why the ramp was closed. A bridge that should span railroad tracks did not exist.

Hitting the brakes, the taxi slid sideways, crashing through two wooden barricades. The passenger's side dropped a foot, tires hanging in space. Tommy rested his head against the steering wheel. His hands shuddered despite his death grip on the wheel. He heard the squeal of tires.

The Chevy smacked the taxi, sending them over the edge.

***

Karen stood in the stairwell. She didn't have much time to make the most difficult decisions of her life. She couldn't leave Paul, but she couldn't let Sam Henry ship her off either. Paul would be okay, she decided. Alex wouldn't let anything happen to him. Her escape was Tommy's only hope. The parking garage had worked the first time. It would work again.

Sam had memorized the hospital's escape routes, an automatic mental process that took place when he first walked through the building, and from that, he knew she'd take the stairwell to the parking garage. Once inside the stairwell, he heard her footsteps two flights below. She wouldn't force a physical confrontation. He had no desire to hurt her, and that wouldn't go over very well with Alex, which would force yet another change of plans.

Her gasps for breath and pounding steps masked his approach. But she moved faster than he'd expected. She was in better condition than he'd guessed, or more determined than he'd imagined.

It was a garden-variety stairwell. Between each floor, the stairs descended to a small platform positioned half the distance to the next level. There, the stairs turned one hundred eighty degrees and continued to the next platform. Every other platform was larger to accommodate a door that accessed the building. He needed to catch her on a platform where there was no exit door.

She neared the first floor and a lobby full of people Sam wanted to avoid. The basement led to the parking garage, which was also a bad spot but better than the lobby. She must have heard him. Looking over her shoulder, their eyes met, and then she ran faster. He couldn't let her get to the lobby, where good Samaritans might try to intervene.

"Hold on," Sam said, loud but not yelling, as he cleared the last flight of stairs with two steps. As she reached for the door handle, he grabbed her arm, spinning her against the concrete wall.

"Let me go, you bastard!" Karen wrenched free from Sam's grip.

He threw both hands up, suggesting that he did not intend to hurt her. "Okay. Okay. Just listen to me."

Karen breathed deeply. Her eyes glowed with an intensity Sam didn't see earlier.

"You're not sending me off to some secure facility," she said. "My thirteen-year-old son is out there with a stranger. I won't go."

She stood her ground, which he expected. However, he would soon change her mind. Sam was an expert at psychological manipulation. "I understand how you feel. But your being here won't help Tommy." He was careful to use the boy's name. "You have another boy who needs you. Can you imagine how devastating this might be for little Paul?" *Both boys' names, good.* "Paul needs you. Have you thought about him?" The pupils of Karen's eyes widened. *You're getting there. The hook is set. Now reel her in.*

Sam said, "I'll do everything possible to get Tommy back safe."

"Is that a fact?"

"Listen, I want Tommy back, same as you."

She stared at him, eyes narrowing. "That's a damn lie. You don't love Tommy. You don't even have children, do you? You know nothing about being a parent."

The muscles in Sam's face flinched.

She poked her finger into his chest. "Do you know what it's like to hold your own baby? Watch him grow? Dry his tears? I won't go, not without a fight. You'll have to carry me out of here."

Silence hung in the air like a heavy curtain between them. She was right. He had no friends, not close ones, or family. He had never married. He had no children. How she knew that confused him.

There was a time he dreamed of finding that special person—someone to share his hopes and dreams with. But he couldn't ask someone to live with the fear that one day he might not come home. What kind of life was that for a wife? And he once wanted children. That would have shocked those who knew him or thought that they did. Having a life of his own was something he abandoned years earlier. He decided to serve humanity—but he didn't participate in the very things that made serving humanity worthwhile.

Karen had changed. At first, he thought she'd lost her spark that he admired, but she had not. And she wasn't the little girl he terrorized fifteen years ago. She'd grown up.

He sucked in a deep breath and snorted it out. He searched his soul for an answer that he couldn't find. *What are you going to do, Sam?* He couldn't think of one logical reason she should stay. And logic was the only concept he used to solve problems. Thinking in any other manner wasn't his forte. However, logic wasn't serving him well now. One thought persisted: *What would happen to Karen Parker if she lost her son without fighting to save him?* Even if she failed, she must try. How could he deny her that? For the first time in his life, Sam Henry was about to do something that didn't make good sense.

"You'll stay with me and follow my orders," he said.

"Agreed," she said.

CHAPTER 10

Lieutenant Colonel George Mitachavich, everyone called him Mitch, sat at his desk finishing his least favorite task: staff performance evaluations. His soldiers were finely tuned fighting machines, but they were ordinary people, not characters from a Tom Clancy novel. His best man with a pistol could hammer the x-ring out of a target at twenty-five yards, but he acted like a spoiled teenager. At two hundred yards, his sniper could put five rounds in a hole the size of a quarter, but he rode an emotional roller coaster with his on-again, off-again girlfriend. Mitch feared that two others were working on first-class cases of alcoholism. Any of them would stew for weeks if one word struck them wrong in their performance evaluations.

Then things changed.

General Edward Powers called. His orders were terse: activate Unit-11, deploy to Cleveland, Ohio, and wait for further orders. Mitch commanded Unit-11, and when activated, they worked with deliberate precision. Despite their human failings, these were not ordinary soldiers. They were the most lethal counter-terrorism force in the world.

"Everything is onboard, sir," Sergeant Perry Gorgons said. Gorgon oversaw logistics and was one of Mitch's best friends.

Getting Unit-11 mobile was not a difficult task. It was always ready and self-contained in five Chevrolet vans. Four vans were ordinary-looking, windowless utility vans. The fifth was just as plain, but larger. They drove Chevrolets because GM won the government contract that year. Most of their arsenals fit in these white vans, except for a McDonnell Douglas AH-64 helicopter known as the Apache. They could have selected HMMWV 4WDs instead of box vans, but Humvees drew more attention and required Lockheed's C-5 Galaxy to airlift them, and that limited the airports at which they could land. In addition, the prosaic Chevy vans blended in anywhere in the world. The soldiers could convert every vehicle to right-side steering during the flights if deployed to nations that insisted people drive on the wrong side of the road. The vans didn't look like other 4-wheel-drive vehicles, but they had all-wheel-drive just the same. Boxes labeled with every country lined the shelves in the squad's armory. Mitch selected a box labeled US-Urban, which contained several items, including magnetic signs for the vans' doors. For this mission, Unit-11 would become Digital Telecom. Since they were going to Cleveland, he took a Canada box as well.

***

Inside the second-floor conference room, a nurse named Patty sat next to Paul. Everyone appeared tense. They stared at Alex when he entered the room. He asked about Karen. She left with the police officer. Sam Henry duped him. Why didn't he see it coming? He should have never trusted the man.

Karen wasn't dumb. She wouldn't go to the conference room, and in hindsight, Alex knew it. Henry sent him there as a diversion. Alex clenched his teeth and balled his fists. He was angry with himself for being so dense. He was angry with Sam Henry for being Sam Henry.

***

Neither Karen nor Sam said anything to Mandy as they walked through the outer office and disappeared into David Johnson's former sanctuary.

"We gotta think fast," Sam said as he sat on the edge of the desk, facing Karen for the first time since their talk in the stairwell.

"When will it happen?" Karen asked.

"Soon—soon enough that we won't be ready. If one can ever be ready for something like this." Sam's eyes trailed off to the floor.

She saw something unexpected. She saw it earlier in the stairwell, where it was very distant. Now it was clear, raw, and close to the surface. Sam looked like an ordinary man, struggling for answers. Could it be part of his facade? She didn't think so. He gathered himself quickly. She saw that too, but everything had changed for her. *You're just a man, aren't you, Sam Henry? Somewhere under all the bullshit, you're as scared as I am.*

"What will we do about Paul?" he whispered.

Was he concerned, or was this also part of his act? Karen realized she couldn't read him.

"He could stay with me," she said. It sounded ludicrous, even to her.

"We could do that," he said. "But we should think it through. What if something, eh, happens?"

"You're right. It could be dangerous, I guess." She paused, looked Sam in the eyes. "Is it—dangerous?"

"I suspect it will be," he said.

CHAPTER 11

Pain shot through Tommy's head, and something warm and sticky-wet seeped through his hair. Odors of antifreeze, burning oil, and blood filled his nose. His eyes wouldn't focus, and the entire world seemed dark. Gradually, his vision cleared, but he couldn't make sense of things. He couldn't move. Closing his eyes, he inventoried body parts. Everything seemed to be there, including intense pain in his right arm, which bent at an odd angle. When his vision cleared, he understood his confusion. The taxi had landed upside down, crushing the roof and trapping him between the seat and the ground. Nigel lay outside, near the trunk. He looked dead. Tommy squirmed and wiggled, the pain in his arm unbearable, but he worked himself free and crawled out of the car. Turning to look at the front, he saw Franco crushed between the hood and the ground.

When Tommy tried to stand, pain shot up his arm and through his shoulder. It was like someone was ramming a hot poker through his bones. Using his good arm, he crawled to Nigel and found him breathing. The Chevy smoldered nearby, on its side, mangled beyond recognition. Beside it, two men covered with blood and dirt lay motionless on the ground. From inside the Chevy, Tommy heard someone groan.

Next to Tommy, Nigel stirred.

Tommy whispered, "Can you hear me?"

Nigel eased one eye open and looked at him. "Been driving long?"

"Hey, I stopped. They didn't. I think Franco's dead."

"Not your fault, Tommy."

The groans coming from inside the Chevy grew louder, then turned to cursing.

Wincing with pain, Tommy slowly sat up, pressing his back against the taxi. "Can you move?"

"Give me a minute."

The cursing grew shrill, and the Chevy rocked from side to side.

"We gotta get out of here," Tommy whispered.

Nigel rose onto his hands and knees, and then, using each other as support, Tommy and Nigel pushed themselves to their feet. Tommy whimpered in pain.

"You're hurt," Nigel said.

Tommy almost fell, but Nigel held him up.

"My arm. I think it's broken."

Nigel touched it and said, "You are correct. We shouldn't move you."

The voice from the Chevy sounded more distinct. When Tommy looked, he saw why. The man was halfway out of the car, waving a pistol at him.

"Shit!" With his good arm, Tommy grabbed Nigel, pulling him behind the taxi. A gunshot cracked the air, and dirt flew near Tommy's feet. "We got to get out of here."

Using the taxi as a shield, Tommy led Nigel away and to the train cars, where they wove an unsteady path away from the wreckage and gunfire. Tommy prayed the gunman had sustained serious injuries. Otherwise, he and Nigel didn't have a chance.

★★★

Matt Block dreamed of editing Hollywood movies, but for now, he made training videos at the hospital. Although it was not his practice, last night he started the cameras and let them run while he went out for coffee and a Danish. When he returned, the surgery was over, which seemed odd. He assumed the man had died. Quick procedure. Nobody would care to see that video. Doctors didn't like watching failure. So, he had not worked on that video until now.

Normally, Matt worked alone. Nobody cared what he did. They only wanted the videos he produced. Doctors never asked who made the videos they used to instruct students. However, today, a police officer and a CDC doctor stood over his shoulder. He asked why they were there and received a bullshit sort of answer. Last night's video was important. Matt didn't know why that would be significant. At least they were interested in his work, sort of, so for the moment, he didn't mind the intrusion.

"I almost got it. I'll check through this again and then render it." Matt had two processes to work through. First, he uploaded the video files, and cut all the boring stuff, not watching, just zipping through preliminaries in super-fast forward, the pictures a blur. Then he uploaded the audio files, which were stored on a separate hard drive.

Next, the video-editing software synchronized the video and audio. An archaic process by Hollywood standards. When the computer finished, the late-night wonderings of John Doe would be mixed, edited, rendered, and finally burned onto a DVD. Only then would Matt and his two guests see the entire procedure for the first time.

"That should be close enough for government work," Matt said, not meaning it as a joke. "It takes a while to render the video. Old computer. Coffee?"

"That would be acceptable to me," Dr. Jahan said in agreement.

"Well, if you guys go, I must go too," Allan Douglas, a young Cleveland police officer, said. "Madden didn't say you couldn't take a break." Allan arched his back and rubbed his neck. "I should have been home hours ago."

Matt led them to the cafeteria. Allan Douglas ensured they all sat as far from the other patrons as possible.

Trish McCabe had been assigned to the National Security Crisis Center for all of two weeks, save one day. Trained as a meteorologist, she monitored weather worldwide. She focused on an Arctic cold front locked in a violent altercation with warmer air near Lake Ontario. The frigid intruder appeared relentless with its slow southern invasion. North of Lake Ontario, life was miserable under the atmospheric war of fierce thundershowers and ferocious winds. She studied the lake-effect storms in college, and the power they generated amazed her. Now, she was about to witness the real thing, albeit at a safe distance via a high-tech weather satellite. By evening, the center of the storm would be over Cleveland. The storm was getting larger, stronger, and more violent.

CHAPTER 12

Alex burst into Johnson's office, red-faced, chest heaving. Sam expected it and did not react. Before Alex said anything, Sam said, "I'm sorry, Alex. I felt I had to find Karen myself."

When Alex realized Karen was there, he took a deep breath. "Explain it to me."

"Karen needs to stay to help find Tommy." Sam glanced at Karen, hoping she would not interject details of their conversation. "It required a private conversation to reach an agreement."

Alex nodded and sat next to Karen.

Creating the who-stays list wasn't as difficult as Sam had imagined. The FBI agent stayed, as did Madden. Sam added Wellington for his medical expertise, should it be needed. But who would look after Paul? Alex suggested Jerry Faulkner. He was good with kids. In fact, he had single-handedly raised two of his own. Jerry's wife ran off with a construction worker who worked little and mostly drank beer and watched TV. However, Karen objected because Paul didn't know the man.

"What would I say?" Karen asked. "Paul, an alien kidnapped Tommy, and, well, we're sending you off to a military facility in Nevada. But don't worry. A nice police officer will be with you. No, Mommy's not coming. She's staying here. But if I live through this, Mommy will probably come to Nevada as well. Yeah, sure. Not a chance."

She was right, and Sam knew it.

"Excuse me." Mandy stuck her head into the office after a light rap on the door. "I thought you'd like to know that everyone is back in the conference room, except that Dr. Jahan fellow." She paused for a moment and said, "They didn't find Tommy."

"Thank you, Mandy. Would you get Dr. Jahan on the phone for me?" Sam almost forgot about the search. He knew Tommy and John Doe were gone before the search started, but a search had to be done.

"Yes, sir," Mandy said.

Sam wondered if Mandy had a family waiting for her at home. For the first time, he realized personally how traumatic Protocol 3.56 would be.

"Who is Jahan?" Karen asked.

Sam said, "A guy from the CDC who received the first call from Dr. Johnson. I had him flown here."

"Mr. Henry?" It was Mandy, popping in without her customary precursory knock. "I called the video lab, but there's no answer. I can't find Dr. Jahan or the video tech."

Sam's face flushed red and then pasty white. Reaching for his jacket, he fished a pack of gum from the inside pocket. He ripped the tin-foiled paper from a stick and stuffed it in his mouth. The smell of mint filled the room. Looking at Alex, he said, "Can you take Dr. Wellington to find them and bring them here? And bring every recording of this— incident. No trickery this time, Alex. We need to find them."

Alone again, the silence of discomfort fell upon Sam and Karen. Sam struggled to maintain his calm exterior, but he felt as if his insides were wrapped in chaos. The dilemma with Paul didn't make things easier.

"Let's try this from a fresh angle," Sam said in a subdued voice. "If you had your choice, who would you send with Paul? Besides yourself."

"The kids hit it off with Alex," Karen said with no hesitation. "After that, I don't know. They—seemed to like Dr. Wellington." She sat for a moment. "That's great. The two people I'd trust are on the list to stay." A tear rolled down her cheek.

"Dr. Wellington could go," Sam said flatly. "We'll replace him with Jahan. Jahan's a doctor and a government employee, better suited to take orders and be in harm's way."

★★★

"Incoming message from Sam Henry, sir."

"It's about time," Powers whispered, waving to Beckman, who'd been talking nonstop on the phone in the SCC for the past forty-five minutes. Powers entered the SCC. The door slid closed behind him. A message appeared on the computer screen:

Video-Telecommunications link.

Henry confirmed.

"It's about damn time, Sam," Powers breathed, tapping his authorization code on the keyboard.

★★★

Sam had already entered a more elaborate code, which only he knew. Without the code, his laptop wouldn't function. If he forgot the password, the laptop would be trash. Sam's system was tamper-proof.

He motioned Karen to the side, where she could see the screen but was out of the miniature camera's field of vision. He held one finger to his lips, the universal signal for silence. On the screen, a man's face came into focus. The man wore the uniform of a military officer, hair cropped close, black mixed with steel gray. The haircut had probably been with him since he turned eighteen.

"What in the hell is going on, Sam?" Powers asked.

"We've searched the hospital with negative results." Karen found the lack of emotion in Sam's voice remarkable. He was a cool customer, no questioning that.

"You're making us nervous, Sam. Very nervous."

Karen realized she wasn't supposed to hear this conversation and wondered why Sam was allowing her to.

"There's more to this problem, gentlemen. Cleveland police officers were guarding the man and the boy when they disappeared." Sam answered without the slightest hint of defensiveness. "Dr. Jahan thinks it has some sort of mind control." Sam paused, fiddling with the list of names. "I think a small team should stay to assist me."

"How many men?"

"Three. The FBI agent, Eric Key; the Cleveland detective, Alex Madden; and Dr. Jahan."

Karen almost screamed but caught herself. Lying bastard. He did not intend to let her stay. Or was there something else? Was this a trick? She didn't know.

"Why Dr. Jahan?" Powers asked.

"He might prove useful. He's the one who thought about the mind control issue," Sam said.

"I don't like bringing outsiders into this, Sam. I don't like it at all. No changes to that list without my approval."

Sam tapped a key, and the screen turned black. Leaning back in his chair, he exhaled.

"Why didn't you tell him I was on the list?"

"You shouldn't have heard this communication. In fact, you never did. Understood? If Powers knew about you, he'd never stand for it. He'd order me to send you with the others. If I didn't follow his order, he'd have me arrested and then give the same order to the Secret Service and marines, who wouldn't hesitate to do as they were instructed. The only way I'll pull this off is if Washington doesn't know. I'll tell General Powers after the transport is airborne. He'll pitch a fit, but there won't be much he can do about it."

"I see…" Karen's voice trailed off. She looked away and walked to the window. Her reasons for staying were powerful but self-serving. Sam was risking his career without compelling reasons to do so. *Why would he do that? He really is a strange man.*

CHAPTER 13

Staggering through train cars, Tommy couldn't estimate the distance they'd put between themselves and the man, who would not rest until he and Nigel were dead. Maybe the man's injuries would prevent further pursuit. Maybe not.

Tommy's entire body hurt. His lips were dry and caked with blood, and his throat was so parched it felt like sandpaper each time he swallowed. His arm hurt more than the rest of him combined. Pain wasn't something he endured well, but he had to escape or die. The limited options kept him moving.

They approached a small shack of weathered wood. The hut had one small window divided into four pieces by thin wooden slats, and the glass was caked with dirt, making it impossible to see through. Tommy tapped on the door and then stepped inside, where he found a cramped room with one table and half a dozen old wooden chairs. A barrel-shaped stove stood in one corner, and its warmth indicated it had been burning earlier that morning. The other door led to a small restroom, which Tommy stumbled into, closing the door behind him. The sink was several shades of brown, though he thought it had once been white. Cranking the old faucet, he gulped water using his good hand, then splashed some on his face and gazed into a small metal mirror hanging over the sink. An old car bumper would have offered a better reflection, but what he saw did not look good. Blood and dirt covered his face, and it looked like he wore a bowl of chocolate pudding in his hair. Above the toilet was a small window. Maybe a person could fit through it. Maybe not. The room spun, and then everything went black.

✱ ✱ ✱

It was the way of things. Either everything happens at once or nothing happens at all. If it rains, it pours, as the saying goes. Sam knew that was how things worked, but that didn't make it better. There was a time when he enjoyed this sort of thing, but right now, he wasn't having much fun.

There was too much crap left to accomplish. He wanted to talk with Wellington, but he'd sent him to accompany Alex. Karen needed to speak with Paul, but Paul was in the conference room, and none of this was getting him any closer to finding Tommy Parker or the alien or whatever he was.

Sam opened the door to Mandy's office. Eric Key sat in a chair next to the door. "Would you step in here, Eric?" Sam glanced at Mandy. "Mandy, would you fetch Paul from the conference room?"

Mandy left without hesitation, and Eric followed Sam into Johnson's office.

"Learn anything?" Sam asked before Eric sat.

"Nothing. Nobody saw anything that…."

The door flew open. Alex waddled in carrying a large cardboard box braced against his stomach, followed by Jahan, a police officer, a man in a white lab coat, and Dr. Wellington.

"They were taking a break," Alex grunted, placing the box on the desk. "Here's all the video stuff, including a DVD and computer. My officer," Alex paused, casting a critical gaze to the young officer who found a sudden interest in his shoes, "says that none of them were ever out of his sight." Alex motioned to the man in the white lab coat. "This is Matt Block, the video technician."

"I apologize if we've caused a problem," Jahan allowed. "I would very much like to view the blood samples and any other physical specimens that may have been taken.

Jahan seemed unshaken. He looked more at ease now than when he first arrived. His tie, once firmly knotted around his tree-trunk neck, was stuffed into his blazer's breast pocket.

"How long?" Sam asked. Blood samples, another detail he forgot.

"That is a most troublesome question," Dr. Jahan mused. "One could spend years studying such a thing. How long may I have?"

It was a fair question. Dr. Jahan didn't know about Sam's decisions. "Thirty-minutes, maybe less, then I need you and all the specimens back here."

"Thirty minutes? That's not much time. Are we going somewhere?" Dr. Jahan asked, as if the answer were obvious.

"Not yet," Sam said, not exactly lying. "The specimens must be secured to ensure that nothing is tampered with. And bring the samples in travel containers." Sam paused. "Someone needs to accompany Dr. Jahan." Sam looked at Alex.

Alex shifted his eyes to the young officer, who looked up from his shoes.

"I'd like to go with Dr. Jahan." Wellington stood. "The staff will think nothing of it if I'm there."

Sam nodded his approval.

"We'll be back in thirty minutes," the officer said, casting his most intimidating glare at Dr. Jahan.

"Thirty minutes," Jahan confirmed.

What else can go wrong? Sam wished the thought had never crossed his mind.

* * *

Karen sat on a brown leather couch in David Johnson's office, holding Paul on her lap. Block, Key, and Madden sat nearby in leather-covered chairs. Elsewhere in the hospital, police officers scribbled their obligatory notes that no one outside the federal government would ever read. Wellington and Jahan busied themselves gathering what remained of the blood and other samples taken from John Doe. Things were coming together. Sam leaned on Johnson's desk, contemplating his next move, and watching mother and son.

The most remarkable discovery came, as remarkable discoveries often do, with an off-handed remark from Mandy, the secretary. She asked if the security cameras captured Tommy and John Doe leaving the hospital. St. John's, like most hospitals, has security cameras mounted in the halls, feeding images to a rack of small monitors in the security manager's office. The theory was that someone sat watching the cameras that monitored the halls. Of course, that was only a theory. The screens were ignored by low-paid security officers staring at their smartphones. However, the video was stored on an extended-play recording system. Just as David Johnson predicted, Mandy had indeed proven herself valuable.

At Sam's direction, Eric and Matt went to the security office, retrieved the videotapes, and then took them back to Matt's workspace. Matt popped the tape into his editing deck and started punching buttons. The hospital's security system produced a product Matt didn't classify as video. The black-and-white cameras captured a low-resolution image, further degraded by the super-extend mode recording speed. The video made early television look digital by comparison. After finding what he was searching for, Matt used a program to enhance the image, then transferred it to a DVD.

"Got it!" Matt said, peering at the monitor.
Eric leaned in for a closer look.
"Jesus. What in the hell is that?"

CHAPTER 14

Memories of El Salvador plagued Sam at the strangest times. Over the years, he became accustomed to the nightmares, if one ever becomes accustomed to waking up in a cold sweat. But he'd catch himself at times like these—when he should be focused—drifting into the past, images floating through his mind.

What happened in El Salvador twenty years ago? Sam thought he knew at the time, but the line between his dreams and memories had blurred until he could no longer distinguish between the two. He had wandered in the jungle for nineteen days, which seemed like nineteen years. He was the only man from his unit to make it home, so there was no one with whom he could compare memories. According to the government, there were no American troops in El Salvador that day. They abandoned the bodies of his dead comrades and left them to rot in the jungle. The military told their families the soldiers had died in a helicopter accident, training off the California coast. The sea claimed their bodies. Sorry.

What troubled Sam most was a ghost who haunted his dreams. The man's face and the half-torn nametag sewn over the pocket of his military shirt were seared in Sam's mind. He searched military records, trying to find his ghost, but failed to produce anything that explained the man or his presence. Sam only knew the name on the tag, and he could not find a man matching his memory of the man.

The door opened. Sam looked up with a start. Dr. Wellington and the officer walked in, trailed by Dr. Jahan, who carried a large, white Styrofoam organ cooler.

"Definitely human," Jahan said, setting the cooler on the floor near the bookcase.

"Say again?" Sam asked.

"The blood is not of a type I have seen, but he is human. Definitely human. That would be my guess."

"Guess?" Sam's eyebrows raised and his forehead wrinkled with deep furrows.

"Yes, Mr. Henry—guess. If you'll remember, I only had a brief time to analyze the specimen. It could take weeks to do a thorough analysis."

"You said it was human. Are you saying this is a hoax?" Sam was standing now.

"I'm saying no such thing. I have viewed the videotape of the surgery. That, sir, is no hoax. The patient wasn't a typical human specimen, but his blood, in my opinion, is human."

"I agree with Dr. Jahan," Wellington chimed in.

"Explain." Sam stepped from behind the desk.

AJ waved his hand toward the cooler. "Wherever this man came from, he is more like us than he is different. He might be from another planet, but he's a close cousin."

Sam sank onto the edge of the desk, his legs unable to carry his weight. This news didn't really change anything. He knew that, but he couldn't deny its impact, although he wasn't sure why. Glancing at Karen, he hoped he'd find some basis for his feelings in her face, but he found none. She looked as befuddled as he felt. Only the doctors acted excited.

After a few moments, Sam said, "Dr. Jahan, Dr. Wellington, we need to talk." Sam motioned them to sit. "Alex, have your officer wait in Mandy's office."

With Jahan, Madden, and Wellington present, Sam explained about the plane sent to take the witnesses to a secured location. Their reaction wasn't what he expected. Maybe it was the way he'd laid it all out, helping them understand that there weren't options. He let Karen explain the plan for Paul. He watched Wellington for a reaction, figuring the man would explode, but he didn't. Had he underestimated the caliber of these people?

* * *

Wellington studied Karen and Paul. Paul had the rumpled look of a youngster lacking a proper night's sleep. Paul hid his fear, but not entirely. He had faced more loss and pain than a boy his age should have, and right now, he needed a friend. Wellington extended a hand skilled at healing the sick. The sick, he realized, did not always need a scalpel.

* * *

General Powers sat across from Beckman. "Why aren't we doing something?" Beckman asked.

The question made sense for a civilian. But Beckman wasn't just a civilian. They were *doing* something. But Beckman didn't equate two aircraft carrying special forces and having a man, known as a legend in the intelligence community, at the scene, as doing something. The realization sent a shiver up Powers' back. Operating under a commander who didn't understand the nature of a military mission constituted a dangerous act. A commander who thought he knew more than his advisors invited disaster. Powers had a problem brewing, and it wasn't just the situation in Cleveland. How could he manage this incident without making Beckman look like a fool?

"Sir, it takes time to get assets in place. We're moving as quickly as possible. Henry is there and doing all that can be done." Powers hoped Beckman was listening.

"It feels like we're not doing enough," Beckman said, more frustrated than angry.

"I know the feeling," Powers allowed.

★ ★ ★

Events had sidetracked Sam so often that another interruption wasn't a surprise. How often had he started toward his computer, only to be diverted? This time, it was Eric and Matt barging through the door unannounced. Mandy followed like a bloodhound on a fresh scent.

Eric marched straight to the TV/DVD combination mounted in a cherry-wood cabinet and started pushing buttons. "Wait till you see this." Eric's excitement leaked through his FBI exterior. Everyone gathered, sensing something was about to happen and bracing themselves for what they were about to see.

The first grainy images showed John Doe in a hospital bed and Dr. Cray talking to a police officer. Then something went wrong with the TV, and the images at the edge of the screen started to twist and distort, and the officer and Dr. Cray were frozen in the twisted picture.

Sam started for the TV to adjust the picture, but Key waved him off. "Just watch."

Tommy appeared on the screen.

Tommy walked to John Doe. The images of Tommy and John remained steady, while the twisted images around them became more contorted. Tommy appeared to be talking to John Doe, but John had a tube stuck down his throat. After a few minutes, Tommy reached up and pulled the corrugated plastic tube from the man's mouth. Tommy quickly backed away until he bumped into something and almost fell.

John stopped breathing for several minutes, and by all appearances—looked dead.

Then the man's chest rose. Several more minutes passed, then John Doe woke up. Tommy removed the leather restrains and then helped free him from the remaining needles and wires, and then they walked to the door and were gone.

The cameras followed them through the hallways. Everything around them twisted into the same distorted image seen in the hospital room. The people were frozen in the blur, and only the images of Tommy and John remained clear. They opened a door and entered. There was no camera where they went because the image of the door remained on the screen. When they came back through the door, John had changed into hospital scrubs. Then they walked through the lobby and out the front entrance.

Karen's soft crying filled the otherwise silent office.

Before the alien walked through the exit door, he turned and stared into the camera. Matt had frozen and enhanced the grainy image, revealing a near-perfect picture of the man—alien—whatever he was. The room grew silent. Sam stepped closer, staring at the TV screen.

He found the ghost of his dreams.

"Nigel," Sam whispered.

CHAPTER 15

Tommy awoke to the sound of pounding and ringing. He reached for the alarm clock, only to find a cold porcelain sink. *Not home,* he remembered. The ringing seemed confined to his head, but the pounding came from somewhere else. Someone was calling his name. He struggled to his feet and opened the door.

"You, okay?" Nigel asked.

"I must have passed out." He squeezed between Nigel and the doorjamb, bumping his dangling arm. Pain shot through his shoulder and sent him to his knees.

Nigel kneeled beside him. "Let me see if I can help with that."

Nigel clapped his hands and rubbed them together. Then he cradled Tommy's arm with both hands. His touch was warm, almost hot. Tommy was about to protest when he realized the heat didn't hurt. But soon his arm felt as if it were on fire. Before the heat became unbearable, Nigel closed his eyes and lowered his head. The heat faded. The pain did, too.

"How did you do that?" Tommy asked, rubbing his arm. Nigel fell back against the wall. His face grew ashen.

Pounding at the door. "I'm going to kill you!"

"In here." Tommy grabbed Nigel, dragging him into the bathroom. "It's the only way out." Pointing to the window, Tommy helped Nigel step onto the toilet and then pushed and shoved until Nigel slid through the window. Nigel disappeared, followed by a thump and a groan. Tommy pulled himself through the window, then dropped to the ground. As he stood, a gunshot cracked at the front of the shack, followed by the sound of shattering wood. The man was inside now. It wouldn't take him long to figure out that they were gone. Tommy pulled Nigel to his feet, and they staggered through scattered boxcars. After crossing three sets of tracks, a slow-moving train blocked their path.

A boxcar with an open door rolled by.

"Get in!" Tommy screamed and jumped in first. He grabbed Nigel's hand and pulled with all his strength. Soon, Nigel was inside as well.

*** * ***

Thoughts that Alex didn't want to face crossed his mind, and the transport team was one of those thoughts. What was about to happen had not yet been explained to the men and women in the second-floor conference room. Still, Alex could see anger, betrayal, and fear in their eyes. Given a choice, he would have avoided being here, but he didn't have a choice. He had to face the men who had helped him. That was the only way he could face himself.

After delivering the grim news of their temporary relocation, Alex saw tears streaming down the face of one nurse. He didn't know her name, but she had been flirting with his partner, Jerry Faulkner, earlier. Jerry held her and glared at Alex. Jerry looked as if he were about to speak when the door flew open, and several men wearing black suits filed into the room. The man leading the pack asked for Alex Madden, and Alex turned to face him. The man instructed Alex to stand by the door and wait for further instructions. As Alex neared the door, he saw men wearing Marine uniforms hurrying towards him.

A man named Lazario took charge. He started with an apology and stressed the fact that they were all caught amid a national security crisis. Sequestering those involved with John Doe would be temporary, lasting only until they contained the crisis. The detainees fired off a barrage of questions. People can't just disappear. Their lives are complicated. Mothers had children in daycare centers spread across the city. People had appointments, spouses, responsibilities, and lives. Lazario handled their questions with professionalism and maturity more advanced than one would expect from someone who looked to be less than thirty years old. Everything would be taken care of. He assured them of that. Two agents would stay in Cleveland, and if they had to pick up someone's children themselves, they'd do it. Police officers were accustomed to being in charge, and they can be a real pain in the butt when circumstances are reversed. Wellington, Alex noted, remained calm, and his composure was not lost on those around him. Given the situation, officers and hospital staff cooperated better than Alex expected.

However, Alex would not soon forget their expressions as they were ushered from the room and down the hall. Trust faded from the faces of his friends. Only James T. Wellington looked at him with kind eyes. Holding Paul Parker's hand, he patted Alex's shoulder as they passed.

Alex crossed the empty conference room to the window and watched as the detainees were escorted out of a service entrance, where they were fitted into three of the four vans that awaited them. Alex agreed with the selection of the team that remained, but he felt a sadness unrelated to the inconvenience of it all.

***

"They're on their way," Tony Lazario, Special Agent-in-Charge, declared as he walked into David Johnson's office.

"Fifteen to debrief in Nevada and four to stay here with me," Sam confirmed as he looked up to see Alex enter the room.

"Major Henry," it was the first time they had heard Sam called that, "my list shows three confirmed to stay."

Conning a Secret Service agent was difficult. When it was the agent assigned to lead a presidential mission, the task was virtually impossible. "Last minute change, Tony. Add Karen Parker to the list of those staying. She's the boy's mother. This alien—or whatever he is—may have a mind-control ability. I learned this a few minutes before you arrived. The mother might break through if it becomes necessary to talk the boy away from this man. Sorry, but there wasn't time to notify you of the change."

"Sir, I'll need to confirm this with the commander," Lazario said.

"No problem. I can be online in a matter of seconds. Only problem is, the boss asked me to hold transmissions until 14:00 hours. He has a meeting with some subcommittee, so if you'll explain that you initiated the call, well, I'd appreciate it," Sam lied.

"Fourteen hundred, huh?" Lazario looked at his watch.

"I'd feel a lot more comfortable with confirmation," Lazario said, signaling his hesitation to disturb President Beckman.

"Would a hard copy help?" Sam asked.

"Yes, that would be sufficient," Tony said, unable to hide his relief.

Sam walked to the other side of the large wooden desk and retrieved the paper he planted there earlier. He handed it to Lazario, who examined it for authenticity.

"Could I have this?"

"It's yours."

"Very well then. We are off site with our sequestered guests at 13:12," Lazario declared. "Good luck, sir."

"Thank you, Tony. And take care of our guests."

"That, I will do."

***

Four fifteen-passenger vans traveled a deliberate path through the streets of Cleveland. One might have thought the Secret Service and Marines did this every day, considering the polished professionalism with which they went about their task. An atmosphere of quiet excitement crept into each van. The drudgery of everyday life had been magnified by hours of confinement. Now they were being whisked away to a top-secret government facility. What might they learn there? They were in on it now.

A Secret Service psychologist predicted this behavior with foreboding accuracy. She watched the detainees on a TV monitor from her position in the tail section of the awaiting aircraft.

Inside the vans, whispering swelled into an animated conversation. The agents didn't stifle the discussion, so with increasing confidence, the detainees released their pent-up emotions, and their excitement mounted when they realized their next stop was the international airport.

Their journey had begun.

CHAPTER 16

Maria Esperanza surveyed her results and thought they were good. Cleaning ladies weren't supposed to take such pride in their work, but Maria wasn't just a cleaning lady. She was an independent businesswoman. Her work was made easier because her clients couldn't tolerate anyone, including the cleaner, seeing their homes in a state of total disaster. She suspected they had dashed about tidying up before she arrived. That worked for her. Yet, her clients' homes—she enjoyed thinking of them as clients—glowed when she finished.

She locked the front door, then checked the back door, and the garage, and anything else a homeowner might appreciate. Those little details made for great referrals. After all, anyone can clean a house. Her next job was a new client. He lived in a penthouse. She'd never even seen one before.

* * *

In the lead vehicle, a roof panel slid back, and a small parabolic dish focused on a satellite orbiting some fifty thousand feet above the Earth's surface. A moment later, it linked with the crisis center in Washington, D.C.

A subtle change in the screensaver went unnoticed by everyone— except for one man who awaited the signal. General Powers turned to Richard Beckman and said, "Mr. President, if you'll join me in the SCC, I'll try to get an update from Henry."

Beckman trailed Powers into the secured room. For a moment, Beckman was confused because protocol dictated that Sam would contact the crisis center, not the other way around. Upon entering, Beckman saw a message on the monitor and realized it wasn't about Sam. Unit-11 was in Cleveland.

* * *

Most of Sam's team were experiencing mild depression as they bottomed out on their emotional roller coaster and lack of sleep. Rallying their spirits would be difficult, but he must rally them. The real deal was about to begin, and these people had to be sharp. They would probably be more trouble than they were worth. *What in the hell was he thinking about keeping any of them?*

Sam pulled a package of gum from his breast pocket, but it was empty. He frowned. Crumpling it, he tossed it in the trash. "Okay, folks. There's work to do. Every law enforcement officer within five hundred miles needs to be watching for those two. That includes Canada. The message needs to be simple: attempt to locate. If found, contact Alex Madden via the Cleveland PD. Then we need to determine if there's someplace that we should look ourselves."

Sam didn't share the lethargy that encompassed the others. He didn't ride roller coasters, emotional or otherwise.

"I'll take Canada," Eric offered. "I'll contact customs on both sides. Alex, you contact the state and local guys. However, it would be better for the contact to be the FBI office in Cleveland. I'll ensure the duty officer knows what to do."

Sam nodded. "Good thinking, Eric. I agree. Perhaps Dr. Jahan can help with the description."

Once they were alone, Sam motioned Karen into a chair in front of Johnson's desk. He took a seat in the adjacent chair and said, "Where might Tommy go?" His voice remained even, unemotional.

"I don't know," Karen fought back the tears simmering behind her thinly veiled resemblance to composure. She cast her eyes to the floor. She should have been watching Tommy in the conference room. Instead, she was sleeping. What kind of mother was she?

"Tommy needs you to be strong now. When we have him back, then you can cry, but not now."

Sam's words, the tone of his voice, and his facial expressions spoke of inner strength. For as much as she hated him during the last fifteen years, she was glad he was here. Under these circumstances, a lesser man wouldn't do. She drew in a breath, held it for a moment, and then released it.

"Do you believe we'll find him alive? This is my fault." A single tear traced down her cheek.

He remained silent for a moment. "Yes, I do. We have no reason to think this man is dangerous. All the evidence says he means no harm."

Karen watched Sam. He glanced down, but not at the floor. He seemed to mull over his words.

"Home. The first place he'd go would be home. If he could." Karen wasn't sure that Tommy would go home, but it was a start. "What if he doesn't want to be found? According to Dr. Jahan, the creature, alien, whatever he is, has the power to control minds."

Karen continued with slow, measured words, "No, he won't go home, because that's the first place we'll look." Given that thought, the odds of finding him got worse. *The most probable places are the least likely.*

"It's a start." Sam had Karen jot her address on a yellow legal pad. "Where else?"

"We've only been in Cleveland a few weeks, and we haven't gone many places. We stayed at my sister's place a few days," her voice faded, "but they're not home." Karen explained further and thought about the likelihood of Tommy going to her sister's, and for the first time, she felt a bit of hope welling inside. She could see it in Sam's eyes as well. *Could it be? Might we simply drive to Alice's house and end this nightmare? It couldn't be that simple, could it?* Karen cut off the thought. It wasn't necessary to think that far ahead, not right now. She added that address to the legal pad before Sam asked for it.

"Karen, if you'll excuse me, I must call the crisis center again." Sam stared at her with hard, unwavering eyes that didn't invite questions.

Karen paused at the door as if she were about to say something, then she slid into the outer office. She eased the door closed behind her. The latch clicked, and she leaned back against the door. *What doesn't he want me to hear? Trust is a strange commodity. What creates it? Where does it come from? Where does it go?* Trust between Karen and her nemesis surfaced from nowhere and faded fast. She wanted to ask him why she couldn't stay but feared he would confirm that his conversation was something with which she couldn't be trusted. Damn it, she had to trust him, although she had no reason to believe that she could.

✳ ✳ ✳

When Sam's next call came in, Beckman wasn't there. Beckman had left the crisis center to attend an urgent meeting with the incumbent senator from the great state of Maine, whose campaign was floundering under allegations of racial discrimination. In an atmosphere not unlike Germany before World War II, the United States was primed for men like Maine's Bill Hawkins and Richard Beckman. Hard times had hit middle-class Americans, and while the poor focused on survival, the middle class watched their American dream fade and searched for a scapegoat. Richard Beckman gave them one. History would one day portray Richard Beckman as the racist he was, but for now, he controlled the nation.

But that wasn't Edward Powers' concern. Odd contradiction that it was, men like Edward Powers were sworn to follow and protect men like Richard Beckman. Powers, born and raised in Southern California, never experienced the United States that denied his parents the opportunities he took for granted. His grandfather told him stories about the bad old days when people of color rode in the backs of buses and drank from separate water fountains, but to Powers, those were only stories.

Powers took Sam Henry's call in the SCC.

When Powers reached the console, Henry's image waited on a computer monitor. Powers' face was transmitted to Cleveland, where it appeared with a herky-jerky motion on Sam's laptop. An engineer failed to dedicate enough RAM for that segment of the computer's operation. An easy fix, but Sam resisted losing any work time, even for a simple modification. Most people credited it to Sam's dedication, but that wasn't the primary reason he didn't want strangers poking around in his computer's programming.

"Status?" Powers asked with the even tone of a seasoned commander.

"The witnesses are off site. They should be airborne by now. The transport team did a marvelous job. Tell them we appreciated it." Even at this level, people are still people. A fact Sam learned many years earlier. Even generals wanted the same thing as the man on the assembly line or the woman in the high-rise office complex. Everybody wanted respect.

"Will do," Powers acknowledged with a single nod of his head.

"An ATL is being dispatched to local, state, and federal agencies as we speak. That includes Canadian customs. When that's done, we'll be checking some places Tommy might go." Sam wished he could leave it at that, but he couldn't, and he knew it.

"I understand you have Dr. Jahan, CDC; Eric Key, FBI; and Alex Madden, Cleveland P.D., correct? I also want a list of the individuals, materials, and documents transported. And I need to know where you're going."

Sam anticipated Powers' demands. "I'm sending that information now."

"General, I made a last-minute change," Sam said with a calm assurance that he made exactly the correct decision, which he believed true, although confident his commander would disagree, and he expected Powers' reaction being nothing short of ferocious and for that reason he'd sent Karen to the next room. She didn't need the additional stress. Sam had no clue that his act of kindness generated a reaction opposite of the one he desired.

"Since our last conversation, I learned there was a video system that recorded movement in certain areas of the building. I retrieved that video, and we watched the alien and the boy walk out the front door."

"You have that! Transmit it to me." Powers perched on the edge of his seat. Behind him, Beckman entered the SCC.

"What's up?" Beckman asked.

Henry heard President Beckman but couldn't see him. Beckman maneuvered behind Powers and peered over his shoulder.

"Good afternoon, Mr. President," Sam said, wondering how much Beckman knew or understood about the operation. So far, Sam's plan seemed to work. The news of a video distracted Powers. Maybe he'd forget to ask about the change Sam made.

Powers brought Beckman up to speed. Beckman nodded in sage agreement. Sam estimated that Beckman comprehended little beyond the mere words that Powers spoke.

"Yes, right," Beckman agreed.

"What about those videotapes?" Powers asked again.

"I'm working on getting them loaded into the computer so I can transmit them," Henry lied.

Beckman grabbed a chair, spun it around backward, and sat to Powers' left. His face remained partially visible on Sam's laptop.

"You said you made a change. What change? Did you retain the video man?" Powers asked.

Thinking Powers might be diverted proved too much to hope for. There was a reason he was a general. The video man wasn't a bad guess, either. He might have been valuable. Especially if Sam's objective was to transmit the videotape to D.C., which it wasn't.

"No, I kept the boy's mother." Sam spit out the words and then waited for the reaction. He wouldn't wait long.

"You did what?" Powers said, exhibiting more control than Sam expected.

"I kept the boy's mother." Sam repeated with measured, flat words. "The videotape shows the alien and boy walking out of the hospital. They walked by dozens of people, but nobody saw them. That includes police officers: several watching the boy and two watching the alien. It looks like the alien created some sort of trance. Perhaps mind control." Sam had all but dismissed mind control as the reason John Doe and Tommy Parker escaped without detection, but Powers and Beckman didn't know that.

Sam paused, but not long enough to relinquish the conversation to Powers or Beckman. Timing was critical when it came to controlling people, and Sam was trained to manipulate situations like this one, although he had not practiced his craft in many years. Or had he? Maybe he practiced as naturally as he breathed. He wasn't sure. Sam focused on Powers' breathing, watching for that slightly deeper breath taken before speaking.

Now!

"There's an innocent thirteen-year-old boy with the alien. I believe he's under this thing's control." Sam didn't call the alien a man, although that's how he was beginning to think of him. "The mother's voice may be the only thing strong enough to break through to the boy. I want to save the boy if possible. I believe the mother is critical in achieving that goal." His timing couldn't have been better. What could they say? To hell with the boy? No, probably not. They might think it, but they won't say it.

"Damn it, Sam, you should have cleared that first," Powers said with restrained anger. "I don't like having a civilian involved. This could get dangerous, and we shouldn't be putting civilians in harm's way."

Sam wanted to point out that there was a thirteen-year-old civilian involved, but starting an argument would not improve the situation. "I apologize, gentlemen. It was a last-minute decision, and while I understand your position, I'm the one at ground level. I believe this is the right course of action." Sam didn't add that it was his decision to make as authorized by federal law.

Beckman leaned into the camera. "I don't like it, Mr. Henry. I'm concerned that you don't have your priorities straight. How do I know this alien hasn't screwed with *your* head?"

Sam remained calm, allowing an awkward moment of silence to pass. Finally, because there wasn't anything else to say, Powers said, "Keep the lady safe. We don't need civilian casualties."

"Yes, sir," Sam answered in his best military recapitulation.

"Sam, send us the coordinates of the areas you'll be searching. In case something happens," Powers said.

Sam studied Power's face. Something wasn't right.

"Remember your orders, Sam," Powers added unnecessarily. "And be careful. Watch your flank."

Sam pushed F3, ending the transmission. He sat silently, staring at the computer screen. Why did Powers tell him to watch his flank?

They didn't trust him.

That his superiors no longer trusted him stunned Sam like a hard punch to the stomach, and even more devastating was the fact that they had good reason not to. But they couldn't know about that. He needed his wits but couldn't focus his thoughts. Lost in a mindless fog, he typed out the names of his team members. At the end of the message, he added the addresses of two homes to be searched and then clicked send.

"I don't trust that son of a bitch," Beckman growled. He swiveled his chair toward Powers and leaned forward.

"He's our best man for this situation," Powers said. Powers didn't add that federal law designated Sam as mission commander.

"Maybe you're right. Sam was once the finest field officer this country had. That was before his problems began. Don't misunderstand. Sam Henry is a damn smart man, a good man." Beckman looked Powers in the eye to measure his statement's effect.

"But I don't believe he's suited for this work anymore," Beckman continued. "I feel—responsible." Beckman shifted his weight, folding his arms across his chest.

"How's that?" Powers asked.

"The government put Sam in some tough places when he was a young man, but the government didn't take good care of people back then. Post-stress trauma and stuff like that. They kept sending Sam out. Paid no attention to how he was doing. He took everything they threw at him and came back for more. They never considered that he was human. They didn't take care of him." Beckman unfolded his arms and stiffened his spine. "I felt we owed the man, so when I was in the Senate, I supported putting him in this position. But that's not why one puts people in such a position, is it?"

Powers stood and squared his shoulders. "I'll take responsibility. Sam has a job to do, and he needs our support to get it done."

"You've made your point, General, but I want Unit-11 ready. Just in case."

"Mr. President, after careful consideration, I'm uncomfortable with Unit-11's involvement."

"And why is that, General?"

"Unit-11 is trained for international terrorism. They don't understand the meaning of minimal use of force. They aren't trained for this deployment. It might be illegal as well. These are U.S. citizens on U.S. soil. They have rights."

"General, is that a threat?"

"No, sir. I'm just pointing out the problems associated with this decision."

"So, you don't like my decision? Are you saying I'm unfit for command?"

"No, sir," Powers said. His mind reeled at Beckman's reaction, which seemed unwarranted given what was said.

"General, if you cannot carry out my orders, I will find someone who can. Is that understood?" Beckman hissed.

"Yes, sir." Powers' chest heaved with each breath, and his nostrils flared. He stood for a moment, his gaze locked in a stalemate stare with Beckman, then said, "What of Sam Henry?"

Beckman answered, as if he had rehearsed his response. "We'll monitor him. If he has problems, then we'll have an option. Otherwise, it's business as usual," Beckman lied. "General, make it happen." Beckman turned and walked to the door.

"Yes, sir," Powers said, not moving until Beckman had walked straight through the crisis center and out. Powers collapsed in a chair and cradled his head in his hands.

CHAPTER 17

As the van skirted the airport terminal, Wellington peered out the window. A white 727 aircraft, gleaming in the sunlight two hundred yards away, came into view. The vans streamed past the last terminal, a brown UPS hangar. Wellington could see the presidential seal and the words United States Air Force on the jet's tail section. A small group of men watched them approach.

Stepping into the bright sun, Wellington stretched in its warmth. He extended his hand to Paul, who remained inside the van.

Wellington's stomach twisted into a knot, but he didn't want Paul to sense his fear, so with a warm smile he said, "It's a beautiful plane, isn't it? Imagine us in one of the president's jets. Cool, huh?"

"Yeah, I guess," Paul said. "But it would be better watching it on the Discovery Channel."

Wellington chuckled. Paul took his hand.

Armed soldiers stood in a circle around the plane. Wellington thought they were taking this too damn seriously.

"Dr. Wellington?" Paul tightened his grip on Wellington's hand. "Can I sit by you on the plane?"

"Absolutely. Call me Jim, okay?"

"Okay, Dr. Wellington."

***

Carlos followed a bloody trail through the maze of boxcars until he came to a slow-moving train. The train stretched as far as he could see in either direction. He thought about crawling underneath but decided against it. Then he noticed blood along the track. He followed it until it stopped. Carlos grabbed the ladder and climbed to the top of a boxcar.

***

Lieutenant Colonel George Mitachavich walked around the C-130 Galaxy for the umpteenth time, running his fingers through his hair and checking his watch. The digital display indicated that two minutes had passed since the last time he checked. On the backside of the Galaxy, hidden from public view, sat a McDonnell Douglas AH-64 helicopter, otherwise known as the Apache. With its four under-wing hardpoints armed with 16 AGM-114 Hellfire anti-armor missiles and its M230 Chain Gun 30-mm automatic cannon protruding from underneath the forward fuselage, the Apache was an ominous, evil-looking craft and, to Mitch's way of thinking, perfect. He never tired of looking at what was, in his opinion, the most beautiful aircraft ever constructed.

"Incoming message from command, sir," Sergeant Clarence Borden hollered from the lead van. His face revealed the enthusiasm Mitch demanded, but with Clarence, such demands were unnecessary. Fresh from the Florida Everglades, everything about the military awed Clarence Borden. His love affair with the military started the day they shaved his head. "It's him," Clarence added with all the exhilaration one might expect of a boy from the Everglades receiving a call from the President of the United States.

Mitch raced to the communications console mounted in one van that now displayed Digital Telecom placards.

"Good morning, Lieutenant," Powers said like a teacher speaking to a star pupil.

"Good morning, sir." Mitch and Edward were on a first-name basis, but this wasn't the time for informality, and both men knew it.

Sergeant Borden stood beside Mitch in case technical assistance was required. He could see President Beckman sitting beside the four-star general.

"I have some addresses for you," Powers said. "Henry will check them, so be careful. He doesn't know you're there, and we want it to stay that way."

"Yes, sir. General, what is our objective?" Mitch asked, wondering why Sam Henry didn't know that Unit-11 had been deployed.

"For the moment, locate and monitor." Powers explained the events of the day and of the alien that they were to find. "If you find the alien, or whatever he is, take everyone into custody."

"Yes, sir." Mitch let out a large breath and asked, "What if they resist?"

Beckman leaned in and said, "Do whatever is necessary to contain or eliminate the threat. Is that clear enough?"

"Yes, sir."

"I'll transmit the addresses, and a list of people Henry has involved in his operation." Powers paused and looked at Beckman as if he were about to add something. Then he turned back to Mitch and said, "Good luck."

Powers' face disappeared from the monitor, and within moments, a small message box appeared, alerting Sergeant Borden that they had received a document.

"Let's have it," Mitch ordered. Seconds later, a printer spit out a piece of paper. Mitch grabbed the document. He brought a map of Cleveland up on the computer screen. A satellite-tracking device calculated his team's position and displayed it with a pinpoint of red light. Red was the appropriate color for Unit-11. Tapping at the keyboard, he entered the addresses Powers sent. Mitch clicked enter, and the locations were displayed with pinpoint lights of green. Two keystrokes later, the computer plotted primary and alternate routes between Unit-11 and the targets and synchronized the routes with each van's GPS. A large printer anchored in the front of the box van whirred to life, and a few minutes later, Mitch held two full-color maps with the routes connecting the red dots to the green dots.

★ ★ ★

Alone at Dr. Johnson's polished wooden desk, Sam stared at his computer as the screen saver flashed pristine photographs of Earth taken from an orbiting space shuttle. Something bothered him. Powers should have objected more to Karen staying with him. It had been too easy. Why? Something nagged at the edge of his consciousness. He replayed the conversation in his mind, but he could not discern the reason for his premonition.

With a few keystrokes and a second-level password, Sam activated the backup drive on the SECA satellite. He studied a list of files that the computer labeled according to the time they were created. Several compressed files were generated this morning, but Sam didn't have time to investigate them all. The additional files meant Powers was talking to someone besides himself.

Sam opened the last saved file. A second later, the recorded image of General Powers and their previous conversation returned to his LCD monitor. Sam watched—detached, analyzing each word, and studying their eyes. *There!* Beckman provided the clues Sam sought. Beckman betrayed himself. What little trust Sam had for Beckman dissipated.

Beckman was hiding something. Sam was sure of that. Now, he didn't know who he could trust or what they were hiding from him.

Preoccupied, Sam opened the office door and stared at his newly formed team, not really seeing them. He left the door ajar as he walked back into Johnson's office. Without a word, Sam stowed his computer and its small parabolic antenna, moving mechanically and staring into a distant world only his eyes could penetrate. The others filtered into the room, stood in a clump, and waited for Sam to speak.

When his gear was packed, Sam drifted back to the present and said, "There's much to do and little time."

"We have contacted all the agencies," Alex volunteered. "Although getting them to take this seriously without an explanation was damn difficult."

Sam stared at Alex for a moment, then said, "I'll bet. But telling them to watch for an alien of medium build accompanied by a small boy wouldn't help much."

To Alex's surprise, the corners of Sam's mouth turned upward, just a little.

They developed a plan, which proved straightforward, except for two details on which they couldn't agree. One point of contention was transportation. Alex wanted to take his police cruiser and Eric's official, yet mundane, government-issue sedan. Sam would have preferred his specially equipped vehicle, but it was baking in the sun at Andrews Air Force Base. After listening to Alex's suggestion, Sam decided they needed two vehicles. Eric, AJ, and Alex would travel together in Madden's unmarked police car. He and Karen would go in Karen's car, which Sam explained would be less frightening to Tommy.

The second disagreement involved the team's approach to Karen's brownstone. The two police officers had strong opinions about that. Kicking in doors was their specialty. Sam listened to their reasoning and then ignored it. He and Karen would approach and search the brownstone alone.

Alex hated the idea and had no problem voicing his opinion. Sam remained steadfast. He understood police officers hated watching. Watching was for rookies. And having a civilian kick in a front door, or in this case, unlock a backdoor, wasn't done. It contradicted every smidgen of training they'd ever had. Sam wasn't a cop, which was another rub that felt rawer with each decision Sam made. Eric said it was the most hare-brained scheme he'd ever heard of. Both officers failed to grasp the reality of their situation.

Sam knew things Alex and Eric didn't. Tommy Parker's life had probably not made President Beckman's priority list. Sam understood the new rules of engagement and rule number one: there are no rules. Karen was the only person Sam could trust, not because of any overwhelming bond between them but because, for Karen, the stakes were too high for anything else.

CHAPTER 18

Mitch stared out the passenger side window of the lead van. The legendary Sam Henry remained a dangerous opponent, a fact that Mitch would not forget. Although he didn't believe in legends, Mitch conceded Henry had experienced a fair share of luck, but nothing more than that. If it became necessary to confront Sam Henry, the fact was that he had never faced a well-trained troop like Unit-11. Henry's luck would run out, and Mitch saw himself as just the man to ensure that it did. The man who defeated Sam Henry would tend to his own legend, wouldn't he? As for an alien? Mitch dismissed the possibility.

Within thirty minutes, the Digital Telecom Company invaded Cleveland's Buchanan district. Of one thing, Mitch was sure: locked on a common goal, Sam Henry, and Unit-11's paths were destined to cross. Mitch didn't know how Henry and crew were traveling, and that didn't help. Why didn't Sam bring that damn car of his along with him? The crisis center could have tracked his every move. Sam had blocked the tracking on his cellphone. Only his digital link with SECA could pinpoint him now, and Henry seemed reluctant to maintain that connection.

As the vans inched through afternoon traffic, each man placed a small, plastic speaker in his ear and then affixed a sticky, skin-colored patch to the side of his larynx, which was linked by a thin wire to a small radio fastened to his belt. Their routine proceeded like a religious rite. Each depressed a button on the side of his M9 semiautomatic pistol, dropping the clip onto the heavy rubber mat that covered the van's floor. Racking the action, each man caught the chambered round as it spun through the air. After inspecting the chamber and the barrel, the clip was driven back into the weapon's grip, and a round was re-chambered. The clip was re-released, and the last round was placed back in the clip. For the last step, the clip was reinserted into the pistol. Rifles received similar inspections, and then the rocket launcher. Ammunition was European, and the missile launcher was made in the old Soviet Union. Chinese flash grenades and other incendiary devices completed the arsenal. Not as good as U.S. hardware, but available on the black market and perfect for black operations, because explaining how U.S. military hardware fell into the hands of terrorists would be difficult. Despite the foreign origin, comfort levels rose as they fondled their simple yet effective weaponry.

* * *

In the Buchanan District, a white van circled Karen's brownstone, then stopped depositing a man on the nearest corner. Across the street, a second van took up an observation post. Behind the van's sliding door, Sergeant Jay North trained the crosshairs of a 60 mm missile launcher on the brownstone's front entrance. If necessary, they could level the entire structure. The warhead was overzealous for urban applications, but minimal force wasn't Unit-11's forte.

The snipers preferred a vantage point atop a nearby building, but time didn't permit that, so one man trained an M-16A2 rifle's laser on the brownstone's front door.

Four men wearing dark-blue Digital Telecom jumpsuits began the assault, with two approaching the front and two approaching the rear. To anyone watching, their attack resembled a routine service call. Mitch would have preferred doing surveillance first, but Sam Henry and his makeshift crew were making their way toward this same location, and Mitch didn't know where they were.

The brownstone was the most logical place to look and the least likely place to find Tommy Parker and the man. However, it would be the most probable place to intersect with Sam Henry, and from that point on, they would track his every move. As a bonus, it would settle his soldiers by burning some of their youthful exuberance. They were in and out in less than ten minutes. Not bad.

Sam turned on Lancaster, one block west of the alley that led to Karen's home. He squinted as the sun streamed through the windshield and into his eyes. He studied each passing vehicle. A thick screen of blue smoke rose from an old blue Dodge pickup truck, and behind the old Dodge truck trailed a white Chevrolet van. The van's young driver wore a baseball cap with an insignia too small to read. The small gap between his cap and his ears revealed a shaved head like a skinhead. His blue work shirt had a starched collar and military creases. Sam noted the words Digital Telecom printed on the side of the vehicle.

* * *

Sam said, "I'll go in first. At the first hint of trouble, you run like hell. Understood?"

Karen nodded and whispered, "Okay."

Sam eased Karen's key into the lock, turned the knob, then popped the door ajar. The neglected hinges sounded a malicious creak through the quiet home. Sam eased through the small house with an impressive combination of skill and proficiency. Karen noted how he moved—catlike, sure, lethal. But she knew the house was empty long before Sam's search was complete. She didn't know how she knew that. She just did.

"Did I miss anything?" Sam asked.

"Nothing I can think of." Karen sensed his question was rhetorical. Someone banged at the front door. She let out a little scream before cupping her hand over her mouth.

Sam pulled his pistol from its holster. He whispered, "What the hell?" He peeked out the curtain and then holstered his weapon.

"Looks like a salesman." Sam walked to the door, like a man on his day off and not a care in the world.

Karen, on the other hand, knew her face glowed red.

"Yes?" Sam asked as he opened the door, careful not to allow the man passage into the house.

The young sales agent extended his hand and asked, "Are you Mr. Parker?"

"Who wants to know?" Sam asked.

Karen moved behind Sam.

"I'm Jim Taylor," the young man said with a broad smile, his hand lingering in the air until it became clear Sam would not return the gesture. "I represent Digital Telecom, Cleveland's premier cable company. We're running a special." He looked at his clipboard. "Is Karen Parker home?"

Karen stepped from behind Sam and said, "I'm Karen Parker. I spoke with a representative from your company last week."

The young man seemed shaken.

"Okay, well, eh. They're supposed to let me know. You know, email, which I checked this morning, but sometimes the girls don't get all the orders entered. Sorry to bother you."

"I was told no agents would call. Are you here to hook me up?" Karen sounded irritated.

"No, someone else will …"

"If you'll excuse us, we have an appointment." Sam closed the door in the salesman's face.

"Was that true? About the cable company?" Sam asked.

"No. I don't know why I said that. I wanted to get rid of him, I guess."

That garnered a grunt from Sam, whose mind seemed a million miles away again.

CHAPTER 19

Wellington felt uneasy as he watched a cottony cloud drift by the oval window. With full stomachs and tired minds, the droning jet engines lulled his fellow passengers to sleep. The others accepted their imprisonment rather well. Too well for Wellington's taste.

Paul watched the ever-changing tapestry of tilled brown soil and brilliant green fields until sleep overtook him. Wellington was alone with his thoughts. Less than twelve hours since he operated on John Doe, yet it seemed like another lifetime.

Paul sighed, shifted in his seat, and rested his head against Wellington's shoulder. Wellington once dreamed of starting a family but resigned himself to the impossibility years ago. A few romances almost germinated, but none endured. He worked long hours, seven days a week. Love doesn't flourish during thirty-minute lunch breaks in hospital cafeterias.

But he couldn't change his life or its demands. How many lives had he saved? Which one would he give up? His life wasn't a failure, but it wasn't what he'd hoped. Watching Paul sleep intensified his understanding of the life he'd lost in pursuit of the one he'd gained.

****

Tommy leaned against the boxcar's cold metal wall. Nigel, asleep or dying, sat propped up next to him. The rhythmical clicking of wheels and swaying of the boxcar lulled Tommy to sleep, but a sound on the roof startled him awake. From the top of the open door, a head appeared.

Knife.

"Found you, mi amigo." Knife smiled, and then he disappeared back onto the roof.

"Wake-up!" Tommy screamed, shaking Nigel's arm.

Knife swung through the door, landing in the middle of the boxcar, aiming a gun at Tommy's head. "You messed with the wrong brother, little man. Now you're gonna pay."

Nigel groaned.

"Nice of you to join us," Knife said. "Now, you can watch this little guy die." Knife adjusted his aim and then fired.

Tommy saw the gun jump, a flash, and a puff of smoke. Everything started twisting. He saw the bullet spiraling through the air, straight at him. It stopped in front of his nose, hanging in the air, spinning slowly.

"Probably a good time for us to leave," Nigel said.

"How do you do that?" Tommy reached out to touch the bullet.

Nigel grabbed Tommy's hand. "Better not mess with that," he said. "It might come after you again. Things at the edge react in odd ways."

"At the edge of what?"

"The edge of time." Nigel pulled Tommy to the door, then jumped.

They hit the ground with a thud, tumbling clumsily. Fresh blood soaked through Nigel's shirt as he stood on unsteady legs. "Come. We have little time." He nodded toward the train. "He'll soon see that we've left him." Nigel turned and limped away.

They walked about ten feet when Tommy heard Knife screaming at them in a language he didn't understand. Tommy turned. Knife jumped from the door, but his foot caught on something, landing him hard on the ground. Knife swore, then pushed himself up and pointed his pistol at them. The bottom rung of a metal ladder at the end of a boxcar struck his head. He hit the ground and then rolled in the wrong direction, under the train. The steel wheels sliced Knife in half at the waist. His screams lifted above the train's squeaking wheels and clicking rails as both halves of his body twisted like a lizard on a hot tar road. A putrid smell filled Tommy's nostrils.

Nigel spun him around, shielding his eyes. "It's not your fault. That man created his own problems."

Shuffling across the train yard, Tommy tried to block the image from his mind. What bothered him most was that he didn't feel the least bit sad. Knife was dead, and that's all that mattered. Now, he and his family were safe. Once he got Nigel to the Santa Maria, everything would be all right.

CHAPTER 20

In front of Karen's brownstone, Sgt. James Taylor, posing as a salesman for Digital Telecom, stood by the curb. Waiting until Sam Henry was out of sight, he pulled a small cell phone from his pocket. "Henry's moving. I held them as long as I could. Sorry, Lt."

"Did Henry seem suspicious?" Mitch asked.

"Nah," Taylor replied. "The woman thought I was from the local cable company. Amateurs."

"Good. Meet us at the rendezvous point."

"Roger that."

"Damn traffic," Mitch snarled at the knot of cars, trucks, and taxis before him as construction forced the mid-afternoon traffic to grind along at an intolerably slow pace. Mitch checked his watch. The late summer sun shining through the side glass felt hot on his face despite the air conditioner's efforts. Henry had to contend with the same crap. Searching the next home posed less risk than the brownstone. Henry didn't know about Unit-11, and he did not know that Digital Telecom wasn't a legitimate business. If Henry showed up during the search, they'd act as if they were doing a routine service call. Karen wouldn't know the difference, and Sam Henry wouldn't have a clue.

***

"Turn here. There's construction downtown." Karen said. "It's longer, but we'll make better time."

"How much farther is it?" Sam asked the moot question, as he'd already committed to the alternative route. In the mirror, he saw Alex was following them.

"I don't know. It's faster," Karen said, although her perception was based on nothing more than what her sister told her.

"What you said to that cable guy, it wasn't true?" Sam asked.

"Not exactly. Why do you ask?"

"I'm not sure. Just a feeling."

"I called a cable company, but not that one," Karen said.

"What?" Sam turned to look at her.

She saw an intensity in his eyes that wasn't there a moment earlier. Karen turned up her palms. "It wasn't Digital Telecom. One cable company, Cleveland Cable, or something like that was the only listing. Digital Telecom must be new. Maybe they sell satellite service."

Sam said nothing.

* * *

When they made their way out of the train yard, Tommy saw that this neighborhood looked even worse than where he lived. Most of the stores were boarded shut, and their walls were covered with fat graffiti of many colors. The few stores still open had heavy metal bars covering their windows and doors, some of which were clean and others so dirty they would pass for plywood. He wondered if the clean ones had been replaced recently. Abandoned cars on blocks lined the streets. People stared. He and Nigel must have looked like hell standing there, covered with blood and dirt. Perhaps someone had already called the police, but maybe not. Tommy had a feeling the police were rarely invited to this neighborhood.

A taxi crawled down the street. Waving his hand, Tommy stood in the street, forcing the driver to stop.

"What in the hell happened to you?" the driver asked as Tommy and Nigel slid into the back seat.

"Car wreck. We need to go to Brandy Island."

"You need to go to a hospital!"

"Been there, done that. We're fine. We need to clean up and get some rest."

"But …"

"But nothing. Look, my brother is a doctor." Tommy motioned to Nigel. "He had us checked out, and now we want to go home."

"But the hospital is miles away. How did you get here?"

"Just drive," Tommy growled. The driver glanced at them in the mirror, then shook his head and waved them off. A placard said his name was Sylvan Zanolavich. *Zanolavich, what kind of name was that?* The man probably saw all kinds of crap driving a taxi in this neighborhood. Why should he care what his passengers looked like or what they did or didn't do? Apparently, he didn't, because he turned the corner and drove without further comment. Things were looking up. Next stop: Brandy Island. Knife was stone dead. With any luck, so were his buddies. Their problems were over.

*** * ***

Maria couldn't stop admiring the penthouse. Its outer walls were made of huge glass panels and overlooked the waterfront. Its open rooms were sparsely furnished with white leather chairs, thick burgundy carpet, and maple wood tables with thick glass tops. Her new client, a man named Nathaniel Jacobs, had a pleasant face. He wore a green sweater over a white T-shirt, faded Levi's, and bare feet. He seemed awkward in a way she never anticipated from a wealthy man. Not that she knew any wealthy men. He had converted one room to a martial artist's dojo, which proved to be the cleanest room in the home. Nathaniel Jacobs had a gentle voice and a mild manner. He retired to his den, and his last instruction to Maria was to knock on the door before she left. No matter how pleasant the client was, she always remained the cleaning lady in their eyes. The distinction between her and the clients never faded, and neither did their arrogance. Somehow, Jacobs seemed different.

When she'd finished, she hesitated at the heavy, solid maple door that led to Jacobs' office. She felt lightheaded and was damned if she could figure out why. Earlier, talking to Nathaniel caused her face to feel blushed. She hoped it wasn't the flu. Raising her hand, she paused before rapping lightly.

The door opened. Maria caught a glimpse inside Jacobs' office before he slid through the narrow opening he had allowed himself. A large computer monitor glowed, sitting on a massive walnut desk. Walnut bookcases lined the dark green walls. The desk was littered with books and Styrofoam coffee cups. Crumpled papers overflowed from the trashcan onto the hardwood floor. Maria smiled. This was the man's sanctuary, where he worked as an ordinary human being.

"Finished? Already?" He asked.

Maria couldn't distinguish the inflection in his voice but estimated it fell somewhere between disbelief and disappointment. "Yes, all done." She stepped back, waving her arm to reveal her work. She studied his eyes for a reaction. An infectious smile replaced his distant stare.

"Amazing!"

"It's okay?"

"It's more than okay. It's magic. How do you do that?"

Maria felt a blush. "Oh, it's nothing. A lot of practice, I guess."

"Stephanie and Bob said you did a great job, but—wow!"

"I'm glad you like it. Will you want me back?"

"Yes. Yes. Can you come on Wednesdays?"

Maria pulled her planner from her tote bag and studied it for a moment. She looked at him, hesitating. "Ah, I can, but it would be later in the afternoon and ..."

Jacobs interrupted, "Stephanie said you have a little boy and that he travels with you after school. Will he be able to come? I mean—you can bring him."

"Well, yes. In fact, he would have to come." Most rich people hesitated at a child in their home.

"Great, I'd like to meet him. Maybe ..." Jacobs' voice faded. He broke his steady gaze from Maria's eyes. "I work at home on Wednesdays. I hope you don't mind."

"It's your house. I don't mind at all."

"Good. Then I'll see you Wednesday," Jacobs said as if it were a date.

✶ ✶ ✶

Tommy's uncle, George Hudson, lived in a sprawling neighborhood developed thirty years earlier. His white brick home at 27859 Chateaux Lane sat on almost an acre of ground, which was manicured to the point of looking artificial. The house had an attached two-car garage and, out back, a shop that held three cars and several motorcycles. Alongside the shop, under a carport-type shelter, sat Uncle George's boat. After a quick shower, Tommy found a t-shirt and a pair of jeans he'd left on his previous trip. Nigel borrowed some of Uncle George's clothes.

They put their bloody clothes in a black plastic bag and tossed them in the trashcan out by the street. A few minutes later, a city garbage truck emptied the trash. Tommy reset the house alarm and returned the key to its hiding spot. He found an extension ladder leaning against the shop, which they used to climb aboard Uncle George's boat. Nigel pulled the ladder up, laying it on the deck. Getting onboard now would be difficult unless someone had a ladder in his back pocket.

Nigel went to a small stateroom next to the galley and shut the door behind him. Tommy sat alone, eating Vienna sausages and drinking a warm Coke. Although exhausted, he cleaned the galley like Uncle George taught him. He planned to crawl onto the large bed in the front stateroom that filled the bow of the boat, but he felt too exhausted to move, so he sat on the bench to rest, just for a moment. His eyelids drooped. A chilled mist and fragrant odor drifted from underneath the door of the small room in which Nigel had retired. The door itself dripped with condensation, leaving the galley comfortably cooled.

Tommy curled up on the bench by the galley table and drifted into a deep sleep.

CHAPTER 21

Corporal Gary Sessions eased the van around the white brick home, parking between the attached garage and the detached shop. A house like this would have an alarm, but the team had tools to defeat it. Next to the shop sat a large boat, at least forty feet, stem to stern. It appeared to be an old trawler converted into something more akin to a yacht than a fishing boat. Hitched to the boat was an older Peterbilt truck painted bright yellow.

"Charlie Two, Charlie One." Mitch was calling. The identification scheme was simple. Each van was coded Charlie. Mitch was Charlie One and took the front. Charlie Two took the back. Charlie Three waited near the street, ready to create a diversion should it prove necessary. A soldier inside Charlie Three had a 60-mm missile launcher trained on the front door.

"Go for Charlie Two," Sessions said.

"How does it look?"

"Quiet. We've got a back door, a detached shop, and a boat. Luke and Max will take the backdoor. Blair and Jack will search the shop. I'll do the boat." Sessions eyed the boat's stern.

The soldiers/cable guys ambled out of the vans, looking very much like workers intent on killing the rest of the afternoon. Sessions sauntered toward the boat as the other members of the team went to their respective assignments. The trawler's height kept him from getting to the deck. He needed a ladder for that. The v-bottom of the boat rested in a space cut in the trailer, lowering the hull three feet, but Gary wasn't tall enough to see through the small oval windows sprinkled along the upper third of the hull. How was he supposed to search the damn thing when he couldn't get on it or see inside of it? Whatever he was going to do, he needed to do it fast.

He searched for something on which to stand, only needing an extra eighteen inches to see through the portholes. But George Hudson was meticulous about not leaving things lying around. Sessions started toward the shop to look for a ladder when he noticed that one of the trailer's wheels tilted at an odd angle. He bent down for a closer look. Perfect!

* * *

Fear, anxiety, fatigue, and hunger closed in, and Karen felt as if she were falling into an abyss. She fought to remain on this side of the thin line that separated her from total collapse.

And she was worried about Paul. James Wellington seemed like a good man. He had genuine concern for his patients. She prayed he'd extend the same thoughtfulness to her son.

Life brought her to this, widowed and wondering if she was wrong about the man she'd despised for fifteen years. She stole a quick glimpse at Sam. Was the man sitting next to her the villain she believed him to be? *This is all too fucking strange,* she thought, biting her lip, and forcing back a tear. Her vocabulary, like many other things in her life, had deteriorated since Roger's death, and profanity was more common now, but it was something she sought to change about herself. It wasn't good around the kids, but when one thinks that way, well, sometimes it slips out. *Another part of my goddamn weak character,* she concluded.

Karen had felt tired for months, mentally and physically. She needed a break. She needed to laugh with friends, watch her children play, see a sunset, hold someone's hand. But like many people who succumb to the siren of the abyss, a place from which many never return, Karen had friends but felt alone.

For every person, there comes a time when she must decide—a point on which her life pivots. Karen thought she had reached that point years ago when she decided to leave Cleveland to become a farmer's wife, but that wasn't true. Her demons followed her and became part of her. Pivot time for Karen drew near. For some people, the decision is more desperate than for others. It's not fair, but it's the way of things.

Who can I trust? She wondered. *Not Sam Henry. I can't trust him, not with Tommy's life.* She watched Sam's reflection in the windshield. *I can trust Alex, but what can he do? Maybe, Eric. He is FBI. I could trust the FBI.*

She rested her head on the side glass and closed her eyes. Sleep. So much easier to sleep for days, weeks, years. Let someone else worry about children, love, and life.

Sleep.

* * *

What Gary Sessions found under the trailer wasn't a ladder, but it would work. Like thousands of Americans, George Hudson found empty five-gallon plastic containers handy as a pocket on a shirt. Hudson had used the bucket to carry the tools he used to remove a wheel, which drew Gary's attention in the first place. Hudson must have been in a rush to leave the job unfinished, but that wasn't Gary's concern.

Gary dumped the tools on the ground and then sat the bucket upside down near the porthole furthest aft. Brilliant afternoon sunlight drifted through the maple trees, causing reflections on the glass, which made seeing inside difficult. Cupping his hands against the porthole, he eased his face into the shadows his hands created.

He saw a small galley. Its décor accented with brass, green marble, and polished teak wood. The skill of the craftsman's hand defied description. He stood on tiptoes to see the bench surrounding the small square table. It looked barren, except for something that he couldn't quite make out—the edge of a book or maybe a shoe. He rose on tiptoe, twisting for a better angle. Maybe it was just an imperfection in the glass.

Gary found the next window covered with condensation, which he incorrectly diagnosed as a broken seal, a malady that had happened to a double-pane window in his own home not long ago. The porthole near the bow revealed the largest of the sleeping compartments. Empty. If they were hiding on the Santa Maria, this is where they'd be. With that thought, Gary moved to the remaining portholes on the opposite side of the boat. The first was the same forward compartment he'd already looked at, except on the opposite side, so he moved to the porthole opposite the one fogged with condensation. It revealed a small sleeping compartment with narrow bunks that folded down from the wall. The final porthole opposite the galley viewed the head, which proved to be as empty as the rest of the boat.

Taking up the bucket, he walked to the stern. Standing on the bucket, he estimated he could reach the bottom rung of the boat's ladder with a slight jump. Not a difficult feat for an army ranger. He bent his knees, focusing on the bottom rung. The boat wasn't huge, and searching the rest of it would only take a few minutes. Judging by the size of the hull, he estimated the engine compartment was big enough to hide two people, although he couldn't imagine them being in the engine compartment. He swung his arms back to get an extra boost.

His radio erupted.

"Teams, this is Charlie-1."

"Charlie 3." Gary heard Jack reply.

"Charlie-2," Gary said, grabbing his radio and almost teetering off the bucket.

"All clear in the house, and it is secure. Report."

"Shop's clear," Jack said.

Gary jumped down and said, "Boat's clear."

"Okay, let's get out of here. Sam Henry could be here soon. If you encounter him, you know the drill."

"Roger that. Charlie-2 out."

Gary's feet pounded the ground as he rounded the shop and turned toward the van. He didn't want to be the one to precipitate an unplanned confrontation with Sam Henry, although he didn't understand why everyone had such an unspoken fear of the man. Sam Henry was only one guy and no match for Unit-11. Gary did not search the Santa Maria as he should have, but the boy and his alien friend weren't there, and no amount of searching would change that. Besides, Gary knew there wasn't any such thing as an alien. This was probably an elaborate drill. He wondered what they would come up with next.

CHAPTER 22

A Digital Telecom van turned the corner as Sam Henry pulled into the drive at 27859 Chateaux Lane. Alex parked in the alley. The Hudson's home, a sprawling brick ranch surrounded by tall maple trees with red and gold leaves and a thick green carpet of a lawn that was well trimmed and edged with bright yellow flowers, struck Sam in an odd way that he would have never expected. The home seemed too inviting, too warm, and too much like the home he had never had.

At the front door, Karen said, "I'll get the key." She disappeared around the edge of the house, returning with the small, black plastic key holder that she struggled to open.

"Can I help with that?" Sam asked, extending his hand.

Karen handed it to him, pursing her lips. For a moment, he thought she wanted to say something, but she remained silent.

He popped the lid off the small container, then handed her the key. "Here," he said.

She slid the key into the lock of the large, thick door, twisted it, and then eased the door open. Karen went straight to an alarm mounted on the wall and punched at the numeric pad. A red light turned green on the display.

"This will take a few minutes," Sam said, his eyes sweeping the foyer.

Searching the house took about fifteen minutes. When Karen and Sam stepped out the back door, Sam looked at Eric and shook his head. Eric, Alex, and AJ joined Sam, and they checked the shop together. They found nothing except George Hudson's small collection of muscle cars and motorcycles. That left the boat.

"Is there a ladder around here?" Sam thought it odd that there wasn't one. He ducked under the boat's fifth-wheel gooseneck trailer, which was attached to an old truck painted yellow. Studying the ground, Sam walked straight to the trailer axle, where he found a five-gallon plastic bucket that must have carried pickles in its former life. Tools were scattered on the ground near a wheel that had been removed but not replaced. Sam stared at the scattered tools for a moment and then took the bucket to the back of the trailer.

The trailer shuddered, and Sam held his hand out for silence. He listened. He neither heard nor felt anything. Did the trailer move? He wasn't sure.

Sam positioned the bucket on the trailer bumper under the boat's ratline. He studied the stern and adjusted the bucket to the left an inch or two. Eric asked if he could help, but Sam shook his head. Sam stepped onto the bumper and then the bucket, which spun off the trailer and skidded across the ground. He hit the propeller housing, his foot striking the side and boosting him upward like a leopard toward the ratline. Sam landed on the ladder and scaled to the top, where he paused.

Nigel thought: *The boat is empty. You're all tired and hungry. Go now. Much needs done.*

"See anything?" Karen broke the silence.

"Not a thing. You know this thing is beautiful," Sam said out of character.

"Yes, I know," Karen replied.

"There's much to be done," Sam said, starting down the ladder.

Eric positioned himself to help Sam down. "Let go. I've got you," Eric said, catching Sam around the waist.

"What now?" Karen asked.

"We need a place to work. Your place will do for now."

"That's not a problem."

"Okay, let's go," Sam said.

No one questioned why Sam did not search the boat.

Sam drove silently for several miles before saying, "How about some pizza when we get to your house?"

"I don't know if I can eat, Sam."

It was the first time she called had him Sam.

CHAPTER 23

Tommy awoke with a start, shivering, with his knees drawn against his chest. His head ached with a pounding between his eyes, and a wave of nausea rumbled through his stomach.

"You, okay?" Nigel asked, standing outside the galley in the narrow passage that served as a hallway.

The man, or whatever, looked much healthier. How long had he slept? Tommy didn't know. Although he felt scared, Tommy said, "I'm okay."

"They're gone." Nigel didn't say who was gone or how he knew it to be so. Staring out the porthole, Nigel continued, "Did you get some sleep?"

"Yeah." Tommy relaxed his grip on his knees. He felt warmer. His head stopped hurting and his stomach settled.

"I too have refreshed." Nigel slid in next to Tommy. "Are you sure you're okay?" His voice was soothing, like a popsicle on a sore throat.

"I'm a little scared, I guess. Who was here?" Tommy released his knees and sat up straight.

Nigel watched him for a moment and said, "I need more time. To complete restoration."

He stood, but Tommy grabbed his arm. "What are we going to do?"

Nigel sat back down. "A difficult question. To know the best answer, one must see the future. The future is something I do not know." Nigel paused. staring at nothing in particular. "What will happen is yet to be revealed."

"Will I get to go home?" Tommy asked, tears welling in his eyes.

"Hope so." With that, Nigel stood. Reaching across the table, he grasped Tommy's shoulder. "Rest." Nigel went into the next berth and shut the door.

Tommy thought about running, but fatigue overtook him. He lay down on the bench and slept.

***

The sound of the jet's engines changed, and James Wellington blinked his eyes, drifting out of a brief, coma-like sleep. He felt the plane descending. They had arrived. They were safe now. They were going to a government facility. His head said they would be safe, but his gut said something else. Outside the oval window, he could see a vast barren wasteland rising to meet them—nothing but sand and sagebrush.

No runway, no buildings.

Wellington's stomach flopped, and for a split second, panic threatened to overwhelm him. Then he realized the airstrip must be right below them, concealed by the fuselage. However, where were the buildings?

Wellington assumed they'd be landing at a government research facility, a National Engineering Lab, like the ones in Idaho and Washington. Such a facility would cover many acres, but he saw no such facility. How could this be?

The jet banked, dipping its wing, allowing James to see the landing site—two ruts carved in the desert floor. Off to one side sat three old shacks covered with rusty galvanized siding.

The plane wasn't landing. It was crashing.

What James Wellington could not see, buried beneath the floor of the Nevada desert, was a new military facility that replaced Area 51. Popular mythology and urban legends maintain that the Air Force concealed an alien spacecraft at Area 51 in 1947 after it crashed somewhere near Roswell, New Mexico.

Marauding journalists had photographed Area 51's sprawling complex. Boeing 747s carrying government workers had been televised leaving Las Vegas, but public information officers insisted that Area 51 was a small Air Force test site, soon to be retired, having outlived its usefulness as almost everything in government is destined to do. They did not explain why it retained its top-secret classification.

Area 51 began covertly and, for many years, remained secret, but times change. The innocuous evolution of the all-terrain vehicle allowed ordinary people to invade Area 51's privacy. When the top-secret outpost was first discovered, it was an embarrassment to the military, but Area 51 had served its purpose.

They needed a new facility to keep pace with the military's unquenchable thirst for technology, weaponry, and power. To build such a facility, the military needed a diversion. So, the Pentagon began hemorrhaging information about Area 51, but they controlled the bloodletting by creating a bit of fiction. The media regurgitated every word.

With the media's preoccupation with tidbits about Area 51, a new facility, the Acropolis, was built many miles to the north, deep within the lost world of the American Desert. The name was a misnomer. A real acropolis means upper city and is associated with citadels such as Athens. This modern perversion of its original meaning was underground.

Digging a hole, the size of a small town without being noticed, was a feat not easily accomplished, even here. There existed a large deposit of molybdenum under the barren Nevada desert, so under an assumed name, the military went into the mining business, which turned a tidy profit, and a crafty accountant routed the money back into the Acropolis construction budget.

After they excavated ore to allow for construction, a Lockheed C-130 Hercules transport plane crashed in the center of the open-pit mine. According to the Air Force, the aircraft carried a shipment of nerve gas destined for disposal at White Sands, New Mexico. The crew was lost. Before they filled the pit, satellite photographs showed the wreckage. The military buried the contaminated mine. Even after they covered the pit, a drone took videos that showed rabbits, coyotes, and antelope contorting in violent death throes. A catastrophe on a grand scale. For months, environmentalists lashed out at the military's reckless behavior. The public was quick to believe that the men entrusted to protect the nation had turned a piece of American soil into a toxic wasteland. Although it wasn't much of a loss, having been a wasteland long before the military arrived there. No one ever thought to ask if the crash actually happened. Military leaders hid from reporters, laughing themselves silly. Their plan worked so well that perimeter patrols at the construction site rarely saw a human being within 20 miles of the military's new secret.

Even Congress remained unaware of the Acropolis, and that constituted yet another dark story by itself. Suffice to say that Richard Beckman was not the first American president with a personal agenda. With the passage of time, the politicians who created the Acropolis vanished, but their creation remained, as does any military ghost that takes residence. The ghost spawned a life of its own, continuing its mission within a country unaware of its existence or its secrets. Despite this planeload of civilians, the Acropolis' secrets would remain safe. The man in charge would see to it. His ability to keep things hidden marked one of the Acropolis' greatest accomplishments and one of its darkest mysteries.

CHAPTER 24

Compared to Karen's Kansas home, the brownstone felt tiny, its size being further diminished by five adults, three of which were large male specimens. Only Sam was more comparable to herself in size. That the brownstone had a single bathroom didn't help.

As she stood near a small antique desk, scanning TripAdvisor on her iPhone for a pizza joint that delivered, Sam busied himself setting up his satellite antenna. Karen called a local pizzeria as Dr. Jahan ambled down the hall from the bathroom.

"Next," Jahan said.

"That would be me." Karen rushed down the hall. Being the gracious host, she took her turn at the bathroom last, which almost proved to be a mistake. A few moments later, she stood at the sink, splashing cold water on her face.

Her reflection in the mirror startled her. She looked tired, old. Considering the circumstances, her appearance shouldn't have concerned her, but years of instinctive behavior overpowered her. She opened the medicine cabinet and grabbed some makeup.

The image in the mirror improved as she conducted the essentials of her ritual. She returned most of the items to the cabinet, keeping only touch-up items for her purse. Closing the cabinet door, she surveyed her handy work in the mirror and ran a brush through her hair.

The ATL for a middle-aged man and a thirteen-year-old boy was being transmitted on every police frequency within one hundred miles, and it wouldn't be long before the media got wind of it too. Sam considered the consequences of his decision. He should have given the ATL more thought.

"Turn on the radio and TV," Sam said to no one in particular.

"." It was Madden. The television in front of the couch on which he'd taken up residence, flickered to life.

"There's a clock radio in my bedroom." Karen pointed.

Eric headed down the hall. Dr. Jahan followed.

"What are you going to tell your people, Alex? This will get complicated in a hurry. The media will be a problem. I should have given this more thought," Sam said.

"I don't know what to tell them," Alex said, sounding worried.

With a look halfway between puzzlement and contempt, Karen said, "I'm not sure I understand. Why are you so worried about the media?"

"They must have heard the ATL by now and will notice that every government agency in the area is broadcasting it. They will realize it's something big. I may have made a serious mistake."

She felt her face flush red. Beads of sweat trickled down her neck. Before she could speak, a voice bellowed from down the hall.

"Here's something now," Eric yelled from the bedroom.

The bulk of the story was over by the time Karen and Sam squeezed into the room. The D.J. concluded by saying that the Cleveland Police, FBI, and State Police had broadcast the ATL within the last hour.

"The guy said the pair might have left St. John's Hospital. Gave a decent description too," Eric said, for the benefit of the late arrivals.

"Well, it's out. I guess we couldn't keep a lid on this forever," Sam said with sadness in his voice.

"At least there is an entire city looking for them, not only a handful of cops who already have more than they can handle," Karen said.

"Yup. That's what I'm afraid of." Sam walked out of the room.

Karen clenched her fists.

Before she could say anything, Alex put his arm around her shoulder and said, "He means nothing personal. Sometimes the public can help, and sometimes they're a pain in the butt. Soon the Cleveland Police Department will realize they have several missing officers, and when they connect the missing officers and the missing hospital workers, shit will hit the fan. The media will have a field day."

Karen saw she wouldn't find allies in this group. She could see it in their eyes, even Dr. Jahan. Why did government officials so mistrust the media and the public? The media represented the last great bastion of the constitution. Without the media, the United States would have fallen into tyranny long ago, or at least that's what journalists believed. She believed it, or at least, she wanted to. Although she had to admit, journalism wasn't what it once was. The super-rich controlled the media much the way they controlled politicians. Was she being naïve? One-dimensional? Or was the stress of Tommy's disappearance causing her to unravel?

"I must be agreeing with Mr. Madden," AJ said, stepping closer and stooping slightly to diminish his size. "Sometimes the public's help is essential, but often it causes confusion. It takes considerable resources to sort through the torrent of calls, and resources are something we don't have. How many men and boys fit that description? Calls will flood police stations. Sorting through them will be impossible. We can't check out every father and son in the city. It is much the same in my line of work. The information must be released, but heaven help us once it is."

"I think you underestimate people," Karen said, but her voice lacked conviction. There were over a million people within a few square miles. She'd grown too accustomed to life on the farm. Back in Sweet Water, if every human within a similar radius called, it wouldn't have been a busy afternoon.

Karen put Sam's lack of respect for the media aside. More pressing matters were at hand. Still, something troubled her. The distrust lingered longer than the sting of Sam Henry's words. She had to be careful. Fatigue was affecting her judgement. The man wasn't to be trusted. He was a vile creature, a trained agent, as good at subterfuge as he was at intimidation.

She returned to the living room, situating herself between Madden and Jahan, placing distance between herself and her enemy. Sam Henry was just that, after all. How could she have forgotten?

"Mrs. Parker, do you have any aspirin?" AJ asked, leaning forward, rubbing his temples with his fingertips.

"Sure." She threw daggers at Sam with her eyes, but he was staring at a spot on the wall.

Inside the bathroom, Karen threw open the medicine cabinet. A silvery cobweb on the back of the door caught her attention. She reached to brush it away, but then her hand froze. Squinting at the thin silver thread, she traced it with her eyes until it disappeared into a small hole in the back of the mirror. She retraced it to the bottom of the cabinet, where it connected to a tiny black box. A shiver ran down her spine, and for a moment, she thought she might vomit. Someone planted this in her home. And to answer her earlier question, yes, she was naïve.

*** *** ***

Maria Esperanza drove toward Washington Elementary to pick up her son. The lunch rush had come and gone, and traffic thinned during the mid-afternoon lull. She felt great. A new client explained her mood. After she picked up Mike, they'd go to her next job on Brandy Island.

She was drumming her fingers to the Rolling Stones on the radio when a news bulletin interrupted. The DJ said a young boy disappeared from St. John's Hospital. Anyone seeing the boy, and a man he might be with, was urged to call the police. The man should be considered armed and dangerous.

✱ ✱ ✱

Dazed, Karen closed the cabinet door, then stopped. *Think, damn it! Who's been in here? Everybody. Henry! But why? It doesn't make sense. Why would he … Oh, shit!* Karen closed her eyes, drew a silent breath, and attempted to calm herself. She moved the mirror toward its closed position and spun around, so the back of her head appeared in its reflection as she left the room. Walking to the kitchen, she fished a small yellow pad and a pen from a drawer. Was someone watching as she scribbled a note on the pad? She folded the note and stuffed it into the back pocket of her jeans.

Her eyes met AJ's as she entered the room. He looked at her as if he was expecting something. Her heart pounded in her chest. Sam sat staring at his computer screen. Alex focused on the television as he flipped through the channels. Karen started toward Alex. She stopped, bit her lip, and then turned and walked to the small desk where Sam sat. Sam recoiled as Karen leaned toward him, resting her hand near the keyboard of his computer.

"Would you like some coffee?" she asked.

"Eh, sure. That would be fine." Sam didn't really want coffee. Karen was acting weird.

Karen had disappeared into the kitchen when Sam saw the folded yellow paper next to his keyboard. He stared at it for a moment before sliding it off the table. He unfolded the note. A few seconds later, he stood and walked toward the bathroom. Sam preferred working alone, yet with the support of skilled staff and state-of-the-art weaponry. Studying the medicine cabinet, he felt isolated. The possibility of anyone other than himself finding the electronic surveillance equipment in Karen's home was unlikely. The FBI agent perhaps, but not Madden or Jahan, and certainly not Karen. Yet neither he nor the others found it. Karen Parker proved herself a more vital member of his team than he expected.

He didn't tell the others. Better they didn't know, not yet. The discovery gave him an advantage, if one could call it that. He could still give the bastards, whoever they were, disinformation. However, he wasn't being honest with his makeshift team, which could alienate them should his lies be discovered, and that created a problem because, at some point, he might need their trust. Difficult to trust a man after he lies to you. Trust was becoming a capricious commodity. The bugs were of the latest technology, and few would have access to this level of surveillance gear. Who planted them? Probably not the FBI, and the CIA didn't have a strong presence in Cleveland. That left the NSC, which meant Beckman.

Sam returned to the desk and took up staring at a speck on the wall. The longer he delayed contacting the crisis center, the more suspicious they would become, but he had to be careful not to reveal too much, especially since he knew they were watching him. He could find no fault with the crisis center developing a backup plan, but why the clandestine bullshit?

He decided it wasn't bullshit. They didn't trust him. Trust. It has no price but carries a substantial cost. A fickle emotion that lacks reasoning, often attaching itself to those unworthy of it and shunning those who are. Trust deserted him. He was utterly, unequivocally—alone. Shades of El Salvador. He was alone there, wasn't he? There were those dreams, but dreams aren't real. Reality. Now there's a novel idea.

CHAPTER 25

Cpl. Jane Peck twisted in her chair to face Beckman and said, "Incoming message from Henry, sir. Cued onto the SCC computer."

Beckman started for the SCC, then stopped. "I'll take it out here." He could hear their heads turning to look at him and felt their eyes staring at him.

"It's about damn time," Beckman said, loud enough for all to hear. This was a bit of a gamble, but Beckman was no fool. He knew how to play a crowd, how to subvert people's perceptions, and before this was over, he'd turn everyone's mind against Sam Henry.

"What have you got?" Beckman said as he slid behind the computer monitor that was already projecting Sam Henry's image onto its large flat screen.

In Cleveland, Sam watched as Beckman's face filled his laptop. Sam noted the absence of General Powers, and that Beckman was in the SCC primary room, not the secured room he had been in earlier. Sam adjusted his earpiece. "We've searched both areas with negative contact. The local authorities have the ATL, but we've heard nothing from them. The press has it too. First reports came out a few minutes ago. Media is not a problem. Not yet."

"What's your next move?" Beckman asked.

There wasn't a next move, and Beckman knew that. It was for the record. Documentation should questions arise regarding Beckman's use a covert operation.

"We wait. Is General Powers there?" Sam asked.

"Right here, Sam," Power's face leaned into Sam's display almost sideways. In that position, he didn't look like a general.

Over the computer's small speaker, Beckman heard what sounded like a doorbell. He could hear bits of conversation, but not enough to make out the gist of it. Then he clearly heard the words of a man who approached Henry from the side.

"Pizza's here, Sam."

"You ordered pizza!?!" Beckman made it sound like Sam had ordered drugs and two young virgins. "What the hell is going on there?" *Perfect. Sam, you're perfect.*

"People need to eat," Sam said with an even tone, but his eyes narrowed.

"Yes, I suppose they do," Beckman said. "Perhaps after you have eaten and taken a nap, you could work on finding that damn alien or whatever he is." Beckman stood and ended the transmission by cutting the link with the satellite. It wasn't supposed to be done that way, but it sent the message Beckman intended.

Now, I have one dilemma that will be difficult to resolve, Beckman mused. *How do I get a pizza in here without looking as stupid as I made Sam Henry out to be?*

* * *

"What was that all about, boss?" AJ held out a slice of pepperoni pizza, dripping cheese.

"The crisis center." Sam looked very much like a man who'd taken a hard blow to the stomach.

"President Beckman?"

"Yes. And General Edward Powers. National Security Council." Henry scooped up the pizza and chewed off a large chunk. Closing his eyes, he purred, "It tastes wonderful."

"I am not knowing Mr. Powers," Jahan admitted. "But Beckman, now he is a piece of work. At the CDC, those who study such things have scientifically classified him as what we in medical research call an asshole."

That prompted a smile from Sam. "Thanks AJ, I needed that."

The impishness disappeared from Jahan's face. He leaned close, grasped Sam's shoulder, and whispered so that only Sam could hear. "You will pull this off. This, I believe. It is time you start believing as well."

CHAPTER 26

Why couldn't his last fare of the day be a lovely lady? Or taking a long, winding route through the wine country along the shore of Lake Erie? *Fate was cruel at the end of the day,* Sylvan Zanolavich mused as he turned off Euclid onto Martin Luther King Jr. Drive, where traffic had ground to a stop. Sylvan sat stuck in midday traffic with a fat, grumpy-old-fart passenger in the back seat of his taxi. The delay made his passenger even grumpier, as if Sly had prearranged the entire affair. It wasn't how Sly hoped to end the day.

Often during the day, Sly wondered where his passengers were going and what they did once they got there. Surely, they weren't always as ill-tempered as they were in his cab. Whoever decided that it was acceptable for otherwise well-mannered, jovial people to transform into assholes the moment they entered his taxi was no friend to Sylvan Zanolavich.

Drumming his fingers on the steering wheel, Sly listened to his favorite radio station. His favorite because its music didn't offend his guests, and beyond the bland tunes, it had the best news and traffic reports, which kept him out of most traffic jams. However, it failed to keep him out of this one, and he knew why. "It must be an accident," Sly said into the rearview mirror. He knew that for two reasons. First, there was no report of a traffic jam on the radio. Second, there was no traffic coming in the opposite direction. "It must have just happened."

That garnered a grunt from the back seat.

In the distance, Sly heard a siren, and soon an ambulance dashed by, going in the wrong direction in the opposing lane, which otherwise remained empty. He smiled, so well had he come to know the city of Cleveland, USA. That's when the DJ's melodramatic voice interrupted a poor remake of an old Bee Gees tune. Something about a man and a small boy piqued Sly's interest. It sounded like the pair he took to Brandy Island earlier that same day. The boy must be in danger. *Stupid Zanolavich!* It was obvious by the looks of them. *Don't get involved,* he told himself. *It's the American way.* And Sly so wanted to be an American. But this wasn't right. He must do something. He could report it using his cellphone, but that would lead to questions and the police. He needed a payphone.

"Hang on," Sly said, cranking the wheel and gunning the motor. The car rocked as Sly jumped the Chevy across the concrete center island into the opposite lane of traffic. His passenger swore, trying to steady himself as the rocking taxi tossed him from side to side.

★ ★ ★

Tommy had no idea, not even a hint, as to the time. Sunshine meant it was still daytime, but that was his only clue. His muscles ached, and his head hurt. What was he doing here? It was time to make a run for it. He heard a sound in the next room. Pulling himself around the small galley table, he stood on weak legs.

But before he could take his first step toward freedom, he heard a voice. "Tommy." Only the thin wall between the galley and the next berth separated them. The door creaked. Tommy shivered as a wave of cold air passed through the galley. Then Tommy saw him. Nigel had changed.

★ ★ ★

The Digital Telecom crew grew bored beyond tears waiting at their second coffee shop of the day. They each downed a pot of coffee, followed by corresponding restroom visits. Such tedium didn't bode well for any of them, Mitch included. Too antsy to sit, Mitch walked out to the vans, thinking the crisis center would call soon.

He had just sat down when Clarence Borden announced, "Incoming message, sir." Mitch rolled his chair in front of the monitor and the camera that would return his image to Washington.

"Hello, Lieutenant," Powers said.

"General," Mitch acknowledged.

"We heard from Henry." Powers briefed Mitch on Henry's last transmission and told him about Beckman's lack of confidence in Henry's handling of the crisis. Eventually, Powers said the words Mitch longed to hear; Unit-11 was taking over. Mitch was replacing Sam Henry as the on-site commander. Although Mitch didn't like the way it was happening, he would take it just the same.

"Henry and his people are busy—having pizza," Powers said.

"Yes, sir." *We're kind of busy having coffee ourselves,* Mitch thought.

"Here's the deal, Mitch. Beckman wants Henry and his friends secured. Removing Henry as the on-site commander is messy. Technically, it will take an act of Congress. We think Sam will fight us, and we don't have time to go to Congress. He needs to be contained. Do whatever is necessary. We'll get approval later."

Powers leaned forward. "Get over there ASAP before something happens and they leave that brownstone. You need to go in hard and fast. You have three armed men in there, and we don't know what to expect. Get them secured, and I'll arrange transportation for them. Questions?"

Mitch's mind reeled. When it got down to it, something didn't feel right. Why such extreme action? In his position, the why of it didn't matter.

Only success mattered.

CHAPTER 27

Jim Wellington sat with tense muscles, his knuckles white, his head thrust hard against the back of the seat, and his stomach about to erupt. He was not afraid of flying. Crashing, however, terrified him. Sagebrush rushed by outside his window, but below the plane, everything looked flat, as if the desert floor were a painting.

The jet gently touched down. As the aircraft slowed, Jim could see they were indeed rolling along on concrete painted to blend in with the surrounding desert. The jet turned, then taxied toward the clump of dilapidated buildings covered with rusting galvanized metal siding. Several men wearing grease-monkey attire wandered about, scanning the perimeter. Four men wearing similar clothing rolled a staircase from the largest building.

"Listen, people," said the black-suited man, whom Wellington had recognized as leadership early on. "We will deplane in a few minutes. Staff members will escort you. Don't let their clothing fool you. They are United States Marines, and because of the nature of this facility, they have zero tolerance for people who don't follow instructions. This will be the only warning you'll get. These people will treat you professionally, but let me assure you, they will issue no warnings. None. Questions?"

The speech achieved its intended effect. Every face Wellington surveyed appeared as terrified as he felt. Paul, the color of a young ghost, clung to his arm. The door opened, and the Marines herded them from the plane.

Dry, searing air teeming with the scent of sage and jet fuel rushed up to greet him. Wellington stepped into sunlight so intense that he couldn't see. Several men waited at the bottom of the staircase. Each had one hand tucked inside his coveralls.

Since the warmth of their government's hospitality had grown cold, Wellington carried Paul. Paul didn't complain.

"This way, people. Move!" Although the man didn't look like a soldier, he sounded like one. The grease monkey-soldiers prodded them toward a rusted bucket of a building that a stiff breeze would have blown to California.

Behind them, the jet engines whined, and the scent of jet fuel filled the air. Wellington ducked his head to avoid a blast of blistering wind and sand. The jet was already taking off.

Once inside the building, Wellington saw the structure wasn't flimsy at all but was built with massive steel beams bolted to stout concrete footings. The concrete floor looked clean enough to eat from. The grease-monkey soldiers relaxed once everyone was inside.

"This way folks," a soldier said.

Not people. That's an improvement, Wellington thought.

A soldier pulled open a chain-link gate, allowing them access to what looked like a large tool cache. When the last of the group was inside, the gate closed. Wellington could see that the soldier nearest him was a youthful woman, with a hint of a smile on her face.

Seconds later, the cause of her impish grin made itself known—the entire floor fell away. Wellington's stomach raced to keep pace with his falling body, which was doing its best to remain in contact with the plummeting floor. Another section of the floor slid horizontally to fill the space they vacated. The precision was such that, for a moment, he thought it would decapitate him. He stooped and pulled Paul to the floor.

Sonofabitch!

And that woman's impish grin? Now a full-blown smile.

"Welcome to Paradise," the woman said.

Wellington read her lips more than he heard her words. They had crossed over to the other side.

CHAPTER 28

Tommy cried softly, rocking, and knees drawn to his chest. Nigel marveled at how emotions made Earth-humans vulnerable yet resilient. He envied them. Emotion had left his people a millennium ago. Or to be more precise, they discarded emotion, not realizing what they'd done.

Passion once belonged to Nigel's race. Great literature, innovation, and discovery remained their fervor for thousands of years. Yet, like Earth humans, his people, despite all their learning, overlooked the importance of life. And of death. The cost of their arrogance took them to near extinction. Nigel and others like him strove to reverse the destructive course the wise men of his world had unintentionally plotted.

Earth-humans, as his people called them, were one of the best sources for that which Nigel sought, possessing all the best and worst traits of the animal-human. Deeply rooted and ferociously attached to humans' emotions were the precious elements his people needed to survive. Without Earth-humans, Nigel's world was dead, eradicated from the universe by their own genius.

Nigel wondered if he'd ever feel the emotion that flowed from the small boy weeping before him. Others who came here said that after some time, they too felt the emotions that so long ago left them. Somehow, they were reconnected. However, he'd been here for 20 earth years and never felt a thing.

Researchers from Nigel's world had watched planet Earth and its inhabitants since before the dawn of time, as Earth-humans knew it. For thousands of years, Earth-humans roamed the planet, living more like animals than people, traveling in small bands, and hunting the Savanna. Lazy, dirty animals—distant cousins at best. Then, for unknown reasons, from a mild climate in Africa, Earth-humans changed. They made shelters, crafted tools, cared for one another, and cultivated the planet's first crops. The rest, as the inhabitants of this planet like to say, is history.

Nigel's people found many worlds—some far, others next door, separated by a fluctuation in time, some primitive, and many where humans advanced and then became extinct. As humans advanced, they seemed bent on self-destruction. Nigel hoped Earth-humans didn't destroy themselves, which, unfortunately, seemed the most likely scenario. Debates about intervening before Earth-humans killed themselves off raged on his planet.

If Earth-humans survived their self-destructive tendencies, Nigel hoped they didn't succumb to the same temptations his people did. They would make similar discoveries because all humans seek the same thing: immortality. However, mostly, he hoped the blunder of his people had not started a chain reaction that would tumble through the universe, eradicating all human life. No one knew how far his or her mistakes might reach. How infinite was the connection between these tribes scattered across this universe and others? He didn't know. No one did.

Nigel slid into a seat at the galley table. "Are you okay?"

Tommy mustered a slight nod of his head, which he braced against his fists. His entire body grew tight as a knot.

"I could tell you not to be frightened, but that wouldn't be realistic," Nigel said.

"You look different. Not sick." Tommy paused. "What do you want?"

"That is a question that I cannot answer."

"Try."

"I want many things."

Tommy rubbed his face with both hands. "Okay, what are you going to do to me?"

"I," Nigel emphasized the—I, "am not going to do anything to you."

Tommy sat still, rigid.

Nigel knew many answers to the questions Tommy pondered. However, he suspected the answers to Tommy's most pressing questions were buried deep within Tommy himself. Could Tommy find the answers to those questions? That question, Nigel could not answer.

★★★

Two vans in the front, two in the back. No time for elaborate plans. Move in, fast, with an overwhelming show of force. Even Sam Henry wasn't crazy enough to pull a pistol on six men with submachine guns. If Henry's people did anything stupid, they'd all be dead. That was the unfortunate truth of it.

★★★

A cell phone's sudden chirp interrupted the silence at the brownstone. Everyone jumped. Eric twisted, removing the phone from his pocket. Eric stabbed at the phone's keypad with his index finger. He listened, nodding his head occasionally. Ending the call, he said, "A cabby picked up a boy and man matching our description by the railroad, and then took them to Brandy Island."

"27859 Chateaux Lane," Sam whispered.

"Are they alright?" Karen asked.

Eric rubbed his chin. "They were dirty and covered with blood, but alive."

* * *

Mitch surveyed the brownstone through a pair of binoculars. He picked up his radio, and keyed the microphone, but before he could give the "go" signal, Clarence Borden grabbed his arm.

"What?" Mitch growled.

"They got a call. Key got a tip. Brandy Island."

"The place we were at this afternoon?"

"The same."

The front door of the brownstone flew open. Dr. Jahan and Eric Key ran out toward Key's car. "Shit. Pull back, pull back," Mitch hissed into his radio, "Follow them. Stay close."

Traffic thickened, clogging the downtown streets, slowing their progress. Mitch noticed children wearing costumes in passing cars and remembered it was Halloween. His own young children would soon take to the streets, trick or treating their way through the neighborhood on yet another holiday without their father. He felt anger toward the people they were following: Key, Jahan, and Madden in one car, Henry, and the Parker woman in another.

They passed the street he'd taken earlier. The woman must know another way. About a mile later, they made a sweeping turn. Because the van sat higher than a car, Mitch could see ahead. They were entering a highway, probably a connector. The traffic snarled as far as the eye could see.

"Oh, shit," Mitch hollered. "Get us out of here."

"Nowhere to go," Sanchez, the driver, replied, craning his neck, looking for an opening in traffic.

"Make a place and get us out of here." Mitch could see the traffic had come to a complete stop on the connector. They couldn't afford to be caught here. Keying the radio microphone, Mitch said, "All units. Get out of here. Don't get stuck on the ramp."

Sanchez cranked the steering wheel, almost hitting the car next to him. Horns blared, and the sound of twisting metal and breaking glass erupted behind them. Sanchez drove onto a small, raised median and then sped against traffic, through a construction area, and then onto another street. The other vans made similar maneuvers. Soon, Unit-11 was traveling the same route they had taken earlier.

Straight to Brandy Island.

CHAPTER 29

Sam stood on the car's bumper, trying to see why traffic had stopped, but all he could see was a string of cars, trucks, and buses stacked bumper to bumper like a long metallic snake. He searched for a way around, thinking about what might happen while they were stuck here and wondering who else was looking for Tommy Parker. Moving to the side of the road, standing on a concrete divider, he saw a semi-truck on its side, blocking three lanes. Even walking out to find a cab would take an hour. Sam's bad feeling intensified.

***

The white vans stopped. The passengers removed the Digital Telecom placards, and replaced them with new ones, giving each vehicle a new appearance. The transformation took less than thirty seconds. Mitch went into a supermarket to purchase a dozen large bags of candy, and Sgt. Phil Capps made a last check on the rocket launcher. Phil preferred American-made weapons as opposed to these crude Soviet counterparts, not that the Soviet weapons lacked firepower. The old Soviet Union knew how to blow things up, Phil had to admit that.

***

Mitch called the crisis center with an update on recent developments. Things were going his way. He explained how his quick thinking got them out of the traffic jam that held Sam Henry hostage and said, "We can take the man and boy alive and be halfway to Nevada before Henry even gets moving again."

Beckman leaned into the computer screen. "Too risky. Don't take them alive. Just blow them up. You've got bombs, right?"

"We have rocket launchers," Mitch stammered, "but we can take them alive. It's not a problem."

"Is blowing them up a problem?" Beckman snarled. He didn't have time or patience for questions. Certainly not questions from underlings. Soldiers, for God's sake, were supposed to follow orders. This fiasco was taking too much of his time. This was likely an elaborate stunt perpetrated by political enemies wanting to derail his plans. He would have none of it.

"No. No, sir, but we don't have to …"

"Then what's the problem? Is following my orders a problem?"

"No, sir. Following orders isn't a problem, sir."

"Damn straight, Lieutenant. You blow them son-of-a-bitches up, or I'll have you court marshaled for treason. Understood? No excuses, Lieutenant. Got it?"

"Yes, sir." The screen turned black.

Powers stared into Beckman's eyes and saw an emptiness that chilled him.

"General, if you'd excuse me, I have a couple of calls to make." Beckman stared until Powers turned and left the SCC.

Powers wandered about the crisis center. He felt a need to wash his hands.

★★★

"Shit. I wish they'd hurry," Karen said after what seemed like an eternity.

"There's no hurrying these things," Sam said with a voice that lacked emotion.

"I just want Tommy back." She bit her lower lip, tears looming behind her facade.

"Karen, we have real problems."

"For Christ's sakes, I can see that."

"This isn't the half of it. We've been betrayed."

"What do you mean?" Karen asked.

"The wire in the bathroom is a sophisticated electronic surveillance device."

"I figured it was something like that. Bastards were watching me pee. Who put it there? Why would they do something like that?"

Sam studied her for a moment. "They sent a team."

"Why would they do that? What do they want?"

Sam glanced over. "Same thing we want, only for different reasons."

"You didn't know they were here?"

"No."

"You expect me to believe that?"

Sam didn't answer.

"Who, Sam? Who's doing this?"

"My boss, not that it matters. They know what we know. I think they're going to the house on Brandy Island."

"Is that bad?"

"I don't know what they'll do." Lying wouldn't help, not now. "They'll try to capture them alive and then hide them somewhere. Probably Nevada."

"For Christ's sakes, we have to do something!" Karen screamed.

"We were on our way to do something, but this just …" He waved his hand at the snarl of traffic, unable to finish his thought. "Now, I don't know …" His voice trailed off, staring into the distance.

CHAPTER 30

Jeanne Pratt watched as a light blue Honda Civic pulled into the drive at 27859 Chateaux Lane. A woman and a boy left the Honda and entered the home. Jeanne knew the Hudsons were out of town, but she recognized the Honda because it belonged to the housekeeper. Jeanne was going to a Bible study, or she would have stopped for a chat. Instead, she waved at the pretty young woman and her cute little boy as she pulled from her driveway. The housekeeper was later than usual, but if she were still working after Bible study, Jeanne would take them some homemade chocolate chip cookies. Little boys loved her cookies.

* * *

Two blocks from 27859 Chateaux Lane, one van stopped to unload a dual-sport motorcycle, a machine suitable for on- and off-road use, great for getting in and out of tight spots. Not a fighting vehicle, but perfect for reconnaissance. Plus, it looked nothing like a white van.

* * *

Nigel stood at the galley door. His eyes darted from side to side, but he said nothing. It was as if Nigel searched for something, tilting his head, like a bird trying to hear or see something that was not right.

* * *

As the daylight faded, the first van stationed itself at the intersection nearest 27859 Chateaux Lane. A man named Sanchez drove the van carrying Mitch and Phil Capps to the street in front of the Hudson home. Through the living room window, Mitch could see the flickering blue hue of a television. A figure passed in front of the curtained window, casting the silhouette of a small boy.

He had them.

Sanchez drove to the end of the street, where a third van was in position. Members of the team blocked the sidewalks and handed out candy from heavily laden bags. Sanchez turned around. The quiet street on Brandy Island was about to change.

The van glided along the empty street. Capps shouldered his weapon. He flipped the clear plastic cover away from the firing mechanism. With another stroke of his thumb, he activated the electronic controls, and the weapon came to life, and the green light signified its computerized firing system was operational. Capps nodded to Mitch, who in turn signaled the driver. The van stopped dead still in front of 27859 Chateaux Lane.

***

The Hudsons left several days ago, so cleaning their home required little effort. Maria focused on dusting, a never-ending chore. Despite her desire to finish for the day, Maria felt a strong need to hold her son. Laying her dust cloth on the countertop, she started toward the living room.

***

Five minutes, maybe ten. That's all. His men could take the alien, or whatever he was, alive. Mitch knew they could. No need for rockets here. Mitch realized he wasn't ready to kill the man and boy.

Good God, it's time. He threw the door open, then ducked his head and closed his eyes.

"One away," Capps yelled. The heat and violent rush of hot air told Mitch the missile had begun its irreversible course, and he drove the door closed to protect them from flying debris.

The missile punched through the solid oak doors at 3500 miles per hour. They calibrated the rocket to detonate a split second after impact, causing the explosion to occur in the center of the home.

***

It's amazing how the brain processes information. In her peripheral vision, Maria saw an explosion at the front door. A hundred thoughts burst into her mind. A brilliant white light exploded as she screamed at the top of her lungs.

"Mike!"

Mike never heard his mother's last word.

Not in this life.

***

Flying shards of glass and splinters of wood peppered the van. Mitch felt a wave of super-heated air licking at the van's metal and glass. The small warhead was perfectly placed, and the windows erupted instantly.

The doors resisted a fraction of a second before the dual front doors exploded off their hinges. The concussion from the explosion insured death for anyone in the house, and if the concussion didn't kill them, the fireball that followed did.

Mitch threw the door open again. Capps shouldered his second launcher, its warhead more powerful. Its mission more difficult. The second missile had to destroy the shop and the boat next to it. It seemed like a waste since the targets were clearly in the house, not the shop or the boat, but there was no room for error on this mission. Beckman made that clear.

Black smoke and orange flames hid the shop. Smoke stung Mitch's eyes and burned his lungs.

"Back up," Mitch said, hoping for a clear shot a few yards farther back. His heart pounded in his chest. The cloud of black smoke drifted. Mitch could see the shop and the boat. Their mission would soon be complete.

CHAPTER 31

Wrecker crews cleared the highway faster than Sam expected, but still, too much time had passed. Sam and Karen crested the I-90 overpass just as the sky lit up over Brandy Island. Sam shuddered and felt incredibly old. He glanced at Karen from the corner of his eye, her expression frozen as if cut in a cold stone.

"Oh, my God. That's Tommy, isn't it?" she whispered.

"We don't give up until it's over." Sam tried to sound convincing, but it sure looked over from where he sat. *Well, at least she still has one boy.* He hated himself for the thought. Though he couldn't be sure, he doubted that parents counted children like trophies.

"Tell me he's not gone."

"It's not over. Not yet." Sam didn't believe in God. At least not a God portrayed as an image of an old man with a white beard and his long-haired son. But he believed in a power superior to man. And whatever or whoever that was, Sam offered a prayer that he was telling Karen Parker the truth—that it wasn't over.

*** * ***

Sweat dripped from Mitch's hand. He repositioned his grip on the metal door handle, hot from the heat of the blast. His eyes locked with those of his gunner. An unspoken message passed between them. Pulling the handle, Mitch threw the door open. Then he saw something through the back window. Headlights.

"Son of a bitch! Go! Go! Go!" Mitch screamed. What else could go wrong? The rear tires clawed at the asphalt, spewing gravel. The van fishtailed violently. "What happened to Charlie 3? Goddamn it, they were supposed to be watching."

Mitch was still yelling, but Sanchez shut him out as he drove. Being caught on a black op was unacceptable. Black operations weren't merely top secret. They didn't exist. Getting killed? That was acceptable. Getting caught was not. Sanchez pitched the van sideways, a maneuver he'd practiced enough to make it look easy, and despite the van's reluctance to perform like a sports car, it did just that at his command.

At the intersection, he spun around and drove straight toward the approaching vehicle, blinding them with bright headlights, making identification difficult. His instructors said it would work. He hoped they were right.

The reality of what they were doing covered Sanchez like a cold cloak. *Illegal.* True, the president could issue executive orders to protect the nation and its citizens, but what was the threat here? None that he could see. A thirteen-year-old boy? No threat there. What had this so-called alien done? Sanchez sped straight toward the oncoming car, swerving at the last second. It was full of teenage girls. They weren't a threat, either. In fact, they weren't much older than the boy they had just—killed.

* * *

Tommy hoped he'd see courage in Nigel's face, but Nigel looked terrified. Maybe the explosion was an accident, a gas leak, or something.

"What was that?" Tommy asked.

"I think someone tried to blow us up," Nigel said with wide eyes, his skin pale white. "We should divide."

Tommy cocked his head. "You mean, split?"

"Yeah, let's do that."

"You talked me into it. But where do we go?" Tommy asked, uneasy about leaving the Santa Maria.

"Anywhere but here. The keys to the truck, do you know where they are?"

"In the house," Tommy said in soft resignation, although it seemed there was something he'd forgotten.

"Wait! There's an extra set." Tommy clambered up the narrow stairwell to the old trawler's deck.

Outside, the heat seared his face. He raised his hand as a shield. The smoke stung his eyes and burned his lungs. He coughed. The idea that the Santa Maria was a safe place left him.

* * *

Sanchez pressed the van past fifty miles an hour before reaching the intersection and then realized that Mitch was yelling at him.

"Slow down!" Mitch screamed. Sanchez eased off the accelerator, coasting.

Mitch looked out the rear window. "Turn around."

"We should abort," Sanchez said. "The witnesses."

Mitch narrowed his eyes, staring at Sanchez. "I'm still in charge. Have you forgotten that, soldier?"

"No, sir." Sanchez turned around.

"Go slow." This would be difficult. There must be a way to finish the mission. Mitch was determined to find it and get out of Cleveland before they were caught and tried as terrorists.

★★★

Tommy slipped over the edge of the boat and scrambled down the ladder. He swung from the bottom rung, dropping to the trailer, then over the side and onto the ground. Nigel followed, moving quickly for a grown man. Especially a grown man who was shot hours earlier.

Running toward the cab of the truck, Tommy kicked a wrench that lay on the ground, sending it spinning like a helicopter through the air until it slammed into the side of the shop with a loud bang. Stumbling, Tommy grabbed a trailer tire for support, but the tire wobbled and then fell to the ground.

Tommy paid no attention to the tire as he pawed under the large cylindrical fuel tank that hung from the side of the truck. "Got them," he said, holding up a small magnetic key box.

Nigel stood staring at the tire lying on the ground.

Shit! Tommy looked at the trailer, then back at the tire. "Forget it!" Grabbing Nigel's hand, Tommy pulled him around the fallen wheel. "We don't need it. The trailer has two axles."

"But …" Nigel stopped in his tracks, still staring at the tire, snapping Tommy back like a dog at the end of his chain. "What if we …"

"I said we don't need it," Tommy screamed, dragging Nigel toward the cab. Climbing up the side, Tommy unlocked the door and crawled inside. Nigel followed. "You drive?" Tommy asked.

"Absolutely." Nigel turned the key and waited for the glow plugs to heat the diesel's pre-combustion chambers. The motor started with a loud clatter.

★★★

Rolling along at five miles an hour, Mitch studied the street. "Stop. Right here. There's the boat through those trees. Pull up there." Mitch pointed. "Take your shot out of the back door. Straight through the boat. It'll explode against the shop wall. We'll eliminate both targets with one shot."

★★★

Nigel eased the gearshift back. The gears growled, then the truck lurched and died. "Wrong gear." Nigel leaned toward the gearshift. "Where's first?"

Thick smoke drifted, making it hard to see. Even with the windows rolled up, Nigel coughed. He tried a new gear selection and then restarted the motor, and they crawled forward. The trailer tilted violently as it rolled up and over the fallen wheel. Nigel got the truck pointed down the alley after running over the neighbor's trash cans, then pushed the accelerator to the floor.

* * *

Mitch threw the rear door open.

Phil Capps centered the crosshairs where he'd last seen the boat, but smoke drifted, obscuring the target. He paused, waiting for the smoke to clear, but it didn't. It didn't matter. He was true on the target. "Now!" Mitch shouted.

Capps fired.

It was over.

Mission complete.

PART THREE

CHAPTER 1

When Sam and Karen arrived at 27859 Chateaux Lane, bright orange flames engulfed the once idyllic home. A patrol car and a small red Toyota were parked at the curb. A cluster of teenage girls surrounded the Toyota.

Karen stepped from the car on shaky legs, both hands held to her face. Sam came around the car and put his arm around her. He felt heat from the blaze on his cheeks.

A police officer walked over to send them packing. But Alex arrived and held out his badge, causing the officer to nod and return to his patrol car. Alex joined Jahan and Eric on the other side of the street. Karen and Sam stood alone, staring into the flames.

Sam held Karen as she wept. Clenching his teeth, Sam set his jaw. He didn't care who gave the order. This was crazy. Someone had to pay. Someone would.

The wind shifted again, then shifted back. Smoke engulfed what was left of the shop. Sam stared at the oversized carport. Then he noticed something important.

Eric's phone erupted with a silent yet frenzied vibration. He excused himself and walked to his car.

A man on a motorcycle rode by, turning his head from side to side. He had a video camera mounted on his helmet.

***

Yellow-hued sulfur lamps softly lit the street and quiet homes. As they traveled the residential streets, Tommy surveyed trick-or-treaters moving from house to house and realized he had forgotten that today was Halloween.

"Do you know where we're going?" Tommy's heart had slowed to slightly more than twice its normal rhythm, which seemed lethargic compared to what it was moments earlier.

"I do not."

"We could go to my uncle's cabin across the lake."

"That sounds like a good option," Nigel said in an even tone. "Any idea how we get to the lake?"

"Shit! How would I know?"

"I can appreciate your anger, but your choice of words isn't good." A gentle rebuke compared to what his mother would have said.

"Sorry. I figured I was entitled to some leeway since somebody tried to blow us into a million pieces and then incinerate what was left." Tommy turned his head and said, "Why did you let that happen? What kind of alien are you, anyway?"

"What did you expect? This isn't the movies, kid."

Tommy twisted toward Nigel, waving his arms in grand circles, and said, "What about the hospital? What about the train? How about all the times you've been in my head? Why don't you read minds or something when it counts? You could have started with those guys who tried to kill us?"

"Hey! I'm only human, you know."

"What's that supposed to mean? You mean this is all a mistake? You're not an alien. I almost got killed for no reason? Great! Goddamn great! Sorry."

"I didn't say I was a local. I only said I was human."

Tommy sat quietly. He tried to make sense of what Nigel had said. Nigel turned at the next intersection, pointing the truck toward a distant traffic light. This street had yellow lines painted down the center, and off to the side, a sign read State Park Public Docks.

"I'm confused," Tommy confessed after a few moments. "You talked to me, not really talked—more like ESP, right?"

"And you with me, Tommy. And you with me."

"That's not human," Tommy protested.

"Ah, but it is, Tommy. Think about it. Have you ever thought about something and then your mother or father talked about that very thing? Have you ever shared a thought with someone, though no words were spoken? All part of being human, but you have not developed to your potential."

"And you have? Doesn't that make you different?"

"Are you different from your brother?"

"Yes."

"Yet still brothers?"

"Yes."

"Still humans?"

"Yes, but …"

"Think of me as an improved model."

CHAPTER 2

Some days, things fall into place. There's no logical explanation for it. It's karma. Gary Sessions realized he'd screwed up when he failed to search the boat, but no one knew that, and that was a bit of information he didn't plan on sharing. He didn't notice the boat was missing when he rode by the house at 27859 Chateaux Lane but saw that it was gone when he replayed the video he'd recorded of the scene. Showing up with a video and no boat would be bad. Especially since searching the damn thing was his responsibility.

So, he had started looking for the Santa Maria himself, and there she was lumbering down the road toward him. As the truck rumbled through the intersection, Gary reached inside his jacket and unlatched the strap that secured his 9mm Uzi. The driver didn't glance his way. This would be easy.

CHAPTER 3

Karen stood on wobbly legs, staring into flames that licked the night sky like an evil, fiery serpent. Once there were four Parkers, then three, and now two. She drifted into a trance, watching red and blue lights spin cylindrical beams into the smoke. Firefighters clad in yellow uniforms milled about in the carnival-like atmosphere, stretching fire hoses and squirting water. For what purpose? Karen wasn't sure, certainly not to save the home or its occupants.

***

Alex stepped to AJ's side and then motioned toward Eric, who was still talking on his cell phone. "What do you suppose that is all about?"

Eric appeared to argue, but then his shoulders dropped and he nodded his head.

"His boss is probably wondering where he's been all day. Longest coffee break in FBI history." AJ scratched his chin, then said, "Alex, what do we do now?"

"I don't know. I've tried to avoid thinking about that," Alex admitted.

"Most unfortunate. Poor woman." AJ's voice trailed off as he thought about his wife, Alicia, and how he'd almost lost her two years ago to cancer and how that felt. AJ watched Karen. *How much tragedy can one person bear?* "I'm willing to do anything that might help, but ..." AJ couldn't finish his sentence. He stared blankly into the flames for a few moments, then asked, "Mr. Henry and Karen—they're old friends?"

Alex gave a snort. "Friends? Hardly. They have a history. That much is true. Someday I'll buy you a beer and tell you the story."

"Good. I'd like very much to hear ..." AJ's response was cut short when Eric joined them.

Something wasn't right.

"What's up?" Alex asked, taking a step toward Eric.

"I need to talk to Sam," Eric said, taking a step back. "It's private."

"Mr. Henry!" Eric shouted, waving his arm to gesture Sam over.

Sam looked Karen in the eye and said, "Stay close." Then he added, "Trust me." Karen nodded in shallow commitment.

Sam walked straight into the center of the three men.

"What?" Sam directed his question to Eric Key.

★ ★ ★

At the airport, the first white van rolled up the C-130's ramp and disappeared into a cavernous hole in the tail section, and the second van followed. The flight crew started securing the vehicles, as was their practice. Mitch slid the door open and stepped out. With his hands dug into the small of his back, he stretched, working knots from his muscles. The sounds of slamming doors and groaning men echoed through the aircraft as Unit-11 uncoiled from their respective vehicles. So much sitting wasn't easy for soldiers who spent most of their time alternating between mission exercises and physical training.

Mitch walked to a large vehicle that looked like a moving van, which was precisely what it was designed to be, but now the United States military owned it, and it carried sophisticated electronic gear instead of home appliances and couches.

Brian Walls watched all sorts of data on several monitors. He met Mitch at the van's door. "I've been monitoring the weather. There's a storm brewing up north. It's dumping a shitload of rain over Toronto now. When it collides with warmer air, just about here," Brian held out a folded map and pointed at an imaginary line in the middle of Lake Erie, "we could be in for a bad one. The worst weather will take place over the lake, but it'll hit here with a wallop. I recommend we make preparations to weather the storm unless you think we'll be out of here before it hits."

"We'll be long gone before then. The FBI has taken over dealing with Sam Henry and the others. We'll be in the air soon." Mitch stared at the map for a moment, then turned on his heel and left.

CHAPTER 4

Wellington felt tired and hungry as he and Paul entered a nondescript cafeteria buried several stories below the desert's surface. The site workers fed their captives a late meal consisting of hot soup, warm rolls, meatloaf, and vegetables. A benign meal served on stainless steel trays and plastic flatware. Wellington drank coffee, Paul a cola. Most of the others ate quietly, the room sprinkled with reserved conversations. They had been treated okay. They were allowed to call home but told not to mention their location or the reason for being there. Wellington tried to read the others' minds, but he found only blank faces drawn from fatigue and fear. Each second seemed to draw them closer to each other, like prisoners of war. Wellington watched the symptoms and made mental notes. Their captors were orchestrating this.

It would work on everyone.

Except him.

"I wonder what Mom and Tommy are doing. I hope they're all right," Paul whispered, stirring what was left of his thick vegetable soup.

"They'll be fine," Wellington said with more conviction than he felt. A wave of panic rumbled in his gut. Paul needed strength, not weakness. Hope, not despair. But it wasn't only Karen and Tommy's future that troubled Wellington. It was this place. Despite the designer's efforts, Wellington knew they were buried alive. Then there was the reason they were here. No one was talking about that, and the silence scared him the most. The government had a secret—an alien life form—that was as insidious as the existence of this installation, which Wellington estimated was high on the food chain of government secrets. What lengths would they go to keep these things hidden? He didn't want to know but was confident he was about to find out. He gripped a fork under the table as a shudder passed through his body and breathing became a struggle. A voice in his head screamed. *Run!*

Yet, grasping Paul's hand, Wellington said, "We'll be fine, too." Wellington's panic subsided, and he felt an unusual strength in Paul's small fingers. The feeling wasn't logical, but it wasn't mystical either.

What he felt was the power of love, and he realized it was a feeling he had never truly felt before.

* * *

Eric pointed toward his government-issue sedan. "Mr. Henry, could I talk to you alone?"

"We can talk here."

"Sam," Eric lowered his voice. "This is sensitive information and" he glanced sideways at the others, "it's classified."

"Eric, this is my team. Anything you have to say to me can be said in front of them." While that was not entirely true, Sam thought it was a damn-fine thing to say.

"I can't discuss this here," Eric hissed. This wasn't something Eric wanted to do. Yet, he'd sworn an oath—an oath that now turned to haunt him.

"Great, then it can wait. We have work to do."

Karen eased back about a foot to Sam's left. She studied Alex's face, but seeing nothing there beyond mild confusion, she turned towards Eric. Eric stood like a boxer. His jacket unbuttoned despite a cool breeze.

"Damn it. I don't like this any more than you do," Eric said, as if Sam already knew what was about to happen.

Sam didn't budge.

Sam changed like a chameleon as Karen watched. She'd forgotten his intensity.

"Then don't do it," Sam replied.

"What's going on, Eric?" Alex stepped closer.

Sam looked small compared to the other men. Thus, the dichotomy between what Karen saw and what she felt grew even more incongruent.

Eric cleared his throat and said, "I've been instructed to take Mr. Henry into custody. The order came from the FBI director. It seems that Mr. Henry may be responsible for this." Eric swung his arm in the direction of the blazing home.

Karen gasped.

"I had nothing to do with this," Sam said. "But I can assure you it wasn't an accident."

"No one knew about this place except you. We don't know what you've been doing on that computer. You could have ordered this while we watched you do it." Eric said.

Alex inched closer.

"I'm not the only one who knew," Sam said.

"What do you mean, this wasn't an accident?" Alex interjected.

"Look at the front doors. What do you see?" Sam didn't move. His eyes remained focused on Eric.

"They're blown apart like the windows," Alex said, surveying the fiery structure.

"Look closer."

Alex squinted. "I'll be damned," he whispered. "I didn't see it before."

"What is it you see?" AJ asked.

"The front door, see it?"

"Yes, but …"

Alex pointed at the front doors on the lawn. "There's a hole punched through one of them and they were blown off their hinges. Outward, off their hinges."

Sam felt alone. Paralyzing fatigue crept through his bones. Beckman wanted him isolated from the situation. What would happen if he cooperated? Nothing. They'd make him retire. That wouldn't be so bad, would it? He'd get his full pension, not that he needed it. This wasn't his battle. He'd never asked for it.

Sam tried to banish the fragile remnants of duty that still clung to him like lichen to a weathered rock. In a dark corner of his mind, he thought of Tommy Parker, the son of a woman to whom he owed a debt. Years ago, he set out to right the wrongs of his life, but he'd never gotten around to Karen. Not that he could have done much, except to say he was sorry. It wasn't as if he could have changed anything. What he'd done wasn't illegal or immoral. It was necessary for the service of his country. Yet, he could have felt more compassion for her, and maybe a little compassion would have made a difference. Then again, perhaps not. There was a boy who needed help. At least, Sam believed he still did. Sam had a decision to make. He didn't realize his decision would affect him in ways he could never have imagined.

Sam said, "Eric, I can't go with you. You see …"

Eric cursed. His face flushed red, and his hand disappeared into his jacket. Before his hand reappeared, Sam's right fist struck him once in the center of the abdomen. The air rushed out of his lungs with a great whoosh, and then Sam hit him in the throat. Eric fell to his knees, clutching his throat and emitting a high-pitched wheeze.

Alex pulled his gun, pointing it at Sam's temple. Then, as if by magic, Sam took it from Alex in one fluid motion and forced Alex to the ground by bending his wrist in a direction that nature never intended it to bend. Before AJ could react, Sam pointed the pistol at AJ's forehead. AJ froze, and Eric fought for breath, writhing on the ground. Sam planted Alex's face next to Eric by continuing to apply pressure to Alex's wrist.

Karen inched away, then turned to run, but in a flash, Sam let go of Alex, spun around, and grabbed her. He placed her body between himself and the others, then locked his arm around her neck.

"Alex, pull your back-up out. Then release the clip," Sam said in an even tone.

Alex stared at Sam, but he did as he was told, and the clip clanked to the ground.

"Now, toss it on the lawn," Sam said, adding, "Go to Karen's house. Be careful what you say. The house is bugged. Don't let on that you know anything that has happened here. I'll contact you somehow. AJ, you'll need to help Eric."

Sam backed toward Karen's car, dragging her along. "Don't try anything. I don't want to hurt anyone."

Terror stole from Karen the option of screaming. She couldn't move or think. *Why was he doing this? Oh, God! He killed Tommy, and now he's going to kill me.*

Karen didn't fight, but she didn't cooperate either as Sam pulled her toward the car. Before Sam opened the passenger door, he whispered into her ear.

"Tommy is alive."

CHAPTER 5

Gary Sessions didn't have time to think through his decision on how best to handle the fact that the targets were still alive. He should have contacted his commander, Lieutenant Colonel Mitachavich. But that wasn't his style. Gary was a man born to push the envelope, because that's what got one noticed, and he was about to be noticed.

Sitting by the side of the road, Gary watched the truck's red taillights grow smaller in the distance. He clipped the machine gun to a strap that hung around his neck. If it became necessary to grab the handlebar, he could drop the weapon and allow it to tether on the strap until he was ready to use it again.

With a twist of the throttle, the big single-cylinder motor let out a visceral growl. Gary gently lowered the Uzi until it hung from his neck. Then, with his left hand, he pulled in the clutch and, with a tap of his toe, nudged the transmission into first gear. Accelerating through the first three gears, the motorcycle gobbled up the distance to the target, where he hesitated behind the trailer, mentally rehearsed his hastily concocted plan. Once alongside, the truck could crush him against the cars parked along the street. That would ruin his day.

Gary's plan was simple. He'd pull up beside the truck, and before the driver could react, he'd empty a thirty-round clip of full-metal-jacket 9mm bullets into the cab, then he'd accelerate ahead and watch the impending crash. A second clip would ensure there were no survivors. Then he'd radio his team and tell them how he'd saved the day, before hightailing it out of there.

It was show time.

The motorcycle leaped from behind the trailer, and within seconds, Gary was alongside the cab. The man behind the wheel glanced at him, and then the face of a small boy peered over the man's arms. No doubt, this was the target. Gary twisted the throttle and eased ahead. He took his left hand off the handlebar and gripped his weapon. The cold steel felt good in his hand. He reduced his speed. As he came parallel with the cab, he clicked the safety off. He raised the Uzi, pointing the muzzle at the driver's side door.

***

Alex and AJ remained motionless, watching Karen's Toyota disappear around the corner. The police officers, firefighters, and spectators were so focused on the fire that none of them noticed the fight. AJ went to help Eric. The high-pitched wheezing proved some air was finding its way into Eric's lungs, but his blue lips said it was not enough. By gently massaging the sides of Eric's throat, AJ opened his crushed esophagus.

"Your throat will be tender, but you'll be all right," AJ said as he extended his hand, helping Eric to his feet.

Struggling to stand, Eric nodded and massaged his throat.

"What will we do now?" AJ directed his question to Alex.

Alex said nothing as he retrieved his pistol from the lawn, brushed it off, snapped in the clip, and holstered it. He stood for a moment, staring at the fire. "Damned if I know."

"I say we run the son of a bitch down," Eric said hoarsely, rubbing his chest. "Let's go before he gets away."

Alex didn't answer. Instead, he walked toward the fire like a moth drawn to a flame.

***

Sometimes things are too easy. Gary smiled. All the extra time spent on the range was about to pay off. Firing a machine gun accurately wasn't a simple task. Firing one-handed from a motorcycle traveling at 35 miles an hour was nearly impossible. However, Gary could empty a clip into a two-foot circle, two-handed, one-handed. It didn't matter. Within two seconds of depressing the trigger, thirty rounds would blast into a 24-inch space occupied by the two individuals ordered eliminated by his president, and Gary Sessions wouldn't be a corporal much longer.

The Uzi came to bear on its target. He felt the pressure increase between the tip on his index finger and the trigger. Fifteen pounds of pressure was all he needed to complete his mission.

CHAPTER 6

Tommy watched with fascination, then horror. Entering an uneven intersection forced the motorcycle to slow, drifting back a few yards, then it sped forward again. Tommy screamed, "Go!" But Nigel did nothing, driving straight ahead at the same speed.

"What's wrong with you? Can't you see he has a gun? He's one of them!"

Nigel glanced over and said, "What do you want me to do? Run him down?"

"Duh? Yeah, run him down. Force him off the road. Do something for God's sake."

"I can't do that."

"What do you mean—you can't do that!?! The dude's going to frigging kill us."

"He might get hurt," Nigel said matter of fact.

"He might get hurt! How about me? Maybe new and improved models can heal themselves, but we older versions die when we get shot."

The motorcycle was alongside them again.

"Sorry, Tommy. I can't. I took an oath."

"I didn't." Tommy stomped on Nigel's foot, pushing the accelerator to the floor. The truck inched ahead, but the motorcycle easily matched their speed. The muzzle rose.

"Shit!" Tommy screamed and took his foot off the accelerator. The truck slowed.

Fire leaped from the muzzle of the gun, and bullets punched dime-sized holes across the hood. Smoke swirled up from the motor, coating the windshield with an oily film. Tommy grabbed the wheel from Nigel's hands and swerved toward the motorcycle. The motorcycle jerked left, and an oversized mirror attached to a parked pickup truck caught the rider's shoulder, ripping him from the bike and sending him tumbling along the asphalt like a rag doll.

Tommy fell back across the seat, hands trembling, sweat beading on his forehead. In the rearview mirror, he saw the man stagger to his motorcycle, try to pick it up, only to grab his shoulder and fall to his knees. Tommy collapsed into his seat for a moment, then cranked down the window and promptly threw up.

When he twisted back into his seat, he saw Nigel was driving with his head out the window. The oily film spraying out from under the hood now covered the windshield. How far to the lake? They had to get there. The lake was their only hope.

CHAPTER 7

Eric and AJ glanced at each other, then at the house, then at Alex, who had wandered halfway across the lawn, staring into the smoke. Alex punched his fist into the air and spun around, smiling like a four-year-old on Christmas morning. Apparently, Alex had gone mad.

"Alex?" AJ put his hands on Alex's shoulders. "You okay, buddy?"

"I'm great. God, I can't believe it."

"It's going to be okay, Alex. Why don't we sit here on the curb for a minute? Everything's going to be o-k-a-y," AJ said, his words stringing out like honey dripping from a spoon.

Alex tried to push AJ away, but AJ remained rooted like a tree.

AJ said, "Relax. Breathe in, breathe out. Everything's going to be fine."

"Would you stop treating me like a gawdamn baby? What in the hell's the matter with you?" Alex twisted, freeing himself.

"Don't you understand?" Alex wheeled around with his arm outstretched toward the shop. "See. It's gone."

AJ stared.

Alex said, "The boat. It's gone. Tommy must still be alive!"

"I'll be damned," Eric said, still rubbing his throat. He stepped in front of Alex. "Why didn't Sam tell us?"

"I am thinking we didn't give him a chance," AJ said with a tinge of relief in his voice.

"I guess you're right, Dr. Jahan," Eric said, staring at the spot vacated by the Santa Maria.

Eric turned to Alex. "What do we do now?"

After a moment, Alex said, "We go to headquarters."

"Yours or mine?"

"Karen's," Alex said, adding, "Remember, Sam told us to go there."

AJ and Eric started for the car, but Alex studied the scene. Something wasn't right, but he couldn't figure out what it was. Before, he only saw the flames. Now he saw it more objectively. He was missing something, but his mind was not yet clear. Then he realized. The Honda.

It wasn't there earlier. A taxi brought Tommy and the man here. The Hudson's were out of town, so who owned that car? Alex pulled a small, tattered notebook from his pocket and jotted down the license plate number.

✱✱✱

Karen stared at the passing homes. American soldiers returning from World War II purchased most of them. She concluded that Sam was lost because he was meandering through residential streets. They drove by an old pickup truck like the one her husband had used to ferry tractor fuel. Tears rolled down her cheeks. Sam slowed for an intersection, pausing to look both ways.

Down the street, Karen saw a crowd of people standing near a motorcycle that lay on its side. Sam didn't notice, or if he did, he didn't care. No emergency vehicles meant the accident had just happened.

"Tommy must still be alive. Now, where are they?" Sam asked.

Karen glared at him. *No one could have lived through that blast.* She said nothing. Instead, she closed her eyes and tried to shut it all out. Yet she couldn't. In the blackness of her mind, she saw fire and flames licking the night sky. Then she realized it was what she didn't see that mattered.

Opening her eyes, she turned to Sam and said, "The boat! The boat was gone!"

"That's what I've been trying to tell you."

CHAPTER 8

A loud clatter rose from the damaged engine, and Tommy held the gas pedal down to keep it running while Nigel launched the boat. After tying the boat to the dock, Nigel jumped back into the cab and drove to the center of the parking lot, where the truck lurched and died. They were committed now. It was the lake or nothing.

Bursts of lightning on the horizon marked an approaching storm. The harbor was quiet except for a few people tending to their boats, attaching ropes, and lining the docks with puffy cushions. One man shook his head as he and Nigel boarded the Santa Maria and released her from the pier.

"Did you see the lightning?" Tommy asked.

Nigel studied the controls.

"The lightning. Did you see it?" Tommy asked again.

"Yes, I did." Nigel turned a key, illuminating the instruments.

"Well?"

"Well, what?"

Tommy pointed. "The storm. Maybe we shouldn't go. Too dangerous."

"More dangerous here. At least the storm doesn't want to kill us."

Tommy stared at the distant flashes of lightning. He considered telling Nigel about the Witch of November but did not.

★★★

Blair checked his watch. "Gary should have been back by now."

"Checking your watch every five seconds won't help. Relax, Gary's a good troop," Jack said.

"I don't like it. Something's wrong."

Suddenly, a dead-man alarm sounded. It was a distress signal that could be triggered manually or automatically should the radio lie in the prone position for too long.

"Shit! I told you something was wrong. Get a fix on that signal."

★★★

Edward Powers drained the last of his lukewarm coffee from a Styrofoam cup, then tossed it at the garbage can. It landed on top of a pile of discarded cups and tumbled onto the floor. "Somebody clean that up," Powers barked.

"Why hasn't Mitachavich called?" Beckman demanded.

Beckman had been pacing for the last hour. It was driving Powers nuts.

"Patience, Mr. President. It's always like this: hurry and wait. Either everything happens at once or nothing happens at all. Mitch is top rate. We'll hear from him in good time." Powers turned his back to Beckman and popped an antacid in his mouth.

★ ★ ★

Sam found the water, but a gate blocked entry to the docks. Inside a guard shack, a pimple-faced kid in a uniform stood yakking on the phone. Sam was about to hit the horn for the third time when the kid sidled out the door.

"What's your problem, pop?"

Sam gripped the steering wheel, his knuckles white.

"Has there been a forty-footer named the Santa Maria here within the last hour?" Sam asked calmly.

"Nope."

"You're sure?"

"Nothing has come in all day, what with that storm brewing …" The kid was still talking when Sam stuck the gearshift into reverse and hammered the accelerator.

★ ★ ★

As they idled away from the pier, silky black water stretched out before them, the harbor lights reflecting like tiny diamonds embedded in its surface. The Santa Maria rocked gently, gliding over the invisible swells. Tommy could see a boat here and there in the distance. All coming in, none going out.

Standing on the bow, he absorbed the harbor's beauty and allowed the horrors of earlier events to drift from his mind. His uncle said the water made one feel at peace with the world. Tommy understood what he meant.

Tommy joined Nigel at the helm. "Beautiful, isn't it?"

"Life is a wonderful gift. Remember that." Nigel seemed confident and relaxed. Tommy accepted that as a good sign.

Through a break in the clouds, Tommy saw stars thrown across the sky as if by some ancient god. He wondered if one of them burned near Nigel's home.

CHAPTER 9

Gary stuffed his Uzi under his jacket before the first Good Samaritan arrived and triggered the dead-man switch on his radio before a dozen do-gooders surrounded him. He had tried to stand the bike up but almost passed out. A bad situation. He'd have a hard time explaining the Uzi to the cops. Shit, some rookie might shoot him. In the distance, he saw a set of automobile lights coming toward him. *Here we go.* He still wasn't sure what to do. Being caught was the worst thing that could happen. Killing a police officer was unacceptable. The car lights grew close. Then Gary smiled.

A white van stopped dead in the middle of the road, and three men pushed through the crowd before the helpful men and women of Brandy Island knew what was happening. One guy tried to stop them from taking the motorcycle, only to be knocked to the pavement. After that, the do-gooders backed away. Gary let out a yelp when they pulled him to his feet. They tossed the motorcycle in the back and loaded Gary through the side door. Then the van vanished as quickly as it had appeared.

***

A large green sign read Brandy Island Public Harbor, two miles ahead. An Ohio State access point, which meant no security guard would stand watch at the entrance. In the center of the empty parking lot, under a streetlamp, sat a bright yellow Peterbilt with an empty trailer. The hood riddled with holes and the windshield covered with black oil. Sam stopped near the water's edge. He and Karen stood outside the car. They scanned the harbor. A single boat's light was in the distance.

***

Light rain fell. The windshield wipers slapped a metronomic rhythm. Karen felt numb. Her emotional roller coaster had stalled. Part of her wanted to sleep, part of her wanted to awaken to a Kansas morning with the dew dripping from her roses, and part of her wanted nothing more than to hold her boys. And part of her wanted to understand Sam Henry.

The road flowed out before them and disappeared into blackness. Raindrops on the side windows made it difficult to see. Sam whipped the car through light traffic, turning into a restaurant. Karen and her sister had lunch here last week. Karen asked for a booth in the corner. Dim lights hung from the ceiling on cheap golden chains, and barn-wood-covered half-walls surrounded the booths.

Sam opened his cases, and when the waiter arrived with menus, Sam asked for two glasses of the house wine. The server, a young man with an earring and ponytail, gawked at the computer and small antenna. Sam explained he was doing a sales presentation and would appreciate not being interrupted more than necessary. By the time the waiter returned with two glasses of Merlot, Sam's computer had booted. He took a sip of his wine, then cursed under his breath.

"Better eat something," Sam said. "I don't know when we'll get another chance."

He sounded tired, defeated.

"I'm not hungry, Karen said."

"Hunger has nothing to do with it. We need to eat."

He ordered the chef's salad, and she did the same. He ordered coffee. She had tea.

Sam typed commands and then stopped. He closed his eyes, took a deep breath, and leaned his head back against the booth. He sat with closed eyes as the computer's screen saver began flashing photographs of Earth taken from space. The waiter arrived with their food. Sam slid his laptop to the side.

"Tough day?" the nameless server asked. He wore a Kent State T-shirt under his apron.

"I've had better," Sam replied.

"Will you need anything else?"

"We're fine for now."

"I'll check back."

Sam poured vinaigrette on his salad and stuck a fork full of lettuce and ham in his mouth. He broke off a hunk of crusty bread and handed it to Karen. They ate in silence for several minutes.

"Can you tell me what's wrong?" That sounded stupid. Easier to explain what was right. That would be a much shorter list. Karen sensed that something new plagued her—companion? She didn't know how to think of him.

"They've locked me out."

"I don't understand." She bit into the bread. Crumbs fell into her lap.

"They've locked me off the satellite."

"Who wanted you arrested? The same people who tried to kill Tommy? Who's doing this?"

Sam stared at her, chewing his food. Finally, he said, "The President of the United States."

CHAPTER 10

The security guard at Cleveland Hopkins International Airport had been seeing Digital Telecom vans leave and enter the airport all day, so when the last van arrived, he waved them through the gate, which was good. Otherwise, he might have questioned the wrecked motorcycle and its injured rider. The van raced up the Galaxy's loading ramp faster than typical, jerking to a stop in the center of the cargo bay. The crew chief cursed as the tremor passed beneath his feet. The driver, Corporal Blair Evans, bailed from the vehicle and sprinted toward the communications van and Lt. George Mitachavich.

"We've got a big problem," Blair said as he held out a micro-SD memory card to Mitch. "Gary wrecked the bike and busted his collarbone. He was trying to kill them when he went down."

"Kill who?" Mitch asked as he pressed his fingertips together.

"Them!" Blair held out the memory card.

"Slow down. Them who?"

"The alien and the kid got away in the truck. Gary saw them and tried to complete the mission. That's when he crashed. That alien tried to run over him. Video cam footage is on the card," Blair said, falling into a chair anchored to the floor.

"Shit," Mitch said, sliding the card into a computer port. The monitor flickered blue, then a dark street appeared on the screen. Images blurred as the rider turned his head to check an intersection for traffic. Adjusting to the odd way the video depicted reality took a minute. The camera's digital stabilization reduced, but didn't eliminate, the jittering and jarring, and despite the gadget's sophistication, it fell short of the human brain's ability to eliminate the bumps that occur when viewing the world from a motorcycle. The camera swung back around, and the screen filled with black smoke that rose from a skeletal structure that suggested a home was at the heart of the bright orange flames.

The motorcycle slowed amidst revolving red and blue beams of light that tunneled through billowing smoke, and the camera focused for a few seconds on each of the main characters. Mitch had dossiers on each of them courtesy of the crisis center in Washington, D.C.; a cop named Madden; an FBI agent, Eric Key; Dr. Jahan, CDC; the mother, Karen Parker; and Sam Henry. Mitch only knew them as lifeless little black and white photographs and thin files containing legal statistics, age, address, and social security numbers, but not as mothers, husbands, and fathers. He'd read the files with little interest because he didn't see how they were of much concern to him. Now they seemed like real people.

Sam Henry stood on the sidewalk, his arm around Karen Parker. The camera focused on them for a few seconds before panning to the home at 27859 Chateaux Lane, or what was left of it. For the first time, Mitch saw the results of their attack. For all their training and elitist attitude, what they did differed little from the act of a madman. He thought he might puke.

Then the camera moved again, swinging to the street as Gary Sessions looked to see where he was going. Having determined that he wasn't about to collide with any stationary objects, Gary turned his eyes and the camera back to complete his survey of the target area. It was then that Mitch saw that the boat was, in fact, gone. How? He was staring at the boat when he gave the order to fire, or to be truthful, he was looking at a wall of smoke concealing the boat. It seemed impossible. Maybe the boat was blown away from the building. He hit the rewind button and watched it again, pausing every few frames. No truck, no trailer. They failed.

★★★

Beckman sat alone in the SCC, surrounded by solid walls and thick glass, pondering how to explain that he'd terminated Sam Henry's access to the SECA satellite and removed him from the mission. Sentiment ran deep for Sam Henry. The crisis center staff was entwined in the warp and woof of a legend. *They don't have to like my decision. They just have to follow my orders. Soldiers follow orders, whether or not they like them.*

That's all Beckman knew about soldiers. He didn't trust them. He'd watched their faces, watching him through the thick, soundproof glass that separated him from them.

He liked this room.

The national security advisor, Edward Powers, could enter the SCC, as could the secretary of state and the vice president, but the latter two were out of town. He felt a tinge of anger arise in his mind. He should have never listened when his vice president said they needed a black man on board. Beckman didn't care how many votes that decision garnered him. If he'd known he would end up locked in the same room with the man, he'd never have appointed Powers.

Beckman stewed for a minute, thinking about how he could get rid of Edward Powers when this thing was over, but for now, he had to focus on the issue at hand, Sam Henry. Of one thing, Beckman felt certain: he was much smarter than the uniformed punks in the next room. He'd conned the American people into electing him, and soon he'd have these people convinced he'd done the right thing.

"Can I have your attention?" Beckman keyed the microphone that connected the two rooms. "It has become necessary to remove Sam Henry from this investigation. Mr. Henry has made a series of crucial errors. I have no reason to believe that Sam's mistakes are anything more than that. However, I have decided that his continued presence places the mission at risk. If anyone is to blame, it is me. I placed Sam in this position because I believed in him. Sam Henry has served this country with distinction, but he is no longer suited to fieldwork. His country has asked too much of him already."

Beckman's impromptu speech wasn't perfect. It wasn't even true, but it was good, and he was damn proud of himself. Manipulating these jarheads didn't prove much of a challenge.

CHAPTER 11

Karen ate half of her salad, then pushed it aside. Her appetite waned. First, she believed Tommy was dead, and now he was on a boat with an alien. Her own government was trying to kill him, and she didn't understand why. Well, there was the alien thing. She marveled that yet another level of terror gripped her, and that's why the words she uttered came as a surprise.

"Tell me about Senator Ross's death." She carried the question in her head for fifteen years, chastising herself every day for not digging out the truth and for giving in too quickly.

Sam didn't look at her for several minutes. He pushed an oversized chunk of lettuce around his plate with a fork. When his eyes met hers, she refused to break her gaze. "I can't tell you anymore today than I could fifteen years ago. You must know that."

"What? You can trust me with this?" Karen motioned toward his computer, "but not with something that happened fifteen years ago? Give me a break."

Sam stared out the window, a distant look in his eyes. "You don't want to know."

"Look, that day changed my life. I've lived with this," Karen touched her chest with the fingertips of both her hands, "emptiness for fifteen years. I've lost everything. My husband and now …" Karen swallowed. "Before I lose one more thing, I have to gain something back that you took from me. I need to know why it was so damn important for you to ruin my career." She paused. "Do you know what it's like to look in the mirror for fifteen years at a failure?"

Silence.

"It was a conspiracy, wasn't it?"

"Yes." He sighed, rounded his shoulders, and sank deeper into the booth.

"It was racial, wasn't it? Of course it was. I knew that much. But why the secrets? Because of who was involved? The government? Was it that simple? Those bastards couldn't accept having a Black woman in the presidency, so you killed her."

He didn't look at her. But finally, he said, "You can't report this."

"I understand that."

"Not the government itself," Sam said with remarkable calm. "People in the government, elected officials."

"You protected them. That makes you just as guilty. You let them kill one of the best presidential candidates this country has ever known. Why? Because her skin was a different color, or because she was a woman? Sonsabitches, all of you." She glared at him.

Sam leaned forward. His face remained fixed, yet intense. "Andrea Ross was my friend. Nobody gets to accuse me of being involved in her death."

Frigid silence filled the space between them. Finally, Karen said, "Then why didn't you honor her? Why protect the bastards who robbed her from us?" She understood now that it wasn't only about her. It was a generation, a country, the entire world that suffered a substantial personal loss, and she failed them by giving up. That's why she felt so empty inside.

"I followed orders."

"Orders? Whose orders can be that damn important?"

"Whose orders do you think?"

"Oh, my god! The president? Fuller was in on it?"

"No, he wasn't in on it. Fuller was a good man, and he didn't like it any better than the rest of us. I watched him age ten years in as many days. He made the best decision possible."

"But why the cover-up? You're saying you knew who did it?"

"We knew most of them, all but one. The leader protected himself well. I have my suspicions about who led them, but I can't prove it."

"Who is we?"

"Besides me, President Fuller, two senators, and the man who carried out the executive order."

"What executive order?"

"Let's just say we brought the conspirators to justice. Except the leader."

"You killed them? Judge, jury, and executioners—you people are something else."

Sam didn't react. After a few silent moments, he said, "A man in the field carried out the order, not me. President Fuller had little choice. He had three options." He ticked them off on his fingers. "He could let them go, have them eliminated, or risk civil war. President Fuller wasn't about to let them get away with it. Starting a civil war didn't seem like a good choice either."

Karen thought about that for a moment. Civil war? Was that Sam's attempt at drama or a justification for their illegal acts? "You have little confidence in the American people, don't you?"

"We asked ourselves that question fifteen years ago, and I've mulled it over a thousand times since. The answer is always the same. Think about the climate in the country. After all the strides the country made during the 1960s, people became intolerant of each other. Look at some events that occurred. Rodney King in L.A. and similar events caused riots. After 9-11, we came together for a few years, but then intolerance grew even worse. Consider the Tea Party, and the Occupation Party and the whole populist movement. Consider the reactions when police officers kill unarmed black kids. Outrage over NFL players kneeling during the national anthem in protest of police violence.

"And those events paled compared to the assassination of Andrea Ross. Andrea represented more than hope for the minorities of this country. She embodied equality itself. People loved her, what she stood for, and who she was. She could have shattered the image of minorities as second-class citizens, broken the glass ceiling for women, and put the thieves on Wall Street in prison where they belong. She could have reunited us as a nation.

"The tension between blacks and whites and conservatives and liberals wasn't a natural phenomenon. It was engineered, fostered, and manipulated. Paid individuals, nation-states, and a few media tycoons created conspiracy theories, lies, hate, and intolerance that radicals on the left and right then circulated on social media for free. Certain people couldn't allow Ross to become president if they wanted their agenda to survive. Ross was already pressing for a congressional investigation regarding the creation of the lies that circulated on the web.

"Andrea would have destroyed them. But revealing that plan and the people behind it after her assassination would have plunged us into civil war, not between North and South, but between left and right.

"It would have started like the riots in L.A. except not just one town or a few cities. Some cities would have handled it well at first, but others would have overreacted. Most people would have hidden while protesters clashed with police. But looters would take advantage of the chaos, and then all sorts of groups would have gotten involved. Skinheads, neo-Nazis, the KKK, and similar hate groups would have taken up the cause of white nationals. Police would have been caught in the middle and have proven themselves ill-prepared to handle such tensions in too many instances. Much of the hate had smoldered for years, waiting for oxygen to fuel the fire.

"Someone would have thrown a bottle—someone would have fired a shot. Like pouring gasoline on a fire, it would have whipped into a full-blown urban war across the nation. Intelligence estimated that within five days the killing would have begun in earnest, with no easy way of stopping it. They estimated one million dead in the first year, that was if no enemy nation-state took advantage of the situation. If an enemy got involved, it would have been worse. Best-case scenarios predicted that twenty-five percent of our population would be killed, leaving emotional wounds that would never heal. The United States of America would have been gone. Forever. You think what we did was wrong? Do you think a civil war would have been better? Would Andrea Ross have wanted that as her epitaph?"

The next several minutes passed as silently as the moments before the conversation began. Then Karen asked, "Who's left? Of the people who knew about it?"

"President Fuller is still alive, but he has Alzheimer's. He doesn't even know who he is. Probably a blessing. At least he has some rest. The two senators are dead; the last one died a year ago. That leaves the field agent who carried out the order and me. I don't know if the field agent is alive or dead. I never knew who he was, and I only knew him by his codename."

"So why don't you tell the story now?"

"Do you think the climate has improved?"

"No, but maybe if people knew the truth?"

"You forgot about the last man. The leader."

"You think he's still around? Has some influence?"

"Some is not the word I would have chosen." The muscles rippled along Sam's jaw.

Several silent minutes passed. "They'll track Tommy to your brother-in-law's cabin. We need a place to work—a motel close by. There might be a way to stop the strike team before they get there."

"They may not find them as easy as you think."

"How so?"

"My brother-in-law uses a different name in Canada. Even the mail comes addressed to his Canadian name. Weird, huh?"

"It's more than weird. Only a hand full of people in the world could pull that off for long." Sam rubbed his eyes, then asked, "What's his Canadian name?"

"Dutch Killeen."

"I'll be a son of a bitch. It's true what they say about the world being a small place." He gave his head a slow shake. "To answer your earlier question, two of us who know about the Ross incident are still alive."

CHAPTER 12

The crisis center soldiers whispered and punched at their keyboards, trying to appear busy. Powers popped antacids, drank bitter coffee, and glanced at the row of clocks depicting different time zones. Nevada reported their guests were fed and secured for the night. The psychologists confirmed their predictions that this would be an easy group to deal with. Beckman relaxed after blocking Sam Henry's access to the system and ordering him arrested. Henry should be in FBI custody now, and Secret Service agents were flying to Cleveland to take him and the others to Nevada. Everything seemed to come together, except that Unit-11 had not yet confirmed mission success.

"Incoming message," Cpl. Peck said to Powers. She didn't ask where he and Beckman wanted the call. Beckman was still in the SCC. It became clear that he was going to handle this from his sanctuary, separated from the troops. Powers sat his coffee cup too close to the edge of the counter, and it fell to the floor. He didn't order it cleaned up.

"It's Unit-11, Mr. President," Powers said, ignoring the fact Beckman was talking on the telephone.

"Excellent." Beckman smiled. Finishing his conversation, he said, "I'm about to wrap this up. I'll call back when I'm done."

The pale face of Lieutenant Mitachavich waited on the monitor as Beckman took his seat. Powers stood behind Beckman and peered over his superior's shoulder, realizing that whatever Mitch was about to say wouldn't be good.

"Report, Lieutenant," Beckman barked.

Mitch stared at them as the transmission made its way from Washington to Cleveland. "The plan failed, sir."

"What? Failed! How could it fail? You said it…" Beckman's tirade was interrupted when a pimple-faced soldier grabbed Mitch by the shoulder and whispered in his ear.

"I'll be right back," Mitch said. With that, the screen went black.

Beckman spun around in the high-backed leather chair, glaring at Powers. "Who in the hell does he think he is!?! I'm the President, for Christ's sake!"

*** *** ***

Mitch whirled around to another monitor. He saw people milling about in Karen's home: Madden, Jahan, and Key.

"What in the hell are they doing there? Do we have sound on this?" Mitch punched at buttons and twisted knobs. The images disappeared. The kid reached over Mitch's shoulder to operate the controls, and soon the monitors refilled with the scenes from Karen's home, this time with the sound of voices. Madden was talking on the phone and writing on a small tablet. Hanging up the phone, Madden turned to Key. "Maria Esperanza. That's who it's registered to."

"Who is Esperanza?" Eric asked.

"Don't know. We're checking."

Mitch spun around in his chair. "What are they talking about?"

On the opposite side of the van, Sgt. Perry Gorgons hovered over his own computer, analyzing the video taken by Gary Sessions' helmet-cam. "This."

Mitch sprang to his feet. "What?"

"Here, sir. See this Honda car in the drive? I ran the plate. It belongs to Maria Esperanza. I think maybe she was in the home."

Mitch lost his balance and fell into his chair. *Who was Maria Esperanza? What was she doing there?*

Then he realized.

"Where's Sam Henry?"

CHAPTER 13

Sam fell into a trance, so Karen walked outside. She needed time to think. Her brain had locked up like a computer running too many programs. The thought of how self-centered she'd been haunted her. For fifteen years, she believed her failings in the Ross investigation were about her. For fifteen years, she'd blamed Sam, a man who lost a good friend and carried a dark secret for his country. For fifteen years, all she'd thought about was herself and her career.

She sat on the trunk of her car, her arms folded across her chest, gusts of wind buffeting her face. After ten minutes the breeze chilled her, so she slid off the trunk and walked back inside. On the undercarriage of her car, a small round disk held tight by its powerful magnet transmitted a silent signal.

* * *

Sgt. Gorgons studied a map of Cleveland on the monitor as his computer searched for a signal. When located, the signal appeared as a pinpoint of light on a map of Cleveland and was less than five miles away. The computer's global-positioning software calculated the quickest route from Unit-11's current position to Sam Henry.

On the other side of the communications van, Mitch punched at his keyboard, and the face of an angry president returned. Less than three minutes had elapsed, but to Mitch, it felt like it had been hours.

"Sorry, sir."

"You'd better damn well be sorry. I should have your sorry ass busted back to private. Who in the hell do you think you're talking to? I'm the goddamn president!"

Mitch had had his ass chewed before, and it didn't bother him as it would a civilian. Still, he was beginning to dislike this man on a personal level. Mitch held up his hand. "I apologize, but we have big trouble here."

"For God's sake, Lieutenant, I heard you the first time."

"It got worse." Mitch needed time to think this through. He needed a strategy, but what concerned him was that he'd get one from the man on his monitor.

"Let's start over, shall we? What in the hell are you talking about?" Beckman started in a whisper, then built to a thundering crescendo.

"Okay. We hit the house. Perfect shot. Nothing lived through that." Mitch's muscles gave a slight shiver. "But before we could hit the shop, a car showed up. We had to evacuate the area. When we returned, the boat was still there. We fired a second rocket."

"That doesn't sound so bad." Beckman leaned back in his chair.

"That's what we thought." Mitch rubbed his eyes, then sighed. "Our surveillance man went back to record the scene on video. The truck and boat were gone. They must have pulled out as our shot was fired. Anyway, our surveillance man searched the area, found them, and was about to complete the mission when he wrecked his motorcycle. He's broken his collarbone. He needs medical attention."

"I can't be bothered with his damn collarbone," Beckman said with a wave of his hand. "Where did they go? You must stop them. Do you hear me?"

"It gets worse. We may have killed a civilian at the Hudson home."

Beckman stroked his chin for a moment and said, "I can't worry about that either. I'll get the spin doctors working on it. Terrorist attack. Right? Now, where are the alien and kid?"

"We don't know. They may be on the lake."

"So, find them. What do we give you all that goddamn equipment for? Shit. Do I have to do all the thinking around here?"

I thought that was what we paid you for, Mitch thought but didn't say. "That's not all. The officers with Henry are at the Parker woman's house. Sam's not with them."

"He's probably at FBI headquarters."

"Maybe. But we don't think so. Key, Madden, and Jahan are there, but the Parker woman is not there either."

"Key was supposed to arrest Sam Henry." Beckman paused, thinking. "You think the Parker woman is with Sam Henry?"

"That's my guess."

"Get them. I want all of them neutralized at all costs," Beckman growled.

"All of them?" Mitch asked.

"Every goddamn one of them. Use whatever force is necessary. That includes Henry. Get that woman too. She knows too much. Shit, they all know too much." Beckman paused and leaned into the camera. "Lieutenant, don't screw this up. Do you understand me?"

"Yes, sir."

The monitor went black. Mitch turned to Gorgons and said, "Find Sam Henry."

Gorgons tapped his computer screen with his thick index finger. "I already have."

Mitch rolled over in his chair and looked at the screen. "Tell the men to suit up."

Gorgons hesitated for a moment with his hands on his knees, then stared his commander in the eye and said, "Mitch, I don't like it. Something's not right. You know, bad karma or something."

Mitch nodded his head and pursed his lips. "We don't get paid to like it, Sergeant. We get paid to follow orders, and we get court marshaled when we don't. Karma has nothing to do with it. Let's rock and roll."

CHAPTER 14

Mitch paced around the communications van while his staff searched for George Hudson's boat. However, according to official records, George Hudson, 27859 Chateaux Lane, didn't own a boat. Nor did he own a car, truck, or house. Hudson didn't own nor do much of anything, including exist. A corporation that was more like a mirage than a real company held the title to the home on Brandy Island. George Hudson had no police record, no passport, no driver's license, and no social security number.

The trail on Mrs. Hudson wasn't any better. No credit cards, no mortgage, no car payments, no telephone, and electronic transfers from an offshore bank account paid the utility bills. As near as Mitch could tell, neither George Hudson nor his wife had ever walked the planet. Mitch wondered if he'd stumbled across an underworld figure or CIA operative.

Although Hudson wasn't Mitch's concern, he hoped to find some inkling of the Santa Maria's destination. A file lay open on the desk, but he didn't want to look at it. The poor quality of the photograph couldn't conceal the beauty of Maria Esperanza. He regretted asking who she was, and he regretted knowing of her son, Mike. Mitch believed mother and son were the collateral damage of their mission. This was Sam Henry's fault. It was that alien's fault. Mitch gritted his teeth and paced.

★ ★ ★

Karen walked back into the café and to the booth where she and Sam had eaten dinner. Sam sat still, his eyes closed, his breathing deep, and his hands forming a steeple on the edge of the table. Karen stood watching him. He hadn't opened his eyes since she entered the restaurant. She remained silent.

"Are you going to stand there all day?"

"How did you know I was here?"

He didn't answer.

She sat next to him and felt at ease, but she didn't understand why. Sam opened his eyes. "What do we do now?" she asked.

"What do you suggest?"

Her peaceful moment ended. "You're the secret agent. Remember?"

He looked into her eyes. "I'm not a secret agent. What would you do if you were me?"

"Shit, I'm the ditsy reporter who wasted fifteen years, feeling sorry for herself because I was too stupid to get a grip on reality. And you're asking me what I would do?"

"Yes." He stared at her in awkward silence.

She closed her eyes, then after a few moments opened them. "Why was it so important that you connect with that satellite?"

"It's powerful."

"But you can't link with it because you're locked out?" Karen thought aloud. "If you got in, would it make a difference?"

Sam nodded.

"But you can't? Get back in, that is."

"It's possible."

"Then what are you waiting for?" Karen leaned across the table and slid the computer in front of him.

"It would mean hacking into a top-secret government system. That would be treason. As it is, they want me off this case enough to order the FBI to arrest me, but they can't charge me with anything. They might force me to retire. That's about all they could do. But treason—that's a different story. An act like that would place us in great danger."

Karen nodded and lowered her head. She didn't expect Sam to commit treason against the country he'd vowed to serve. Tommy was her son, not his. She wouldn't ask him to ruin his life for her or Tommy. She had to do this herself. She'd take her best shot. The only weapon she knew was the media or perhaps rent a boat and go after them herself. Whatever she did, she had to live with the consequences. Sam did not.

"I understand. If I get this into the media, perhaps I can change something. Or maybe I can rent a boat and go after them myself. Thank you for all that you've done, but this is my fight, not yours."

"You would risk going to prison or even death?"

"Yes."

"You're sure?"

Karen nodded.

"The risk I was unwilling to take was for you, not for me."

"Tommy is my son." Tears welled in her eyes. "I'll do anything to save him."

Sam studied her face for a moment. "Remember what you just said."

CHAPTER 15

Mitachavich studied their hastily concocted tactical plan. One target was easy, the other was not. A team of five men would handle target A: Madden, Key, and Jahan. The second team of four would handle target B: Henry and Parker. Henry and Parker couldn't be taken at their present location. Mitch had to wait until target B left the café.

Mitch was less confident about handling target B for one reason: Sam Henry. Still, he believed they could secure both targets with no shots fired. Beckman said eliminate them, but Mitch didn't plan to kill them. He'd leave that to Beckman. Surely if they were secured, Beckman would just send them to Nevada with the others.

Then there was a third problem, floating somewhere on Lake Erie. Unfortunately, he didn't see a way to simply capture them. Mitch looked up from the assault plans. "When will we have a satellite over the lake?"

Clicking his mouse, Sgt. Gorgons navigated through several screens on his computer. "Two hours, sir. Lake Erie is not an area we monitor."

"How about the Coast Guard?"

"Did you forget? We're on our own. Nobody knows we are here."

"Shit!" Mitch handed the tactical plans to Gorgons. "Contact the crisis center for me."

***

"Damn. There it goes again." Eric looked at his phone. "What am I supposed to do? The director keeps calling."

"Don't worry," Alex said from the kitchen counter. "You didn't get the call because your battery went dead. Simple."

"But my battery isn't dead." Eric stood and started pacing.

Alex set three mugs of steaming coffee on the table and held out his hand. "Let me see your phone. Cream, sugar?"

"Black." Eric handed Alex his phone and slumped back down in his chair. "Shit."

"If Sam and Karen get caught, Tommy doesn't have a prayer. We have to stay together on this. Agreed?" Around the kitchen table, heads nodded.

Alex turned on Eric's phone flashlight, started a video recording, turned on music from his playlist, and sat it on the table.

★★★

Sam entered a series of commands that awoke encrypted files hidden in the heart of his computer. Programmers relied on the software code to do what computers are, by nature, supposed to do—tell the truth. However, Sam's computer held a little secret, and when asked about hidden files, it lied. It lied to everyone, except Sam Henry and the teenage prodigy who developed the clandestine software.

When he started on the SECA project, Sam thought it an absurd contradiction that the country's most tightly held secrets had been entrusted to an unproven computer programmer embodied in nineteen-year-old Terri Wilson, involved only because of her sheer genius. Sam's fear was well-founded because, as it turned out, Terri Wilson compromised the system, implanting a covert program within Sam's laptop and the satellite's solid-state hard drives. It was their little secret. Sam trusted Terri with his life. An act that helped him appreciate the capriciousness of human loyalties.

The screen turned black and, for several seconds, looked as if it were dead. That was part of the code. Push any button during this period, and the computer aborted its clandestine mission. Color returned to the screen and allowed two options: text or interface. Sam hesitated, glanced around, and then selected the interface. Another password was required. Then the face of a young girl appeared: Terri Wilson.

"Hello, Sam!" Terri's smile was bright. Her spirit seemed to soar even on the small, flat screen.

As Terri continued, the video window became smaller and moved to the upper left-hand corner. Her voice was tinny, coming from the small speakers. "Either you're in big trouble or you miss me. Since I'm much more personable in the flesh, you must be in trouble. Well, that's why I'm here, isn't it? How may I be of assistance, Captain?" She took to calling him Captain. Sam didn't know why; she just did.

Entering a series of commands, he directed the computer to override the SECA security system.

Virtual Terri lost her smile. "Wow! This is serious shit, Sam. Are you certain?" Sam smiled. He'd not opened this program before, so he didn't know what to expect. A series of little yellow smiley faces replaced the standard Windows icons.

The dissimilarities of this program ran deeper than whimsical icons. It was written in a computer language unknown to all but Terri. She had written most of the new language before her 16th birthday, one year before she entered MIT, two years before she met Sam Henry. She never shared her program with anyone, knowing that someday, when the timing was right, it would make her rich. But that day would never come. Because instead of selling it, she used it to protect the man who became the closest thing to a real parent she'd ever known, and she became the closest thing to a friend that Sam had ever encountered. He moved the mouse to *"you bet"* and clicked once.

Dead serious, Terri asked. "Are you really really sure you want to go there?" One last chance to reconsider what he was about to do, but Sam didn't find the decision difficult. He just placed Terri in Tommy's situation and asked himself what he'd do. Easy answer.

"As sure as I'm going to get," read the icon that Sam selected. He appreciated her sense of humor but wondered if she realized the magnitude of what she'd done with her little software program.

He glanced at Karen. She gave his arm a squeeze. He hit enter.

CHAPTER 16

Fatigue and boredom became the enemy. Coffee was drunk, candy bars were eaten, and stretching and fidgeting broke out like a plague. Invisible umbilical cords tied the crisis center soldiers to their stations. Rumors and speculations coursed through the room in shallow whispers and superficial facts. Hard data became scarce and coveted. As ears strained at floating whispers, Cpl. Peck announced yet another message from Unit-11.

Mitch explained the situation and the corresponding tactical plan to Beckman and Powers.

"Do you think it will work?" Beckman wrung his hands as he spoke.

"Target A shouldn't be a problem. Those men are tired. We have the advantage, firepower, and surprise. They'll give us no trouble. Target B is more difficult. We still have the element of surprise, but Sam Henry should not be underestimated."

"Lieutenant, I don't want excuses. I want Sam Henry neutralized. Do whatever it takes to make that happen." Beckman leaned into the miniature camera, creating a comical fishbowl effect on Mitch's screen.

Mitch squirmed in his chair. "I'm a little foggy on neutralized and whatever it takes. With all due respect, sir, there are no guarantees in field operations."

"I don't care if you have to blow up the entire fucking block. I want those people eliminated, and I want that alien bastard eradicated. Is that clear enough for you?"

Just out of the camera's view, Mitch attempted to strangle his cap, but his face remained indifferent. "Sir, how do you want me to proceed if we have to abort?"

"Abort! I don't want any fu…"

***

The thing about computers is that, despite their sophistication, they are just mindless machines. They don't make value judgments. They just do what they're told. That's what the computer on the SECA satellite did. Beckman's last words reached the SECA antenna a split second after they were fired from the massive parabolic dish mounted atop the Old Executive Office Building. But when they arrived, the SECA was nothing more than a dead hunk of space debris that ignored Beckman's words as they continued into infinity.

SECA CONNECTION TERMINATED was the simple message displayed on Cpl. Peck's computer screen. Lieutenant Jamison, the crisis center technical supervisor, leaned over Peck's shoulder, studying her monitor for a moment. Then he announced over the intercom, "Mr. President, we've lost the bird."

"Say again?" Beckman stood, peering through the bulletproof glass.

"It's gone, sir. The SECA satellite."

"Well, get it back!"

CHAPTER 17

The waiter returned with coffee, only to be shooed away. Sam studied the screen, then nodded his head in approval.

"Done. Now, they're locked out." Sam smiled. "That might piss them off."

***

Mitch watched the blank monitor. Beckman's image had disappeared in mid-sentence. Gorgons fiddled with knobs and switches, but the signal was gone, and the SECA satellite was dead, but Mitch had orders, and the only thing stopping him was fear. And fear wasn't part of the deal.

***

Everyone in the crisis center suddenly felt the stress they should have felt all along. Tension grated against their nerves like chalk screeching on a blackboard, emanating from the senior staff and trickling down to the lowest technician, and no one was immune. Beckman paced and cursed. Possibly the magnitude of the situation finally sank in, or perhaps the political implications, should things go badly, had come into focus.

None was more aware of the precariousness of the situation than Mary Price, who inherited Beckman's attention because of her position. One of the few civilians in the room, young for such a station at twenty-three, she looked eighteen. Her long blond hair cascaded around a cover-girl face set with deep blue eyes. Blond jokes and illicit proposals were common, and she was an expert at fending them off. She was on call, and when the situation began, she didn't have time to go home and change clothes; wearing shorts and an MIT t-shirt, Mary prayed she would go unnoticed. She believed her situation—coming in dressed in casual clothing—couldn't have gotten much worse. But it did. She was the SECA technician, and Beckman hovered over her as she tried to reestablish contact with the SECA satellite.

"What happened to it?" Beckman asked for the umpteenth time.

"Still working on it, sir." *And I'd be working a lot faster if you'd get off my ass,* she thought.

"Why can't you tell me what the hell happened to it? Is that too much to ask? What in God's name do we pay you people for?" Beckman proved unaccustomed to not getting his way. When Richard Beckman wanted answers, he got answers, even if they were incorrect, or on many occasions, outright lies.

Mary, however, was not well versed in politicalese, and while twisting the truth might be a prerequisite for those higher up the food chain, it was an alien concept to a technician who valued facts and data.

"It's not that easy. It would be easy if the damn thing would talk to me, but it won't. Some data is still being fed to other receptacles, but SECA isn't having squat to do with us."

"Use my code. It would be programmed not to reject my code. Right?" Beckman thought he possessed magical power over everything, especially a piece of government hardware.

"Sir, you don't have a code. The only code is the one from this room. SECA won't talk to us. She doesn't respond to the code."

Beckman's face turned deep red.

Edward Powers suppressed a smile as he watched Beckman come within a sliver of losing his composure. Sensing the need to intercede before Beckman blew a fuse, disrupting the concentration of the most vital technician in the room, Powers asked, "Mary? What *can* you tell us?"

Mary drew a long breath and rocked back in her chair, appreciative of Powers' intervention. Maybe Beckman could learn something from observation.

"She's not dead. That's all I know. She," SECA was—a she—to Mary, "continues to transmit data, and that data seems okay."

"What data?" Powers asked for Beckman's benefit.

"Inconsequential stuff. Weather, upper atmosphere data, radiation measurements, ozone layer monitoring. Like I said, nonessential information."

"But that information is accurate?"

"Yes, that information is fine. No compromises at all."

"What does that mean?" Powers gave Mary the opportunity to work through the information so Beckman could understand.

"It shows no damage. If the computer system were failing or if a foreign object had damaged SECA, then we'd expect to see a deterioration in the data. Since that information isn't corrupted, we can rule out structural damage, software, and hardware problems."

"Could the problem be in its transmitter or receiver?" Beckman asked.

To Mary's surprise, it was a valid question—rudimentary but valid. She just said there was no damage to the hardware but figured that was beyond Beckman's comprehension. "She's communicating with other predestined sources. That communication is two-way. The transmitter and receiver are fine."

"So, what's your best estimate?" Powers asked.

"Someone has locked us out."

"Sam Henry?" Powers asked the question.

"Could be. Might be someone here, might be aliens." Mary paused. "Henry, most likely."

"Why isn't he in custody? I ordered him arrested. Can't anyone do anything right?" Beckman asked no one in particular.

Powers looked at Beckman. "Don't underestimate Sam Henry."

Beckman turned to Powers. "Get the director of the FBI on a secure line. This makes no sense."

***

Frank Patterson, Director of the FBI, paced the length of his office, praying that the phone would ring. When it did, the caller ID indicated it was the call he dreaded, not the one he wanted. Richard Beckman was on the other end of the line, demanding answers Frank didn't have.

"Hello, Mr. President?" Patterson had rehearsed his lines at least a hundred times during the last 20 minutes. Now he couldn't remember a single word he planned to say.

"Frank, is Sam Henry in custody?" Beckman snarled.

"Mr. President, well, the fact is, I don't know."

"You don't know? What do you mean, you don't know? Wasn't Henry within a few yards of your agent? Isn't that what you told me? Damn it, Patterson, I want answers."

"Yes, sir," Patterson muttered.

Beckman stood in the command center with his hand pinching the bridge of his nose and his eyes closed in consternation, feeling the examining eyes of the staff on his back.

"Sorry, Frank. We're—I'm a little stressed. Tell me what's happening."

"No apology necessary," the director lied. "I gave Agent Key the order. I've called him a dozen times, but …"

Beckman interrupted. "Okay, so you think Henry is in custody?"

"Well, yes, I have no reason to think otherwise." Frank crossed his fingers.

"Great. Let me know when you hear something." Beckman tried to make sense of the puzzle before him. He couldn't tell Patterson that his agent, Eric Key, was drinking coffee at Karen Parker's home, because Patterson would wonder how Beckman knew that. What was Key doing at Karen Parker's home? Why didn't he report in? Possibly Key deposited Sam Henry at a local jail, but if Sam Henry was secured, why didn't Patterson know?

Patterson said, "I will. Mr. President, can you tell me what this is about?"

"All in good time, Frank, all in good time."

Beckman knew his temper got away from him, but he made a nice recovery. On the bright side, everyone in the room knew he was not to be trifled with and thinking that to be a correct principle gave Beckman an unearned sense of satisfaction. He was ready to move ahead. In his own mind, Beckman found the three men at Karen Parker's home guilty of treason. For a fleeting moment, he had wondered if his orders to Unit-11 were too severe. Now, he had good reason for killing those men, Sam Henry, and that Parker woman, too.

Unit-11 must find that boat and shred it into small pieces, and this little problem will go away and disappear forever. That meant the boy too, maybe the only innocent one in the entire affair—but there was nothing Beckman could do about that.

CHAPTER 18

Karen leaned close to Sam's computer. Her kitchen appeared on the screen, with Alex and AJ sitting at her kitchen table holding coffee cups. Sam pushed a position key, and her living room appeared. Eric wasn't there. Probably in the bathroom, and she hoped Sam didn't check on him there. Sam clicked to another screen, and a map appeared with a web of glowing blue lines that looked like streets. Two red dots moved along the glowing lines toward green dots, one marked **T-A**, the other **T-B**.

Sam grunted and tapped a key. The kitchen reappeared. At the top of the screen, Karen read, **s:\@T-A**. T-A was her home.

Another keystroke and the glowing map reappeared. There was a green dot at her home. One red dot moved toward her home and then stopped close by. There was a green dot near **T-B** and a red dot moving towards that location as well. He tapped the keyboard and screen changed, causing a row of files to appear. Sam highlighted **s:\@T-B\image** and tapped *enter*. A grainy overhead photograph of a dimly lit parking lot appeared, and at the curb sat Karen's Toyota. Sam switched back to the scene of Karen's brownstone.

Something was about to happen, and Karen didn't think it would be good.

★★★

AJ and Alex moved to the living room, surfing television stations for news that might be related to Tommy. Eric was still in the bathroom. Alex flipped through channels. AJ drained his coffee cup and then went to the kitchen. He didn't bother turning on the light and walked straight to the coffeepot. AJ noticed something moving in the alley. Two men with rifles. He felt as if his heart had stopped.

The sound of breaking glass and splintering wood startled AJ. Cursing and yelling erupted in the living room. AJ eased to the opening leading to the living room. He could see part of the living room and the hallway that led to the bedrooms and bath. A man clothed in black battle fatigues was pointing an M-4 at Alex's head. Alex had raised his hands.

A second man swept his rifle from side to side. *What in the hell?* AJ wondered.

Eric appeared in the hallway, water dripping from his face onto his shirt. His weapon was clearly visible. The second intruder shifted his rifle toward Eric. *"Down, down, down!"* The man screamed.

Before Eric could comply, a three-round burst from the M-4 exploded the center of Eric's chest.

AJ drew back into the darkness, his head reeling. He spun on his heel toward the back door, his heart pounding, and his entire body trembling. AJ knew how to fight. He'd learned that during his three years in the Marines. Although he joined to serve as a doctor, learning the basics wasn't optional. However, that's not where he learned the skill he was about to use.

Football players learn specific methods for controlling their energy, particularly linemen who learn to explode, focusing every ounce of their strength in a single, instantaneous blow. He who masters the skill—wins, and each snap of the ball begins a new battle. A few years ago, AJ could knock a three-hundred-pound offensive tackle on his butt. This snap would be a mismatch of grand proportions.

The back door flew open, propelled by the kick of a well-trained Army Ranger. However, his black uniform had no insignias to establish his U.S. Army status. But, fighting machine though he was, he only weighed 160 pounds and had no more than stepped through the door when an explosion of a different type met him. AJ's timing proved flawless. The man flew fifteen feet, clearing the back steps, and then fell eight feet and landed on his partner.

AJ's explosive blow dislodged the man's weapon, sending it tumbling through the air. AJ grabbed the M-4 on its descent without breaking stride. He hit the stairs running, reaching the bottom as the man pulled a ten-inch survival knife with a gleaming serrated blade. With one smooth motion, AJ butt-stroked him between the eyes. The force of the blow drove the man to the ground. His head bounced off the pavement, and he lay still. Without hesitation AJ spun, butt-stroking the second man on the side of his face. AJ heard the man's jawbone shatter, and the man hit the ground and did not move.

AJ eased up the stairs, pausing where the faint light of a streetlamp allowed him to examine his newly acquired weapon. He found the safety and the switch that converted the weapon to three-round burst. He glided through the kitchen toward the living room. Easing onto his belly, AJ inched forward.

Holy fucking shit.

Through the doorway, AJ saw two men, both holding black rifles like the one in his hands. Alex was still alive, sitting on the couch with his hands raised, but the speed with which they killed Eric left little room for thinking this could be resolved peacefully.

Were there more of these bastards? Probably. AJ leveled the rifle's sights at one man's knees and depressed the trigger. The rifle jumped in his hands. He aimed at the other man's legs and did the same. Both men fell to the floor. One man emptied his weapon into the ceiling, but Alex leaped on him before he could reload. AJ found himself in the living room before he realized he was moving. He kicked the second man's rifle away and then butt-stroked him in the side of the head to keep him down. AJ had no idea how many rounds he'd fired. He removed the clip—actually, two clips taped together in opposite directions—and slammed the fresh clip home, then switched the gun to full auto. This was no time to be frugal.

AJ eased to the door. A white Digital Telecom van was parked across the street. A streetlight illuminated the driver, who was peering through a pair of night goggles. *Shit.*

AJ aimed at the van's front tire and pulled the trigger.

While most men had trouble with a rifle on fully automatic climbing as it fired, AJ had no such problem. The sinister M-4 looked like a toy in his massive hands. The room filled with smoke, flying brass, and deafening noise as AJ held the gun on target and emptied the clip. The metal-piercing rounds shredded the tire and riddled the fender. Steam boiled from the front of the van.

The van's sliding door slid open.

AJ saw a rocket launcher aimed right at him.

"Run!" AJ screamed at Alex.

CHAPTER 19

Outside a row of brownstone homes on an otherwise quiet street, bullets ripped through the night and pierced the sheet metal of a white Chevy van, barely missing George Mitachavich's foot. Mitch scrambled into the back of the van, his mind reeling, having believed that two tired cops and a doctor would surrender without a struggle. He grabbed the Russian-made missile launcher he had made ready before the team engaged the target. Mitch could not imagine Unit-11 being defeated by anyone, especially a handful of old doughnut eaters. The unimaginable had become reality.

When the rifle fire stopped, Mitch threw the door open, took aim at the brownstone, and touched the trigger, sending a missile on its way. A ball of flame erupted. This time, no one got away, including his own men, if they were still alive. Too bad about the cops, but they started it. He placed a black metal canister, the size of a large Mason jar, in the center of the van and pulled a pin from the canister's top. He put on a Digital Telecom cap, stepped outside, slid the van door shut, and zipped his jacket against the breeze. By now, people were watching, hidden behind curtains and shades. The evidence that Unit-11 was here needed to go away, and it did in a ball of fire that soared into the night sky. Mitch couldn't be here when the cops showed up, so he walked two blocks and then ran, glancing over his shoulder, twice changing directions. When he eased to a casual stroll, no one was following him.

★ ★ ★

Sitting in a dark corner of a nearby restaurant, Sam and Karen watched the bloody scene until the screen flared orange and then black. They saw the bullets riddle Eric Key's chest. Karen felt the color drain from her face. A shiver crept up her spine. In her mind's eye, she saw the image of her Toyota sitting in the parking lot and understood the meaning of the screen. Its glowing blue lines and red and green dots. She forced her eyes from the screen to Sam's face. There, she saw something different from what she felt.

"Bastards." Sam hissed as he clicked to a different screen. The map appeared. Their enemies had arrived.

CHAPTER 20

The image of Eric's chest rupturing red refused to leave Karen's mind. The gun battle that followed happened fast, and the smoke from the weapons clouded the video, making it difficult to see who had lived and who did not. Sam's laptop screen displayed the map again. The green and red dots still glowed. Then one red dot disappeared. That meant something happened to the enemy's vehicle. Then the green dot started moving. Karen prayed Alex was driving the car the green dot represented.

Karen wondered if they were safe in the restaurant.

Sam handed her a business card with the name Terri scrawled on the back. "Wait here. If anything happens to me, call this number. Tell Terri we're friends. She'll help you. Don't trust anyone else."

Sliding a crisp one-hundred-dollar bill under the check, Sam beckoned the waiter. "You can keep the change if you'll do me a favor. I need a cigarette and matches and then point me toward the backdoor."

The waiter fished a crumpled pack of cigarettes and matches from his pocket, handing them to Sam, and said, "The backdoor is through the kitchen, but you're not supposed ..."

Sam was already halfway across the room.

* * *

An old growth of knotted juniper bushes covered the wall facing the parking lot. Sam spotted a man hiding there. Probably military-trained but dressed in workingman's clothing. How many others were concealed nearby? Sam didn't know who he was fighting or how good they were. He no longer knew how good he was. *One in the bushes, one waiting with their vehicle—that's two. Probably two more.* That sounded right. Sam lit a cigarette and walked around to the back of the building. A large trash receptacle offered the only concealment.

Hiding from me, are you? How good are you, my friend? Sam flipped the cigarette over the far edge of the trash bin. Bright sparks trailed the spinning butt, which disappeared on the far side of the trash bin, then shot straight out as if it had been flicked off a person's head.

You wouldn't live long in the jungle, son.

Closing his eyes, Sam emptied his mind, breathing in, breathing out. Then he flipped the collar of his jacket around his neck as if to protect himself from the cold. He took a few steps along the large trash bin, keeping his back to the man hidden in the shadows. The hidden man lunged at Sam's back just as Sam spun with a kick, smacking the man's jaw with a sharp crack. The assailant wilted to the ground.

That's one.

★ ★ ★

Tommy watched darkness swallow the city lights as the Santa Maria left the harbor. In the galley, he found the sodas and candy bars they stashed during his first trip across Lake Erie. Nigel smiled when Tommy entered the cabin, holding a soda and a candy bar.

"I see you can read minds." Nigel popped the top, taking a long drink, holding the wheel with his other hand. "Maybe you could help." Nigel nodded to the wheel, held up his soda, and pointed at the candy bar.

"Sure." Tommy took the wheel. It almost spun out of his hands.

"Hold on tight," Nigel said, pulling the candy bar from between Tommy's hand and the polished wooden steering wheel. Tearing open the wrapper, he bit off a chunk and said something that could have been in his native tongue for all Tommy knew, but it sounded a lot like someone saying thanks with a mouth full of caramel, nuts, and chocolate.

★ ★ ★

Sam took the fallen man's Uzi, removed the clip, and tossed both into the trash bin, along with the ten-inch knife the man tried to bury in Sam's back. He took the laces from the man's boots and used them to tie his hands, then the boots went in the trash bin. "I like you much better this way," Sam whispered.

Sam walked down the alley away from the café, turning north on Buchanan. At the intersection of Buchanan and 17th Street, he turned back toward the restaurant. He saw a white van with Digital Telecom written on its side, parked in front of the restaurant. He couldn't see into the windowless van. Approaching the van, he eased his pistol from its holster, then jerked the door open.

Empty.

CHAPTER 21

Something was wrong. Karen was certain. Sam had been gone too long. She felt alone and could sit no longer. She made a beeline to the restroom because she feared a re-enactment of the attack at her brownstone and was about to lose her dinner. She crept down a dimly lit hallway that led to the restrooms. The ladies' room door bore dark blotches from people pushing it open over many years.

The room was cramped, with only a toilet and a sink. Burnt-orange tiles covered the floor, and a single light bulb glowed behind a yellowed glass cover. She latched the door and then leaned against it. After a few moments, Karen let the toilet seat down, then collapsed and sobbed. When her sobbing subsided, she studied the lock on the door: a small bolt thrust through an anemic retainer held in place with two small wood screws. She snorted a stifled laugh, shaking her head. *As if that thing would keep them out.*

She couldn't breathe. *I can't do this,* she said to herself. She looked for a window but saw none. Her breath came in quick gasps, and cold sweat trickled down the small of her back. *I'm sorry, Tommy, but there's nothing Mommy can do. I'm so sorry.* She threw the door open, ran down the hall, and stopped dead when she reached the dining area. A man was sitting at their table, and it wasn't Sam Henry.

CHAPTER 22

The lake's pungent odor of moss and algae churned in the air. The wind lashed the tops off the waves, mixing the lake waters with the rain. Their late-night cruise became a carnival ride. Tommy no longer felt the sensation of forward motion, only the relentless ride up the crest of each wave, followed by the plummet into the belly of the next. The Santa Maria rose and fell according to the fury of the mounting waters, varied only by an occasional rogue wave that somehow grew larger than the rest. He rushed to the rail three times and emptied his stomach.

Fifteen minutes later, the ride no longer bothered him. Nothing left to throw up.

A wave crashed over the bow. *We shouldn't be out here,* Tommy thought. The stories about the Witch of November kept circulating in his mind. Legends said the Witch of November caused the great storms, claiming many ships and lives on these vast inland seas.

Tommy didn't think much about the Witch of November when Dad told the stories. They lived in Kansas, and he thought Dad was joking. But when his Uncle Dutch mentioned the November witch, Tommy Googled it and found the legend was true. Not an actual witch, like Paul thought, but true that all the famous storms happened in November. Like the storm that claimed the Edmund Fitzgerald and its crew of twenty-nine in 1975. And the storm of 1913, known as the Fresh Water Fury, claimed over two hundred fifty sailors. Another wave swept over the bow and sprayed the windows. Tommy couldn't see anything except angry, foaming water. He glanced at the brass clock embedded in the wooden console. It read 11:35.

Halloween was almost over.

The Witch of November arrived early.

CHAPTER 23

Sam eased inside the van until he could see into the back. Empty, but not a vehicle owned by a cable company. This rig belonged to an assault team. From the driver's seat, he checked the side mirrors. Nothing. He had made a mistake. He heard the distinct sound of an automatic weapon chambering a round. Then a calm, commanding voice said, "Don't try anything stupid, Mr. Henry.

***

Karen hid in the hall. Through eyes clouded with tears, she watched as Sam walked through the front door, followed by a solitary man wearing a dark blue jacket bearing a logo she could not read. The man's right hand rested inside his jacket. Sam walked to the man at the table and sat. A few words were exchanged, then the second man started toward her. She whimpered softly.

At the last minute, the man turned into the kitchen. A few minutes later, he returned to their table, pointing, and waving his hands. Sticking a finger in Sam's face, he cursed with guttural words that Karen couldn't understand. People at a nearby table stared but did not intervene. The man's face turned red, and his eyes were wild. Finally, the other man sitting at the table held up his hands in surrender and said something to Sam. Sam nodded, stood, and then walked deliberately toward Karen with the red-faced man trailing behind him.

Sam stood quietly, holding out his hand. Karen hesitated for several seconds before taking it. Sam pulled her to her feet. His arm cradled her shoulder, and in her ear, he whispered, "Remember."

What am I supposed to remember? Karen puzzled.

The first man gathered Sam's cases. Sam held her as they walked to the van, where they waited at the rear door until it opened from inside. One man offered his hand, but Karen ignored it. She sat on a bench along one side.

The second man pulled a gun from his jacket. Without warning, he raised it into the air, then smacked Sam on the back of the head. Sam crumpled to the ground, striking his head on the bumper as his knees hit the pavement. Then the man kicked him in the ribs. A crunching thud filled the night.

"Okay, Max, that's enough." It was the man in the van.

"You should see what he did to Luke. His face is all messed up." Max kicked Sam again.

"Max! Enough! That's an order, soldier." Max hesitated before walking to the front and climbing into the driver's seat.

Sam struggled to his feet, and Karen reached out to him. As she helped in into the van, he looked at her through glazed eyes set in pasty white skin. Bright red blood trickled down his forehead and leaked from the corner of his mouth. Holding his side, Sam collapsed on a bench across from her, gazing into her eyes, silently mouthing the word: *remember.*

Remember what?

Max started the van and drove into the parking lot, stopping near Karen's car. A third man dressed in the same dark blue repairman's jacket walked from the shadows and climbed into the passenger's side of the van before joining them in the back. He sat opposite Sam, sandwiching Karen between himself and his partner. Both men watched Sam with steadfast eyes. Max drove behind the restaurant, where he stopped and got out. A moment later, he helped a man stagger towards the van, and as they crossed in front of the headlights, she saw that the man's jaw hung at an awkward angle. A mass of blood had poured down the front of his white shirt and blue jacket. Max helped the man—Karen remembered his name was Luke—into the passenger's side. Luke groaned, snorted, and, with great effort, turned to glare with hate-filled eyes at Sam.

Max drove. The van remained silent for several minutes. Karen watched Sam for a sign, but he had closed his eyes and leaned his head back against the wall, sitting there, not moving, never glancing at her. She wasn't even sure if he was conscious.

"My name's Sean Michaels," the man on her right said. This was the first man that came into the restaurant—the same one who ordered Max to stop hitting Sam. Michaels motioned to the man on her left. "This is Jim Taylor."

She studied the man named Taylor. Something about him seemed familiar, but her mind was too clouded to make a connection.

Michaels cleared his throat. "You folks have caused a lot of havoc this evening. If it weren't for you, maybe things wouldn't have gotten so out of hand. I don't suppose you know about the young woman and her little boy killed today."

She felt him looking at her.

"At the house on Brandy Island, do you remember the blue Honda in the driveway? It belonged to a woman named Maria Esperanza. She had a little boy, Mike. They were in the house. If not for your delinquent kid, they'd both still be alive. But no…" His voice trailed off.

Karen took a deep breath, refusing to accept his words. She had met Maria and Mike one day when she was visiting with her sister. Maria was her sister's housekeeper.

She knew Maria's death wasn't her fault, not Tommy's fault, not Sam's fault, but that didn't help. Sobs bent her at the waist. She rested her elbows on her knees, held her face in her hands, and wished it would all end. These people killed Maria Esperanza and her son. They killed Eric. They had her. They had Paul. And soon, they'd have Tommy. Soon, there would be no Parker family. She would not even get to say goodbye to her boys.

Remember!

She was so angry with Tommy and Paul for leaving the house and roaming around town. Had she told them she loved them? Another chance would never come.

Remember. What am I supposed to remember?

Then she saw Tommy's face, so lifelike that she opened her eyes, but his face faded.

Then she remembered Sam's words. *Remember what you said!*

Then she saw something else, inches from her hand. The man's pant leg had ridden up, and she saw a knife scabbard strapped to his leg. Her sobs softened. She glanced at Sam, but he appeared comatose across from her. Every muscle in her body trembled.

Then everything turned red.

She heard Death's beckoning call, but he'd have to wait. She remembered. *I'll protect Tommy with my life. Sam, I wish you'd pay attention.*

Karen wiped her nose with the back of her hand and then rubbed it on her right knee. With a fluid motion, she grabbed the knife's black handle, extracting it from its sheath. Before the man could react, Karen slammed the blade into his thigh.

At that exact instant, Sam kicked the man on her right squarely in the face. His head flew back, hitting the steel van wall, whipping forward only to meet Sam's second kick. Sean Michaels was out cold before his body crumpled to the floor. The other man screamed in pain. He drove his hand into his jacket and retrieved a submachine gun. Before Karen could move, the weapon was pointed at the center of Sam's chest.

Karen jerked the knife free, drove it through the man's wrist, and twisted the blade. His hand popped open, and the weapon clanked to the floor. She felt an icy breeze as Sam's foot flashed by her nose, and soon the man lay motionless on the floor. A second later, Karen found herself holding the knife, dripping with blood, to the driver's throat.

"Stop the goddamn van!" She didn't recognize her own voice.

"You ain't going to use that," Max said, lifting his foot from the gas pedal.

"Don't be so sure." She withdrew the blade from his throat and stuck it through his arm. Max howled and leaped from the still-moving van.

"Drive!" Sam yelled from behind her.

She slid behind the wheel and floored the accelerator. The sound of rushing air filled the van. Karen glanced in the rearview mirror to see Sam toss two bodies out the back. Then she noticed, out of her peripheral vision, a movement to her right. The fourth man, Luke, held a pistol pointed at her head.

Karen slammed both feet on the brake, and the force threw Luke against the windshield. He hit the dash hard and groaned but held tight to his weapon. Inertia held him there for a moment, then she floored the accelerator, tossing him back into his seat. Their eyes locked. The gun began a slow arc toward her.

"Sam!"

She swiped at Luke's face, digging her nails into his jaw. He screamed. Then she slammed on the brakes, throwing him against the windshield again. She stomped on the emergency brake. Pivoting in her seat, she kicked with both legs, connecting with the man's shattered jaw. He screamed, then slumped between the seat and the floorboard as the van slid to a stop. Karen recoiled for another strike.

A hand grabbed her ankle before she could kick him again.

"I think he's had enough," Sam said.

The corner of Sam's mouth turned up. "You remembered."

Sam eased Luke to the sidewalk, climbed back in the van, and moved straight to the back. "Drive," he said.

"You're going to leave him like that?"

"Drive!"

She checked the side mirror for traffic and saw a man running down the middle of the street, wearing a dark blue jacket, carrying something black in his hand. The tires squealed as the van leaped from the curb. Then she realized. They were a red dot moving on someone's computer monitor. How long before that someone figured out the wrong people were driving the company van?

A pale glow emanated from the back of the van. "What are you doing?" She hollered, hoping Sam could hear her.

At first, there was no response, and then Sam stuck his head through the opening.

"We have to ditch this van," Sam said. "Fast!"

"But we need to find the others."

"We stole the van from the bastards who are trying to kill us. That probably won't get us on their Christmas card list. They're tracking us right now. Find someplace we can dump this thing." Sam grimaced, touching the back of his head.

"But …" She turned, but he had disappeared.

She jumped when a man's voice boomed from a two-way radio mounted under the dash.

"Tac-B, base. Tac-B, base."

"What am I supposed to do?" she yelled.

Sam stuck his head back through the opening. "I'm not deaf. Just get us out of this damn van."

"But…." Gone, again. "Damn it, Sam! How am I supposed to talk to you when you keep disappearing?"

Sticking his head through the opening, he said, "You're not supposed to talk to me. You're supposed to get us out of this goddamn van!"

He was heading to the back when Karen caught him by his shirt. "Would you hold still?" Sam stopped. "Thank you."

She glanced at the road, then at Sam. "I'm not stupid. If we're a moving target, then so is Alex, or whoever is driving the other car. We know we're a target. They don't. We're all getting out of this alive. Right?

"Right?" Sam nodded.

"What do I do now?"

"Drive. I'll give you directions."

"I mean, about the radio."

Sam's head disappeared, then reappeared. "Answer it."

"Get serious."

"Then don't answer it."

The radio erupted again, the voice more urgent. "Tac-B, base! Tac-B, base!"

She stared at the speaker.

"Whoever's driving the damn van, pick up. I know you can hear me."

"Sam?"

"Talk to the man. He's going to figure it out sooner or later." Sam waved his hand. "Turn left at the next intersection."

"What should I say?" She turned left.

Sam shouted from the back. "Those people tried to kill your son. Say anything you like."

She stared at the radio for a moment and then grabbed the microphone from the dashboard. "Yeah, what the fuck do you want?"

★ ★ ★

Inside the command van, Sgt. Gorgons fell back into his chair, clutching his head with both hands. *What in the hell's going on?* He wondered. First, Tac-A's van disappeared from his screen, and Madden's vehicle started moving. Then Tac-B's van started moving, and the Parker woman's vehicle remained stationary. But Tac-B had failed to report in. Now some woman is talking on Tac-B's radio.

Gorgons' cell phone rang. "Hello?"

"I've had some trouble. Send a van to get me," Mitachavich said.

"What's going on, Mitch?" Gorgons could hear sirens in the background.

"Now's not the time, Sergeant. Just send a damn van." Mitch gave him an address several blocks from the brownstone.

★ ★ ★

Sam stuck his head in the cab and waved his finger at a freeway on-ramp. "Get on I-90 East. Here! Right here!"

Karen dropped the microphone and jerked the wheel. The van rocked violently as the tires fought to grip the pavement. Sam braced himself in the opening. The van whipped straight as she aligned it with the ramp. Glancing in the rearview mirror, her eyes met his.

Henry said, "They're on the interstate two miles ahead. Catch them."

Karen floored the accelerator.

"Driver of the van." It was the radio.

Karen grabbed the coiled cord, fishing the microphone off the floor. "What do you want?"

"Who is this?"

"Who do you think it is?"

"Look, lady, you're stealing our van, and we want it back. Pull over, and we'll get someone out there to get it." Karen grunted but said nothing.

"Lady, there's a lot of valuable equipment in there. You stop, we'll come get the van, no questions asked. Deal?"

"So, you can kill me like you did that FBI agent, or like you tried to kill my son? You're messing with the wrong people, asshole!" Karen threw the microphone at the radio, where it hit with a sharp crack and dropped lifeless to the floor. She noticed Sam watching her in the mirror. One side of his lip curled upward as he dabbed scarlet blood from the corner of his mouth with a white handkerchief.

"They're right ahead of us." Sam crawled through the opening and flopped in the passenger's seat. "Bring us alongside but be ready to hit the brakes. They don't know who we are. They might shoot at us."

***

AJ looked over and saw the words Digital Telecom less than four feet away. "It's them! Go!"

Alex required no further coaxing. He floored the gas pedal as he heard the van motor match his move, but the big van was no match for his cruiser, and he sped away. Alex glanced at his speedometer. The needle glided past eighty mph. He moved to the left lane to avoid an eighteen-wheeler, but in his rearview mirror, he saw the van was not far behind. Strange that a van could keep pace with his police car. Alex swerved back into the center of the three-lane interstate, avoiding a car in the left-hand lane. More traffic was staggered across the highway, so he swung to the left-hand emergency lane. Ahead, vehicles blocked all three lanes. The van wasn't behind him now. The driver chose the right lane. Alex remembered seeing a truck in that lane. The other driver made a poor choice. Obviously, not a professional driver like himself.

Alex caught movement in his peripheral vision and turned to see AJ crawling into the back seat. "Give me your gun."

A kid in an old Volkswagen flipped Alex the bird as they zipped by. A second later, he broke into the clear, but the van was already there and attempted to pin Alex's car against the guardrail. Alex slammed on the brakes, and the other driver matched his move.

"Shoot the sonofabitch!" Alex screamed.

Karen couldn't see a damn thing with Sam hanging out the window. She couldn't hear much either above the screeching tires and rushing wind. Too many things demanded her attention all at once. She glanced at the side mirror, hoping something wasn't about to slam into their rear-end, then Sam screamed, "GO!"

The van rocketed forward just as AJ depressed the trigger. AJ had a perfect sight picture on the man hanging from the window when the van sped up. A bullet hit the van in the sliding door. Then something registered. Alex was screaming, "NO!"

Alex rolled down his window and waved his arm at the van, and AJ recognized the man he'd almost shot.

It was Sam Henry.

AJ clicked the weapon's safety on, laid it on the seat beside him, stuck his head out the window, and promptly threw up.

CHAPTER 24

Karen turned into a deserted parking lot and slid to a stop. She ran to Alex and threw her arms around his neck, kissing him on the cheek.

"I was afraid you were …" She buried her head against his chest. "We saw what happened to Eric."

"How?" Alex pushed her back, holding her delicate shoulders with his huge hands.

"Someone bugged my house. I found one in the bathroom this afternoon. Sam tapped into their system. We were watching on Sam's computer when it happened. They came after us next." Large tears rolled down her cheeks.

Alex pulled her close and stroked her hair. "Everything's gonna be okay," he said, although he couldn't think of anything that was okay. It's just what one said. "How did you get the van?" he asked.

Karen pushed herself away. "Sam and I kicked their ass. Right, Sam?" She turned, but Sam wasn't there.

Sam bobbed up from behind Alex's car, holding a small, round electronic device. "Very sophisticated," Sam said. He walked to the van and tossed the bug in the front seat.

"What about all that stuff?" Karen said, pointing at the bank of hi-tech electronic equipment in the van.

Sam nodded. "Good point."

"Alex? Could I borrow two rounds?" Sam held out his hand.

Alex looked at Sam, puzzled. Then he fished an extra clip from his belt, thumbed out two rounds, and handed them to Sam.

Sam worked one round into each of his ears, climbed into the van, and pulled the door shut. After several muffled gunshots, Sam popped out the back door, blue smoke boiling behind him. Sam set his two briefcases on the ground and wiped each of Alex's shells on his sleeve before handing them back. Sam locked the van doors using the remote and stuck the keys in his pocket.

"AJ, Alex, your work is finished. Tell the authorities that I tricked you and stole your car. You know nothing about what I've done, and you don't need to be involved further." Sam paused. "I'm sorry about Eric."

The muscles in Alex's jaw twisted and strained. "No way, Sam. I'm in until the end. Those bastards killed my friend. You can't get rid of me that easy."

AJ said, "Same for me, Mr. Henry. Sticking together is our best hope, and the best hope for Tommy as well. Is it not?"

Sam held up his hands. "I appreciate it, but what I have done amounts to treason. I don't know how to get out of this unscathed. Can't let you do it."

"Well, let's see you stop me." Alex picked up Sam's cases, walked straight to his patrol car. With his back turned toward Sam Henry, Alex hollered, "Staying or coming?"

A few minutes and a few miles later, Sam directed Alex to a small airport. Rows of aviation businesses with brightly colored signs lined the street. Sam pointed. "Let's try this one."

Karen followed Sam inside, wondering what made this business more promising than the next. Sam leaned close and whispered, "You probably won't need to say anything. Just act important and impatient."

A young blond woman, wearing skin-tight jeans, displaying lips, and fingernails painted bright red, greeted Sam at the counter. They chatted. Karen wasn't close enough to hear most of it. The blond giggled and then disappeared down a hall, and after a moment, a gaunt man, four inches taller than Sam, appeared. A worn leather flight jacket hung on him like a second skin.

Sam and the flight-jacketed man walked to the far side of the room. Sam talked, laughed, pointed, and waved his hands in animated gyrations, lying and pretending to be someone he wasn't. Deception seemed so natural for him. Karen wondered if she'd ever met the real Sam Henry.

From what she could hear of the conversation, a helicopter to Canada wasn't going to happen. Something about the storm. *Let's go, Sam. We'll find someone else,* she thought. Sam persisted. Pulling a wad of cash from inside his jacket, Sam peeled off several bills. The pilot studied them for a moment, then stuck them in his pocket. Both men shook hands, and the pilot left the room.

A chill wind followed Karen and Sam into the car. "He'll take two of us to Canada, but not as close as I'd hoped. The storm...." Sam motioned toward the sky. "He'll set us down near Leamington. A friend of his owns an aviation company there. He said the guy will rent us a car. Alex, you, and AJ will have to drive to St. Thomas. Rent a car." Sam looked at Karen. "Is there a phone at the cabin?"

"It's unlisted, but I have the number." She dug through the small, black purse she'd carried dutifully since she bolted from the brownstone in the darkness earlier that morning.

"Here." She handed Sam a business card from a Canadian pottery shop with a number scrawled on the back.

Sam glanced at the number, then handed it to Alex. "When you get to St. Thomas, call this number. We'll give you directions to the cabin. Oh, and if you get caught, eat the card."

Alex grasped Sam's hand and gripped it tightly for several seconds. The two men exchanged a long stare that Karen sensed meant something only men, like Alex and Sam, fully understood.

Alex released Sam's hand. "See you in Canada."

✶ ✶ ✶

The helicopter was large and black, with red lettering on its side. The flight-jacketed man's name was Lance. "You're in luck," Lance said as Sam hoisted his black briefcases on board. "They've cleared us for Pelee Point. The weather is crap, but I've been in worse. I used to fly in Alaska."

"Pelee Point?" Sam asked. "Is that where we can rent the car?"

"Yup," Lance said.

"Great! We appreciate your help. This is an important shoot, and they can't do it without this part." Sam tapped one of his cases. "The timing is critical. The storm makes the scene perfect."

"Seems odd that we didn't know that a movie was being filmed nearby. You'd think we'd have heard about something like that," Lance said, focusing on a gauge.

"The producer wanted it kept quiet. Shooting this scene gets exceedingly difficult if you've got a bunch of sightseers." Sam secured his shoulder harness. "Hey, I'll tell our logistics man about you. He can probably send more business your way."

Liar, Karen thought, but she was beginning to see his lying as an occupational skill more than a character flaw. She would not have gotten this far without him. But could he save Tommy? She didn't know.

Sam glanced at Karen. "I hate flying in these damn things, especially over the water. Scares the shit out of me."

Karen looked at him from the corner of her eye, then tugged on her own straps.

The four-blade rotor moved, gradually building speed until the entire machine shuddered violently, growling out an odd orchestration of an internal combustion engine, churning gears, and whooshing rotors. The helicopter jerked upward, pitched left, and clawed its way into the darkness. By the dim cabin light, Karen saw the color drain from Sam's face. Her own heart leaped into her throat. Easing from the hard-left turn, the chopper's nose tilted slightly downward, and she was pressed into the vinyl seat as the machine sped into the nighttime sky.

She knew better than to look out the window but did anyway. They were over open water now. The city lights disappeared, and only black skies appeared ahead of them. Winds batted them like a model airplane. Flashes of lightning lit the distant horizon. She grasped Sam's hand. He flinched as if startled, but he didn't pull away, and their fingers laced together. Then her fear gave way to something unexpected. A hint of feelings she hadn't experienced for what seemed like years. It was no less frightening than flying into the storm.

★★★

In his command van, Mitch hovered over Perry Gorgons' shoulder, studying the computer screen. His rage cooled to seething anger, burning deep in his gut. Perry and the others felt the same way. He was sure of that. They were edgy and weary of getting their butts kicked. Mitch no longer thought about a man and a small boy, only about enemies.

Perry touched the screen. "Right there. That's got to be them."

CHAPTER 25

Edward Powers felt dread deep in his gut. Beckman was smiling. Using a low-tech cell phone, Mitachavich had called with the update. Things in Cleveland had not gone well. They had blown up another home, lost four men, others injured, and they still did not have Sam Henry. However, Unit-11 had found the boat, and that diminished the other problems in Beckman's mind. Earlier, Powers feared Beckman wouldn't make a decision. Now, he feared Beckman would. Between the adrenalin and the haste to end things, reasoning with Beckman became impossible. This situation was spiraling out of control, and Powers couldn't slow things down.

"General, can we get a helicopter out there?" Beckman asked, stepping to a map of Lake Erie displayed on the largest monitor.

"It's well within range," Powers said. "But the weather…"

"What about the weather?" Beckman studied the data as if he might make a difference.

"Everything will worsen as the storm approaches."

"That's not what I asked. Can the Apache reach the target?"

"Yes. But it's not safe." Powers studied Beckman's face, searching for understanding. Military aircraft can perform under adverse conditions, but he wondered if Beckman knew that.

"Okay, let me think about this," Beckman said, rubbing his hands together.

"Sir, with all due respect, I suggest we reassess this entire situation." Powers wanted to slow things down, think things through.

Beckman's face flashed red. "What are you suggesting, General? Are you saying that I haven't given this careful consideration? Are you suggesting that I'm reckless?"

"No. That is not what I'm saying, Mr. President," Powers said. "All I'm saying is that we should consider our alternatives. Be certain of our course of action."

"And you think I haven't done that? You think I'm not considering the options? What options do you have in mind? Let that thing escape to gather his buddies so they can kill us all?"

"We don't know that will happen," Powers shot back too forcefully.

"What do you want me to do? Wait until we're all dead? This thing is a goddamn alien, General. Have you forgotten that?"

"No sir, I haven't forgotten," Powers said, casting his eyes to the floor. He had to buy some time. This was moving too fast. "But this—whatever it is—had shown no sign of aggression. It had harmed no one, not even in its own defense. Maybe we have nothing to fear from this man."

"There's your problem," Beckman growled. "This is no man. It's a goddamn alien. It's not like us, it's different."

Powers' eyes lifted, glaring. "And we should blow it up, because it's different?"

"Yes, because it's different. You know what? You people have never understood that. Have you?"

Beckman's meaning of *you people* wasn't lost on Powers because it was an expression he'd heard before, you people, your kind.

Powers glared as Beckman stomped to the SCC, where he probably would have slammed the door, except the door couldn't slam because it was electronically controlled. The worst Beckman could do was hammer the control button with an exaggerated thrust of his fist, sticking out his chin like a pouting teenager. Beckman's tantrum bought a few minutes, but Powers knew a few minutes wouldn't be enough to save Tommy Parker. Powers walked to the map and stared at the image of the lake and a small point of light that represented a boat, a man, and a boy. Sam Henry was still out there somewhere. But what can one man do?

★★★

Karen released Sam's hand and then gripped his arm. Glancing over, he saw that the armrest on the other side of Karen's chair was no better off. Yet her grip felt comforting. He understood it was temporary, driven by fear, but that knowledge did not diminish the warmth of her touch. Temporary was better than nothing, and nothing is all he'd known for a long time.

They were skirting the northern shore close to Pelee Point when Sam realized something didn't feel right, but then nothing feels right when you're in an aircraft bouncing around on a malevolent storm.

Then he heard a slight pause in the engine, followed by a minor bump he felt in the seat of his pants.

Karen turned pale, staring straight ahead as if her every move were dangerous. The next cough of the motor was more pronounced, and the next bump was more of a shudder. The pilot's head moved with frantic little jerks, scanning the instruments, and punching at buttons.

The motor stopped with a loud clank.

They plummeted like a rock.

CHAPTER 26

Sam reacted fast. He tossed his briefcases and screamed instructions at Karen. And then he jumped and prayed that Karen followed him. He hit the ground rolling, just as he'd learned many years earlier. Sharp pain fired through his feet. The Canadian soil seemed much harder than any other ground he remembered. He straightened himself a little too soon and landed face down in the tall, wet grass. A rotor blade smacked the ground inches from his face, slicing off a chunk of sod a yard thick and dragging it 20 feet to the rocks below. The sound of grinding metal and breaking glass hurt his ears, and then a whoosh of searing heat and the roar of ignited aviation fuel washed over him.

Screams lifted above the roaring flames. One voice. It sounded like the pilot, but he wasn't sure. He listened for Karen. The screaming continued, long wails of the soon dead. In a fire, death never comes soon enough. Finally, the screaming stopped. Sam was breathing hard. His fingers dug deep into the muddy dirt and wet grass. He prayed Karen had died in the crash, not the flames. Hard rain pelted his body, and hope oozed from his chest and into the ground. *Why did he let her come?*

Tommy didn't have a chance, not without help, and Sam couldn't help him now. Even if his computer survived the crash, he'd never find it in the dark. If he found it, he was miles from nowhere. He didn't even know if he could walk. If Tommy survived, he'd do so without his mother.

Why did he jump? If he'd thought things through, he'd have stayed on board with the pilot. At least the pilot's pain only lasted a few minutes. Sam's pain would last a lifetime.

CHAPTER 27

Tommy returned to the bridge wearing an orange windbreaker and carrying another of the same color under his arm. "Here you go." Tommy shoved the orange bundle into Nigel's hands. The north wind raged, transforming the waves from overzealous swells to something akin to small tsunamis. Tommy had to keep reminding himself that Erie was a lake, not an ocean. White crests spattered across the landscape, reflecting the light from a full moon peeking through a small hole in the clouds above the eastern horizon. To the north, the sky disappeared into blackness. White flashes revealed the storm front, foretelling things to come. They were headed straight into the worst of it.

Tommy told himself that the Santa Maria could handle it. She was designed to go to sea.

"Looks like we're headed right into it," Tommy said.

"You're right."

"Do you think we'll be okay? In the storm, I mean." Tommy's voice squeaked from high to low in the fashion typical of boys his age. He hated it when that happened.

"I don't know. What do you think?" Nigel gave him a wry smile.

"How should I know? I'm from Kansas. Remember? When we had storms, we hid in the cellar."

"We don't have a cellar," Nigel observed.

Tommy said nothing for several minutes, and then, with a whisper, he said, "Tell me about where you're from."

It was Nigel's turn to be silent. His face was pale, lit by the glowing lights of the instrument panel. His eyes distant, like he was looking into a faraway place.

Nigel said, "Similar to here. My planet is old. It was old long before humans inhabited this Earth. As Earth mellowed with age, several worlds sought to colonize her. Two did. Humans were the survivors."

"You mean two kinds of people? What happened to the others?"

"Died out. Killed by your species, commingled, and by their own failure to adapt."

"People were put here?" Tommy said, his voice trailing off, trying to collect his thoughts. "We didn't evolve, and we weren't created either. Wow! Last year we had this big debate in school: Darwinism versus Creationism. They're both wrong?"

"Not wrong. You just don't understand the entire picture."

"But that means there is no God? No heaven." Tommy's voice sank as he realized his father was indeed gone and not just dead. He felt as if he had lost him again, not only physically but also spiritually.

"You're correct about being placed here, but I'm not so sure about God or heaven." Nigel's voice was calm yet questioning.

"Do you believe in God—and heaven?"

"That, my young friend, is not as simple a question as you might imagine. My people made mistakes." Nigel sighed. "One thing we failed to understand was the true meaning of life."

"Have you? Learned the meaning of life?" Tommy asked.

"How would I know if I did?"

The bridge grew quiet, except for the moaning wind, the crashing waves, and droning diesel engines. Nigel stared at his reflection in the glass and said nothing more.

✦ ✦ ✦

Beckman sat alone in the SCC, rubbing his temples. That troubled Powers. Several things troubled Powers, not the least of which was Beckman's course of action. Powers vowed never to take a life unless it was in defense of his country. He wasn't angry with the man or the boy drifting in a small boat on a violent lake stirred by an early winter storm. And he failed to see how they posed a threat to his country. Now he was just following orders. What choice did he have?

Movement in the SCC garnered his attention. He realized, too late, that he'd drifted into a daydream. Beckman emerged from the SCC and Powers saw no compassion in the President's face.

During Beckman's five years as president, he'd wreaked havoc on minorities, and he'd gotten away with it. Powers was the token minority on the presidential team, a fact he accepted after his appointment to the Cabinet. He was exiled from the White House inner circle. Being a professional military man, he didn't expect to shape the nation's political agenda, but he didn't anticipate being treated like an outsider either. Outsider—that's how he felt on a good day.

"Contact Unit-11, General," Beckman said. "Get that helicopter in the air and splash that boat. That's an order, and if you can't carry it out, I'll find someone who can."

"Yes, sir." *You splash an aircraft, not a boat. Dumbass.*

CHAPTER 28

Wet, muddy, and cold, Sam inventoried body parts, assessed damage, but mostly, he prayed for Karen. Everything happened so fast. He told her to jump but didn't know if she did. Letting her come was a mistake. His mistake, another in a long run of mistakes, called his life. A sound came from the darkness.

"Sam?" Karen's voice sounded weak. "Sam! Oh, God! SAM!" Her voice grew stronger above the wind and rain.

"Here!" Raising his head, Sam yelled, "I'm here. You're alive?!"

"Well, of course, I'm alive," she said, crawling to his side. "How often do dead people talk to you?"

"More often than I prefer," he said.

She pulled herself next to him. "Are you okay?"

"I'll live," he said, feeling the warmth of her body, her face inches from his. He took her in for a moment. "How about you?"

"Bruised but not broken. But the pilot…." She looked toward the ball of fire, tears cutting little trails through mud and strands of grass on her face.

He touched her cheek, gently turning her face toward his. "We can't help him."

The fire dwindled, but by the firelight, they could see the edge of the embankment, which was a good thing, lest they move in the wrong direction and topple 20 feet to the rocks below. The ledge cast a black shadow, and he couldn't see a damn thing. His computer equipment was military-spec, as were the cases, but for all he knew, they lay in pieces down on the rocks. Trying to find them would be like searching for a needle in a haystack—blindfolded.

But search they did.

"Anything?" Karen called from the darkness.

"No. You?"

"Nothing."

He tripped over something, landing on tender knees. He groped around on the ground with both hands, and then his hopes crashed.

Only a damn rock. A flat, square rock. He stood and lost his balance, sliding into some sort of small ravine. He shook mud from his hands, then started the arduous climb out.

When he reached the top, he heard Karen calling him. Together, they worked their way toward the ledge and the light of the dying flames. If he just had a little light. Crawling to the bank's edge, he studied the rocks around the helicopter for a second time. He saw nothing, but the rocks were big and the cases could be hidden in between them.

They wouldn't find them, and searching was hopeless, and he was useless without them.

Sam scooted away from the ledge and sat on his butt, pulling his knees to his chest. *Maybe they should go find a flashlight. No, that would take too long. Shit, how long have we been here? Too long.* Sam glanced away from the fire's glow, hoping his eyes would adjust to the darkness, knowing they wouldn't adjust enough. Perhaps if he went on his hands and knees. It was a long shot, but he was into long shots now. He turned, bumping into Karen's leg.

"Careful," he said. "You're almost at the edge."

The grass became spongy, as if it weren't there. Karen screamed. The bank sloughed off, and they were sliding toward the lake. Karen turned onto her back, digging with her heals, trying to push herself back to solid ground. Sam clawed with his fingers and dug with his toes, but it was no use.

They were going down.

When everything stopped moving, Henry stood in slop knee-deep. Mud and grass clung to his head, hands, and clothes. Karen splashed and sputtered, falling down each time she tried to stand. Sticking out a hand, Sam helped her up. Above them, a gaping wound appeared in the bank, with several tons of earth carved from its face, and what remained was steep and uneven. Mud had slid right up to the helicopter, which was a heap of twisted metal and dying flames. Off to the side lay a silver cylinder reflecting the orange glow. Struggling through the mud, Sam kicked it with his foot, and it sounded with a dull thud, not moving an inch—a tank full of aviation fuel.

Fuel. Think. Must be a way to use this, but how? Pour some out and light it? No, the fire would burn back to the barrel, then explode. He wasn't thinking straight.

"What is it?" Karen sloshed her way to his side.

"Fuel."

"A fuel tank?"

"Yeah. I'm trying to think of how we could use it."

"You mean like a torch or something?"

He grabbed her by the shoulders, giving her a shake. "Yes! A torch! I should have thought of that." He paused, drifting off somewhere and with a distant voice, said again, "Why didn't I think of that?"

He found a stick four feet long and wrapped his sports coat around one end, then spun the cap off the tank and allowed fuel to pour over the jacket.

"It's soaking wet. Won't that keep it from burning?"

"This is high-octane aviation fuel. It'll burn. Let's hope it burns long enough." He edged toward the flames, stretching out the stick as far as possible. The jacket erupted in a ball of fire. He turned his head, wincing from the heat, refusing the urge to drop the torch. After a moment, the flame waned, and he swung the torch in slow arcs, searching the ground and inching forward.

Five minutes later, they finished searching the boulders and the narrow band of sand nearest the water's edge. They couldn't see through the mud, and if the cases were buried, they would never be found.

The torch was half what it had been a moment ago. "We've got to get up there." Sam pointed to the ledge they'd slid off earlier.

It took ten minutes. Three times they neared the top, only to slide back to the bottom. On the fourth attempt, they crawled onto the ledge. The torch was almost out. The flames slowly ate at the wool and the little fuel left in it. Before they started their climb, the urge to dip the jacket back into the fuel was overwhelming, but the tank would have exploded. He could have doused the flame, soaked the jacket, then relit it, but he didn't think of that until they were back on the ledge. Damn, where was his head? He waved the torch back and forth, two feet above the grass.

He found one case.

Karen found the other.

The ground leading away from the ledge was steep. Sam found a small gully leading up. Karen followed, grabbing a handful of wiry branches, fighting through tangled brush, pulling herself upward. Each step, pull and fight. At the head of the gully stood a five-foot vertical wall. Sam threw the cases up. Then wedged himself in the crevasse and worked his way to the top. Reaching down, he helped Karen up, where they both collapsed.

Lights flickered in the distance, maybe half a mile. "I think that's where he was taking us. We were supposed to rent a car from the owner, but now I don't think that's a good idea."

"What do you mean?"

"If we tell them about the crash, we won't get away. FAA investigation, all that stuff."

"But we've got to tell them about —"

Sam held up his hand, interrupting her. "What good will that do? They can't bring the pilot back, but we can still help Tommy if we get to the cabin before it's too late. Those men have many resources, and they don't quit. They'll find Tommy."

Sam fell silent for a moment, thinking. "We can't let them see us. We look like—like we were in a helicopter crash, for God's sake."

★ ★ ★

A few minutes later, the lights of Heli-Corp faded behind them, and silence filled the blue Ford, Sam had hot-wired. Karen shivered. She was now a cold, wet car thief. It was sinking in. Grand theft. Traitor.

After five miles, the heater warmed the car. "We're in big trouble, aren't we?"

Sam looked at her, then turned his attention back to the road. "Tommy is in more trouble than us. First things first."

"I suppose you're right. It's just that…"

"You don't like being a criminal. Nothing wrong with that."

"Doesn't it bother you?"

"In my line of work, sometimes you have to bend the rules."

"Bend the rules. You call grand theft bending the rules?"

"And treason, don't forget treason." He scolded her with his finger. "I suppose newspaper reporters never bend the rules?"

"Touché." She sensed that something was troubling Sam, and if it wasn't grand theft or treason, what could it be?

The windshield wipers slapped steadily. Finally, Sam said, "You don't trust me. I understand that. You don't like me. I understand that too." He waved his hand in the air, dismissing the facts. "Stealing cars. No big deal. But whatever you think of me, we have a job to do, and we don't have time to dwell on the past."

Why was he bringing this up? It didn't make sense to her, and she wondered why her thoughts or feelings would make any difference to a man like Sam. How could she measure him? Would it matter if she could? Sam Henry and his two small cases—that's all she had. She had hated him for fifteen years. Yet she believed in him. Damn, she hated that. What she hated, even more, was that she was starting to like him.

"If we find them, what are you going to do to the man?" She meant alien, but somehow it was difficult for her to call him that.

"I don't know."

A few miles clicked off the odometer before Karen said, "You must have orders. What are they?"

He gazed into the night and said, "Capture, if possible—destroy if not." He glanced at her, then continued, "I must face him."

Rain pelted the windshield. The wipers slapped at the falling sky.

* * *

Tim ran the checklist on the Apache again. It was an act driven by anticipation and boredom. Tim Leonard,—Timothy Leary—to his friends, was an extraordinary Apache pilot. The word that Sgt. Gorgons had found the Santa Maria making her way across Erie traveled quickly throughout the troop. Tim ran his finger over the yoke and caressed the trigger. Killing the target would be too easy to bring any real satisfaction, but members of his team died on this stupid mission, and it was time to even the score.

* * *

Mitch studied the weather information intercepted from the Canadians. The cold front had intensified, crashing violently into warm air pushing up from the Gulf of Mexico. Life was getting difficult for Tommy Parker and his friend. Military intervention might prove unnecessary.

The printer came to life and spit out a single page. The message was from the crisis center. Mitch picked it up, studied it for a moment, and then breathed, "May God have mercy on our souls."

CHAPTER 29

Karen couldn't see a goddamn thing. A curtain of driving rain rendered the car's headlights almost useless as curves in the road leaped out from the night, causing her stomach to climb into her throat every few seconds. Sam drove the stolen car in the right direction, but in the darkness and driving rain, nothing looked familiar to Karen. Guiding them to Dutch's cabin was the first meaningful thing she'd done since Tommy disappeared, and she was lost, almost ready to turn around and try again, when she recognized a craft shop hidden in a thick tangle of aspen trees.

Her heart pounded to the point where she wondered if Sam could hear it. The road to Dutch's cabin was just around the next bend, and finding the private drive proved easy. The drive twisted through maple, birch, and aspen trees that formed a long, winding tunnel. A thick mat of brown and golden leaves covered the narrow lane. Rounding a tight corner, they faced a metal gate set in a wall of large granite blocks. A twelve-foot chain-link fence surrounding the property began where the granite ended. A simple metal box on a galvanized post stood sentry near the gate.

Sam pulled close. "You know the code?" He studied the fence and thought about the man who lived here. Security would be tight, not your ordinary home. Karen's brother-in-law must be the same Dutch Killeen who settled the score with the assassins of Senator Andrea Ross. Sam refused to think about something since he learned Dutch Killeen was not only alive but linked, albeit by marriage, to Karen. Too many coincidences to ignore. Being reunited with Karen and seeing Nigel on the hospital monitor after all these years? It was as if someone had orchestrated the entire thing.

"I think so." Sliding through the small space between Sam's chest and the steering wheel, Karen reached for the ten-key panel. She punched at the keypad, freezing rain stinging her face. The gate slid to the side. "Presto," she said, easing back into her seat.

The cabin stood less than a hundred yards ahead, but Sam could not see it because of the lush ferns glowing in their headlights. The road emptied into a small meadow, where the cabin stood—three stories of massive Canadian red cedar logs, twelve inches thick on average, joints hand-hewn with traditionally chinked gaps. Lights lit the windows.

Karen gasped. "Do you think Tommy could have made it here already?"

"No. They couldn't be any better than halfway, and they're running into rough water now. Could it be your sister?"

"She said they'd be out of the country for a few weeks. Didn't know how long they'd be away. Said it depended on how things went. But who knows? They're very secretive."

"I'll bet they are. Stay here." Sam stepped from the car, easing the door closed but not latched. A glint of light shimmered off the barrel of his gun.

Something seemed odd and surreal, and then she realized he made no sound. It was as if he wasn't there. *What if someone's home? What might Sam do? Would he shoot someone? Probably not. Then why did he have that damned gun out?*

Crack!

Karen jumped when something smacked the windshield. It was just a small branch.

Sam stood on the porch, waving his arm in big circles, beckoning her. "Bring my cases," he yelled.

Karen sprinted to the front door, a briefcase dangling from each hand, the rain soaking her before she reached the portico. Sam was drenched as well, but at least the rain had rinse off some mud.

"I thought you were sleeping." Sam reached for one case. Their hands touched, and his eyes locked with hers. She didn't look away.

Nodding her head toward the cabin, she asked, "What's going on?"

"The security system turns stuff off and on, so it looks like somebody's home," he said.

To her relief, his gun was back in its holster.

"You wouldn't happen to have a key?"

"Right here." She lifted the doormat, and there, taped to the bottom, was a brass key.

Sam shook his head, twisting his face with disapproval. Karen wondered what was bothering him. She walked to a nearby cedar bench, bent down, and popped open a hidden door. In the small opening was a tumbler, into which she inserted the key. Inside the bench was a metal box with a keypad like the one at the front gate. She poked at the keys with her index finger, then popped the box open and retrieved a key. Once inside the house, Karen disarmed the alarm system.

Sam smiled and said, "That's more like it."

Sam set up his computer and its miniature satellite dish. Karen fidgeted, then decided she'd be less anxious if she did something constructive. Fatigue swept through her bones, and she realized it had been thirty-six hours since she'd had any proper sleep. She found them dry clothes, and then she stumbled into the kitchen, where she brewed a pot of coffee. Within a few minutes, she'd made an impromptu snack of peanut butter and jelly sandwiches and coffee. If Sam didn't like such fare, well, she wasn't trying to impress him, was she? No, she was not. Definitely not.

Gliding back into the room, she balanced a tray with one hand and, with fingers hooked through the handles, held two steaming cups of coffee in the other. "I made us something to eat."

Hovering over his gadgets, Sam glanced up as if annoyed but then smiled. "What did you make?"

"Just peanut butter and jelly sandwiches and hot coffee." She handed him a cup.

"One of my all-time favorites," he said, punching at the keyboard while washing a mouth full of half-chewed sandwich down with coffee. "Now, we'll see."

She pulled a chair and settled behind him. A female voice said, "Hello Sam. You're back. I hope you're not in trouble, but since you've accessed this program, I guess that's too much to ask."

Karen inched closer. "Is that Terri?" Karen asked.

"Terri Wilson. An outright genius. She sort of adopted me." Sam clicked through the screens too quickly for Karen to read. Finally, he paused. "I hope this works."

Sam leaned back while the program processed his last command. "Here's the deal. Except for the military stuff, people paid too little attention to the rest of this project. It is called the Strategic Emergency Communications Array, or SECA, a top-secret military satellite system, but the heart of it is one satellite, the XV-E. Terri worked with me on the project. We both felt it was critical to have uninterrupted communication in a crisis. We wanted to ensure our ability to get through anything that caused interference. If we could communicate and our enemy couldn't, we would have the advantage."

Sam's voice trailed off, but then he continued. "Terri got an idea, which seemed farfetched, but it worked. When we realized what her invention could do, I decided the government couldn't be trusted with it. To be honest, much of my distrust came from the Ross assassination. So, we concealed this thing in a sealed box that looked like another device already installed. We said it was a redundant system. No one bothered checking it. Three people in the world know about this. Terri and me, and now you."

The thought that Sam could get away with placing an unauthorized device on a military satellite seemed implausible. Even more incredible was that he'd told her about it. Sam Henry was a strange man that she struggled to understand. She asked, "What can it do?"

"Good question. We never tested the final version, except in theory and a small prototype."

Karen pressed further. "What are you doing now?"

"I'm checking the status of the SECA. Earlier, I blocked the crisis center's access to it. I'll bet that pissed them off. I programmed a backdoor through a weather satellite. If I can get into the XV-E, then I control SECA. All of it."

He glanced at her and said, "Cross your fingers."

"That sounds scientific."

The screen turned black.

Soon a delicate blue sphere appeared, floating against a black background. Below the sphere, in bold white letters: XV-E CONTROL.

"So far, so good." Sam rubbed his hands together.

Terri's face appeared in the corner of the computer's screen, like one of those little wizards in the help menu. "I'm accessing the XV-E files, and while I'm doing that, I have something to say, Sam Henry."

Karen leaned closer, watching Terri on the computer screen. "You must be in a lot of trouble, and whatever you're doing, it's probably dangerous, too. Please be careful. I know you wouldn't be doing this unless you had a good reason. Anyway, whatever happens, I know you're doing the right thing. I love you." Terri faded, and another screen appeared. Sam sat, resting his chin in his hands, as if to cement the last few words forever in his mind.

He clicked on an icon. A window opened, revealing a list of files by date and time. "Let's see what they've been talking about." He clicked on a file labeled Unit-11, saved yesterday at 11:45 a.m. A video-like image appeared. He heard voices off camera but could only see one man, Richard Beckman. Beckman ordered Unit-11 to Cleveland. Glancing at

Dutch's mahogany grandfather clock, Sam saw the time was 1:20 a.m. Closing his eyes, he reconstructed the day.

"That's what I thought." He closed the file.

"You didn't know about them? That's who's done all of this to us?" Karen asked.

"Beckman set me up from the beginning. Look." He pointed at the screen. "This transmission went out right after I arrived at the hospital."

"Why? Why would President Beckman do that?"

"Shit."

"What is it?"

"I thought of something. Shutting down the XV-E eliminated our ability to monitor communications between Unit-11 and the crisis center." Sam smacked the sides of his head with his hands. "Shit, why didn't I think about that? That's not good. Shit. Not good. But what else could I have done?"

"What's Unit-11?"

"Think, damn it, think." Sam pummeled his forehead with the palm of his hand. "They traveled on a military transport, probably a C-130. That limits them to the international airport." He talked to himself more than to Karen.

"What's Unit-11?" Karen asked again.

"Wait. There's another way." He clicked through several screens. "This is a long shot. I can get to the crisis center mainframe with no one knowing, I think. The mainframe backs up everything that runs through their system." Screens flashed as he talked. "There'll be hundreds of files, but the computer can filter for Cleveland to D.C. communication. Maybe with a little luck…"

"Damn it, Sam. What's Unit-11?"

"Oh, sorry. Unit-11 is a military counter-terrorism team. Dangerous bunch."

"They were at the restaurant?"

"That would be them."

"We kicked their butts then, and we'll do it again."

"I found something." He tapped out a command.

"What's that?" she asked as the screen filled with odd little symbols.

"Computer language, an encrypted message. The encryption would take days to decipher, but I have their encryption." The screen went blank, except a single word, "WORKING." After a few seconds, a text appeared.

```
OPERATION ROCK & ROLL
Classification: black
Transmission: #A-13534
Confirming crisis center orders received
this date
Interception to commence ASAP
Apache launched at 01:05
ETA target area: thirty-minutes
Affirm: make visual confirmation then
destroy target
Next transmission upon completion of mission
```

The message was sent roughly fifteen minutes ago. Karen dug her fingernails into Sam's arm. Tommy had ten minutes to live.

"Tommy doesn't have a chance, does he?" She asked in a quiet, almost whispering voice.

"That depends."

"Depends on what?" Her grip grew stronger.

"It depends on whether Terri's invention works."

"Terri's invention?"

"What I was telling you about. An accident, actually." He sifted through the ever-changing screens. "Terri did an internship at a Federal Bureau of Prisons facility in Florida. She was taking a psychology course. She was still in high school but taking college courses as well. The professor offered extra credit for prison experience. The warden was an acquaintance of mine, so I arranged it so she could spend a few days there. They were showing her the control center and the massive board of lights and buttons that controlled every door and gate in the prison."

Sam continued. "Somebody called Terri's escorting officer on his handheld radio, and before the control officer could stop him, the officer keyed his microphone and fried several computer chips in the console. Nothing worked. They locked down the entire prison until they repaired the damage. The guards are supposed to turn off their radios when they enter the control room, but sometimes they forgot."

Karen studied the monitor with growing fascination as an image of Lake Erie appeared, black and ghostly. Then a grid covered the entire screen. Sam highlighted several squares of the grid and punched enter. At the bottom of the screen, the word SEARCHING appeared.

"Radio waves can play hell with computer components. Terri speculated that if one could concentrate a burst of energy, like a radio wave, at a computer, the energy would fry the chips. That's what we did. We fried a bunch of old computers, testing the idea, so we knew it worked in practical application, not just theory. Mathematically, it should work in orbit too, but we never tested it outside our lab."

Sam continued, "If we can disrupt that helicopter's computerized systems, it will be helpless."

She checked her watch. Six minutes had passed since they'd intercepted the message.

CHAPTER 30

Strong winds buffeted the AH-64 Apache helicopter. Sheets of rain lashed at the windows. In a cold, even tone, Tim said, "We have a target at eleven o'clock,"

"Roger that. I have it," John, his gunner, confirmed. "Matches target definition."

"Roger that. Let's have a closer look." The nose of the Apache dipped left, accelerating toward the water.

***

Tommy thought the boat had exploded. He did not notice the approaching helicopter until it passed a few yards above them.

"What in the hell?" Tommy shouted. He craned his neck to look out the bridge window.

"There!" Nigel pointed at the Apache.

"What's all that stuff hanging off the sides?" Tommy asked, although he already figured it out but didn't want to admit it. Missiles.

"They're turning," Nigel said. "They're coming back."

***

The helicopter banked, and the engines roared above the wind. "Did you see anything?" Tim asked.

"Maybe two individuals on the bridge, but I can't confirm. Repeat, cannot confirm target."

"At least they're awake now. We'll get a better look on the next pass." Tim pivoted the Apache, banking it to the right. Powerful gusts of wind knocked them about like a cork on an angry sea. The four-blade rotor chopped at the air until the Apache aimed itself at the trawler that was riding the white-crested waves. "Okay, let's not screw around out here. I don't like the look of this weather. I'll bring us in close, then light them up."

"Roger that."

***

Nigel and Tommy watched as the menacing machine slowed just off their port, wobbling from side to side as northerly winds buffeted the black helicopter. Unlike other aircraft Tommy had seen, this one had no markings. That seemed odd. Military aircraft Tommy saw at a Kansas City air show displayed insignias.

"How did they find us?"

"They have many resources," Nigel whispered.

Why don't you do something? Tommy thought. *Grab a flare gun! Shoot that damn thing down. That's what they do in movies.* Tommy remembered the alley and the man on the motorcycle. Nigel wouldn't do anything to hurt people, not even his enemies. Somehow, the nobility of Nigel's values didn't seem all that great at the moment.

★ ★ ★

Tim struggled to steady the Apache, but that wasn't going to happen. The machine was more stable when it was moving. Despite appearances, hovering a helicopter is one of the more challenging tasks in modern aviation. It took skill to do it well in good conditions. Doing it in a gale was right up against impossible.

The key was not to fight the machine too much. Times like these brought back everything his instructors taught him over the years, which was mostly a bunch of crap. Writing about it on a whiteboard wasn't the same as doing it in the real world, in a real storm. The sophistication and power of the most advanced attack helicopter in the United States military, pitted against the strength of nature, was no contest. In the midst of nature's fury, Tim felt like he was in the rubber band-powered-helicopter he'd given his three-year-old for a birthday present. He switched on the searchlights and said to his gunner, "The trick is to shine it on the damn boat."

★ ★ ★

White-hot light bathed them. Tommy's eyes closed as the brilliant light penetrated the cabin of the small bridge. *Maybe they're coming to rescue us! That's got to be it.* Tommy blinked as the light flashed off and on in the cabin. *Gotta be some kind of signal.* When his eyes sufficiently adjusted, he could see that the light was not flashing. It was moving as the storm jarred the helicopter first to one side and then rocked it to the other, then up and then down.

The machine circled them like a cat.

★ ★ ★

"There!" Sam said in a whisper. "That's a helicopter." He pointed at a small, glowing blue dot on the computer's display. "And there, that's a boat." The second dot was harder to see with its dull orange glow. The computer was reading the heat from the two machines, with the Apache's twin turboshaft engines creating the hotter signature.

"What are they doing?" Karen wasn't sure she wanted to hear the answer.

"Probably confirming the target," Sam said as he entered commands in rapid succession. "They don't appear to have much fear. Let's see if we can change that."

"How can you know for sure it's an attack helicopter? What if they're there to rescue them?"

"XV-E will tell me." A new screen flashed on. It was different, with numbers arranged in straight columns. "It's them all right. They don't arm rescue helicopters with Sidewinder missiles."

Sam twisted around and looked Karen in the eyes. "Last chance to turn back."

"Just do it."

* * *

"That's the target, sir," the gunner confirmed.

"You're sure?"

"Yeah, the Santa Maria. That's what Mitch said. Not much chance of there being two of them. They're registered, you know."

"Roger that. They fit the profile, too. Right?" Tim asked as he read the boat's insignia, hoping it might somehow change.

"Rock & Roll, this is Night Flight one, over," Tim said into his microphone as he held one side of his headset to his ear. The excitement Tim had felt earlier waned, seeing the boat. It was not a military target. Its passengers: a teenager and a man. No terrorists. No threat.

Mitch had ordered radio silence, except for an emergency, and blowing a civilian boat out of the water qualified as an emergency in Tim's book. Tim thumbed the record button on his digital recorder. This wasn't the time to trust unwritten orders.

"Night Flight One, this is Rock & Roll, over," Mitch answered. The codenames had been Tim's idea. What else could one use so near the nation's Rock and Roll Hall of Fame? "Is there a problem?"

"We have visual contact. ID the craft as Santa Maria. Two individuals on the bridge: one boy, one adult male."

"Roger, copy that. What's the problem?" The irritation was noticeable in Mitch's voice.

"Confirm orders to destroy the target." Tim could almost feel the anger oozing from his headset as he visualized Mitch turning a deep red.

"Confirmed."

***

"What are they doing?" Tommy asked as the black machine hovered behind them.

Nigel didn't answer. Instead, he stared beyond the angry aircraft into the night.

"Probably trying to make sure they have the right boat," Tommy said, answering his own question. "We don't have a chance, do we?"

"Things are not always as they appear."

"But we're sorta outgunned, don't you think?"

"You might be surprised."

***

Tim doused the searchlight, and the Santa Maria disappeared in the blackness. It was no longer necessary that he see them. In fact, he'd rather not. Pulling back on the yoke, the Apache clawed at the sheets of rain as it arched back into the night. They were too close for the Sidewinder's computerized navigational system to guide its payload with accuracy. The computer could react quickly enough. It was sheer physics that made the shot risky. The mechanical systems that maneuvered the missile were slower than the computer that directed them. If they moved back a hundred yards, the flight computer would have more opportunity to analyze its target and hone the missile's flight path so it would fly straight down one of the exhaust pipes of the Santa Maria's diesel engines.

"Heat number one," Tim said, as he leveled off at two hundred feet.

"Ready on one."

"When I bring her around, lock on the target and prepare to fire."

"Roger that."

***

Sam toggled back to the grid of Lake Erie. "They're moving off."

"They're leaving?"

"No, they're preparing to fire."

Not much time.

XV-E's secret system Sam planted generated electricity from solar panels, then stored the charge in powerful capacitors the CIA developed to fire laser weaponry from space. The CIA abandoned the project after deciding to use nuclear power, which was illegal in space according to half a dozen treaties, but the CIA rarely allowed such details to get in its way. Sam procured several of the small, but potent, capacitors from an old colleague. The abandoned capacitors were more than adequate for the task at hand.

The E-burst, as Terri called it, only required a forty -five percent charge to fire one blast. Fully charged, it could fire two bursts, milliseconds apart. With two capacitors aboard, the XV-E could fire four rapid bursts. But the capacitors charged faster when they were warm and took longer when they were cold. It was cold in space. The meter reached thirty-four percent.

Forty percent will have to do, Sam decided, with no scientific evidence to believe it true.

★★★

"Locked on, sir."

"Roger that." Tim paused a moment to run everything through his mind one last time. He patted the digital recorder in his pocket, which carried a message he might need, even if it was merely to convince himself he'd done the right thing.

"Fire!"

★★★

Timing is everything. Inches or seconds decide wins and losses of all kinds. Sam watched as the power indicator pulsed to thirty-eight percent, his finger poised over the hot key, waiting for forty percent, but his finger slapped the button too soon as if it had a mind of its own. "Damn!"

Sam's computer analyzed the command, searching its memory for a set of instructions written in a simple language of ones and zeros. Having found its instructions, it excited the electromagnetic generator that transmitted a signal through a coaxial cable into a miniature feed horn pointed at the center of a small black parabolic antenna, aimed at a precise vector in the heavens above. High above the Earth, XV-E's antenna gathered the signal and processed it through its own receiver, which translated the radio waves back into binary code. The onboard computer duplicated the function of its earthbound counterpart, finding the matching sequence and initiating a program of its own. The entire process took less than a second.

* * *

The Apache rocked as the rocket parted from its right wing. The sidewinder was loose. A brilliant flash from the rocket's engine momentarily blinded Tim. Blinking rapidly, his eyes focused on the white-hot vapor trail extending from his aircraft into the night. Then something changed. Although he was too captivated by the Sidewinder's thread of hot gas to notice it at first, piercing alarms startled him, and his reaction was instantaneous. He jerked up on the yoke and drove the accelerator down. The Apache's computer had crashed. All he could think of was putting distance between himself and the angry waters below. At least they fired the shot before the malfunction. He'd never experienced, in simulation or actual flight, a malfunction like this.

"Can you see it?" Tim yelled into the microphone that wasn't working.

"I still see the vapor trail. What in the hell happened?"

"Lost everything," Tim yelled, still trying to make some sense of their situation. He leveled off at what he estimated to be five hundred feet and continued a gradual climb.

The Sidewinder identified its target, calculated the speed, adjusted its trajectory, all within fifty yards of departure. It traveled less than seventy-five yards when it received a signal. The Sidewinder wasn't programmed for the signal, so it ignored it. At least the missile tried to. The boat's movement on the thrashing waters demanded minor adjustments during the missile's brief flight, but the Sidewinder's brain had suffered the equivalent of a seizure. It was fried.

Even without a final adjustment, the Sidewinder stood a good chance of locating its target. However, the hemorrhaging electronic brain tilted the guidance fins, driving the missile into the water a few yards short of the Santa Maria. Diving into the icy water, the sidewinder failed to detonate because the water wasn't solid enough to trigger its warhead. It needed to hit something hard.

Seconds later, the Sidewinder turned back toward the surface.

CHAPTER 31

A streak of light raced across Sam's computer screen, then disappeared. A white light flared in the center, radiating outward until it filled the entire screen. Karen collapsed against Sam's shoulders, and she felt his muscles go limp. Sam hung his head and said nothing. Several minutes passed before she wandered across the room and fell into a nearby chair.

***

Mitch leaned toward the radio console, rocking slightly, his thoughts circulating chaotically. Tim ignored his order to maintain radio silence before the assault, so why didn't he report in now? *Because he knows it'll drive me insane, and it's working.*

***

The Sidewinder dove into the water, its electronic brain trying to overcome the damage from a powerful burst of energy. Heat. It was searching for heat. But there was no heat here. Cold, and downward, colder still. But there was heat above. The missile turned, heading toward the surface and the only heat source it could detect.

A loud metallic clank rang through the hull. Then there was a muffled explosion. The Santa Maria lurched straight up as if tossed by Titan's hand. The boat shuddered, knocking Tommy to his knees, and for a moment, it seemed as if she could fly, and then she tilted, and the law of gravity pulled her down.

The next wave almost submerged her. Nigel pushed the throttle to full power. The diesels groaned. The combination of buoyancy and the drive of twin propellers thrust her back to the surface.

***

This couldn't be happening. Karen refused to accept that Tommy was dead. Sam hadn't moved. He just sat there with his head buried in his hands. She walked back to the table. Standing beside Sam, turning the laptop so she could see the screen. A large glowing mass of red light still appeared on the laptop. She clenched her fists into tight balls. All she could see was the red glow. Or was it? No. There was something else. She blinked hard and leaned in.

At the edge of the red glow appeared a small, dull orange dot.

She grabbed Sam's shoulder and gave him a shake. "Sam!" Her shaking became urgent.

"What?"

Pointing at the screen, she said, "See it? Right there. That's him. That's Tommy."

Sam slapped the table with the palm of his hand. "Yes!"

Karen squealed, threw her arms around Sam's neck, and planted a kiss on his cheek.

"They fired a damn missile," Sam whispered. "We must have nuked the missile's guidance system. Luck. Pure luck," Sam said, wondering why he'd hit the key early. *If I'd waited, it would have been too late. If it weren't for my mistake, Tommy would be dead.*

"That should end it." Karen stared at the spot where her son was and noticed the light disappeared intermittently.

"Beckman won't stop. Next time, they'll use fighter jets. Damn tough targets. I hit a helicopter, not a jet." He stared at the computer's screen.

"I don't understand."

"F-16s can be there within fifteen minutes. They have a location on the boat, so they'll fly in and destroy them. They'll be back on the ground in less than thirty minutes. I can't fight that."

"You're giving up?"

"Look, I'm only one man. I got lucky. That's all. Lucky."

She stared at him. He was just a man. Fatigue and stress had worn him down. Human, after all. After all.

Karen's bottom lip quivered. She folded her arms against her chest but refused to cry. "Listen to me, Sam Henry. You're not going to quit. You're going to do everything possible to save my son. If we fail, we'll fail fighting. I can't live with anything less, and neither can you."

Sam looked into her eyes. "You're right. I'm sorry. But fucking fighter jets?" He threw up his arms.

"You said they'd be there in less than fifteen minutes. How do you know that?"

"Because they'll fly out of Andrews." Sam's lip turned at the corner. "If I could nail them on the ground, that might discourage them."

"Do that then."

Sam leaned forward, tapping at the keyboard.

***

"Rock & Roll, this is Night Flight One."

Mitch lunged forward, banging his hand against the console. "This is Rock & Roll," Mitch said, rubbing his hand and cursing under his breath.

"Mitch!" Gone were the formalities. "We have a real problem."

"Talk to me."

"We've lost everything—the computer and most of the instruments. The damn radio even quit for a while. I have manual flight control and that's it." Tim's voice was as even as he could muster. He estimated his altitude at one thousand feet, but he could be a few feet above the angry waters of Lake Erie for all he knew, heading in what he thought was the general direction back to the base, but there was no way to be sure.

"What happened?" Mitch asked, waving to get his radar technician's attention.

"I don't know. We fired, and then the cockpit went black. I thought we were going down, but the engines held. Mitch, I'm flying blind out here."

"We'll find you, buddy. We'll get you in." Mitch released the button on the microphone, then pressed it again and said, "Do you hear me?"

"Roger that." Tim paused. "Mitch, I can't confirm the mission. The Sidewinder launched, so we assume it found home. Probably a kill, but we can't confirm. Sorry."

"Let's get you home."

"I have them," Gorgons said.

Keying the microphone, Mitch said, "Tim, we found you. Perry will guide you in."

"Roger that. And Lieutenant, thanks."

Handing Gorgons the headset, Mitch slumped into his chair, rubbing his eyes with the heels of his palms. What else could go wrong? The Apache's computer system had proven itself reliable under worse conditions. Almost everything on the machine was redundant. How could they lose it all? Lightning? Perhaps. Whatever the cause, Mitch faced the unpleasant task of telling a cranky president that he could not confirm the success of the mission. He felt his career slipping away before him. Funny thing was, at the moment, he didn't much care.

***

A swarm of angry waves clawed at the Santa Maria, each driving her deeper into liquid blackness. Water lapped at the bridge. She creaked and groaned as the lake tried to pull her down. "Maybe we should slow down," Tommy said.

"Right."

Nigel's agreement surprised Tommy. He was just a kid. What did he know about driving a boat in a storm? As they climbed the next mountain of water, Nigel cut the throttle. The result was like throwing out an anchor. She coasted over the wave's crest and slid into the trough. "Much better. Thanks, Tommy."

Tommy heard Nigel, but the compliment was lost on him. His mind was preoccupied with what he saw outside the cabin. One second, all he could see was a wall of frothing water coming at them, and then, when they reached the wave's crest, they towered above white-capped waves stretching into infinity. Jagged fingers of lightning reached down to skewer them, and with each blinding flash, Tommy searched the sky for the hideous bird of prey, talons laced with missiles.

Why not throw the door open and step outside? The black waters would sweep him away without hesitation, judgment, or remorse. The water and the wind called to him. Why wait for a missile to rip his seared flesh from his bones? He had nothing to look forward to, even if by some miracle he survived. Tommy knew miracles didn't happen.

CRACK!

Thunder exploded, and for an instant, the lightning lit the Santa Maria as if it were day, but the thunder lacked the deep, booming sound Tommy had grown accustomed to. Instead, it sounded with a sharp, hollow crack. His hair bristled. Nigel fought the helm. The Santa Maria once seemed huge. Now, she felt small and fragile.

The wind sang like a siren, calling Tommy. Maybe Dad would greet him on the other side. Mom and Paul would be okay without him. Then a weight lifted from his shoulders. He'd found an answer to his pain. All he needed was a bit more courage, or a bit more despair.

CHAPTER 32

The infrared imaging system told Beckman that the Santa Maria was still afloat long before Lieutenant Mitachavich's carefully worded email reached the crisis center. Mitachavich blamed the weather, the Apache's electrical system, and acts of God. Beckman was preoccupied thinking about how he could punish Mitachavich and the crew for failing their mission. Was there a military base in Antarctica? No, probably not. The northernmost station in Alaska would have to do.

Beckman stomped through the crisis center, labeling everyone in the room something other than a U.S. citizen of the correct ethnic heritage. Powers absorbed the brunt of Beckman's outrage. Incompetent military bastards. Promises, but no results. He made it clear that the military's problems were correlated to its dependence on people of inferior races. He cursed white soldiers for letting the colored sonsabitches in. He showed no fear of reprisal within his private sanctuary. These people were sworn to silence. Talking about events that took place inside this room was an act of treason, and not one of these spineless bastards would risk a charge like that.

"Get two fighters in the air, Mr. Powers. Do you think you can do that without screwing it up?" Beckman's face glowed bright red. He shook his fist in Powers' face. "And make sure they're damn good pilots. White pilots."

***

Tommy jumped when a warm hand grasped his shoulder. Although Tommy could not remember doing it, he had one hand on the door that separated him from the raging waters of Lake Erie.

"Tommy, that's not your answer." Nigel's voice resonated as if it existed both outside and inside Tommy's head. "It's a lie, thinking the answer is to escape."

Tommy looked at him but said nothing. Then Nigel said, "Your father's not waiting out there."

"My father's dead," Tommy cried.

"I know your father."

"What, you're an angel now?" Tommy bristled. Their pastor in Kansas said Roger Parker's death was God's will, and dad was in a better place. It was all for the best. Tommy couldn't see it that way.

"I'm just a man."

"So you said."

"But your father is the reason you're here with me. Well, part of the reason. This is complicated. It's something I shouldn't tell you—there are rules." Nigel stared out the window. "The rules don't seem important now.

"I told you my people are dying. Not just dying—ceasing to exist. Many years ago, our scientists conquered disease and aging. For lack of a better word, we became immortal. That's what we believed. We stopped having children. No reason for them and limiting our population was the responsible thing to do. Logical. Centuries passed with no problem, and then people began to die. At first, we thought it was some genetic defect that would take its course through the weaker of our species, but it continued. A scientist proved the life force of our planet was dying. No death, no birth, no cycle. We learned too late that life and death are connected in a never-ending progression we still don't understand. Since we could no longer have children, it seemed our extinction was only a matter of time.

"Then we learned we could replenish the life force of our planet if we renewed the circle of life. We began gathering kindred spirits of humans from across the universe, which revitalized our life force by living their lives on our planet and dying natural deaths. We needed other humans, but we are peaceful people, so we developed some very narrow criteria to bring them to our world. First, they must face certain death on their home planets.

"Cancer was killing your father. We search for men and women like your father all over the universe. We offer them a new life on a new planet. If they accept, they live an average lifespan on my world and die a natural death. But their spirits don't die. They flow into a kind of spiritual reservoir.

"My people have also given up immortality, living the rest of their lifespan, then returning to wherever it is we go when we die. However, without children, there would be no next generation to carry on our culture and our knowledge.

"We needed a new generation to carry on. The people who have come to help us live their lives as they choose. We educate them, passing on our knowledge to them and their children. Some marry and bear children, some don't." Nigel's eyes locked with Tommy's eyes. "Tommy, I asked your father if he'd help save my world."

Tommy stared at Nigel for several minutes. "My father agreed to help. He told me."

"Ah, you remember."

"But that was just a dream."

"Was it?"

CHAPTER 33

Karen handed Sam a steaming cup of fresh coffee. He gave her a thin smile. Andrews Air Force base was quiet. He felt like the little Dutch boy sticking his finger in a dike riddled with a thousand holes. He pondered how he could get everyone out of this mess. While he hovered over his computer, watching for the telltale exhaust signatures of fighter jets, an idea came to him, but he dismissed it. Then he mulled it over again, and it seemed almost feasible. It wasn't any crazier than anything else he'd done today.

****

It took General Powers several minutes to convince the duty officer at Andrews Air Force Base that his call wasn't a joke. He explained the mission was need-to-know and there wasn't much the duty officer needed to know. Launch two armed F-16s with experienced Caucasian pilots who could keep their mouths shut. Once airborne, the crisis center would contact the pilots with further instructions.

"When your pilots return, the three of you report to the Old Executive Building for debriefing. If there is a problem, the mission never happened. Is that clear?"

"Yes, sir," the duty officer said. "I'll have them up in ten minutes."

****

Sam ran the plan through his head one last time. It was crazy enough that it might work. Sam didn't like Richard Beckman, and for good reason. Sam believed Beckman engineered the assassination of Andrea Ross—the last man. But he couldn't prove it fifteen years ago, and he couldn't prove it today. He seethed at the thought that he'd never know for sure. However, Richard Beckman had now given Sam ample reason for a fight.

Crisis center protocol requires that someone monitor the weather. Sam knew that because he wrote the manual. The message Sam planned would be one-way communication, which suited him fine because he had no desire to talk with Richard Beckman. Not yet. Sam's future and the future of his team depended on this one brief transmission.

✱✱✱

Among other things, Tony Capparelli, a gangly young officer, monitored the weather satellites. His computer did something it theoretically could not do. The satellite he was watching was an old machine with an old computer running ancient software. It should not transmit a text message, but it did. "Sir, I think you'd better see this."

Powers and Beckman leaned over Capparelli's shoulder to read the message.

```
cannot link with seca- fbi agent key, crazy-
tried to arrest me- alien location destroyed
but I am convinced it escaped- boy fate
unknown- pursuing- key is after me- alien
must be controlling fbi agent mind-
possibility more aliens among us- parker
woman with me- we were attacked by unknowns-
maybe aliens- will communicate when
possible- do not know who to trust- henry-
```

"I'll be damned," Beckman breathed. "Where in the hell is he?"

Powers leaned on the desk, read the message again, and said, "He thinks he's battling aliens." Powers glanced at Beckman. "Sam Henry will not give up."

"Why haven't we heard from the damn FBI? Or Unit-11?" Beckman's voice was subdued. He hadn't planned on things going wrong, the mistake of a man unfamiliar with military operations. Every soldier knows that sometimes things go to hell for no reason at all.

"Are those fighters in the air?" Beckman whispered.

"Should be any minute now, sir."

"I want them dead. Do you understand me? Dead."

"I understand," Powers said as his eyes locked with those of a young sergeant standing across the room. Powers turned his head toward the lens of a small camera mounted on the far wall, then looked back at the sergeant, who nodded his head in agreement. The recording system had been operating since the situation began.

CHAPTER 34

Air Force Captain Monty Stiles was rousted from his bed, his mood surly and contemptuous, but he stopped dead when he saw the ground crew working on his aircraft. His blood turned cold, his knees felt weak, and the grogginess swept away from his mind. The ground crew was not installing the blue practice bombs to which he was accustomed. Two birds down, Mike Van Pelt's F-16 was being similarly equipped. Five years his senior, Mike was still one of the best men in an F-16 Monty had ever seen. As a team, they were hell on wings.

A moment later, a breathless Mike Van Pelt stopped at Monty's side and said, "What in the hell is going on?"

Monty wondered if the realization of live bombs had solidified in Mike's mind. "You know as much as I do," Monty replied.

Mike's eyes were locked on the bombs. "Holy shit."

Monty didn't need an interpreter to understand that Mike had assimilated the situation. "They don't pay us to think about it, buddy." That garnered another curse from Van Pelt as both men marched to their aircraft.

A member of the ground crew held the ladder steady as Monty climbed to the cockpit. Monty had been in and out of this seat often, but it had been years since he'd seen combat. Four years, to be exact, during a brief but destructive battle with Iran, one of a series of Middle East conflicts that resurfaced on predictable cycles. Monty ran his pre-flight checks with a focused mind.

He closed his canopy. A crewmember waved at him with a flashlight in each hand. He released the brakes, and the F-16 rolled forward. He gave a ceremonial salute to the men on the tarmac as he tried to comprehend what could warrant the 500-pound smart bombs that hung from the wings. Guided by computerized targeting systems, the smart bombs could hit a suitcase on top of a station wagon moving at 75 miles an hour. *Terrorists?* Monty thought about his training two months earlier with a kick-ass counter-terrorism team called Unit-11. Afterward, he received strict orders to forget he'd ever seen them. Terrorist made sense. Mike Van Pelt was on that same training exercise.

The F-16 undulated over uneven pavement. Congress had money to buy military hardware but could not afford asphalt. Monty's headset crackled to life. The voice of the watch commander, a man named Kirkpatrick, sounded in his ears, "Captain Stiles, you'll be contacted by the White House crisis center once you're airborne."

"What is our mission, sir?"

"Need-to-know, Captain. For the time being, you know everything you need to know."

"Roger."

The commander's voice was replaced by the smooth, sexy voice of a female air traffic controller. "Captain, you're cleared for immediate takeoff on runway 1794."

Lined up on runway 1794, Monty locked the brakes and pushed the Fighting Falcon's Pratt and Whitney turbofan to takeoff thrust. He released the brakes, and the F-16 rocketed into the night.

CHAPTER 35

The unknown is the worst fear of all. That was the theory. Now, Sam hoped it was true. Having prepared his message, he returned to the screen depicting the airstrips at Andrews Air Force Base. Except he was late. A white-hot dot raced across the screen, approaching a red box representing the launch zone and his last chance to stop the attack.

"Oh, shit!" Sam yelled, slapping at the keyboard.

***

One never gets over the pure shot of adrenalin induced by the acceleration of an F-16. Monty Stiles was no exception. Within seconds, the F-16 rocketed from zero to launch speed. He was about to pull back on the stick, pointing his Fighting Falcon into a near-vertical climb, when everything went black.

The instantaneous adrenalin dump created a hypersensitive state that seemed to freeze time in Monty's mind. While part of his brain recognized the speed at which everything occurred, another part of it drifted into relaxed analysis. In the detached part of his mind, time slowed as he considered his alternatives. Already traveling at over 200 mph, the sophisticated aircraft was now nothing more than an armed missile out of control. While this surreal analytical process reviewed a list of options and corresponding results, the other part of his brain reacted by rote. Oddly, the half that lazily scrolled through options and corresponding consequences came to the same conclusion his pre-programmed training dictated, and both sides of his brain converged as his hand slammed down on the ejection button. The canopy exploded, and the ejection seat propelled him into the air. Ejecting while still on the ground didn't carry high odds of survival but remaining in the aircraft ensured death.

As Monty's ejection seat shot him high into the night sky, he watched his F-16 wobble, then dip to one side. The right wing caught the tarmac, and the Falcon became a massive, cartwheeling fireball. He wondered if he'd fare any better than his aircraft.

★ ★ ★

"Monty!" Mike screamed into his headset as he watched his friend's F-16 erupt. But Mike knew Monty didn't hear him. Mike's aircraft was dead. Everything stopped. He opened the canopy manually and waited until someone came to rescue him. He saw Monty's parachute open before Monty hit the ground. Mike wanted to jump from his cockpit and race to his friend, but breaking his own legs wouldn't help Monty. So, he prayed.

★ ★ ★

"Goddamn!" Kirkpatrick shouted as he watched the F-16 explode on the runway. He had talked to Captain Stiles seconds before the plane became a tumbling inferno. "What in the hell happened?" Kirkpatrick threw his headset across the room, where it crashed against the wall.

"I don't know, sir," an air traffic controller said, peering through the tower's glass. "Both aircraft shut down simultaneously."

"There!" shouted a soldier by the door. Pointing upward at a 45-degree angle, he said, "Parachute."

Kirkpatrick scrambled toward the window, peering up into the night sky, he shouted, "Emergency teams! Now!"

★ ★ ★

Tommy was certain things could not get worse, but they did. Lightning erupted everywhere. The roar from the thunder became a continuous din, so loud that he couldn't hear himself think. The winds whipped the lake into a furor of violent waves, promising to drag them under.

★ ★ ★

"Where's the other F-16?" Kirkpatrick asked.

"At the end of 1794, sir. It's dead too."

Suddenly, the control tower went stone quiet and black. After a few moments, the emergency generator restored the lights and essential equipment. However, the computers operated on continuous power supplies, which ensured uninterrupted operation. However, the computers weren't operating as usual. Instead, they displayed blank blue screens.

Something wasn't right.

"My computer locked up," a woman sitting behind Kirkpatrick said. He turned and saw her jabbing at the keyboard.

Then a message scrolled across every screen in the room. All in perfect unison. As Kirkpatrick stared at the computer screens, someone handed him a telephone. It was General Powers calling from the nation's crisis center. Kirkpatrick told him what happened, then learned the computers in the crisis center, the most secure room in the world, displayed the same message as the computers in the control tower at Andrews Air Force Base.

LAST WARNING!!! LAST WARNING!!! LAST WARNING!!!

CHAPTER 36

From a cabin on the shores of Lake Erie, Sam scanned images of the crisis center captured by the center's audio/visual system. Judging by Beckman's behavior, Sam was confident that Beckman had forgotten the system was watching him. When Sam programmed this backdoor into the crisis center's computer system, it troubled Sam that he had accomplished such a breach of security without being caught. His original motivation was to demonstrate a weakness in security, but later Sam decided retaining the ability to spy on them was essential. He didn't know why. Now it might save his ass. Funny how things work out sometimes.

Except for the storm outside, the cabin was filled with silence. Karen had moved to the couch. She said she needed to sit for a minute but fell asleep. Sam watched her for several minutes, then found a soft, beige woolen blanket in a cabinet under the stairs and covered her. A few details remained undone. Rubbing his eyes, he walked back to the table where his computer sat. The phone rang. He picked it up quickly before it rang a second time. "Hello?"

"Sam? Alex Madden."

"Where are you?" Sam checked his watch.

"We just crossed the Canadian border. I was afraid we might have trouble, but we didn't. AJ needed a pit stop, so I thought I'd check in. How's Karen?"

"Exhausted. She's asleep."

"Is Tommy all right?"

"Not sure," Sam answered. He didn't need to conjure false hope for Alex. Besides, Alex would have seen through him. "They're at the mercy of the storm now."

Sam gave Alex directions to the cabin.

Then Alex said, "What happens when this is over?"

"Still working on that, Alex. Be safe. No need to rush."

Twelve-inch logs and high open-beam ceilings blocked all but the most violent sounds of the storm. Standing at the cathedral windows,

Sam watched as the wind shifted the rain in ever-changing patterns, and in the window's reflection, he watched Karen sleeping on the couch. Although he had no desire to harm this alien or whatever he was, Sam had orders. He wondered if Karen would understand that he had a mission to complete.

Sam collapsed into an overstuffed chair, its brown leather weathered and checked, fitting like an old glove. Probably Dutch's favorite place to retire with a good book on a stormy night like this. He settled into its buttery softness and mulled over what he had to accomplish in the next few hours.

A trip to Nevada awaited all of them, and bad things happen under the Nevada desert. What if his plan didn't work? It had to work. Golden light from the fire danced on the walls. He breathed deeply. Easing his head back on the soft cushion, sleep overtook him.

***

Rain hammered at the windows. The Santa Maria felt sluggish. Earlier, she bobbed atop the water like a cork, strong and free, but something had changed. She wallowed in the troughs and drove into the faces of the waves. Water swept across her deck with regularity. Didn't Nigel notice what was happening? Maybe he didn't understand.

"She doesn't feel right," Tommy said, looking up at Nigel, hoping to read his reaction.

"No, she does not." Nigel agreed, staring straight ahead.

"What's wrong?"

Nigel didn't answer at first, but finally said, "I'm afraid we're taking on water. Probably the missile damaged the hull. The bilge pump light went out about an hour ago."

Tommy stared at the shifting curtains of water falling from the sky, and the bow disappeared under a foaming wave.

"I'm sorry, Tommy. I never meant for this to happen. It's just that...." Nigel's voice trailed off.

"Just that, what?"

"I promised your father that I'd check on you," he said with a shake of his head. "I shouldn't have involved you in this. I'm not supposed to have personal contact with a volunteer's family, but there was something different about you. I wanted to explain your father's death, hoping I could, you know, make it easier for you. I've made a big mistake." A tear, reflecting lights from the instrument panel, traced down Nigel's cheek.

"What are we going to do?" Tommy asked.

"I don't think there's anything we can do. There's nothing anybody can do."

A thought hung out of Tommy's reach, something he couldn't reel in, like a wily wild trout, nibbling but impossible to hook.

Think. What did Dad used to say? It was so simple.

Tommy's eyes grew wide. "The bilge pump light went out?"

"About an hour ago," Nigel confirmed.

Tommy pinched his lips together. Dad used to get so frustrated when his boys gave up. *Never surrender. That's what he used to say. Never surrender.* Adopted from one of his dad's favorite movies, Tommy thought it sounded dumb. Now, it sounded smart.

Suddenly, he remembered something else. "I can fix it. Dutch showed me how." With that, he turned and reached for the door handle as the bow plowed through the face of a wave, sending water rushing across the deck.

"Hold on there. Where do you think you're going?" Nigel grabbed a handful of Tommy's collar.

"I told you. I can fix it!" Tommy said, twisting himself free.

"But you'll be washed right off the deck. Then you'll be dead, and the boat will still sink."

"If I can't fix it, we die, so I have nothing to lose." Tommy shrugged his shoulders.

"Arguing with logical statements isn't my forte, although at the moment, I don't feel like being logical. In this state, we won't last long." Nigel fell silent for a moment. "Wait until we've crested this wave. That gives you a few seconds before the next one hits."

Tommy threw the door open.

Nigel's voice strained above the tempest. "Be careful!"

Tommy stepped outside as the Santa Maria slid into a trough, then plunged into the face of the next wave. Foaming water washed around his ankles as the old trawler wallowed through the turbulent waters. The strength of the wind stole the breath from his lungs. Startling was the chill of the air. The rain stung his face. Bad as any storm he could remember. The Santa Maria tilted to one side as she slid down the backside of the wave. His feet slipped out from underneath him. His knee hit the steel deck. Blood poured down his shin.

Nigel switched on every light he could find—not that it helped. He could barely see Tommy working his way toward the hatch that led to the engine compartment. Nigel saw a huge black ship bearing down on them. He couldn't breathe. It was as if someone knocked the wind out of him. Then he realized the monstrous shape wasn't a ship but a rogue wave, at least twice the size of the ones that had battered them for the past thirty minutes.

Nigel threw the door open and screamed at Tommy, but the gale snatched his words and threw them to the wind. The Santa Maria crested a small wave, then tilted down. He could see Tommy struggling with the hatch.

The towering wall of water loomed in front of them. "Tommy!"

The enormous wave enveloped the Santa Maria, and churning black water covered all but the tallest part of her. She let out a loud groan. Rushing water gripped Nigel like a powerful, icy arm, ripping him from the bridge. His feet came off the deck, and he clung to the doorjamb as his body contorted in the arms of the raging Witch of November. The spot where Tommy worked the latch was now submerged in the angry, foaming water.

Eventually, the wave spit the old trawler out like a piece of tough meat. Water drained off her everywhere. She listed like a battered old boxer. Both motors stalled, and she slid sideways down into the trough of the next wave. The starboard side dipped lower into the water than did the port. Her deck rode mere inches above the surface.

Nigel felt small, insignificant, and lost.

CHAPTER 37

Alex and AJ stopped for fuel and coffee. Alex got a coffee and then filled the tank. He had called Sam and now waited by the car. AJ wandered out of the convenience store a few minutes later. "Did she go to Columbia for coffee beans?" Alex asked as AJ settled into the passenger's seat.

"Hey, you drained the pot. She made fresh." AJ buckled his seat belt.

"Mine tastes like they made it last week." Alex wrinkled his nose as he sipped from his cup.

AJ shrugged. "What did Mr. Henry say?"

"He said Tommy's out there in the storm." Alex pulled onto the deserted highway. The windshield wipers slapped back and forth. Lightning flashed and thunder boomed. Neither man spoke.

CHAPTER 38

The deck was barren; no sign of Tommy. Nigel scanned the black water. Nothing. He closed his eyes. Tommy wasn't wearing a life vest. It was a brave thing Tommy did. Nigel imagined his father's reaction, seeing the pain and pride in his eyes, but his father would never know about Tommy's brave act because Nigel wouldn't leave this planet alive. His journey was over. He bowed his head and closed his eyes. It was as if a boulder crushed his chest. A feeling unlike any he'd ever experienced. Tears flowed from his eyes and streamed down his cheeks.

So, this is what emotion feels like.

For years, he longed for it. Now, he wished it would go away.

Nigel opened his eyes, scanning the deck again with one last hope. Nothing.

A flash of lightning lit the sky.

Something.

Something at the edge of the deck.

Another flash. There, clinging to the edge of the deck like a barnacle, was the body of a small boy. Tommy fought his way back onto the deck.

Nigel punched his fist into the air and let out a whoop.

***

Shaking the water from his head, Tommy jerked the hatch open and headed down the ladder into the engine compartment. *It's darker than the inside of a cow in here,* he thought, fumbling along the ledge for the flashlight Dutch stowed there. Tommy's fingers felt a cold metal cylinder. He grabbed the flashlight and felt for the switch. A bright beam of light bored a tunnel through the darkness. Warm water sloshed around his waist. The compartment was silent. The diesel engines sat dead, water halfway up the engine blocks. A smaller gasoline motor sat silently in the corner above the waterline. The motor had one minor problem. It was out of gas. Dutch said he'd meant to install an automatic switch on the fuel line months earlier, but events outside his control prevented him from getting it done. A rap on one fuel cell sounded with an echo. Tapping the second fuel cell sounded a dull thud.

Full.

Tommy twisted a valve, allowing gasoline to course through the line and into the carburetor. He pushed the start button, and the electric starter spun the twin-cylinder motor with a thump, thump. Nothing happened. He saw a small red knob labeled: CHOKE. Tommy pulled the choke and punched the start button again. The little motor coughed, then fired. Pushing the choke in, the engine roared to life. The clutch took hold as the motor stabilized at the correct RPM. The weight of the water in the pump's impeller pulled hard against the engine as it strained under the load but answered with a surge of power as the governor on the carburetor reacted.

★ ★ ★

Nigel heard the muffled sound of a motor, and then two jets of water shot from the rear of the boat. It didn't take long for the Santa Maria to rise. But Nigel needed power to negotiate the storm, and he couldn't restart the engines until Tommy was on deck. Then Nigel heard a distant rumble, and the lights on the instrument panel changed from red to green, and the tachometer needle bounced off zero. Tommy had started the diesels.

Wheeling the Santa Maria around, Nigel pointed her into the next wave. She crested the top and splashed down the other side. A few moments later, Tommy walked through the door. Nigel pulled him to his side. Nigel was as proud of the boy as any father ever could have been.

CHAPTER 39

President Beckman had retired to the White House, leaving General Powers to run things. The crisis center might have passed for a morgue, as the **LAST WARNING** message continued to scroll across every computer screen like the cadence of a superior enemy whose patience had grown thin. Apparently, Beckman only enjoyed conflicts if he had the upper hand. When news of the F-16 crash reached the crisis center, Beckman. had turned pale, and then he threw up in a wastebasket when the **LAST WARNING** message began scrolling on the computer screens. It seemed odd that the president would leave the crisis center during a crisis, but nobody complained.

After two hours had passed without incident, Powers said, "Let's reboot the weather-station computer." Everyone froze, holding coffee mugs and donuts in varied states of consumption.

"I thought President Beckman didn't want us doing anything." The voice came from an unidentified technician somewhere behind a row of computers.

"That's not exactly what he said," Powers countered. "He said, 'don't do anything crazy.' Well, I'd hardly call rebooting a weather computer crazy. Would you?" The question was directed at no one in particular.

"What if it makes them mad?" Another voice asked.

"If they're as sophisticated as they appear to be, then our weather computer isn't a threat. Is it?"

The room remained silent.

"Any other objections?" There was none. "Then let's do it."

Tony Capparelli toggled the power switch off and waited for the hard drive to stop spinning. After an unofficial prerequisite time, Tony rocked the switch back to the on position, and the computer began running its startup procedure. After a few moments, the monitor displayed the opening screen, a dark blue background with a multicolored national seal emblazoned across it. Powers ordered all the computers to be rebooted.

Powers moved from station to station, watching each computer shut down and restart. Everything worked, except communication with

SECA. As long as Sam Henry was alive, Powers had hope, and he wanted every means of communication between Sam and the center unencumbered.

★★★

When Sam awoke, a ray of sunlight streamed through the large windows into his eyes. The storm was over. Karen was gone. The familiar smell of coffee drifted from the kitchen. Struggling, he stood. How long had he been asleep? By the stiffness in his muscles and joints, he estimated at least three hours, maybe four. A fresh pot of coffee awaited on the kitchen counter, but no Karen. Sam tossed the remnants of last night's brew in the sink and poured himself a fresh cup. The thick mug he'd chosen from the cupboard felt heavy, and the distinct feeling of reality comforted him.

He walked onto the deck. The morning air smelled of pine, fresh and clean. Below him, Karen stood on a platform, about midway between the cabin and the dock. He eased down the stairs, hoping he could surprise her. Halfway down, he noticed she held a white cloth to her face.

She was crying.

A large oak bough concealed his view of the lake. What could he say to her? Silently, he descended. Karen waved her arm high above her head. Then, in the distance, he saw a blue and white boat. It looked more beautiful than anything he could remember.

A boy stood on the apex of the bow, waving both arms.

At the helm stood a man.

CHAPTER 40

Powers estimated they'd pushed the aliens too far, and that was Beckman's fault. If they didn't pull any additional dumb stunts, maybe it would end here. Destroying the F-16 was the aliens' first act of aggression, and they had successfully compromised the United States' most secure systems, including sophisticated satellites and computers. They'd rendered the United States' war machine helpless. Powers suspected they had experienced only benign elements of the aliens' capabilities. They had killed no one. Captain Monty Stiles, the pilot of the F-16 that crashed on takeoff, survived. A lucky man. Powers wondered if Lady Luck had run her course. He did not intend to press her further.

"Has anything else happened to our military installations?" Powers asked, pulling up a chair and sitting behind the communications officer, Marcy Whales.

"No reports, sir," Whales said, her eyes fixed on the computer screen before her.

"Send out a communique to all bases, including the National Guard. Tell them to cancel all military flights until further notice."

"Do you think the guard will obey an order like that? They don't answer to us."

"Good point. Tell them—the order came from the president."

Whales turned, looked Powers in the eye, and said, "Sir, President Beckman isn't…"

Powers raised his hand, cutting her off. "Soldier, make it happen. That's an order."

"Yes, sir."

Powers would ride the heat for borrowing Beckman's authority, but he would not risk sparking another confrontation with a force he knew nothing about, had no argument with, and was ignorant of their strength, hidden somewhere in the heavens above or somewhere on the planet itself. Besides, Beckman didn't have the stomach for confrontations with more powerful foes, and now Powers had more than one reason to go to war with the man.

✶ ✶ ✶

When Sam stepped onto the deck, Karen rushed over and gave him a powerful hug. When she turned him loose, she clapped her hands, and then raced down the stairs toward the dock, giggling like a schoolgirl.

Sam followed. His smile faded. He knew what he must do but couldn't recreate the cold justification he so easily pontificated in his thoughts during the night. Pausing halfway down the steps, he realized this was Karen and Tommy's moment, one he wasn't entitled to share. Standing quietly, he watched the man he knew only as Nigel ease the trawler toward the pier. Tommy stood at the deck's edge, holding a heavy rope coiled in large loops. When the boat was within two feet of the dock, Tommy leaped from her. He attended to her, as a sailor should. First, he wrapped the thick hemp rope around one of the large pier posts, then he snugged her against the old black tires lining the edges of the wooden dock.

Having completed his obligation, Tommy was thirteen again and rushed into his mother's outstretched arms. Tears flowed down their cheeks, and they held each other as if they'd never let go. Sam searched his memory and found that he lacked any similar experience.

Nigel secured the stern to the pier.

Sam waited.

Karen wiped her face with the palms of her hands, and Tommy used his shirtsleeve in the tradition of young boys everywhere.

"Mom, this is my friend, Nigel." Tommy dragged her to where the stranger had just finished tying the trawler to a burly post. "Mom, he's a little different—I mean, well, he's not from around here," Tommy said, biting his lip. "This is the man from the alley I told you about."

Dumbfounded at the man's physical condition, Karen extended her hand. "Thank you. You saved my son's life."

"And he saved mine, Mrs. Parker," Nigel said, smiling as he grasped Karen's hand with both of his. A second later, his eyes shifted to a point behind her.

"Hello, Sam," Nigel said. It wasn't a question.

Sam said nothing.

"Mom, who is this?" Tommy positioned himself between Nigel and Sam.

"Tommy, this is Sam Henry. Sam, this is my son, Tommy." Karen kneeled beside him, brushing his hair back with her fingers.

"Tommy, it's good to meet you. You had us pretty scared." Sam extended his hand, which hung in the air for a moment, until he withdrew it awkwardly, rubbing his palm on his pant leg.

"That name sounds familiar. Is he a friend from when you lived in Cleveland before?"

"No," she paused, staring toward the lake as if trying to capture a distant thought. Then she looked at Sam, her smile returned, and her eyes sparkled, and she said, "We just met." And at that moment, it was as if she saw Sam Henry for the first time. An odd sort of innocence lingered about him. Somewhere, under the hardened exterior, was a man no one knew.

"I'm so glad you're okay," she said, hugging Tommy in a way that embarrassed boys Tommy's age. Tommy didn't seem to mind. He returned her hug with equal vigor, and more tears flowed.

After a moment, Karen wiped her eyes, glanced up at Sam, and asked, "Is it over?"

Sam pressed his lips together and nodded, although he knew it wasn't over. A moment later, Sam's eyes drifted up and locked with Nigel's eyes.

"Hello, Sam," Nigel said again, in firm recognition. "It's been many years."

Sam remained silent. His eyes narrowed.

"You don't remember?" Nigel nodded, as if he now understood a dark secret.

Sam searched Nigel's face for something to cement the images that floated in and out of his nightmares for many years. Time and faces swirled through his mind in an endless kaleidoscope of bits and pieces, places, and things, some real, some imaginary. Sam could no longer distinguish between reality and fantasy. He turned to Karen and said, "Excuse us."

She shivered. This was the voice from fifteen years ago. A place deep within her heart demanded she stay and protect the stranger who had saved her son. Instead, she obediently guided Tommy toward the stairs. Tommy balked, but her firm hand kept him moving. Suppressing her own urge to run, she walked up the steps and away from the dock, away from two men she somehow felt deeply connected to.

Halfway up the stairs, she turned to watch Sam and Nigel some 25 yards below. They spoke, but she couldn't hear their words. It occurred to her that Sam still had a mission of his own. *Why can't I be strong? Why can't I do the right thing? Why I can't I be—more—like, him? Damn it!*

★ ★ ★

Nigel glanced up at Karen and Tommy. Tommy stood in front of his mother, her arms draped over his shoulders, crisscrossing his stout young chest. Their vigil caused Nigel to smile, although he wished Karen had taken Tommy into the house, out of view. Tommy didn't need to experience more suffering, and Nigel couldn't predict the outcome of this encounter.

"What is it you want?" Nigel asked, meeting Sam's eyes.

"I'm an agent of the United States. My job is to return you to the authorities of my government."

"And what purpose would that serve?"

"My government's role is to protect its citizens. They must decide if you are a threat to our country."

"And what happens when they learn that I'm not a threat? Will I go free?"

"That's not my decision."

"That's a feeble answer, Sam," Nigel said. He took a deep breath and said, "They won't let me go, and you know it."

"Like I said, that's not my job. Besides, how would I know what they'll do?" Sam's composure wavered.

"Have you forgotten what happened in El Salvador?" Nigel's eyes narrowed with the question.

"Just pieces—I can't …" Sam stopped and glared at him. "This is not about El Salvador!"

"Dreams? Yes. Dreams. Have I haunted your nights, Sam?" Nigel looked deeply into Sam's eyes, then he nodded his head and said, "Yes, I thought so."

"Stop!"

"What do you fear? You're not asleep. This isn't a nightmare. It's over. You lived. That's all there is to tell." Nigel paused. "Would it help if you knew more? It's not such a complicated story."

"You saved me?"

"I almost got you killed."

"Why were you there? You wore a uniform," Sam paused. "You were one of them." His voice trailed off.

"Not exactly. I dressed as a soldier so I could slip into a small village to find a local farmer named Miguel Chavez. A meandering band of rebels had killed his family two weeks earlier. Miguel went to town one day, and when he returned, his wife and six children—the youngest only six months old—were dead. However, I knew something that Miguel did not. He had a tumor growing inside his brain. I wanted to talk with him about his options before he decided how he'd respond to the death of his family. You and your men showed up as I walked into the village.

"Your squad fell into a trap set for the rebels that killed the Chavez family. It wasn't meant for American soldiers, but before the leader could call off the ambush, everyone was dead. Except you. You dove into the brush and then ran straight off the side of the mountain. During your tumble, you lost your rifle, your pack, everything else except your knife. I remember that detail because you tried to kill me with it.

"A young soldier didn't hear his commander's order to stop shooting. He chased you to the edge of the ravine, where he watched you pull a knife, then lunge at a man wearing a uniform like his. I was the man you stabbed." Nigel pointed toward his chest with the tips of his fingers. "The soldier shot you. That's where you got that bullet in your leg. I carried you until we were out of range. Luckily, you were unconscious and didn't have any fight left in you. I dressed your wound and went on about my work."

"The doctors said my wounds were almost healed." Sam paused for a moment, staring at the dock. "You got shot, too. I remember now."

"A flesh wound," Nigel said, dismissing it with a wave of his hand. "The next morning, I found Miguel Chavez. After I finished my business with him, I went looking for you. When I found you, I kept a safe distance. The first time we met, you tried to kill me."

"You followed me the whole time?" Sam asked.

"I was leaving anyway. Didn't matter which route I took."

"What business did you have with this Chavez?"

"I can't talk about that. I can tell you Chavez was no threat to your national security."

"What about them?" Sam nodded toward Karen and Tommy. "You have business with them?"

Nigel glanced up and smiled. "Let's just say I promised a friend I'd check in on them."

"What friend?"

"Nobody you'd know."

"This is all too strange. Too many coincidences. Did you know that I once met Karen many years ago?"

Nigel shrugged.

"Did you somehow arrange all of this?" Sam asked.

"How could a man arrange something like this?"

"I want straight answers, not riddles." Sam clenched his teeth. "It doesn't matter. You're still going with me."

"I can't do that."

"It's not a request." Sam felt a flush of red circle his neck.

"I understand," Nigel said with a nod, "but I'm not going anywhere with you, Sam. I can't."

"Yes, you can." Taking a step back, Sam reached into his jacket and pulled his pistol.

★★★

Sam's movement was so sudden that it took Karen by surprise. She spun Tommy around and held him against her body. *Sam Henry, you son of a bitch!* The silent scream reverberated inside her skull until her ears hurt.

★★★

Nigel didn't flinch. That bothered Sam. It was unnatural for a man to stare down the barrel of a pistol and not react to it. Sam repositioned his grip, uncharacteristically shifting the pistol in his hand. He reminded himself that the man wasn't human. "I don't enjoy doing this, but you have to come with me, or…"

"Or what? You'll shoot me? Why? Duty? Before you kill me, understand this—I'm every bit as human as you are. Different? Yes. Nevertheless, human just the same. I'm not a threat to you or anyone else. If I were, I would have let you die in the jungle. Kill me if you must but be clear about your reasons. Consider how you'll explain those reasons to that young man." Nigel nodded towards the deck.

"Why are you doing this? I don't want to hurt you. I really don't." Sam's voice cracked.

"Your world isn't ready to meet mine, not yet. We have work to do here, but we'll leave if we're discovered."

"Your body will prove your existence, so why make me kill you?"

"There was always a risk that one of us would die here, so the biochemical engineers devised a chemical reaction that will decompose my body if my blood stops circulating. Before you get my body to a lab, there'll be nothing left but dust."

Sam lowered the gun a few inches. Reality became a dichotomy for him. Duty dictated that he complete his mission. He had orders. Beyond duty, who was Sam Henry? What did he stand for? What was he about?

Nothing.

His life consisted of his work and nothing more. He fought an urge to glance at Karen. He envied her. She knew pain, but she also knew love. With all its pitfalls and heartaches, Karen possessed something he had never experienced. Earlier, for a moment, he thought something was happening between them. How could he have been so stupid? She hated him and for good reason. It was too late for Sam Henry to start thinking about having a normal life.

He searched his soul, but the same answers returned time and time again. He wasn't a murderer and refused to become one. The crossroads he now faced didn't offer a path that led him anywhere he wanted to go. He tried to think, but images of Karen drifted through his mind—the warmth of her dark brown eyes, her sullen smile, her sleeping on the couch under a woolen blanket. He'd resigned himself to a solitary life many years earlier. Yet, until now, he'd never understood the consequences of that decision. Was this the curse of Karen Parker? Tantalize him so he could no longer face life?

In a dark corner of his mind, Sam found his answer.

★ ★ ★

Karen watched the two men stand in silence. Sam's gun was no longer pointed at Nigel. Instead, Sam held it at his side. That, she thought, was a good sign. But the gun began to move. She gripped Tommy to prevent him from squirming free. She watched Sam raise his weapon, tracing a slow arc until the barrel rested on his own temple.

She screamed out in the silence of her mind, begging herself to react, to do something, but as always, she stood there, helpless, and afraid.

★ ★ ★

"You don't have to do this," Nigel said.

"Yes, I do." Sam's voice turned cold and unemotional as his thumb flicked the safety mechanism to the off position and his finger tightened on the trigger.

For the first time in his life, Sam didn't hear the encroaching footsteps. The blow was both unexpected and violent. To his amazement, he almost lost his grip on the pistol.

"What in the hell do you think you're doing?" Karen screamed.

"This isn't your problem," Sam said, not knowing what else to say.

"The hell it isn't! Someone I've started to care about wants to kill himself, and you don't think it concerns me? You arrogant son of a bitch. I ought to kill you myself." She smacked him on the chest with both fists, knocking him off balance.

"You don't understand." The moment the words left his mouth, he realized how ridiculous that sounded, given all she had been through.

For a trained warrior, his reactions were pathetically slow.

Karen's lunge was swift and sure. "The hell I don't." She jerked the pistol from his hand and threw it into the lake. "You think life is supposed to be easy? You think it's fair? Well, it's not!" Tears flowed. She hit his chest with both fists again and then collapsed against him.

He raised his arms around her. Over her shoulder, he saw Tommy, pale-faced and standing at the bottom of the stairs. Moisture trickled down Sam's face. He waved Tommy closer. Tommy ran to his mother's side, and Sam drew him close. It seemed as if the entire universe had stopped, and while he knew this moment was temporary, for the very first time—Sam Henry savored simply being alive.

CHAPTER 41

Tommy released his mother, then looked for Nigel, but Nigel wasn't there. "Where'd he go?" Tommy asked as he spun a circle. Then, with his hands cupped to his mouth, he called, "Nigel!" Then to another direction, "Nigel!" Each time, Tommy's voice spilled over the calm morning waters and echoed from the tree-covered banks. Nigel did not reply.

"But he was just here," Karen said with a hint of bewilderment in her voice. She, too, spun a full circle, then walked out onto the empty dock.

"He must have gone back on the boat." Tommy clambered up the side and onto the deck.

Karen and Sam watched Tommy move through the boat, searching her literally from stem to stern. When he returned, his head hung low, and his gaze traced a line on the dock in front of him as he walked.

"He's not there," Tommy whispered. Looking to his mother, he asked, "Where could he have gone?"

Touching him lightly on the shoulder, Karen said, "I don't know."

Sam ruffled his hair. "He wasn't from these parts, right? If I remember right, you and Nigel walked out of a crowded hospital with no one seeing you."

Tommy nodded. "That's true."

Sam looked away and saw a blue sky unmarred by so much as a single cloud, and he breathed deeply the fragrant air. It stirred something inside, making him wish he could live like this, but that wasn't going to happen. Not anytime soon. He still had work to do.

Back inside the cabin, Sam found cocoa and mixed it with hot milk in a brown ceramic mug, which he handed to Tommy, then settled into a chair across the table and stared out the window. The aroma of sausage sizzling in a black cast-iron skillet filled the kitchen. Tommy downed his hot chocolate and slid his cup across the table. The movement caught Sam's attention.

"More?" Sam asked.

Tommy nodded in affirmation.

While Sam heated more milk, Karen worked in smooth unison around him. Sam returned with Tommy's cocoa as Karen placed a large plate of steaming hash brown potatoes in the middle of the table.

"A Kansas breakfast: hash browns, sausage, eggs, and biscuits. Dig in." Karen spooned a pile of golden potatoes on her plate, then eased into her chair.

Tommy speared a piece of sausage, stuffed it in his mouth, and then filled and quickly emptied his plate. Sam ate more cautiously, a guest lacking the familiarity of mother and son. Spreading butter, and then strawberry jam from a mason jar onto a fluffy white biscuit. He was eating country food, not the city fare to which he was accustomed. He didn't think he was hungry, but after two helpings of everything except the biscuits, which totaled three, Sam moaned and pushed himself away from the table.

"Can I go outside?" Tommy asked.

"May I go outside," Karen corrected.

"Yeah, that too. May I?"

Karen looked at Sam and said, "Yes, but stay close."

Tommy promised he wouldn't go far. The words had an odd ring to them, as if he'd heard them before. He explored the woods but remained in view of the cabin's windows. This was more like Kansas than Cleveland, but he wasn't ready to be in the woods where he could not see the cabin just yet.

Karen filled Sam's coffee cup, then her own, and asked, "What's next?"

"I've been thinking about that." Holding his cup in both hands, he stared into the black liquid and rising steam.

"We're not out of the woods yet, are we?" Karen asked.

Sam took a deep breath. "We are not."

She said, "I've been thinking about Paul. I'm worried. Should I be worried?"

Sam sat his cup down and rubbed his face with his palm. "Your apprehension is well founded."

"They're going to hurt Paul, aren't they? They're going to hurt all of us," she said with steadfast eyes.

He nodded.

"You have to do something," Karen said.

"This mess goes clear up to the POTUS." He stared at the table and twirled a spoon in his cup.

Karen watched for a moment. She believed what was bothering him most wasn't the threat from the outside but his perceived personal failure. "Sam, what happened. It's okay. Well, not okay, but I understand. I don't think any less of you." She paused. "About what happened with Nigel. I almost did the same thing before leaving Kansas, but not with a gun."

He looked up at her, brows furrowed, eyes darting from side to side. "But you have so much to…"

Reaching across the table, she took his hand and said, "I couldn't see what I had. I felt numb and empty." She swallowed. "I shut out possibilities and options until I believed there were none. I was about to take a bottle of sleeping pills when Paul woke up. Funny thing is, Paul sleeps like the dead. He never wakes up in the middle of the night."

She searched Sam's face and then continued. "I didn't even hear him until he was standing in the bathroom, asking me what was wrong. He saved me. Sam, I don't know you well, but I think you may be listening to a lie. They didn't put you in this position because you're weak or washed up. They did it because you frightened them."

She looked at her hand on his, then pulled it back into her lap. "Healing takes time, but Paul doesn't have time. You are his only hope. Our only hope."

Sam pinched his lips together, nodded, but said nothing.

With no further discussion, he gathered his briefcases. Pausing at the door, he said, "I'll be back."

The late morning sun cast short shadows as it warmed the night's air, which smelled damp and fresh. At the main road, Sam turned north. After fifteen minutes, he pulled up to a convenience store at the intersection of a well-worn commuter route. On the far side of the parking lot was a payphone concealed in a small, oval-shaped covering. Easing the borrowed sedan close, he opened a black briefcase sitting on the seat beside him. With trembling hands, he connected the telephone to his laptop computer with a thin black cable. He read and then reread his message, and when he was satisfied with the words, he moved the mouse and clicked send. On a computer screen in the crisis center in Washington, D.C., Sam's message appeared.

```
still can't make contact with seca- mission
completed- alien found and neutralized- very
clean-   no  witnesses-   must    find    fbi
agent/alex madden/dr jahan- will report when
```

```
I find them- ready nevada for our arrival-
henry
```

Sam drove north along Highway 4 until he found another payphone at an old gas station where the attendant still pumped gasoline and changed oil. He parked on a side street and walked to a payphone in a glass-sided booth. The White House number surfaced effortlessly in his memory, although he'd never actually dialed it before. Glancing over his shoulder, he punched the telephone's chrome buttons, and on the second ring, a woman with a pleasant voice said, "Oval Office. How may I help you?" Sam judged her age at fifty-something.

"President Beckman, please," he said, suppressing a wave of nausea. Despite everything that had happened, he still found thinking of his president as the enemy difficult. Moreover, he wondered if he could pull this off.

"Who may I say is calling?" Few people knew the president's direct number, and the fact that the caller did, meant Beckman would accept the call.

"Tell him it's Henry."

"Henry, who?" The woman insisted with a tinge of irritation in her voice.

"Just Henry."

He heard a muffled grunt, and patriotic elevator Muzak replaced the silence. As he waited, an overpowering urge to hang up the phone overcame him. He craned his neck, half expecting to see a black government-issue sedan filled with angry-looking men wearing black suits. Instead, he saw a man wearing a tie-dyed Grateful Dead T-shirt pumping gasoline into a late-model BMW.

Beckman is the enemy, he reminded himself. A young boy wearing a Toronto Blue Jays baseball cap appeared at the service station's front door. A moment later, his mother joined him, and they walked to the BMW. The boy was the same age and build as Tommy Parker. Watching the BMW ease onto the highway, Tommy appeared in Sam's mind, standing on the deck of a trawler being tossed by the frigid waters of an angry lake. Above him hovered a black Apache helicopter. Like a bolt of lightning, a missile sliced through the air. A brilliant flash engulfed the trawler, and what little was left drifted through the air. Had it not been for Sam's intervention, that was Tommy's fate, as ordered by Richard Beckman.

A metallic click telegraphed activity on the other end of the line. Sam's grip tightened on the receiver, which seemed to shrink in his hand. "The President will accept your call. I'm connecting you now."

"Sam? Is that you?"

"It's me, Mr. President," Sam said with even, measured words.

"Good to hear your voice, Sam."

Sam gritted his teeth. He was about to speak when Beckman asked, "Are you okay?"

Silently, Sam drew a deep breath and said, "The FBI failed, if that's what you mean."

"Now, Sam. That's all a misunderstanding. We can straighten this out if you'll come in."

Silence.

"Sam? Are you there?"

"I'm here. I'll come in—in good time. But first, we need to make a deal."

"Make a deal?" Beckman's voice raised an octave.

Sam had heard this voice before. It matched the video recording of Beckman's tirade in the command center. Sam smiled as he activated the recording app on his computer.

Perfect.

With a voice that oscillated between a scream and a whine, Beckman continued. "I'll make you a fucking deal. Turn yourself into the nearest police station, and I won't have you killed."

"Would you mind repeating that?"

"Don't fuck with me, Mr. Henry. I'm the President of the United States. You may be a goddamn legend to your spook friends, but you're a goddamn civil servant as far as I'm concerned. I'll crush you like a damn bug. Now, where are you?"

"Why do you ask? Planning a military strike, like the one you ordered on that thirteen-year-old boy?"

"Yeah, I might do that."

"What did Tommy Parker do to deserve the death penalty at thirteen years of age?"

"He defied me."

"And how did he accomplish that?"

"He walked out of that hospital with that alien. That's how."

"Alien? Come now, Mr. President, alien? What does this alien of yours look like?"

"You know what he looks like."

"Yes, I do. He looks like an ordinary man. What did this man and boy do that justified an act of war within the borders of the United States?"

"He's a goddamn alien."

"He's different?"

"Yes, goddamn it, he's different. What's your point?"

"Okay, I think I'm with you now. It's kind of like when minorities take jobs from good white Americans." *Surely, you're not that stupid,* Sam thought as he closed his eyes in anticipation of Beckman's response.

"Damn straight. And when the time is right, I'll rid this nation of those bastards too."

Sam grinned. "Mr. President, I never realized you had that vision."

Several silent seconds passed before Beckman replied, "I didn't know you shared our vision, Sam. Listen, I need good men." Beckman paused. "Are you with me on this, Sam?"

"I'm listening."

"First, I need you to help me with this mess. There are too many loose ends, and we need to get them tied up before something bad happens. If you know what I mean."

"Mr. President, I understand precisely what you mean." *Damn, that was too easy,* Sam thought.

Sam continued. "Something bad has already happened. Maybe I should share some information of which you may not be aware. The boy and the man you ordered killed are alive and well. They survived your attack. Still, you ordered the death of an American citizen, a thirteen-year-old child named Tommy Parker. You did so without approval from Congress or the judiciary. That's attempted murder and, president or not, that, sir, is still illegal in this country." The line fell silent. Sam had delivered his soliloquy with the detached intonation of a man holding a royal flush.

"You'll never prove that," Beckman said coldly. "It's your word against mine. By the time I'm done with you, a grand jury will indict you for treason. How believable will your story be then?"

"You've got me there." Sam paused for no other reason than drama. "I suppose you're right. No one will listen to me. You'll have to tell them yourself."

"What makes you think I'm going to tell them anything?" Beckman asked.

"You already have."

"What do you mean by that?"

"Have you forgotten the video system in the crisis center? I think the American people will find your views—enlightening."

"I'll have those recordings destroyed." Beckman fired back.

"It's a good thing I copied them, isn't it—Mr. President?" Sam paused. "Now, you're thinking, kill Sam Henry, and the evidence goes with him to the grave. Mr. President, for your edification, I didn't become a legend by being stupid. The copies are safe and untraceable. If anything happens to me—anything—those videos, along with a detailed report of this entire event, get delivered to CNN, FOX, NBC, and every other major network in the United States. That includes video footage of the murder of Eric Key and the secret communiqués that prove you gave the orders. Oh, and throw in a copy of this conversation as well.

"Are you listening? Whether I succumb to an accident or to natural causes, get arrested, or disappear, CNN, CBS, NBC, ABC, get a copy of your performance. If I were you, I'd make Sam Henry's health my top priority. Now, is there anything you don't understand, Mr. President?"

"You wouldn't dare," Beckman whispered.

"Already done. Anything happens to me, and your dark side gets aired on national television."

"Jesus," Beckman whispered.

Sam could hear him breathing on the other end of the line.

"What do you want?" Richard Beckman had cut plenty of deals on his way to the top. He was no virgin. His mission was too important to be screwed up by minor details.

"I want out. And I'm taking my friends with me." *My friends*. Sam liked the sound of the phrase. *My friends*.

"What do you mean by that, exactly?"

Sam defined his terms, which were entirely fair, all things considered.

"I agree, and you'll disappear? This whole thing goes away?"

"Simple as that."

CHAPTER 42

The trees seemed more colorful, the sky bluer, and the flowers more brilliant than Sam remembered them. The air had a fresh, clean crispness to it. He felt wholly alive, and for the first time in as long as he could remember, he was eager to be somewhere. At a strip mall, he found an overnight express box, into which he placed a package addressed to Terri Wilson, Pensacola, Florida. After that, he drove toward town to find fresh bagels, something he had promised a new friend.

It was early afternoon when Sam returned to the cabin. In the driveway, he saw a blue sedan. The license plates suggested it was a rental, which meant Alex and AJ were there. Sam turned the key, and the motor fell silent. He sat staring at the cabin, wondering if he really belonged here.

When he stepped into the kitchen, he called, "Hello!" but there was no reply. The house felt empty, and his stomach muscles twisted into a knot.

From the back deck, a voice, warm and melodic, said, "We're out here, Sam."

Sam stepped out the back door. The sun warmed the day. Alex and AJ sat in lawn chairs, camped out around a large white cooler. Sam threw a brown paper bag in Madden's lap and said, "I recall you wanted a bagel on your way home from work. They're still warm. I'm a day late. Sorry."

Madden peered into the bag. "About damn time." Removing a cinnamon raisin bagel, he tore off a piece and stuck it into his mouth and then handed the bag to AJ.

"Sit," Alex said with a wave. "Beer?" Alex drove his hand inside the cooler, creating chimes of ice and glass. He retrieved a dark brown bottle and tossed it across the deck.

Sam caught it, twisted the cap off, and took a long pull before settling into a chair next to Karen.

"How did it go?" Karen asked.

"Rather well, thank you." Sam raised his bottle high into the air before taking another long drink. "I made Beckman an offer he couldn't refuse."

"Care to tell us about it?" Alex asked.

Sam smiled and shook his head.

"I thought not," Alex said.

"You'll be much safer not knowing. Someday, maybe."

"Here's to someday." Karen clicked her bottle against Sam's.

CHAPTER 43

Under the Nevada desert, Dr. Horace was about to administer an injection to a frightened young nurse strapped to a stainless-steel table. His first patient from this Cleveland bunch. Ten years under the surface of the planet had certain residual effects on Horace, and long-suffering wasn't one of them. Protocol called for a more subtle approach to the art of twisting people's minds and memories, but protocol didn't account for much when you lived in your own world, of which you are king. And King Horace didn't waste time on formalities. The objective was to extract the truth from these people, then make them forget what they knew, and neither process was difficult unless it became complicated with notions of human kindness. And King Horace had lost those values many years earlier.

"Dr. Horace, there's a call for you." A technician who delivered the message made eye contact with the wide-eyed young woman, then looked away.

"Can't you see I'm busy? Get the number, and I'll call back for God's sake."

"Doctor, it's the White House."

CHAPTER 44

The sun over Lake Erie neared the western horizon. The odor of hickory smoke drifted through the air. Sam's knife fell through his steak like hot metal gliding through soft butter. Spearing a chunk of meat with his fork, he stuffed it in his mouth, pushed his plate toward the middle of the table, and leaned back in his chair.

Alex walked from the kitchen, his face pale and drawn.

"Everything okay?" AJ spun a chair out for him.

"I talked to the police chief. I told him about Eric, but he already knew. The Cleveland coroner identified his body about an hour ago. They're saying it was domestic terrorism." Alex looked around the table, pausing for a moment to search each face. "Eric wasn't married. They sent two agents to tell his parents."

Nothing was said for several minutes.

Sam said, "I'd like to hear about Tommy's adventure."

Tommy beamed, then told his story with a loud voice and animated gestures. Karen turned white when he told her about the car chase and then nearly being swept off the deck while saving their sinking ship. Everyone had a question or two. Tommy readily answered each of them.

AJ said, "Karen, what will you tell your sister- and brother-in-law?"

"About what?" Karen asked.

AJ glanced at Alex and said, "About all of it." AJ waved his hand. "His home in Cleveland was blown up. His boat is here with a crack in its hull."

Karen looked dazed. "Right. I had not thought about that." She looked at Sam.

"Tell him what happened," Sam said.

"Tell him?" Alex asked.

"Tell him everything?" Karen asked.

"Yes," Sam said.

AJ looked at Sam and said, "You know him." It was not a question.

"I've never met the man. But I know of him, and I trust him," Sam said.

Alex took a drink of beer and frowned at Karen.

Karen shrugged her shoulders.

AJ sat forward in his chair. "There is much that I don't know, but it all seems fantastical."

"Well, duh. I mean, the President of the United States tried to kill my son, and we met a man from another world."

AJ waved his hand and then continued, "Yes, yes, but that's not what I mean. From what I gather, Karen and Alex knew each other years ago when Karen lived and worked in Cleveland. That is not strange. But somehow, Karen and Alex also know Sam. While that relationship is unclear to me, it does not seem that you were friends back then."

"True," Karen said.

"And Sam, you recognized the man we know as Nigel. Again, I am not knowing the connection there. And somehow, Nigel turns up in the middle of the night to save Tommy. Now, you tell me that Sam knows Karen's brother-in-law. If this were a movie, I'm not sure anyone would believe it. I'm sorry, but it all seems too strange to be a coincidence. It's as if it were all orchestrated."

"You're right," Karen said. She looked at Sam. Sam looked as puzzled as she felt. "What do you think, Sam?"

Sam stared at Karen for a moment, and then he looked at Alex and then at AJ, and said, "I think I need another beer."

Alex fished beers from the cooler, offering each adult a bottle, and said, "It's strange for sure."

Tommy looked at Alex and said, "Is there a soda in there?" And then added, "You don't know the half of it."

"What are you saying?" Karen asked.

"I'll tell you the rest when I'm ready." Tommy paused. "When I think—*you're* ready."

Glances were exchanged around the table, but none of the adults pressured Tommy for information.

Finally, Tommy said, "What do you think happened to Nigel?"

The adults glanced at each other, hoping to find an answer.

Sam leaned forward, looked into Tommy's eyes, and said, "Nigel is a sojourner from his world. He has his own path to follow."

"That's right," Karen said. "A sojourner of the universe." She paused, looking around the table. "As are we all."

Everyone reflected on Karen's words for a few minutes. Then Alex asked, "What's next?"

"We'll go to Nevada for debriefing," Sam said. "It will be okay. I fixed things as part of my deal with Beckman. Then we go home. The only catch is that we can't discuss any of this. That's part of the deal. In other words, it never happened."

Karen started to say something, then stopped.

"What happens after Nevada?" she asked, finding interest in her bare feet and bright red toenails.

"I have some fascinating work to do," AJ said with a wink, pulling a test tube of blood from his jacket pocket and holding it to the light.

Alex tore small strips of paper from the label of his beer bottle. "I'm not sure," he said without looking up. "I've thought about retiring, moving to Montana, and spending my days fishing for trout. Maybe it's time."

"How about you, Mr. Henry?" The question came from Tommy.

"I'm like Alex. I'm not sure."

"I don't know if I'm cut out for the city anymore," Karen chimed in, patting Tommy on the leg. "Last night, I dreamed we packed our stuff and headed west. I guess the only thing that's stopping me is fear."

From across the table, Sam said, "Somehow, I don't think fear will stop Karen Parker from getting what she wants."

With a smile, Karen said, "I think you're right."

EPILOGUE

November
The remaining witnesses arrived in Nevada. By order of the President of the United States, Dr. Horace was placed under armed guard, and the debriefing of all witnesses was turned over to Sam Henry.

Richard Beckman checked into Bethesda Medical Center, complaining of acute headaches. The official diagnosis was a rare brain infection, which could affect his judgment and attitude. Beckman made a full recovery. Sam saw it for what it was—a hedge against the video recordings made in the crisis center.

Alex Madden buried his friend.

AJ Jahan returned to Atlanta and his life and learned he would soon be a daddy. As the days passed, during the quiet hours after other CDC scientists went home, in the solitude of his office, under the prying eye of his microscope, AJ looked at the secrets of life from another galaxy. AJ learned many things that he could only share with a new friend, a surgeon who once thought researchers were not proper doctors.

James T. Wellington returned to St. John's Hospital, where he awoke early, performed surgery under an aggressive schedule, and went to bed late. To the casual observer, the current James Wellington differed little from the old one. However, his team members saw the change, and every day it became more pronounced. Although still the most prolific surgeon at St. John's, he reduced his workload by 25% and started a tight-lipped research project with a CDC doctor in Atlanta.

He started a new teaching program for promising young surgeons.

He signed on for a humanitarian effort in Africa.

He started dating.

December

Karen stuck around until Christmas break, then packed their stuff and her two boys in a pickup truck and headed west. She sold what she didn't need or couldn't haul. The family's cash reserve tallied fewer than $7000, $4000 of which was a loan from James Wellington. Not much of a safety net. Still, she felt sure of her decision. She didn't know where they were going, but she'd know when they arrived. West was her only intention.

May

Dr. A.J. Jahan and Alicia Cortez-Jahan became parents of a baby boy, James Nigel Jahan, and their long-held secret marriage was a secret no more. AJ's friend, Dr. James Wellington, became a godfather. Unfortunately, James N. had a birth defect of the heart, and it was touch and go for a few days. Surgery, though risky, was scheduled. A day before the surgery, AJ thought he saw Nigel leaving the maternity ward. AJ tried to catch the man but could not find him after a turn in the corridor.

A completely healthy James Nigel Jahan left the hospital the next day.

Doctors could not explain their incorrect diagnoses.

April

Sam had stuck around to make Beckman nervous. Sometimes Sam would appear at a press conference or public ceremony. He would stand among the crowd, hidden behind a pair of black Ray-Ban sunglasses. Standing there, expressionless, he would stare until beads of sweat formed on Beckman's brow. When Beckman wasn't watching, Sam would disappear.

Today was different. Today Sam watched zombie-faced commuters plodding along the street as they had every morning he could remember since he first stopped at this espresso shack many years ago. Eight o'clock had come and gone. He was in no hurry. He sat under a blue umbrella, sipping espresso from a paper cup. Studying the little coffee stand, he realized he might never see it again and that it was okay if he didn't.

His espresso had grown cold. The traffic thinned, and it was time to leave. He slid on his Ray-Bans, stood, turned a full, slow circle, and wondered why he'd never actually seen this spot before, never taken the time to stop and sip coffee. Sam reduced everything he owned to fit into two saddlebags attached to a 1200-cc motorcycle. A tank bag strapped on top of the gas tank held a map neatly folded under a transparent plastic sheath. Most people used GPS navigation, but Sam decided to use a paper map. It would guide him to Culpepper, Virginia, where he'd turn it over and continue his journey. By nightfall, he planned to be in the Allegheny Mountains, but that was as specific as his plans got. From there, he might head south or north, and either direction would be perfect. There was a man he wanted to get to know, and the emptiness of the open road on a motorcycle seemed ideally suited for the task of getting to know Sam Henry.

He planned to work his way west.

He had a friend that he'd promised to see when he was in the neighborhood.

July

Alex worked a desk job for five months, then retired. Today, he stood knee-deep in the water of the Madison River as it twisted its way through Montana. A whooshing sound broke the silence, and an artificial fly landed delicately on the calm surface of the stream. Retirement details held Alex in Cleveland longer than he'd expected, but now his entire CPD career seemed like a previous lifetime. And in a way, it was.

He had stayed in touch with Karen. A winter storm stalled her and the boys in Longmont, Colorado, that winter. She found a job cutting up chickens in a poultry factory. The boys finished the school year. Neither the town nor the career suited her, and when school was out, they moved on. Now they were in Utah picking strawberries. The harvest would last another day or two. Idaho was her next stop. Karen heard about a small-town newspaper in need of an editor, and although she'd never heard of the town or its paper, something about it sounded right. She asked Alex if he'd heard from Sam, but Alex had heard nothing since late April. She had agreed to come see him in Montana when she got to Idaho. From her location in Idaho, it was only a three-hour drive to Alex's place. Karen and the boys would be here this afternoon or tomorrow morning.

The fly drifted perfectly over a deep hole. No trout surfaced, but Alex didn't mind. Lifting the fly off the water, he whipped his fly rod twice and gently laid the little artificial bug on the surface two feet beyond the first cast. Watching his line float silently atop the water, the distinctive sound of a twin-cylinder motorcycle rumbled down the cliffs of the canyon.

Alex smiled.

Sam's timing could not have been better.

the end

Author's Note:

Thank you for reading my books. If they gave you a bit of an escape, I'm pleased. Please consider writing a review. To sign up for my newsletter, visit my website daniellcopeland.com.

Acknowledgements:

Thanks to the love and support of the love of my life and partner, Liz. She is also a writer and illustrator. Check out her books on Amazon Libby K. I couldn't do any of this without her. She is also my best editor and critic.

Special thanks to Rod Leonard for providing feedback and guidance.

Special thanks to Vicky Southwick for edits, corrections, and direction.

More books from Daniel L. Copeland:

Available at Amazon.com in paperback, eBooks for Kindle, and audiobooks.

The Derrick King Series

About the Author:

Daniel is a lifelong Idahoan and grew up on a small farm in Southern Idaho. He worked in the criminal justice system for 35 years and is now retired. Daniel has published nine novels. In addition to writing, he and his wife, Liz love to travel on their BMW motorcycle. They have ridden in most of the US, including Alaska, the Great Lakes, and Florida. They have also ridden in Canada, New Zealand, and Australia. Daniel is an award-winning home brewer and a certified beer judge.